CONTINUUM

JIM GILSON

Interior Design by The Book Bureau

Printed in the United States of America.
ISBN: 978-1-960548-30-6 (paperback)
      978-1-960548-31-3 (ebook)

The Book Bureau

CONTENTS

ADMISSION

To all those English language purists out there, and I include myself in your number, I want to explain why my novel has been edited with the now widely accepted American spelling.

In 1906, then American president, Teddy Roosevelt, wanted Congress to agree to a modification of the spelling of the English then in use. He simply wanted the have some awkward, hence hard-to-learn spelling, simplified. Congress did not agree but the seeds were sown and what has crept in just makes common sense.

I love tradition but for the sake of all those trying to learn our beautiful language, I have to agree with Mr. Roosevelt and so here we are.

If our language had not evolved, Mr. William Shakespeare would still have us using words such as "honorifi cabilitudinitatibus" but of course he himself was a revolutionist and I say again. Here we are.

CHAPTER ONE

L ife . . . the relentless continuum of one thing happening after another, sometimes slow, oft times fast, occasionally moving monumentally. History does that. Time does that. Life does that.

The year was 1846, and Christmas was but four days away. The situation in Ireland was described in the Guardian newspaper of that date, Tuesday, the twentieth of December, as apocalyptic. Hunger and typhus were killing people in their thousands. Coffin makers could not meet the demands, and dead bodies were piled one on top of another in deep pits with boards laid to separate each corpse. Babies, so many babies, were being buried in baskets by desperate grieving parents trying to preserve some semblance of dignity.

The Potato Famine, also known as The Great Hunger (Gorta` Prat`a` in Gaelic), had decimated the population for almost two years and was responsible for the deaths of over one million poor souls. Those who were able to remain strong could be seen at the beginning of the devastation desperately helping their weaker neighbors to bury their dead, but as the hunger worsened, many victims were placed in shallow holes in the ground and covered with stones. Despite the care taken, foxes would often find their way to the raw flesh, and the scavenged corpses became exposed. The long hair on many of the dead women could be seen eerily dancing in the wind.

Hunger and hard work will always be at odd ends with one another, and as the population weakened physically, living conditions became the stuff of nightmares. It would be impossible to qualify the mental state of the sufferers, and only those who had lived through wars could possibly identify in any way with the bloodcurdling visions of what had become life on the land.

Food became so scarce and starvation so rampant, many farmers were moving closer to the coast in the hope of being able to flee the torment and seek a safe haven in England. Hungry people were harvesting the abundant kelp brought in on each tide, boiling it into a slurry and serving it as a soup.

Farm livestock was not spared the misery. A major portion of the feed given to sheep, cows, and horses consisted of potatoes. These animals were dying of hunger, and their carcasses were left to rot where they fell. What meat that could be salvaged was eaten by the crofters, but most simply went to waste because the condition of these animals was so poor, they were beginning to putrefy well before death.

The once beautiful rolling hills of productive farmland became a pockmarked terrain of nightmares, and the stench of rotting flesh in combination with the acrid odor emanating from the soil that housed the putrefying potatoes had created an atmosphere that the god-fearing inhabitants had begun to refer to as "hell on earth."

Chapter Two

The Diaspora

Some sympathetic mariners smuggled families across to the English coast, and the major port of disembarkation was Liverpool but those caring mariners were in the minority. People had become desperate, and many corrupt boat owners would pile people on board, relieving them of everything they had of value by way of extracting their fee for passage. A large number of these desperate people would move inland to Manchester by travelling up the Mersey River and into the River Irwell in the hope of reaching Salford and Manchester, a distance of thirty-one miles, where so many of their relatives and friends had already settled and were offering assistance.

The wealthy landowners, most of whom were English, were more concerned about profit than rendering any relief to the victims of this most catastrophic situation. All alternate crops were not affected by the root-rotting disease causing the potatoes to fail, and of course, the potato was the prime source of food allowing these still primitive farmers to subsist.

The sad fact of the matter, however, was that the bulk of these other foods grown were being shipped to England for market pandering to and allowing the "landed gentry" to live their lavish lifestyles either oblivious or, more likely, simply choosing to ignore the problem. It would be extremely hard to put these greedy attitudes down to not being aware of the plight wreaking havoc throughout Ireland, England's closest member of her empire.

Much literature was already in print exposing the slum living conditions of the poverty-stricken English working class. Over the one hundred years that preceded the Potato Famine, England had grown into the most powerful nation on earth. Not down to the innumerable wars that had taken place in that century. Not due to the fact that England had created an empire never before even remotely matched by any previous or present regimes.

England had outgrown its antiquated and primitive feudal system of governance and had transformed itself into a nation with inventions, factories, mills, and rail transport with ordinary men of vision becoming wealthy overnight. This Industrial Revolution brought about a change to the way everything was done, and the demand for workers was extreme. It was said at the time that most workers were regarded by their masters as no more than the coal that fed the fires of the greedy forges catering to the overwhelming industrial development of that time.

Mr. Charles Dickens had written a wonderful book that he entitled *The Parish Boy's Progress*, later renamed *Oliver Twist*, and this told in brutal reality just how desperate the poor had become and describes many of the tragic situations workhouse children found themselves in. The book was serialized, and printing began in 1837 with the complete story told over a two-year period. Some more well-read intellectuals of the day did suggest that the main character Oliver was based on the true story of Robert Blincoe told by the author John Waller and printed in 1832, and from this, a realization arises proving that there were serious concerns being put to the public regarding the cruel treatment of the working class for quite some time.

Queen Victoria began her reign in the same year that *Oliver Twist* went to print in 1837. The British Empire, at that time, was the largest wealth-generating conglomerate in the world, yet it appears that the Queen of the day chose to do next to nothing to intervene and help in any way with aid to assist the rapidly increasing number of her starving Irish subjects. Evidence of a five-pound donation was recorded as coming from the Queen and possibly another two-thousand-pound contribution at a later date. The wealth being plundered out of

India alone during this time in the name of the Empire makes her effort insulting.

England's wealth and financial security had never been stronger. To contextualize the time, consider this. On Sunday, July 19, 1843, the SS *Great Britain*, designed and built by Isambard Kingdom Brunel, was launched at Bristol by Prince Albert, Queen Victoria's German husband. The first propeller-driven, iron-hulled steamship that totally revolutionized shipping. She was over a hundred meters long and weighed in excess of 1,930 tons. Prince Albert was a staunch supporter of the progress and the development he saw all around him and encouraged his Queen to do the same. They did not hide away. They travelled the countryside, and Albert, in particular, was captivated by the rapidly expanding railway network beginning to traverse all of England.

In the following year, 1844, a consortium of wealthy businessmen and engineers was building the railway line from Manchester over the Pennines to link with Sheffield. None of this was driven by tourism. It was capitalism at full stretch.

They must have been aware.

The British government fared no better. The Poor Law Act declared in England in 1834 and extended to Ireland in 1838 offered no assistance to farmers; in fact, it compounded the problem by declaring that all out-of-work able-bodied indigents be sent to labor in the squalid conditions of the workhouses.

This allowed unscrupulous businesses of the time to press all of these able-bodied indigents, so many of whom were merely children, into service. All workers, often complete families, upon being sent to the workhouses, in reality became slaves. They were all made to wear uniforms and slept in overcrowded dormitories on beds no more than two feet wide.

There was absolutely no consideration given to hygiene, health, or hunger. Although cruelty seemed to be the order of the day and physical punishments were brutally meted out for the smallest of rule infringements, the authorities did little to right the escalating list of complaints. Families were segregated and often only saw one another briefly in passing.

The food supplied was barely enough to keep the workers standing upright, never mind provide the energy that would be needed to complete the long day's labor, often extending to sixteen hours.

This appalling fact alone, if considered, paints a picture of the cruelty and inhumanity on open display everywhere and every day in the life of workers, so many of whom were just children. Breakfast consisted of gruel. This stew-like concoction could best be compared to porridge but had additional ingredients thrown in depending on what was cheap and available. Stale vegetables and legumes chopped into pieces were often added.

There was no consideration given to proper diet, but the business overseers did know the value of a full belly when it came to work output. The gruel was served hot. A ladle was used to drop the slop directly into the outstretched palm of the worker. It did not dribble out and fall to the ground because it was so thick. The workers simply ate the slop directly out of the palm of their hands. No plates, no spoons, no dignity.

Many of the shaking outstretched hands could hold no more than a small spoonful. Children aged four or even five do not have big hands. Another meal was served in the evenings, and that barely kept the workforce alive.

Children were harvested from orphanages, and good money could be earned by unscrupulous operators in the child slave trade. Some children were worked so hard that they were no longer productive and therefore returned to the orphanage only to be replaced by yet another child slave.

The owners of many of the mills would house the child laborers on site. They would be locked in cramped and damp dormitories which often lead to the spread of disease and dysentery. They were called apprentices and were only turned free when they reached seventeen years of age. When the female workers were no longer required by the mills, they often found that they were too old for alternate employment, and if they could not marry, many turned to prostitution.

It was reported that in one of the disgusting workhouses, a brawl broke out between workers who were pounding animal bones into powder to be used for farming fertilizer. The bones contained marrow and food was the issue as the starving inmates fought for it.

CHAPTER THREE

The Industrial Revolution in England had begun in earnest almost one hundred years earlier around 1740, and as factories began to spring up all over the English west coast, the demand for labor was exploding and this is what began the rift between the Irish, deliberately imported workforce, and the locals who had been there from the beginning. The Irish were prepared to work for less money, and tensions led to many ructions between the workers. These tensions escalated exponentially as the relentless Potato Famine forced many more thousands of Irish folk to head to England.

In 1844, two men met in Paris and, after finding that they had much in common, became lifelong friends. The philosophies born of this pairing that offered so much to the working class in their lifetimes would over the next one hundred years make the devastation of the Potato Famine appear as a mere hiccup in history. Frederick Engels was the clear thinking, organized, and very astute one side of the same coin that found itself often weighed down by its own reverse face where sat Karl Marx who could bluster on and confuse issues.

The Connellys

In 1846, Joseph and Grace Connelly, through no fault of their own, found themselves and what was left of their seven children living a life that could never have been imagined three years ago. The home they had abandoned several months earlier was all that Joseph Connelly had ever known.

His father, Patrick, had originally rented the small crofters cottage, and Joseph considered himself to be blessed because he and his two sisters, Kate and Tess, had enjoyed a carefree childhood. Joseph's mother, Irene, was always able to set a plentiful table, and although the children worked hard on the small holding, their laughter far outweighed any concerns they might have had due to their modest circumstances.

The small home they lived in consisted of a windowless stone structure with a straw roof. Internally, there was one bedroom, and the remaining area made up a kitchen with a woodstove. Two ancient chairs and a timber slab table were the only items of furniture to be seen. It was customary to sleep as many family members in the one bed as possible, and the remainder slept on the floor. Joseph did not mind his position on the floor as he was able to lay near the woodstove for heat, and he kept it stoked so the warmth was there for all to enjoy each cold morning.

The State education system was in its infancy, and Joseph was able to attend school regularly except during planting and harvesting on the farm. These two events required the participation of the whole Connelly clan, and their very survival depended upon these two labor intensive chores to be carried out no matter what.

Joseph's father, Patrick, died tragically when an infected wound caused his blood to sour, eventually shutting down his heart.

The injury occurred when Patrick had the farm horse, Trot, harnessed to pull the single furrow wooden plough enabling the rows to be dug allowing the potato crop to be sown. The ancient leather strapping in the harness fractured causing the plow to become untethered. Trot, with no weight to pull, ran forward and, because Patrick had fallen into the bad habit of wrapping the reins around his right hand for better control, the leather tightened as Trot lurched forward, tearing away two fingers from the entrapped hand. As Patrick was pulled forward into the wooden plough, one handle broke and speared his right thigh.

A loving and able father, Patrick felt his heart break as he laid helplessly in bed for several weeks until his angels gathered around him and mercifully relieved his pain.

When Joseph's father died, it was expected that Joseph would don the mantle of "man of the house"—after all, he was thirteen years old and those thirteen years of learning under his father's gentle guidance had acquitted him well for the tasks ahead. He was no longer able to attend school but had already learnt how to read and write.

Mr. George Dosset was Joseph's teacher and recognized that the lad was bright and very quick to learn, so although Joseph became bound to the farm, Mr. George Dosset would call at the Connelly's croft, dropping off several books for his young charge and collecting those he had left on his previous visit. The young scholar always found time in the evenings by the light of a small candle, when everyone was in bed, to delve into Mr. Dosset's offerings. He saw each page as a gift and had no trouble at all allowing his mind to be transported to places he knew he would never have the opportunity to visit in reality. Reading by the flickering light late into the evenings was the single comfort Joseph had to look forward to, and he treasured the time. He was alone.

Joseph's two sisters were courted young as was the custom of the time, and at fifteen, Kate, the "baby," married a young man, Mathew Morgan, who worked as a blacksmith in the nearby village of Transbridge. Almost twelve months later to the day, Tess, now seventeen, was betrothed to a man whom Joseph disliked intensely. Nothing remains unknown in small Irish villages, and Marcus Eversall, Tess's betrothed, had a reputation for drunken behavior and brawling.

Joseph met his wife-to-be, Grace O'Mara, at Saint Brendan's Catholic Church, where the Connelly family attended Mass and received the sacrament of the Holy Eucharist every Sunday. She was new to the district, and Joseph willingly threw himself under her spell, believing her to be the most beautiful girl he had ever seen. The first things he noticed on that brightly sunlit Sabbath were her glistening green eyes, as green as the emeralds that had so mesmerized him. The glittering green emeralds that adorned the monstrance in the Dublin Cathedral. The candles that burned either side of that beautifully ornate host carrier caused those green emeralds to flicker, as if taking part in a hypnotic sacred dance. Joseph believed that he would never see anything as beautiful as those green gems again in his lifetime. Grace O'Mara dispelled that myth.

Joseph was awestruck by that object of reverence when he accompanied his father on church business to try to convince Bishop Mannix of Dublin to lower the amount of the tithes being paid by him and his neighbors into the ever swelling coffers of the catholic church. The negotiations ended badly, and it was the first and only time Joseph Connelly ever saw his father angry. So angry in fact that he cursed the bishop using language that Joseph had only sampled previously from the mouths of the seamen to whom he would deliver the farm's potatoes for transportation to the port of Liverpool in England.

"What would be the value of that solid gold monstrance?" Joseph asked of his father as they rode home from Dublin on the roof of the mail and passenger coach through driving wind and rain.

His father's reply lived on to haunt him. "Many meals on many, many tables, son."

Wealth above all else!

After a quick courtship, Grace and Joseph married, with Grace moving in to the Connelly croft.

The parish priest father Riley, who performed the marriage service, was an insignificant little man who looked to be much older than his hard spent forty years. The church building was suffering from lack of adequate maintenance, and all the parishioners knew that the majority of the stipend allotted to Father Riley was being spent on cheap whiskey. He insisted that imbibing the alcohol in large quantities was the only way he could physically cope with the problems of the parish he had, reluctantly, been sent to. It would seem that the same amounts of strong drink were required at all the seven parishes to which Father Riley had been assigned previously. Some parishioners expressed their concerns to the incumbent Bishop Mannix when he bothered to visit, but all was to no avail.

So many parishes, so much whiskey and rumors concerning the inordinate amount of time Father Riley was spending with his preferred altar boys. It was an old trick of the church to move "problem priests" often to other parishes to allow rumors and complaints to subside.

Despite the poor service provided by the catholic church to the parish that Joseph and his family were so devoted to, Joseph depended on his faith and considered himself to be a better man because of it. He was very well thought of by his community and often helped his neighbors with farmwork during the heavy load days.

Grace, nee O'Mara, now Connelly, was true to her given name. She had true grace and was living with her widower father and three brothers in a village near to the Connelly croft. It was on a day that she decided to attend Mass, with her cousin Colleen, at St. Brendan's Catholic Church that she was initially introduced to Joseph Connelly. He was not new to love. He was surrounded by love. His mother, his father, and his two sisters truly loved him, and he knew it to be so. Joseph knew how to receive love and to return it. This grounding afforded Joseph the wherewithal to begin a family of his own.

Joseph's mother, Irene, no longer enjoyed good health and spent much of her time confined to bed. Typically for the time, she smoked a pipe and was seldom without it. Her room stunk of cheap tobacco, lanolin, and illness. Joseph's father had always grown tobacco as a trading crop with the sailors who were able to pay in cash or barter for seafood. Tobacco grew well in the otherwise useless, boggy areas of the farm and required little maintenance.

Irene purchased the cheap clay pipe from a tinker who travelled the countryside carrying a sailor's tote bag overloaded with all manner of kitchenware and small trinkets. Many of the gift items were of a religious significance, and on previous visits to the Connelly croft, Irene had separately purchased three sets of rosary beads. One set she kept for herself, one she gave to Patrick as a Christmas gift, while the third set she hid in the family straw mattress to await Joseph's next birthday. He received those rosary beads on the day his father died.

The clay pipe was given to Patrick by his family in honor of his fortieth birthday. Try to smoke the "bloody pipe" Patrick did, but every time he sucked the smoke into his lungs, he exhaled coughing uncontrollably. Try, cough, try, cough, over and over. Patrick was not a man to give up easily, but he did give up on that pipe. It was an occasion for great laughter when the family came into the cottage altogether at the end of an exhausting day picking potatoes to find Irene Connelly barely visible standing by the woodstove shrouded by the pall of smoke emanating from that bloody pipe.

Irene Connelly became excited every time she saw the tinker headed toward the farm. She would feign interest to purchase some small item knowing full well, as did the tinker, that she did not have the money to complete the sale. The tinker called himself Garret.

Garrett was not old but bent over and well-worn as were his clothes. A small shiny hook sat in the place that once held his left hand. He told stories of wild adventures, and the Connelly children would sit on the ground with their mother as Garrett held court.

Joseph particularly liked the story that Garret told of how he lost his hand. He told of a fight he had found himself in while trying to defend the honor of a young lady who had been set upon by a band of brigands in Manchester dockside. The number of offenders often varied with each retelling of the tale. Joseph would ponder on how he would one day take charge and fare well in a similar situation.

Irene loved the idea of touching the small gift pieces. Touching something new. How fresh they were. With each visit, the pleasure she felt was the same. In reality, most of the trinkets were the same ones that Irene had tenderly stroked and that Garrett had been carrying onto the Connelly farm for the past eight years.

Garrett declared that he was a "proud gypsy; some scholars refer to us as the Egyptian tribe. Yes, our history comes from the land of the pyramids and the pharaohs. I am proudly from the true line of Abraham and his second wife, Keturah. Gajos, that is people like yourselves who are not proud gypsies, sometimes don't take the time to understand our story but not for one sacred second do I include you, Missus Irene Connelly, or any of your beautiful children in that number."

As Garrett spoke, Joseph could not help but notice that he started to gouge at the skin on the back of his right hand with the engraved silver hook that served as his left hand. He was cutting into the skin but seemed to be numbed to the pain.

"I pray that the red heart of my Sacred Black Madonna, Saint Sara la Cali, blesses you all, " uttered Garrett.

Joseph's inquisitive mind was piqued further as he heard Garrett say "Black Madonna, Red Heart" so the question followed: "Who is the Black Madonna?"

Garrett's answer further confused the issue. "The Madonna is a religious statue, young Joey. Her skin is black," he said. "She is our own patron saint and, of course, the mother of our Lord, but sadly, I heard some thieves plucked out her Red Heart. But Joseph, heart or no heart, my people will always pray to her."

Garrett continued. "Missus Connelly, you do listen, and I know that young Joseph here respects myself and people such as myself as his faith tells him to. I tell you now, I share the same faith and return that respect to all mankind, but hear me now and believe it please that amongst my own people, I am in truth a king."

There was something about the guilt in the tone of Garrett's voice when he spoke of the Black Madonna that unnerved Joseph. He reckoned there was more to the tale than Garrett had disclosed.

CHAPTER FOUR

Joseph was not so keen on reading poetry, and when his mentor, Mr. George Dossett, dropped in and gave him the odd tattered book of poetry to read as part of his at home education, he struggled. There was something not right to Joseph's ear as he listened to Garrett stumble out his awkward story of the heartless Black Madonna.

Joseph was not one to dwell on and memorize any lines of poetry that he was given to read, but as he was trying to understand the way he felt about Garrett's explanation, a line from "Marmion: A tale of Flodden Field" by Sir Walter Scott came crashing into his thoughts. "Oh what a tangled web we weave when first we practice to deceive." Mr. Dossett had explained to Joseph that this line was often misquoted as having been written by Shakespeare and had featured in either *Hamlet* or *Macbeth* some three hundred odd years earlier. It never did. Joseph had always held Garrett in high regard. He had no reason not to, but on the telling of the story of the heartless Black Madonna , something changed.

Life for the expanding Connelly family had become incredibly difficult. Rental on the croft had to be paid, and the rigors and hardships of farming the croft, coupled with the rigid constraints and demands for tithes imposed by the representatives of their god, had created a situation where any hope of improvement was beyond imagination.

Joseph and Grace had only been married two years when Irene Connelly passed away. No specific ailment took Irene Connelly. Joseph explained to the folk that had gathered for her funeral, "My loving mother just wore out. I believe she was very happy to say goodbye to this earth. She had simply had enough. She could take no more."

Joseph buried his mother alongside his father. She had lived for fifty years, and nearing her end, she made Joseph swear to look after his sister Tess because she held great fears for her safety after several visitors had related to her the instances of beatings meted out to Tess by her cruel husband. Joseph begged his sister to return home, but she had given birth to a son by this time and Marcus Eversall threatened to harm them both if she moved out.

A few short weeks after the death of his mother, Joseph found himself weeping into another hole in the ground. The roughly hewn timber box being lowered slowly into the grave next to his mother held what was left remaining of his sister Tess. Her brutish husband had beaten her so severely with a small axe she was rendered unrecognizable.

Joseph had never known such sadness, but after gently covering the tiny piece of his god's earth that was now the final resting place of the sister he so loved, he found himself lost in thought as he took in the beauty of that day. Tess loved shamrocks, and the whole of the church grounds was covered in them. They were in bloom. The flowers were pink, and such was the season that the pink glaze almost completely obscured the green carpet from which they had sprung. He imagined he could see Tess plucking up a handful of the delicate pink treasures and bringing them home to place in a vase on the cottage table. Her favorite color was pink.

The local police officer, John Rostan , was a good and diligent man. He was born in Ireland, but his parents had relocated to London in 1813 when John was just three years old. He decided as a young man that he would become a policeman, and now, at thirty years of age, with twelve years in the force, he found himself having to deal with situations that, as a child, he could never have imagined. He was a tall man, well over six feet, with a powerful body that served him well along the path he had chosen. John was respected by his senior officers, and when he was offered the position of senior serving constable at Transbridge back in Ireland, he accepted the challenge but not just for the promotion. John had not married, and when he relocated to Transbridge, his longtime live-in friend Roger Earls moved with him.

Whenever he was able, John would visit his parents in London with whom he spoke Gaelic in a very broad Irish accent, but on his return to Ireland, he transferred back to speaking thunderously with the Cockney accent of London England. He knew this ruse would reinforce the authority required to perform his duties. The friend with whom he shared his home secured a position as pastry chef at the one and only bakery in Transbridge.

Despite significant effort, the police, in particular John Rostan, were unable to find Tess's murderer. He had fled the scene and just seemed to disappear. Tess's son, Peter, was taken in by her sister, Kate, who, by this time, already had two children of her own. Kate's husband, Mathew, had expanded his blacksmith business and now employed two apprentices. Not rich but doing very well, Mathew was a caring man and did not hesitate to receive Tess's son into his home.

The first child born to Joseph and Grace was named Benedict, soon followed by Paul, Mary, Therese, Katherine, Josephine, and Ellen. The arrival of a new Connelly was almost an annual event. Katherine did not see her third birthday. She arrived too early into a world that saw her father and mother beginning to struggle with that unforgiving necessity of coping. Katherine was always weaker than the others of the brood, and during a particularly brutal winter, only four days from Christmas, her mind was soothed by an ever-increasing fever and death was gentle. She was the only other family member to inherit her mother's emerald-jeweled eyes. Joseph took great care as he fashioned her coffin and quietly wept over it as he drove in the last nail. Grace, prior to Katherine's death, had already handsewn a brightly colored little dress knowing that it would only ever be worn once. She wept loudly as she tied off the last stitch.

Without fail, the Connellys, all eight of them, would tend the graves of Mr. and Mrs. Connelly senior and baby Katherine and Tess. Old flowers were removed, and freshly picked blooms were laid ever so carefully in their stead. The graveyard was situated next to the ancient battered old church of Saint Brendan, and several older women who lived nearby took great pride and care ensuring that the grounds were immaculately kept.

CHAPTER FIVE

The self-appointed leading hand of the gardens and grounds maintenance group was a fiercely Irish Catholic stalwart by the name of Molly Malone.

She and her husband took over a croft that had seen the previous tenants evicted. Molly's husband drank heavily, and the croft only survived because Molly was worth two good men when it came to the crofting business of farming. Parish rumors abounded when local folk began to slowly realize that Molly's husband had not attended Mass for quite some time. Only one member of the catholic community of St. Brendan's was brave enough to ask as to his whereabouts, and that was Father Riley. Bravery was not really a strength in the character of Father Riley, but he could emulate bravado by priming himself with enough Irish whiskey, and as was his bent, that is exactly how he managed the pressure he was being put under by his nosy parishioners to find out the whereabouts Molly's husband.

One day, Father Riley found himself looking out from his bedroom window, and he saw Molly working in the church garden. He could see she was alone, and because he had consumed a serious amount of alcohol for breakfast, along with five self-rolled cigarettes, his synthetically produced courage was in overload.

Father Riley's question to Molly was sharp. "Why do we not see your good husband at Mass these lovely days, Molly? Is the poor man ill? Can I arrange for some of the good folk of St. Brendan's to give you both a hand?"

"Jesus Christ himself wouldn't have the cheek for so many questions." Molly became instantly livid at the barrage. "You could have stopped at question number one. You don't see the useless shite that lived with me at Mass anymore and you never will again. He has run off, and I am all the better off for it. I don't need a helping hand from anybody to farm the croft. I have been doing all that needs to be done for a year now, and with that dung pile gone away, I am the happier for it."

There was a venom in Molly Malone's answer, and Father Riley, although drunk at the inquisition, reckoned that the dung pile may not be living at the croft anymore but he was there all the same.

Molly prided herself on knowing what flowers to plant along with the when and the where of it. The planting program that

Molly insisted be used ensured that there was always a ready supply of blooms to be cut and used for decoration in the church when the various masses being said required them— e.g., lilies for the requiems; bright dahlias, ranunculus, violas, calendulas for Holy Days of Obligation; and basket loads of white blooms for baptisms, communions, confirmations, and weddings.

It was primarily down to the extra effort that Molly would make when it came to the presentation of the gardens that nearly all the neighboring parish church maintenance committees decided to no longer enter the annual best church gardens competition.

Molly's motley group had taken out the once fiercely contested competition for three years in a row, which coincidentally equated to the same amount of time Molly had actually been living in St. Brendan's Parish. Molly insisted that the trophy, a small wooded crucifix, that had become detached from its base and that nobody had bothered to repair should be kept in her home at all times, and not even the bravest of the parish horticulturalists were brave enough to raise an objection, fearing the hell inspired admonishment of one Molly Malone raining down upon them.

Sadly it was no coincidence that Molly Malone and her helpers were the consistent winners of the best garden competition.

Father Riley, the parish priest at St. Brendan's, had initiated the "win at any cost scheme."

He was in trouble with his bishop from Dublin who had made him aware that church investigators were looking into complaints made against him by his own parishioners with regard to the misuse of the tithe money they all had to pay. Father Riley was known to spoil himself whenever possible with the most expensive tobacco for his pipe. He drank heavily, and it was always the cheapest alcohol. "Quantity not quality says I," he often mumbled to himself, and then there was the complaints against him for possibly molesting some of the altar boys with whom he was far too familiar.

He felt he could gain some positive recognition from his Dublin-based spiritual leader, Bishop Mannix, by claiming that he had orchestrated the three successive triumphs in the best garden competition. What he did in truth—with the very willing cooperation of Molly Malone—was to pay her to visit the other gardens in the competition and sabotage the soils in the flowerbeds. Salt was the weapon of choice, and Molly would dig it into the opposition's flowerbeds on her visits to these places if no one was around.

CHAPTER SIX

The crofters lot was harsh, and given that the allotted land they tended and farmed was rented from affluent landowners and never owned, their tenure was always tenuous. All improvements to the farm were carried out by the tenants. The homes they built were no more than primitive stone hovels. All outbuildings rose at a cost to the farmers. The meager farm equipment was purchased by the crofters again at their own expense. Implements were often shared by the six to ten farmers who were permitted to live in small clusters, allowing what was to be the beginnings of villages that grew as time passed. If, through genuine hardship and due to no fault of their own, the crofters fell behind in their rent, many landlords saw this situation as a means to improve their own wealth. Rent racking was common. This evil practice took place when a landlord would judge a particular tenant to be doing better than others in his collective. His factor or property overseer would provide overall updates to his employer and decisions could be made to raise rents without giving any reason. The payments demanded of the over-achieving crofter would soon see him unable to meet the debt. He would be evicted without notice, and another desperate family would be installed immediately. Their rent would be considerably higher because the farm already included all the improvements the now-destitute previous tenant had provided. No compensation was paid to the unfortunate evictees, but the landowner had increased his lot considerably.

The year of Katherine's death heralded in the beginning of God's decision to put Ireland to the sword. Desperate prayers fell on deaf ears. Extra masses were said in the hope that the Almighty would be appeased for whatever it was that he considered so wrong. Whatever it was that these peasants had done to cause the divine wrath of their god to be delivered by such a savage onslaught.

The Connellys were not alone in their struggle for survival.

Potatoes were the currency of the day. Sharecropping allowed rent to be paid to the landowners. Part balance of the crop allowed food to be put on the table while the remainder was sold at market for cash and bartered for other necessities.

The croft that adjoined Joseph Connelly's was farmed by the Dennys, Finbar and Helen with their five offspring, Michael, Dominic, Jean, Angela, and Therese.

Fin and Joseph had always been neighbors, and given that Joseph had no brothers, Fin filled the position more ardently than many blood brothers. On the odd occasions when spare time was available to Joseph and Finbar, they would meet to go fishing, throw stones, eat wild berries, and chase down rabbits. Fin looked forward to the times he could spend with Joseph. Joseph was clever. He could read and write. He could add up numbers. Although almost the same age, Finbar had always looked up to the boy he would insist on calling big ugly brother. Joseph had read many books loaned to him by his ever-vigilant mentor and ex-teacher Mr. George Dossett. His imagination knew no bounds, and Fin would listen absolutely spellbound as Joseph retold the story of his favorite hero Ivanhoe, written in 1819 by Walter Scott. Both boys mentally placed themselves within the ranks of the army of Richard the Lionheart, England's king who bravely led and fought in Crusades on behalf of his God to conquer the Holy Lands in Persia. Finbar insisted that he be Ivanhoe, the brave and handsome heroic knight.

The story of Rob Roy, written by the same author, told the true story of Scottish clans struggling against English oppression. The boys could identify with much of the content in this thrilling story. The Irish were being treated no better than the Scots were exactly one hundred years earlier when the Jacobites revolution was quelled, culminating with the battle of Culloden in 1746.

Mr. Dossett secreted a copy of Mary Shelley's *Frankenstein* to Joseph telling him not to let anyone know that he was reading such a book. This was not done in malice; it was done because George Dossett was a man ahead of his time, and he wanted to discuss what Joseph understood about the messages contained within that text. Shelley's book, also known as the Modern Prometheus, contained many parallel meanings, and Dossett was in his element explaining to Joseph all he understood about the novel. He felt he was pandering to his own ego, but by the time he and Joseph had finished their deep discussion on the meanings of the work, he was pleased to reassess his motives and declared to himself that it was indeed education he was promoting and not his own self-worth.

Jane Austen's *Pride and Prejudice*, written in 1813, was another favorite, with its colorful and often brutal descriptions of the Georgian era with all its snobbery and pompous affectations. The historical backdrop witnessed the French Revolution, guillotining of Anne Boleyn, and the rise of Napoleon. All wonderful ingredients being blended well in the minds of two young men who otherwise would have no knowledge or appreciation of anything beyond their own narrow geographical, cultural, and faith-based boundaries.

Joseph quietly enjoyed the hero worship. It was positive, and it made him feel good. In fact, it made him feel so good that he found himself examining his own conscience in case the feeling was sinful. Such was the power over thought that insidiously overpowered the religiously controlled local population.

AN GORTA MOR, the Gaelic term given to the Potato Famine.

In 1844, the potato crops began to fail. The plants would begin well but leaves withered, and although the growth underground attained a usable size, when dug up, it was foul-smelling and rotting. The Irish crofters all planted the same potato type, and colloquially, it was known as the Irish Lumper. Had other varieties been incorporated, the famine may well have been avoided.

Although the potatoes were corrupted and had become soft, giving off a terrible smell, some people—due to desperation—did still try to eat them. If they were actually able to swallow the disgusting mush, it would lead to vomiting, with many diners remaining very ill for days.

Initially, the devastation was not total. Some farms fared better than others, but as time passed, it became obvious that no holding was to be spared, and starvation became the savage reality.

Chapter Seven

Finbar Denny was the first of Joseph's neighbors to abandon his croft in the hope of meeting up with his cousin Matthew in Manchester who was working on the railway line being built over the Pennine Mountains to link Manchester with Sheffield in Yorkshire. Matthew was made aware of Finbar's situation through a discussion he had with a sailor friend who knew them both and worked on the produce transport boats. He asked that friend to advise Finbar that he, Matthew, would provide temporary accommodation for him and his two remaining children, also offering to find work for his cousin on the rail line construction. Matthew had just been made the leading hand of one of the many forty-men gangs that specialized in laying sleepers and rail for the steam train rail transport network growing so rapidly that the overview maps required to locate everything were eerily beginning to resemble the Victorian medical etchings of the veins and arteries that coursed through the human anatomy.

The year was 1845. Finbar Denny was desperate. Only two of his five children, Michael and Angela, still walked the earth. Dominic, Jean, and Therese were buried alongside their mother, Helen, in the graveyard at St. Brendan's, no more than ten paces from the Connelly graves. The children perished from starvation, and along with infections of typhus, they were savagely called to their maker. Helen Denny had been starving herself to feed her children and was no more than a skeleton draped in crimson skin when she breathed her last. The typhus caused her blood to seep into the skin through damaged veins, resulting in swollen flesh that glowed with a bloodred hue.

When visiting the graves of his wife and children, Finbar couldn't help but note that the once-beautiful gardens that surrounded St. Brendan's Church and the adjoining graveyard were no more. The colorful garden beds had been reduced to rows of mud with the odd dead flower stem protruding from the surface like the rent mast of a floundering sailing ship.

Finbar noticed yet another new grave had been squeezed in, almost lapping the grave site of his wife. He immediately realized who had been interred so close to hand and sadly thought to himself that he would have preferred it if this person had been buried well away from his loved ones.

This new grave had been marked by a small wooden crucifix, and the base had actually been reattached. The Great Hunger had beaten Molly Malone and her beloved garden beds with her.

Finbar was told of his cousin's offer to help relocate his family by that mutual friend, and with no alternative available to him, he put together a small bundle of clothes, tying them in the only two threadbare blankets he had left because the remainder he had used as shrouds to bury his dead family members in. He made Joseph aware of his intentions at Sunday Mass, and by the dawn of the following day, he, Michael, and Angela had fled. The covert departure was necessary because Lord Houghton, his landlord, was not a man to be indebted to, and Finbar was indebted.

Lord Houghton, who lived in the family Georgian-style mansion twenty miles from central London, owned over two thousand acres of land in Ireland and held one hundred and ninety-eight crofters under his charge. He had two overseers living on his Irish estate, and it was their job to ensure that all problems were attended to. They were expected to execute their duties heavy-handedly and tolerate no ructions from any of the oftentimes desperately angry, hard-driven farmers.

Collecting rent was a big part of their reason to be there, and if rents did fall behind—and they often did—the guilty tenant could be beaten in front of his family and left with bruises that came as a warning to his neighbors when next they all attended Sunday service at whatever parish church they belonged to.

Finbar had been dealt several of these beatings, but as the famine progressed and his family succumbed to the hunger, paying rent was simply impossible. The overseer, Jonathan Hessings, found himself reluctant to add any further misery to the man that he could clearly see was good and decent. It was he who finally caused Finbar to make up his mind and leave. He even left several pennies with him on their last meeting.

The mutual boat-laboring friend smuggled the Denny family on to the craft he sailed in and hid the three wretched souls in the cargo hold. Prior to their arrival onboard, he had made up a small parcel of bread and cheese which he hid in the place that was to be their safe haven for the voyage. The passage crossing, a distance of one hundred and forty miles, took longer than usual due to lack of wind and a particularly heavy load of food plunder that could have relieved in some small way the strife being flayed on the people of its place of origin.

That small parcel of food looked like banquet proportions to the Dennys as they wolfed down most of its contents within five minutes of unwrapping it. Finbar held some back because he did not know if that was all there would be. His concern was abated when, some six hours later, an unfamiliar seafarer delivered a small portion of rum and a well-battered clay jar of water to the relieved refugees. More cheese and bread also arrived with the drinks, and with bellies well satisfied, the Dennys huddled together for the completion of their short but long voyage.

CHAPTER EIGHT

U pon their arrival in Liverpool, they travelled up the river route along the Mersey to the Irwell and eventually landed in Manchester. Finbar parted with two of the pennies he had been given by Jonathan Hessings to secure a tragically filthy, tiny, and unfurnished room in the tavern, aptly named the Black Duck, where he had arranged to meet his cousin. The hour was late, so he unwrapped the clothing parcel, handing out each item to its owner, and insisted that they put them on over the top of their original rags. He drew his children to him, placing Angela in the center, then taking the threadbare blankets, all three huddled in for a night that was already bitter cold.

Finbar was exhausted but unable to sleep as his mind raced menacingly, creating so many scenarios, none of which were heartening. His main concern was Matthew, his cousin, who had agreed to help him settle and gain work. What if Matthew did not materialize? What if he had been involved in some rail construction disaster? He knew such things happened often. What if he was in gaol? He was known to be a hotheaded hard man. What if, what if? The night travelled more slowly than the becalmed vessel that had delivered the Dennys several hours earlier to this unfamiliar place where Finbar found himself profoundly tormented until his God's sun lit up the heavens to herald in the new day that Finbar desperately hoped would answer all the questions he had battled with during the darkness of that dreadful night.

He had been told in no uncertain terms by the keeper of the Black Duck that the room had to be vacated at daylight because the quiet space was used by sailors to write letters home to family during the day. Still wearing everything they owned, the Dennys found themselves squatted down in a small lane that adjoined the tavern, positioned so as to have good vision of the entrance in the hope that Matthew would be true to his word.

The doorway to the oversized cupboard in which they had spent their first night on English shores was also in clear view. Finbar was surprised to see the first letter writer arrive in the company of a woman who, it seemed to him, was trying desperately to present an image that did not attest to her true age. The letter did not take long at all to write because, within ten minutes, the scribe and his companion exited the room and slowly walked arm in arm back toward the docks. Another short letter and couple number two headed off in the same direction as the first. Within minutes, yet another couple arrived. Indeed a new scribe but the woman who accompanied him was the same person writing letters with the first sailor of the day. Finbar could almost hear the penny drop, and at that moment, he glanced across to Michael to see a much younger version of himself staring back at him with a wry smile plastered across his adolescent face. All of Michael's sixteen years flashed through Finbar's inner thoughts, and turning to thirteen-year-old Angela, he saw the worried look on her tender face and forced a broad smile.

The day had warmed only slightly as the morning dragged on with no sign of Matthew. The streets that bounded the Black Duck had become alive with activity, and the noise was deafening to the Dennys who had never seen or heard the like. As noisy as it was, the volume escalated as a band of five extremely loud and possibly moderately drunk men headed toward the tavern from Manchester Central. There was no mistaking the man who centered the approaching cluster. Matthew stood head and shoulders above his cohorts, and his booming voice could be clearly heard above the din and clatter of all competition.

"So there you are you little bastard," he bellowed.

Fin was not short of stature, but he was dwarfed as Matthew propelled himself forward, taking Fin into an embrace that forced every ounce of air from his lungs. The relief Finbar felt at that moment was almost palpable. Matthew was wearing some nasty-sized scars on his face that were new to Fin. They had not seen one another in over seven years, and if the truth be told, were it not for Matthew's physical volume, he may not have recognized him at all. Matthew quickly barged his way through all the necessary introduction, including Michael and Angela, to his cronies.

That fact that Matthew was able to name Fin's two remaining children without asking greatly impressed him. With the formalities quickly over, Matthew threw his arm over Fin's shoulder and forcefully aligned him directly in front of the tavern door.

"My colleagues and I intend to round off our breakfasts at yonder tavern, and I insist that you and yours join us, cousin. The wee-ens look like they could do with some fattening up, and the sooner, the better, I say. No coins required. You know me as a man of my word, Fin, and what I said I will do for you will surely be done," trumpeted Matthew.

The Dennys one and all could not get through the front door of the tavern quick enough, and it was not until one hour had passed that the adults staggered back out into the street, followed by Michael and Angela who did indeed look well-sated. Matthew suggested that it was time to head for home because he was due back to work a shift on the railway line construction in four hours and would need to get some sleep. It was a considerable distance from the Black Duck to the dilapidated dwelling where Matthew resided with his wife, Coleen, and their two sons, George and Edward.

Matthew's alcohol-fueled enthusiasm did not falter throughout the trek. He began a familiarization commentary and told the Dennys as they walked most of what he thought they should know about their new life.

The area he called Salford, and he insisted they memorize the address. "Old homes boxed in between Brown Street North and Hargreaves Street South," he repeated over and over and then insisted that the Dennys do the same. "North of the river Irk and our church is St. Michael's near Angel Gardens" also repeated over and over by all. "You should know that everyone who attends St. Michael's will swear that it is the ugliest church ever built, and so I welcome you to Little Ireland," he proudly proffered. "We are all Irish around here, so your Gaelic won't be a problem although you will have to pick up as much English as you can as fast as you can because the Protestants hate us Catholics. They call us Taigs and if someone, anyone, calls you a Taig, you best just ignore them because they would like nothing better than to have you start a fight so that they can knock seven sorts of shite out of ya and then have the peelers throw you in gaol and you can't feed yer family if yer locked up. We work harder and longer than they do. We take whatever the bosses offer us. We don't complain, and they bloody well know that our prayers get to God a long time before theirs do because we found him first. You must go about your business, but stick to Little Ireland please. Stay in Little Ireland."

Apart from repeating instructions as Matthew demanded, the Dennys remained silent. Not out of courtesy but born solely out of the horrific attack on every one of their senses that Little Ireland was charging them with. There appeared to be little or no paving in the streets and laneways, and as they walked, it seemed to them as if they were sinking further and further into a quagmire. The mud was as thick as cement and carried within it tons of garbage and rotting material simply dumped there by the residents because no alternative was available.

The homes stood in rows but appeared to be built from a plan conjured up by an addlebrained child whose only motive in doing so was to make his parents angry at the poor effort. It could be seen, through the scramble, that when these old dwellings had first been erected several generations past, a uniformity of sorts had been followed. The present vision however presented like a canvass created by an artist never happy with his effort, so in an attempt to properly please the eye of the beholder, further layers were added again and again. The end result rather than soothing the vision of the spectator shocked as did Mary Shelley's *Frankenstein* when it hit the bookshelves in 1818 and had been read to Finbar by Joseph Connelly.

Every house had pieces added, and the one ingredient missing from the majority of these constructed carbuncles was craftsmanship. All manner of materials had been tacked on here and there in an effort to create more rooms under roof. Every home had grown its own single occupant pig pen. The pork produced offered vital nutrients to Little Ireland's grossly inadequately fed residents.

Matthew noticed Fin's puzzled interest in the bricked up windows of the old homes. "Daylight robbery we call that, cousin," he mused.

The window tax that had been introduced as far back as the 1690s only added to the appalling sight because, to avoid payment of that tax, landlords closed in many of the windows, and in doing so, the interior of the tenements remained in darkness twenty-four hours a day. Oil lamps could be seen flickering in open doorways to light the path into these homes that looked more like caves.

The window coverings were initially made from timber offcuts discarded by the wooden boat builders at the Manchester shipbuilding dockyards. These boards were nailed to the window frames, but the tenants would remove them as quickly as they were erected. Not to be beaten, the government then declared that boards or no boards, the windows were still windows, and when that edict was issued, the landlords went to extraordinary measures and had the costly light givers fully bricked in.

The whole scene was atrocious to look at, but the overriding sensual knockout was the stench. Finbar, not wanting to appear rude, soldiered on beside Matthew, but both Michael and Angela following behind had drawn the collars of their coats tightly over their noses. Angela stopped suddenly, having spied two dogs tearing apart the flesh of a scrawny cat in one of the adjoining hall-sized laneways. All control left her, and she vomited up the feast she had consumed back at the Black Duck Tavern, a mere twenty-eight minutes earlier. Michael did not escape the cascade that came with epic force, and after wiping the offensive matter away from his own clothing with a dirty rag he had produced from his coat pocket, he leaned over Angela to do the same. As he held her, he could feel her body trembling almost uncontrollably.

With everything she had witnessed and been personally part of in Ireland, he could not remember ever having seen her so distressed.

The Irish village devastation they had just withdrawn from had become slow and, in areas, almost static. Nothing much was moving, whereas Salford, like the whole of Manchester, appeared like a scampering mass of men, women, children, dogs, cats, pigs, and chickens seemingly heading nowhere in particular but in a great hurry to get there. Michael drew his sister's ear close and whispered to her in Irish Gaelic "Uafasach." His summary meaning all of "horrible, disastrous, unbearable, and shite."

Finbar realized that the numbing effects of the five ales bought for him by Matthew at the Black Duck had totally withdrawn. He realized with great discomfort that he could not bring himself to turn and look back at his children for fear of how that vision could crush him.

The sense and picture of perfect pandemonium became complete with the addition of noise. The barking of dogs, the hissing of angry cats, the flapping, clucking, and crowing of chickens too many to count, the squealing of pigs, the high-pitched chatter of filthy children, and the calm or raised voices of the adult denizens of the Salford slum all accompanied by the rhythmic clattering of the looms in the countless number of cotton mills powered by the hissing and thumping of the steam engines reportedly invented by Scotsman James Watt in 1786 and continually improved to allow them to power Manchester's industries smoothly from well before daybreak and well into the night.

Every factory was belching out black smoke from the chimneys that extended to great heights toward the heavens. Despite all efforts made to dispel the smoke, it created its own atmospheric capsule, and a gray pall hung over the town causing the sun's shape to be roundly visible through the acrid filter.

Manchester, at that time, was the beating heart of England. Prior to steam power, it was waterwheels that allowed machinery to turn, and the prime industry there was the manufacture of cotton cloth with an unrivalled quality. The canal system that was excavated manually to enable more waterwheels to be incorporated into the system was the human effort that transcended all others up to that time. The cotton, also referred to as soft gold, gave birth to innumerable entrepreneurs, and vast fortunes were made overnight. The nouveau riche ploughed small fortunes into more and more projects that screamed for workers. News spread of the desperate need to keep growing the workforce, and the town population had exploded.

The French philosopher Alexis de Toquaville, having visited Manchester, reported back to Paris that "Manchester was a watery land of palaces and hovels" where "pure gold flowed from a raw sewer" where "man had turned back into a savage."

It was not uncommon to hear people refer to Manchester as the Cottonopolis.

CHAPTER NINE

"And here we are, Fin," shouted Matthew to his nervous companions with all the enthusiasm of a circus ringleader. The Dennys were visibly relieved and hoped, surely, that their situation was about to improve. Finbar and Matthew entered the premises, but Michael and Angela, both unsure of just how to proceed, halted at the entry. As Fin's vision adjusted to the poor light, it occurred to him that he was surrounded by many children and adults. He was led to the kitchen and asked to take a seat. Matthew waved away the seven or more women and children who were occupying that space with a loud "Stop yer mithering us the now," and all but one female immediately cleared the room.

"This is Colleen, my wife, Fin, and she knows everything that I have agreed to do for you, and because I am not home much, what with building the railway line and all, Colleen will help you to get settled in. Loads of people share this house with our family, but they think I pay the rent, so if anyone causes problems, they go back to the streets. You will have to get smart about using the privy. We think that about one hundred and eighty folks have to shite there, and the lineup can take forever. It is a good idea to use it for shite only. If you are looking to do the other, just go up one of the laneways and tell your wee-ens to do the same, but stay well out of the sight of the Peelers," and that being said, Matthew left the room, and Fin could only presume that he was to take the sleep he spoke of during their trek from the Black Duck.

Colleen burst forth with a barrage of questions. Some to Finbar but mostly directed at Michael and Angela. As Fin listened to the interrogations and explanations that Colleen scattered about the room, he judged her to be a good and caring woman who spoke well and was very organized.

"Let me show you where you will be sleeping," she said, and no sooner had the words left her mouth, the Dennys found themselves following her down a set of narrow cellar steps, and she clutched Angela's hand all the way. The cellar was dark, dank, and stunk of the very unpleasant mix of shite and urine. It was also already populated. In the darkness, Finbar could make out the presence of at least four other people. Colleen pushed her way to one corner and exclaimed with mildly tempered pride.

"This is where you will sleep, and as you can see, I have gathered whatever blankets I could lay my hands on for you. The lice will be a problem, so the three of you can search each other, and when you find them come and see me. I have three bottles of tinctures that I use to rub on the skin. A strange little Jewish man named Abraham mixes them for me, but he won't tell me what is in them. Sometimes they work, but sometimes I have to scrub my children until they are red raw to kill them off. There are three doctors in Salford, but all three are Prodies and don't really care much for we Catholics, so I prefer to use the Jew. Abraham also owns his own pawnshop, and he loans money to mothers who have to leave goods with him while their husbands work away, like Matthew does, and there is no money until the men return with wages. His interest charges are dodgy, but he has saved many a family from going hungry. He also has the right stuff for headaches and pains, and his prices are cheap," stated Colleen.

"How many bodies sleep in this cellar?" enquired Fin.

"Sometimes eight but most times ten, including you three," Colleen replied. "I have a friend I would like you to meet later today, Fin. Her name is Mary Burns, and she has told me that her friend Frederick Engels might be able to give Michael and Angela some work in his father's cotton mill. Matthew will find work for you, Fin, but he has asked me to see if Mary Burns could do something for your Angela and Michael. He says the rail work is far too heavy for a young boy just over from the famine, but he wanted you to work with him because although he knew you would be weak, you would insist on doing your fair share, so he wants to keep an eye on you. He is a leading hand now and says he can pick and choose the men he wants for his gang. I am a very lucky woman to have him."

Finbar found himself only taking in parts of the information being provided to him by Colleen. In truth, he was still trying to work out how ten people could possibly sleep in this cramped space. There was no other option available, and he knew it, do or die, the Dennys had to make it work. He felt weighed down with guilt over the first thought that came to him as he stood in the stinking cellar from where he had just ascended into the muted light of Salford. He was glad his wife Helen was dead. He cried within as he admitted to himself that he also felt the deaths of his three children, Dominic, Jean, and Therese, were a blessing. Death had to be better than the existence Fin envisaged he and his children were now to be burdened with.

With still several pennies jingling in his pocket compliments of cousin Matthew, he asked Colleen for directions to St. Michael's church. He needed to pray, and he needed his family to pray with him.

"Up to Aspin Lane and into Gould Street, you will pass Angel Meadow Cemetery on the way. Oh, how stupid of me. You will find it easy. Just head toward the ugliest church you have ever seen."

For several agonizing minutes as the Dennys headed in the direction pointed out to them, no one said a word. Michael was the first to speak.

"That must be the church, Da, and Colleen is right. It looks horrible."

As bad as it did appear, the sight of St. Michael's and his son's exclamation made Fin smile, and that was just the cue his companions needed. The triple cross interrogation just exploded with each of the three participants wanting to know and understand more about where to and what to do from here. After well over one hour of silent prayer at the altar of his creator and with nothing resolved, Fin joined Michael and Angela who had exited the church earlier.

"Top o' the mornin' to ya. I've not seen your faces before. Can I help?" Father Timothy McCordy, the parish priest at St. Michael's, had followed Finbar from within the church.

Fin gave Father McCordy a quick summary of his situation, mentioning the facts that he would be working on the train line and that Colleen's friend Mary Burns was going to help Michael and Angela find paid work at Engels Cotton Mill. The priest asked his new parishioners to join him in a cup of tea at the presbytery adjoining the church and where he lived.

"Everybody calls me Father Tim, and you can do the same if you so wish. It sounds to me that you have a good man in your cousin Matthew. I don't see him often, but his wife comes here and helps with cleaning and placing the altar flowers. You must be careful in Salford. It does not pay to be too Catholic. There are small gangs of young ruffians, English of course, who delight in hurting people of our faith, but they are simply using their faith as an excuse to be cruel. We call them scuttlers. It's an old seafaring term. If you are willing—and please be so—I would like to offer you a small amount of money which you can repay to the church as soon as your wage comes to you from the railway work with your cousin," said Father Tim.

Finbar immediately raised his right hand and uttered a firm but cordial "No. We do not need charity, Father, but I do thank you."

"I am not offering charity, sir. I am offering a small loan, and that is greatly different," explained Father Tim. The sense and fairness of the offer once explained in clear terms allowed Fin to be agreeable.

Father Tim spoke further. "Now I must tell you that I do not know Colleen's friend Mary Burns, but I do know of her reputation, and I would suggest that it might serve you well to avoid having any dealings with her. She is living in sin with one of the mill managers, Mr. Engels, and many of my parishioners see her as a bad example to our younger folk who are already suffering many problems that make living according to our faith hard to understand and follow. There is a lot of unrest amongst the workers, and once you and your children join them, you will understand why. The rich just keep growing richer but see no real need to care a jot about the conditions they expect their employees to work under. There are some who believe that the workers should take a stand and demand that their wages and conditions be improved. Now this Mary Burns person is well-known to be one of those troublemakers, and it has come to my attention that Mr. Frederick Engels has visited the homes of many of the poor folk of Salford and he is writing a book damning the behavior of many of the mill owners with regard to the way they mistreat workers and care little about their health issues caused by factory toiling and all the accidents that happen because the machines are not made safe."

CHAPTER TEN

The prime minister of the day was Mr. Robert Peel, who served in that position for the second time between 1841 and 1846, but prior to that position, he was head of police and actually was responsible for introducing foot patrols to the city streets. They called these patrols beats. The colloquial terms Bobby and Peeler, used to describe the beat police, came from his name. The misery of the slums throughout England was causing huge crime in the towns.

Populations had exploded because of the Industrial Revolution now well into the second century of its exponential growth. Laborers were pouring into the big towns, many fleeing the Great Hunger but also, due to the fact that England was no longer at war with France, thousands of soldiers were no longer required to serve, so that swelled even further the ranks of those seeking work. The majority of the returning soldiers were Irish, but the famine left many with no homes to return to in Ireland, so Manchester became one of the towns where labor was cheap and employers could pick and choose without conscience.

Robert Peel tried to pass acts that would provide food aid to the wretched folks of Salford and surrounding slums, but he was unable to win the battle. Before he became prime minister, it had been decided by parliament to adopt a laissez-faire approach to the problems of the poor. In summary, this simply meant that no assistance would be offered and the attitude of "wait and see" was deemed to be the best option.

After a cup of tea and an oatcake each, the Dennys thanked Father Tim for his kindness and began the walk back to Matthew's place. Along the way, Michael produced one half of the oatcake given to him by Father Tim and placed it in his sister's hand. He knew she would be hungry after vomiting earlier in the day.

Finbar was so lost in thought he failed to respond on several occasions when Michael fired questions at him. He realized that Father Tim had only intended to give good advice, but he now had some choices to make. The last thing he could afford to do was upset Colleen. She held sway over the future of the Dennys.

Matthew would be away a lot, and if things worked out, Fin would be with him. He needs Colleen to look after his family.

If he ignores this Mary Burns person, it would, most likely, not go down well with Colleen.

Arriving back at the Brown Street North home, the Dennys entered and were immediately set upon by an anxious Colleen who did not try to disguise the fact that she was not happy.

"What took you so long? I told you that my friend Mary wanted to meet you all and to talk about work for the bairns. Where did you go to?"

Finbar quickly explained about Father Tim, and after apologizing several times over, Colleen's temper quickly subsided, and Fin thought to himself that her ire was intended to be more of a show for her friend Mary than any real angst with the Dennys.

Mary Burns was an attractive woman, and Fin guessed her age to be around twenty-five years. Without even uttering a word, her visage could not have been any more Irish than if she had been floated into the room on a bed of shamrocks drawn by a harnessed team of leprechauns all wearing emerald-colored tunics and smiling devilishly broad.

She told Fin that she had spoken to her friend Mr. Engels with regard to work for Michael and Angela. She explained that Frederick's father owned several cotton mills in Manchester and he had sent his son to live in the town and to manage one of those mills. Frederick had told Mary that the reason his father insisted that he move to England and accept the responsibility of manager had more to do with the life he was leading in Germany and the fact that his father saw him as too soft.

The cotton mill she referred to was actually jointly owned by Frederick's father and his business associate Peter Erman. The mill was capable of spinning double yarn and employed over one hundred people. Before even meeting Mary Burns, Fin had made up his mind to accept whatever was on offer from her. It would mean security for his children, and the wages they would earn were desperately needed if the Dennys were ever going to survive the unenviable situation he had brought them into.

It was agreed that the Dennys would report to the front gate of the factory at five o'clock the next morning to meet with Mary. She had arranged for the foreman of the mill to show them around and to explain to Finbar just what would be expected of his children. In the back of his mind, he kept hearing the voice of Father Tim whispering to him the warning that he gave when they shared tea and oatcakes at St. Michael's the previous day. Father Tim had expressed his misgivings related to Mary Burns, and priests have to be trusted.

The first night sleeping on the floor of the damp and stinking cellar under Matthew's house did not go well. The Dennys made themselves as warm as they could while trying to get some sleep by huddling close together and wrapping Colleen's three tattered blankets as tight as possible around them. Straw had been piled over the dirt floor, but it had been there so long, it was completely flattened and soaking wet. Fin counted seven other people sharing the ten-foot by twelve-foot black space. These cellar dwellers were very friendly, and Fin went out of his way to express his gratitude to them for allowing the Dennys to join them. Three men and four women made up that compliment. Two married couples and one much older lady that everyone called Granny, and shortly into the introductory conversation, she asked Michael and Angela to address as so.

Their stories were all the same. They were there for the same reason as the Dennys, and like Fin, they were desperate. Fin barely closed his eyes throughout the noisy night. All the sleepers were snoring, and Granny was the leader of the sonorous band. It was still dark when Fin rose. He had no idea of the time but was aware that a small timber-cased clock sat on the mantle above the woodstove in the kitchen. After gingerly picking his way through the sleepers, he ascended the steps, trying as he placed each foot not to make a sound, but that was not to be. Every step tread creaked, and the sound was amplified in the stillness.

"I'll make you a cuppa, Fin," Colleen whispered as he entered the kitchen. She had risen early to ensure that the Dennys got away on time. "I have made a big pot of porridge and was about to wake you, but you beat me to it. Get the bairns up and fed. You don't want to be late. We can't let dear Mary down."

Colleen had scratched out a rough map in pencil on a scrap of paper. None of the streets were named because she was unable to write, but the directions were easy to follow. Her map was a series of lines. Every street along the way had been allocated one of those lines. From the front door, the arrow in the line indicated a right hand turn. Then pass three lines, streets, on the left and turn left at the next line. Pass two lines on the right and enter the third line and on it went.

The Dennys arrived at the mill well before time and huddled up against the factory entry gate. Hearing the constant clacking and clicking sounds coming from the mill, it was obvious to all that the day's production had already begun or at least that was assumed. The truth of the matter was that those sounds had not just begun because they had never stopped. This mill ran continually for twenty-four hours per day, every day, and although other mills did abide with a "no work Sunday" to appease the wants of the church, Mr. Engels's machinery never sat idle. He considered religions to be a load of ill-conceived rot and was never short of labor to carry out the Sunday shifts. All mills ran two shifts per day.

The morning was bitterly cold, and the strong wind just added to the discomfort. Mary Burns arrived as arranged and was accompanied by a tall thin man whom Finbar took to be the foreman. Mary Burns introduced Mr. Snowdon, who was indeed the foreman, to the assembly. Finbar presented his right hand to shake that of Mr. Snowdon, and Mr. Snowdon mimicked the gesture, but as the hands met, Fin flinched. A fine piece of artisan carved fruitwood in the shape of a hand was the cause of the start. The introduction was awkward for Fin, but Mr. Snowdon used his left hand to clasp Fin's grip on to the false appendage in a manner that he was obviously used to doing. The foreman took charge of the situation, and the tour began.

Finbar noticed that Michael seemed distracted by Mr. Snowdon's face as he repeatedly stared at him. The reason for the interest was obvious, so Fin nudged his son's shoulder to disarm the rudeness. Mr. Snowdon appeared to have only one eye. Meer observation couldn't confirm the yay or nay of it because his left eyelid remained constantly closed, so there may have been an eye in place, but given that the area of skin surrounding that eye was so shrunken, it was probably safe to assume that the eye was gone. The nose deviated a full one and a half inches to the left of center and a shabbily healed scar traversed his face beginning high on the left-hand side of his forehead travelling due south in a jagged line to the chin.

With military precision, the unfortunate foreman very systematically walked his charges up and down the length of the ten aisles that ran between the looms, directing his explanations to Michael and Angela. He spoke in English with a strong Welsh accent. Mary Burns listened intently and relayed the information to the youngsters in their own Irish Gaelic.

Finbar was taken aback by what he was witnessing. Hundreds of wheels were spinning at such a rate the spokes that formed their centers were not visible.

Each machine was steam-powered and endless unguarded drive belts bounced up and down dangerously close to the workers at a frenetic pace. Men and women pawed over the machines like worker ants tending a monolithic queen. Strange mirrored light fittings hung down on chains from the roof timbers illuminating the mill like daylight even though the sun had not yet begun to appear.

Like everywhere else in Manchester, this place had an unpleasant odor. In this case, caused by escaping steam mixing with the ingredients used to process the cotton for milling and weaving. The constant motion of the machines was causing lint to be blown all over the premises. It gave the effect of falling snow, but breathing in these soft fibers was in fact causing grave health problems among the workers. Consumption was rampant, and the life expectancy of the mill population hovered around forty-two years of age. Young children, some so tiny, scrambled under the looms, gathering up as much of the deadly lint as they could, placing it in buckets that they rushed to empty every few minutes.

The foreman of works looked to be a mean man, and the children were so obviously in fear of him.

"Don't judge him too harshly, folks. He barks, but he don't bite. Well, he would, but Mr. Engels won't have none o' that," said Mr. Snowdon, who could see the look of concern on Finbar's face.

Finbar Denny just wanted to take hold of his two children and escape. Michael, however, was mesmerized by all that was going on, but he had also tuned into the fear in his father's eyes. "Da, I want to work here. I can do it, and we need the money."

By the end of the tour, Fin had to admit to himself that his son had to make his own decisions. By the standards of the day, he truly was an adult. Mr. Snowdon stated he could offer work to both Denny offspring, and it was agreed that they start on the next morning. Fin thanked him sincerely and held out his hand to shake the wooden replica that the foreman had attached to his arm from where his own hand had been severed. This time, Fin did not flinch but rather found himself puffing with pride when Michael proffered his own right hand to Mr. Snowdon.

Finbar, Michael, and Angela thanked Mary Burns and Snowdon for their help as they left the mill, heading back in same direction from which they had arrived.

As the Dennys returned to Matthew's home, the conversation was buoyant and at times cheery. What a difference the new day had brought. Colleen greeted them and immediately sat them down for a drink. She wanted to know all, and the children were ever so eager to oblige. She reassured Fin that they would be safe with her. Matthew and Colleen had two young children of their own, but there were so many wee ens living in the house, even Colleen seemed to struggle to identify her own, but Fin had a good feeling about this vibrant woman and he agreed to the plan.

CHAPTER ELEVEN

Colleen seemed to tune out of the conversation. She was distracted by the approaching noise from the street that could be heard getting louder and louder. Her smile exploded into laughter. "Sounds like Matthew is home," she yelled, and with that, the twenty-something occupants of the tiny house spilled out into Brown Street North.

It is said that people either love or hate the bagpipes, but if you were Irish in 1845, there was no choice. Every full-blooded Irish Catholic loved the caterwauling, and Matthew was a master piper. He was such a powerful man that he often had to repair or replace the bag of his ancient instrument due to it blowing out under severe pressure as he crushed it toward his chest with his huge arm. He insisted the bag be made of sheep leather. He knew skins from dogs were also used, but he was not having a bar of that. "Bloody barbaric," he would steam.

The approaching parade was indeed a sight to behold. Matthew, playing the pipes, headed the rabble. He was decked out in a kilt and sporran. As he marched up the road toward Colleen, his kilt swayed rhythmically from side to side. His gait was somewhat awkward, and the five men that staggered behind him were faring no better. By now, every occupant living in Brown Street North was cheering in the street. Adults and children alike clapped and waved. Many were even dancing. The Dennys had never seen the like, and they loved it.

Colleen leaned in to Fin and chuckled, "Matthew doesn't own a kilt."

"Well, he does now by the looks of it to be sure," laughed Fin.

"Oh, they are very arfarfan'arf [drunk]," exclaimed Colleen.

The six-man staggering vanguard halted directly in front of Colleen as Matthew threw his right arm into the air. That action allowed the air to be dispelled from the pipes bag, causing the chanter to drop and dangle like a floppy willy between his legs. The humor of the vision was not missed by those who stood close enough to witness the comedy, and Colleen laughed hysterically.

"Oh, what a Benjo [street party] we have here," laughed Colleen.

"Madam, is it you that has charge of this ale house known to all as Mr. Dennys Mud Hole," demanded Matthew of Colleen.

"It has to be said, sir, that I am indeed that person," Colleen replied.

"Then I am here to inform you that my companions and I have been ordered to deliver to you in person several parcels of the most beautiful smoked cod to be found anywhere in Mother Vic's empire," and as he spoke, Matthew turned to his band of extremely merry men, and they in turn lifted five sizable calico-covered parcels over their heads: one bundle of fish per man. The closest bundle was handed to Colleen, and the others were offered out for the street audience to share.

Two of the merry men also carried a timber keg of gin each. "Share it around, men, but see that the wench who runs this ale house has none. I have been told she is a devil with the drink in," and as Matthew made that proclamation, Colleen jumped as high as she could to enable her to deliver a closed fist to the top of his lofty head. As she landed, Matthew took hold of her, and they began to dance. That was the cue for the whole of Brown Street North to join in.

Michael and Angela took the hands of some of the children and formed a circle. They began to swirl around and around and both felt their anxiety begin to lift. Michael yelled, "Can you believe this, Ang?" Angela did not reply. She just smiled, and then that smile turned in laughter. Finbar heard his daughter's laughter and bowed his head to Michael by way of offering thanks.

The merriment continued well into the night, and the later the hour, the more energy and enthusiasm Matthew seemed to be able to muster. Every person in the house, and indeed the whole street, was able to eat far better than usual that evening thanks to what Matthew had now baptized and named his personal "Miracle of the Kilt and Fishes."

CHAPTER TWELVE

True to his word, Matthew stirred Fin early the following morning, and the pair headed toward the depot two miles from home. They boarded a wagon, and in just over one hour, they arrived at the construction site of the railway line that he proposed would link Manchester to Sheffield. The terrain was hilly at best but mostly mountainous. Every foot of ground that the rails would be laid on had to be levelled by hand. It took two heavily laden wagons drawn by teams of six horses each just to carry the tools and equipment to the site. More wagons carried the heavy timbers (sleepers) that had been precut and rough-dressed on which the steel rails would be placed and secured. Countless larger and longer wagons brought up the tail of the procession. It required an eight-horse team to drag these monsters. They carried the steel rails.

Every task was done by hand. The only assistance available to lessen the enormous human effort was black powder, but that assistance often came with a hefty price attached. This explosive had been around since the ninth century where it was concocted by Chinese alchemists. It was made up of measured amounts of sulfur, charcoal, and saltpeter (potassium nitrate). The preferred charcoal came from the willow tree. The black powder was notoriously unstable. Accidental friction could ignite it, and unintended explosions occurred far too often.

While travelling to the site, Matthew used the time to go over and over with Finbar everything he deemed his cousin should know about the tasks he was about to throw himself into. Fin was becoming more and more impressed by the way his cousin saw things done. His rough visage stood in total contrast to the thoughtful, caring, and very clever person that Finbar could see had emerged from within that rough image.

"You only do what I ask you to do. Take orders from no one else. Drink the water every time the water boy comes your way. Do not dip your water from the barrels placed along the line for drinking. I know the Prodies piss in the barrels to make us sick. More jobs for them, don't ya see? I asked Mr. Knore, our boss, to let me pick the water boy, and I told him my reason. He was thankful because many men fall ill on the line, and the water is often the problem. Now my water boy is a big strong lad, and we call him Kuddy because that is what he wants to be called. I know his true name to be Peter Doyle, but to us, he is Kuddy. I did have a Peeler ask if a Mr. Peter Doyle was known to me. Now there is another lie that I must remember to confess. Kuddy carts the water up from the river, and if he can't get it there, he has a large barrel locked in the tool wagon. Mind me now, Fin, we don't want you any sicker than you be now. Our barreled water is safe water. The railway company makes sure of that. A sick workforce is no workforce at all. Do not fight anyone, and definitely do not fight the Prodies. They will make you pay," whispered Matthew.

"My men do not handle the black powder. The boss will offer to teach you how to use the powder safely, but you must say no. He asks every new man starting with the gangs to use the gunpowder, but it is too dangerous. Tell him you have ten children and your wife is dead. You have mouths to feed. Did you meet Mr. Snowdon yesterday morning? The foreman at Erman and Engels cotton mill. The man with all the damage to his face. The man with the wooden hand. I know you did because I told Mary Burns that I wanted him to be there. Now Mr. Snowdon didn't say no to the boss even after I told him to." The question needed no reply. The answer was already there within the context of the question.

Fin was not a healthy man. The starvation due to the famine had left him weak, and he waved away any concern expressed by Matthew with regard to his hacking cough. The gang had been asked by Matthew to keep an eye on Fin. He knew his cousin's fitness was not up to the standard he would normally insist on. Matthew had helped other men, now belonging to his gang, through the same rough start that Fin was about to endure. The essence of Matthew's care was not simply familial. It was tribal. The men did as asked, and although it took several weeks for Fin to gain full strength, it was his tribe that he owed his vastly improved situation to. He had taken to referring to himself and his coworkers as the Mud Hole Men after hearing Matthew initiate the term prior to performing his miracle of the kilt and fishes.

It had not escaped the notice of the Trans Rail project director, Mr. Knore, that the Mud Hole Men had gained a reputation for getting things done in less time than other gangs without compromising standards. He met with Matthew on site one day to present a demand that he euphemistically kept referring to as a proposal. He planned to turn the Mud Hole Men into a mobile gang of troubleshooters. Such was the brutal nature of the labor required from the railway gangs. Many men simply could not cope with the rigors and would simply walk off the job, putting too much stress on those who remained. The other main cause of "stop work" was injury, and these were often horrendous. Broken bones were not uncommon and large lacerations caused by misuse of tools.

This inconsistency of numbers could hold up construction in one area but that in turn could stop the project in its tracks. Consistency of numbers was a problem that Matthew had identified and was able to put forward a solution to Mr. Knore that raised his stocks once again and this time considerably.

Matthew proposed that he and his men could prepare replacement laborers, but if he was given the time, he could get these men work prepared and fit. "If myself and my men could choose the most likely replacement laborers and have them in a camp, we could teach them just what they would be expected to do, and if we could feed these men some good food, they will become stronger and far more likely to cope with the hard graft."

Mr. Knore recognized the brilliance of Matthew's scheme and gave him the go ahead to proceed. Matthew was allocated funds, and the training camp was set up. Who better to select men who would survive the training than Matthew. He had been a hard worker all his life, but the real talent he offered was his honesty and his innate ability to care for and lead his men.

It would not occur to anyone who simply observed the workings of rail line construction that any skill would be required, but Matthew knew that simply was not the case. He recognized that every handheld tool used by the workers could cause injury to handler or, more sadly, to someone else on the gang who just happened to be too close. He taught the dos and don'ts. The major contributor to injury occurred when untrained men were expected to manhandle the heavy timber "sleepers" that were placed at ground level to allow the steel rails to be fixed to them, and of course, if those steel rails were accidentally dropped, the injuries that could occur just added to the proceedings being held up.

Matthew had gained a position of considerable power, and that power enabled him to get things done that did not necessarily fall within the guidelines of railway construction. He moved from one construction site to another. He gathered information and was always ready to help any deserving folk who needed a hand regardless of whether they were rail workers or not.

Chapter Thirteen

On the home front back at Mr. Dennys Mud Hole in Brown Street North, Michael and Angela had become very close to Colleen who treated both on an equal footing to her own two much younger children.

Angela had also made a real friend of Granny, the old lady who shared the cellar floor they all slept on at night. She would make sure that Granny had food to eat and even volunteered to empty the chamber pot that the old lady used.

Granny had much to offer Angela, and the young woman had much to learn. And what a willing student she was. Granny spoke French fluently, and Angela soaked up the intricacies of the language of love with all the fervor of a summa cum laude. Granny insisted that Angela compose short stories both to improve her poor writing skills and, more importantly, to allow her to see her own thoughts on the page. Angela was also taught how to sew, not just sew to repair a garment but to create new items of clothing such as skirts and dresses. She was taught to cut the pattern and then to sew the pieces together with the finest of stitching.

Colleen and Matthew Denny had both noticed how much happier Granny was since Angela had arrived. Six months had passed, and Colleen casually remarked that "I swear that Granny is standing two inches taller these days, and I know for fact that our Angela is the cause."

The old lady would seat herself daily on the front steps of the house in Brown Street North. It was at the same time every evening, and when she spied Angela approaching, her face lit up. For the first time in her life, she knew what happiness was, and she embraced it with all her heart.

Louisa DuBois had lived a life that had afforded her much luxury but had mainly travelled a road that consisted of cruelty and hence the associated sadness that had been devouring her. The kind heart of one young lady had changed all that.

That kind heart was crushed after returning home from work at the mill one evening and finding that Granny was not seated in her usual spot. Angela went down into the cellar hoping to find that Granny was huddled up asleep in the fresh hay that she had bought and spread the day before expressly for the purpose. Granny was not asleep in her usual corner. Angela strained to see in the dark and found the old lady under the stairs. She was dead.

Colleen and Michael rushed down to the cellar following Angela's screams, and she was inconsolable. She was cradling Granny on her lap as she knelt on the floor. She would not allow anyone to come close. She just wept, and as her tears fell onto Granny's face, she gently brushed them away. It was as if she was cleansing her friend in preparation for her entry into heaven.

Granny's funeral came with a twist. Her body had been taken to St. Michael's church for the requiem, and a collection of money had been organized by Angela Denny to hopefully purchase a coffin and if possible some flowers to decorate the "Ugly Church." Angela felt herself and Granny blessed after counting the donations when she realized that she had enough to purchase a plain coffin and a few flowers. Angela asked Matthew Denny, her uncle, to take charge of the money and the arrangements because out of anybody she knew, it was Matthew that would do the job best.

Matthew was nowhere to be found on the day of the funeral, but Colleen assured everybody that all would be well. It was a bitter Tuesday morning, and it seemed to Angela that half of Salford had decided to turn out for the service.

As Angela, accompanied by Finbar, Michael, and Colleen, entered the church, Angela let out an all too audible gasp. So many flowers and the coffin she was sure had been intended for a queen. "How was this possible?" she asked Colleen, who gently whispered into her ear, "My Matthew would never let family down."

Father Tim, who performed the service, let Colleen know that tea and oatcakes would be available for family at the presbytery after the burial. The coffin only had to be carried a short distance to Angel Meadow cemetery, and after a few kind words, a crowd returned with Father Tim to take up his offer of tea and oatcakes. Who could have imagined that so many people would take up the offer. Angela smiled to herself when she realized that the supply of oatcakes seemed to be endless, and she recalled what Colleen had whispered into her ear.

Finbar had arranged time off through Matthew to attend Granny's funeral because he knew how close his daughter was to her and felt he would be needed to help Angela cope with the sadness of the whole affair. He was certainly happy to be spending the time with his two children because, due to his work on the railway track, he was away from home for days at a time. His concern for Angela, however, was quickly allayed when he saw how well his daughter was conducting herself on the day. She spoke to Colleen and Father Tim with all the finesse of a fine lady. She carried herself differently. She wore a dress that modestly flattered her. A dress she had made herself. Fin puffed with pride as he realized his shy little girl was blossoming into a fine young lady.

Fin knew to attribute a sizable portion of his daughter's positive development to Granny. Colleen spoke often to him about Angela. He was told how Granny had taken Angela under her wing and was teaching her all manner of things. Angela's ability to read and write was basic but improving quickly under the tutelage of Granny. She encouraged her young charge to speak English and speak it well. She taught her to sew, and the dress she wore to Granny's funeral was her first but by no means her last effort. Angela worked long hours at the cotton mill but spent any spare time she had with the old woman. Angela considered it to be a godsent gift if one of the steam-powered looms broke down resulting in her being sent home. This meant more time spent learning.

Fin's curiosity got the better of him, and having witnessed the odd goings on at the funeral, when he was able to get Colleen on her own back at Brown Street North, he was determined to find out just who Granny was. She did not fit the norms of the Salford slum. What was she doing living there?

"Colleen," he quizzed, "are you able to talk to me about Granny? You see I don't understand why she was living here. She was a grand lady indeed, but she did not belong in the rough company of Salford. Do you know anything about her? I beg pardon if I speak so bluntly and please tell me to heed my own business if you do not want to talk about her. I will be ever in her debt for how she loved my Angela. Yes, she was part of our family, but if you know she had family elsewhere, I feel obliged to let them know that she died. I feel that I should do something to keep her memory, and I know our Angela would feel the same."

Colleen was taken aback by the reference that Finbar had made. "Our family." She always kept her emotions well-tethered, but when Finbar felt comfortable enough with her to include her in "our family," she was overcome. She moved to him, and with arms outstretched, she held him tightly. Fin was embarrassed for just a split second because as she squeezed him, she said, "I am not able to say much about Granny DuBois, but what I do know will please me to tell, and I promise to do that when the quiet evening comes, but I have something to give you now."

Having said that, Colleen placed a small milking stool in front of the three-tier shelf cabinet that sat next to the coal-burning stove in the kitchen. She held on to the second shelf for balance and stepped up on to the stool. This maneuver allowed her to reach the top shelf, and with a full stretch of her right arm, she clutched something at the back of the high shelf and asked Finbar to take it as she handed it down to him. It was a small wooden box. Colleen climbed down from the stool and asked Fin to take a seat at the table, which he did immediately, still holding the box.

"I have to talk to you about what is in the box, so could you open it and take a peek at what you see inside please?"

Fin did as instructed, and on inspection, the contents of the box looked to be an item of jewelry. Fin knew nothing of fine craftsmanship, but even to his untrained eye, the item looked exquisite. "And what is it that we have here, Colleen?" he asked.

Colleen did not hasten to respond. She had to prepare an answer. She knew full well that the answer she would give could place Angela in danger depending on what course of action this revelation would have her take.

"What you have there is a locket that belonged to Louisa DuBois or, as she preferred to be called, Granny. She was staying with us because her life was in danger. Louisa DuBois was just a child when she was offered work in France by a man who was a marquis. The French are a funny lot. They behead the king and queen but still let the other so-called royals call themselves all manner of fancy names. Anyway, Louisa would refer to him as her Drunk Duke. She was working as an agent in the palace owned by the marquis in Marseille, the largest French port."

The position she held was created by the marquis who saw the value in having someone in his employ who spoke both English and French. He was a businessman who was ever frustrated with the antics of the port customs people. He would ship cargoes of beautiful things in from all over the world to be sold in the two grand shops he owned in Paris and Calais. If the cargo got held up at the docks in Marseille, the Drunk Duke would lose money. The delays in the release of the shipments was usually caused by customs officials at the French docks simply because English wasn't spoken, and the marquis insisted on using English ships and English captains because as he often ranted "The French fleet of cargo carriers were manned by useless dogs and frogs who were such bad sailors that my precious booty could end up in Bombay and these clowns would not know the difference."

As Colleen continued on with the strange tale, Finbar began to feel a knot of anxiousness tighten in his belly. He knew Colleen well enough by now to identify her two modes of storytelling. First, there was the funny tale, and then there was the one of foreboding and portend. There was no mistaking this tone. It was definitely the latter.

"Louisa was English. She was an orphan and was able to learn French at the orphanage she was placed in with the help of a caring nun who saw in Louisa a girl who would do well if given the chance. The marquis had stipulated that the position should go to someone who has no family ties. He did not want the issues and responsibilities of family to impede the performance of his agent.

"It was left to the Catholic Church to find such a person because the marquis had asked for church assistance in the past. He realized that the people recommended by the church would come from poor backgrounds and circumstances. He judged that their loyalty could be readily relied upon, and in the case of Louisa DuBois, his suppositions were well and truly vindicated.

"Louisa had only been working for the marquis a short while when he began to show more interest than she had expected, and that interest was sexual. She explained to me that she never really liked the man. He was overbearing, loud, rude, and extremely cruel to animals, but she was flattered and saw in him a way out of her own poor situation. Louisa said she did not push away his advances, but she wished she had. When he proposed marriage, Louisa said yes immediately. She had shared his bed, and in doing so, her own wealth situation was vastly improved, but she never expected marriage. She believed she was no more than a dalliance, and when he tired of her, she would simply be passed over."

Colleen continued after placing the well-worn kettle back on the stove, an indicator to Fin that there was much more to come.

"Louisa would speak as if in a dream when she spoke of her wedding day. By all accounts, it was a grand affair. She called the church she was married in the Major Cathedral, and all the flowers in the world were picked for this church to show off.

She rode in a beautiful golden carriage pulled by four white horses. Her dress cost a fortune and—"

The storyteller, Colleen, realized that she had transported herself into the fairy-tale unreality of the life of Louisa DuBois. Finbar was simply not interested in the trappings of French aristocracy. Colleen apologized for her digression and continued to the point.

"A few months after the sacrament of matrimony and the vows were heard by all at the cathedral, Louisa began to regret the loveless situation she caused herself to fall into. Because she was now spending much more time in the company of the marquis, she saw and experienced behavior in her husband that she had not been privy to when she was simply his agent and did not see him so often.

"He entertained regularly, often throwing huge banquets attended by everyone that he was in business with or had squeezed favors from, and his performance at these events was extraordinary. He was the ultimate gentleman. He flattered all the ladies but just enough to stir their hearts yet always drawing away just in time so as to not upset their ever-vigilant spouses. His name and title recall was outstanding, and Louisa said he never failed to address his guests by their full names, and in the cases of the now not-relevant royalty, he always recited their correct titles and avoided any shortcuts in his introductions that so many of his contemporaries now deemed good enough."

Coleen drew closer to Finbar across the kitchen table and continued on, almost in a whisper as though the walls could hear every word.

"The man was a right black bastard, Louisa told me. To everyone who thought they knew him, he appeared to be a good man, but when no one was around, he was different. Louisa said that one day, while she was out walking with her Drunk Duke on the estate, he thrashed one of the dogs that accompanied them because it licked one of his boots. He used the walking stick that he always had with him to continually hit the terrified animal, and although she begged him to stop, he continued his frenzy until the poor animal was dead. She told me that he was also brutal with his horses when out riding. She mentioned a particular occasion when he drove the spurs he had attached to his boots into the flanks of the beautiful animal he was riding so hard and so often that by the time they returned to the stables, strips of bloodied shredded flesh hung from the ravaged areas. The animal's only crime was to run too fast and therefore embarrassing the somewhat poorly skilled rider.

"Several days after the cruel event, Louisa sought out the stable manager, and she asked after the poor animal. She was told that the marquis had ordered the horse be butchered and the meat given to the estate workers to eat.

"It wasn't long before the marquis started physically abusing Louisa. He drank too much. His preference was cognac, and he consumed it straight from the bottle most evenings. Louisa started to encourage him to use opiates and kept a bottle of laudanum next to his liquor cabinet where she would add it to his bottle of cognac in the hope that the drug would calm his late night anger.

"The marquis had two previous marriages that ended in his divorce of the first wife and the mysterious death of the second. One son, named Phillip, was born to the first marriage, but the second union produced no children.

"Louisa, who did want children at first, found herself doing all she could to avoid pregnancy when she realized what a brute the only son of the marquis had turned out to be. Even the marquis was afraid of upsetting his offspring and was becoming increasingly concerned about the way his son was treating his stepmother."

Colleen poured out two more cups of tea and begged Finbar to continue listening to her history lesson and pay attention to all the details because the life of his daughter, Angela, will depend on Finbar understanding what was happening.

"This is where it gets interesting, Fin," said Colleen with a look of concern on her face. "Louisa said that the Drunk Duke, despite his faults, did love her in his own cruelly possessive way. He came to her one day with a plan that seemed so bizarre, she thought he had gone completely mad. He told Louisa that he intended to transfer the titles of several of his properties into her name because he was becoming more and more afraid of his son. The marquis had been told by a friend that Phillip was plotting to have his father certified insane and have him locked up in an asylum. He was going to use examples of his father's cruelty to convince the doctors that his father could no longer be trusted to handle his own affairs. Once the Drunk Duke was out of the way, Louisa would be next to go for sure. Louisa said she had no trouble believing that Phillip would plot against his father because the marquis had excommunicated his son from any involvement in the family business as he deemed him to be too reckless after large sums of money seemed to just disappear from the company accounts under Phillip's charge.

"The Drunk Duke and his son were alike in many ways, but Phillip had one fault that his father did not carry. He was a gambler and not a very good one." Colleen chuckled at that revelation because Louisa had told her many stories of Phillip's gambling escapades, and one such tale came front of mind. "He once bet the clothing he was wearing on a split of the deck, and Louisa told of how she laughed when she saw him sneaking home across the palace grounds in nothing but his undergarments.

"The Drunk Duke, true to his word, did transfer three title deeds into Louisa's name. He told her that the total value of the three deeds, if sold, would earn her enough money to pay for her to return to England, live comfortably, and be safe from

Phillip's nastiness. Louisa stayed with her Drunk Duke for ten years until his sudden unexplained death.

"She was able to sell one of the properties left to her and was surprised to learn that Phillip had been able to block the sale of the remaining two. It turns out that one of the tracts of land she owned had become very valuable indeed all due to factories. Marseille, like Manchester, was booming, and land to build more factories on had become hard to find. The chid that the marquis had attached little value to was now five vacant acres with factories built all around it."

Finbar had to slow Colleen down, but on the other hand, there were so many questions still to answer. "How did Granny come to be living here with Matthew and yourself? What of the locket? Why is my Angela in danger?"

"Yes, yes, yes, I will tell you now," Colleen held up her hand to stop the barrage of questions. "Louisa came to live with us because my Matthew is a good man who has many friends. One of Matthew's friends is a ship's captain who knew Louisa through dealings he had with her in the Port of Marseille."

"After the death of the marquis and fearing Phillip, Louisa knew she had to flee the country. The ship's captain organized her passage to England, arranged for her to meet Matthew in Bristol, and he brought her to Salford. She had money with her from the sale of the one property she was able to rid herself of. She asked Matthew to help her buy a small house, and that house is the one we sit in right now. She purchased it, but without our knowledge, she had the deeds written up in Matthew's name as owner. No tenant contract was written, but she asked if she could stay with us, and of course, Matthew agreed. We prepared a bedroom for her, but she insisted on sleeping in the cellar. It was like she needed to do penance: she admitted to me that she was not free of sin because of some things she had to do as the agent of the Drunk Duke. She also really enjoyed having people around her, people to talk to, friends. She would refer to the cellar dwellers as her kind of people and let us not forget her own humble beginning."

Colleen drew a quick breath and continued.

"The locket you see before you belonged to Louisa. She knew she was dying, and she asked me to make sure that Angela received this locket after her burial. She lived for almost nine years with us, but because of the way she was treated by her Drunk Duke over in France, her health was always a bother. She was years younger than she appeared. When she came to stay, all the wee-ens of Brown Street North began calling her Granny. She looked like a Granny and walked with a stick. I would tell the children not to call her Granny, but one day, she told me that she liked the title because it made her feel like she had family and she would go out of her way to help young mothers who had to work and she would care for their children. She did not expect that Angela would keep the locket.

She knew that if it was sold, Angela could do so much for her family with the money."

Finbar could not hold back. "But how does this locket put my Angela's life in danger?" he blurted. "I just don't understand."

"The locket is not the end of the story, Finbar. Louisa DuBois left a will in my safe keeping. As I have said, she still holds the title on two properties in France and one is of considerable value. Her stepson, Phillip, owns the adjoining property, but it has no road access. The properties are at the port of Marseille in France. If he obtained Louisa's land, he could bring a road through and increase his wealth and, most importantly, his power."

"He has used some legal argument to stop Louisa from selling, but recently, Matthew received some terrible news from his friends at the docks in Liverpool. It seems that Phillip has paid some bad people to find Louisa and force her to transfer her deeds to him. From what Matthew was told, it seems that if Louisa was to die or be killed, the titles would transfer to Phillip as Louisa's next of kin. Now this is where Angela may be in trouble. The will I mentioned that Louisa left for me to look after states that Angela will become the new owner of Granny's properties when she died. It would now seem that your Angela is a wealthy woman. But she could be in real danger if Phillip finds out about her and the will."

That being said, Colleen left the room and returned holding another timber box. She carefully lowered the box and sat it on the kitchen table. She lifted the hinged lid toward herself, thus allowing Finbar an unhindered view of the contents. She removed an envelope and presented it to Fin with all the ceremony of a religious offering, but Fin's gaze remained fixed on what still remained in the box. Although not a Freemason himself, Fin recognized the regalia and trappings of a second-degree Mason, the Journeyman. The best friend he had left behind in Ireland, Joseph Connelly, was a Journeyman with the local group of Freemasons, and he wore such items. He assumed correctly that the Masonic items belonged to his cousin, Matthew, and immediately, he realized how it was that Matthew had access to so much information about so many people.

Finbar took the envelope that Colleen had just handed to him and began to remove the contents, but in midmotion, he burst into laughter. "What use is this to me, Colleen? I can't read, and I know damn fine that neither can you."

Colleen immediately saw the humor in it all and also burst into laughter. "Mary Burns will help us, Fin, I know she will. I will have your Michael tell her that we need her to help us with a problem that has come up. She will come here, Fin."

Finbar Denny did not doubt that Mary Burns would be able to read whatever it was in the envelope but had no idea what he should do if, as Colleen stated, the information contained within in any way endangered the life of his beautiful Angela.

Finbar was struck yet again with another bout of laughter. "Colleen, surely the title deeds are written in French, and if that is so, I would doubt that your Mary Burns, as clever as she may be, would know how to read French words."

Colleen was not laughing this time, rather she was deep in thought. "Abraham," she blurted. "The Jewish man who mixes all the tinctures and lotions for our people when we fall ill. He is French. He told me so himself. He had to leave Paris because the real French people had decided to make life very hard for him and his kind. He said that Napoleon had decided that the French folk who owed money to the Jews no longer had to pay them, and many Jewish families had to leave. He will be able to tell us all about the deeds."

Chapter Fourteen

Known to all as Abraham Rothschild, the Manchester medicines and tinctures concoctor who also ran his own pawn broking business had decided to adopt the surname of Rothschild firstly because the reputation of a certain Abraham Rothmann had become badly tarnished prior to him leaving Paris and taking up residence in Manchester, and secondly, because the name Rothschild was well-regarded in Manchester because of banking and investment business overseen by people who had the birthright to legally bear the name Rothschild.

Abraham was sent for and was able to confirm that the title deeds did look genuine. He explained that before leaving France, he owned his own shop, so he had actually seen a title deed and recognized that what he was looking at was the same as the document he once owned but, of course, with different names.

At this point in the conversation, Finbar recalled Colleen telling him that Abraham ran a pawn shop in Manchester. He remembered also that she believed him to be a good and honest man, but he had not been made aware that good and honest may no longer apply. He called Colleen aside and asked her whether Abraham could possibly put a value on the locket now owned by Angela. Colleen thought it to be a grand idea.

Receiving Colleen's approval, which he had become reliant on, Finbar firstly put the valuation request to Abraham but also explained in vague terms that secrecy was paramount due to some family issues. Of course, given that it would be in his best interest to become involved, Abraham assented to the secrecy, and Finbar handed him the locket with all the respect that a priest would show to the Holy Eucharist.

Abraham removed a jewelers magnifier from his pocket and pushed it firmly into place around his right eye. His interest went from cursory to keen as soon as the magnifier enabled him to appreciate the delicate craftsmanship that would have been required in the creation of this outstanding piece. He obviously expected that he would be viewing an item similar to the many worthless trinkets offered to him over the counter of his pawn shop. He forced himself not to be rude to these customers who had been quite convinced by their husbands, boyfriends, or itinerant sailors that the items they tendered may well have come from royalty who had fallen on hard times and were forced to sell the family treasures.

Until recent times, ownership of jewelry fell only into the domain of the rich. Industrialization had led to the invention of machinery that could mass-produce trinkets and attractive baubles by the thousands. The use of inferior composite materials along with gold and silver plating led to the market being flooded with eye-catching bracelets, rings, necklaces, brooches, and earrings all well-capable of deceiving their gullible recipients.

But no, Finbar could tell simply by the look on Abraham's face that this item of adornment was no piece of paste. Abraham looked up at Colleen, and as he did, the magnifier dropped into the palm of his right hand as though the motion was the cue for his face to come alive with a smile that brightened up the room.

"I have seen workmanship of this quality only once before, and that was in a jeweler's shop in Paris that had the best reputation of all. It is exquisite, and only one man I have ever met could have crafted such a piece. Jean Baptiste Fossin is such a man, and I would swear that he made this dream come true. How beautiful it is! This man made jewelry for the family of Louis-Phillippe, King of France. He created for Napoleon himself and the Duchess de Berry along with the Russian prince Anatole Demidoff. Fossin was friend to painters, writers, and sculptors. What you have here, my dear friend, is indeed one of Fossin's masterpieces. Where did it come from, may I ask?"

Colleen very quickly replied. "We cannot tell the story of its travels because it is all a bit blurred, sir."

Abraham was obviously not happy with that answer, but not to be beaten, he plowed on. "Have you opened the locket?" asked Abraham.

Colleen keenly replied in the negative. "I have tried, but it just doesn't work. It must be jammed."

"May I try to open it? I will not damage this beautiful object," asked Abraham.

Finbar nodded his assent while in the same instant, Colleen replied, "We would be grateful for your assistance."

Abraham held the locket, but rather than try to open it in the conventional manner, he slid the front half from right to left, and a click was barely audible as the lid gently slid in the direction Abraham had coaxed it to and then sprung open.

"How did you do that, sir?" asked Finbar, obviously impressed, and believing he had just witnessed a magician's fine trick.

"That is how it had been made, Mr. Finbar. The jeweler has taken special care in the creation of this fine piece, and maybe what we have here inside will tell us why opening the locket was an extra difficult task," Abraham replied while Colleen, thinking to herself, observed that Abraham was not his usual self. Something was wrong. He seemed very guarded. He knew more about this locket than he had admitted to.

"What is that inside the locket?" quizzed Colleen, and as she spoke, Abraham handed her a small red piece of silk that had been wrapped around the prize yet to be revealed. Colleen immediately handed the small parcel to Finbar as she reckoned that whatever it was, it belonged to him or, more truly, it belonged to Angela.

Finbar clumsily unfolded the red silk, allowing two gleaming gemstones to fall onto the tabletop. One jewel was as red as an Irish winter sunset, and as Finbar's gaze shot to the other stone, he imagined he was looking at an angel's tear. He quickly gathered them up, thinking as he did. "What to do?"

Colleen solved that problem in an instant. "Hand them to Abraham, and he will tell us just what they are, Fin."

Abraham received them gently and immediately produced the jeweler's magnifier that he had used earlier to inspect the locket. "My, my, master," he exclaimed as he firstly held the clear gem up for survey. "This is a beautiful diamond of magnificent quality. I do not have scales with me, but I say it is close to being two carats. The value of such a gem would be considerable. Since living in Salford, I no longer get to see beauties of such quality, so I would have to contact some of my countrymen who have fared better than me and own shops in London to have any idea of value."

Finbar cut across the conversation as Abraham was in mid-proclamation, announcing as he held high the Irish winter sunset, "I know this stone is a ruby. The Bishop of Dublin wears a ring that has a ruby stone in it. I have seen it. In fact, I have kissed that ruby." Suddenly, he realized how silly he sounded. Akin to a schoolboy trying to impress his peers. The outburst was so out of character for Fin, and Colleen, realizing that he was totally controlled by the situation he had just found himself in, she steered the conversation back to relevance.

"I believe it is a ruby, Fin. What says you, Abraham?"

"Mrs. Denny," Abraham answered, adopting a more formal approach considering that his services could be needed if the stones were to be sold, "it is a fine quality ruby, but again, I will travel to see my friends in London on your behalf to assess the true value of the gems."

At this point in history, rubies were more valuable than diamonds as silver was once considered more valuable than gold—so attesting to the fickleness of humankind.

It did not escape Colleen's notice that Abraham had initially suggested that he could talk to people in London, but his last remark intimated that he had installed himself as broker for Angela's estate. She concluded that she would discuss the next steps with Finbar and then, with his approval, have Matthew oversee any dealings. She and Finbar, and including Abraham, planned how the revelation should be dealt with. It was agreed that nothing further should happen until Matthew returned home from his position of grand importance with the Manchester to Sheffield railway line. Colleen believed that he would still be away for at least three more days. She asked for patience because Matthew's latest promotion from Mr. Knore meant that his planned time away from home could vary by a day or two.

Once Abraham had left, Colleen expressed to Fin her concerns regarding him. It was not today's events that put her on edge with this man. She told Fin that some of the church ladies who helped her with the flowers at St. Michael's had found themselves in debt to him. It had almost become a custom of the time that the wives of the workers who could be away from home for long periods—e.g., sailors, some railway gangs, and travelling farm harvest laborers—to pawn whatever they had of value and use that money to survive on until their men returned.

One item commonly pawned was the one and only good suit that many of the men had deemed necessary for some modicum of self-esteem and the fact that so many children were dying young resulting in countless funerals. Angel Meadows cemetery had actually become a dumping ground for small corpses whose parents simply could not afford the burial fee. The church would intervene and inter the children. The main reason for this service was to stem the putrid smell of death so close to the church and far less to do with charity.

"That Jewish gent Abraham is a man you must be careful with. I know from friends that he can make redemption of items pawned with him very difficult. We don't read, so the paper he gives us can have any old rubbish written on it, and when these wives I know go to collect the items he holds, they are told that the cost is more than they had agreed to and when they show him the ticket, he tells them that the amount he is charging is written there plain and clear.

"One dear friend Mrs. O'Leary told me that when she called him a crook, he became very angry and used his own language to curse at her. Yiddish, they call it. But that wasn't the end to it, Fin. Mrs. O'Leary told me that one of the men, they call him Asael, that works in the Jews shop got into a fight with her husband at the public house and hurt him badly. She said it was deliberate. We all know that Asael is a bad man, in fact, most of the church women call him Arsehole. Matthew always leaves me with what he calls my trouble money to use if any of our friends need help, and Mrs. O'Leary needed help, so I gave her some of the money."

CHAPTER FIFTEEN

W hen Abraham Rothschild left the meeting with Colleen and Finbar Denny, he hurried home at a pace far quicker than his usual ambling style. He was a man on a mission, and it all had to do with one of the precious stones he had just so enjoyed the vision of. *No, not the diamond* , he thought to himself. *I know who owned that ruby, and I know that someone is here in Manchester offering a reward for its return. The ruby that had the reward on offer was described as a step-cut Burmese Pigeon Blood in excess of three carats.*

The man searching for this precious item had actually spoken to Abraham in his pawn shop. He gave his name Solomon Leyman, and he was employed by some young marquis he called Phillip living in Marseille. The ruby had apparently been stolen from the marquis, and he was prepared to pay a handsome reward for its return. The reward on offer was more than the value of the stone, and Abraham took on the likeness of Mr. Dicken's character Uriah Heap in the story of David

Copperfield as he wrung his hands together over and over imagining just what he would do with the reward money.

He thought of how he could offer to take the stones to London for appraisal. He would convince Finbar Denny that the jeweler offered such a good price he felt compelled to take the money because he was aware of the destitute situation the Dennys were in. "I would be doing them a favor," he convinced himself. "I will then pay them a portion of the reward price and keep the rest for myself. Finbar has no idea of the value or the hefty reward, so he would not be in a position to question me. You are indeed a true Ashkenazi, Abraham Rothschild."

Of course, Abraham was not made aware of the real motive behind the reward on offer. The young marquis, stepson of Louisa DuBois, needed the title deed to the property, now in the name of Angela Denny, to allow a road to be built across it, enabling him to expand his empire as he then would be entitled to build factories and warehouses on his own landlocked deed in the French port of Marseille. Abraham certainly did not know that Solomon Leyman was prepared to kill anyone who stood in the way of him obtaining the deed. The offer of a reward for the ruby was only made to expose the whereabouts of the title holder.

Three days had passed since Colleen and Finbar met with Abraham Rothschild. The existence of the will, the locket, and its contents had been explained to Angela, and her reaction came as a shock. It would seem that Angela knew about Granny's intentions to leave her the estate which comprised the two deeds. She also knew of the import and danger attached to the ownership of the property at the Marseille docks. She certainly had been made aware of the beautiful locket, but the existence of both the ruby and the diamond caught her genuinely by surprise. Angela retold the story of the Drunk Duke and how Granny had been treated badly by him and much worse by his son, Phillip. A plan was desperately needed, but all parties agreed that Matthew should be the one to formulate it.

Chapter Sixteen

Colleen had received a message from one of the Mud Hole Men that Matthew had finished setting up the third training camp near York and was heading for home. She was told to expect him the following day. It was obvious to all that Matthew loved a grand entry, and his return from York was to be no exception. The occupants of Brown Street North, hearing of Matthew's approach, had changed from their usual dour demeanor and had created an atmosphere of cheer and celebration that was so needed.

The sound of beating drums was the first hint that the Mud Hole Men were getting near. The children of Brown Street North all knew that Uncle Matthew would have food with him as that was what they had become used to. This custom began after Granny secretly bought the house that Colleen and Matthew live in and assigned ownership to them. Matthew was no longer burdened with the extreme rentals charged in the area and vowed to himself that the money he saved would be returned to his community by way of cheer-ups. Matthew felt duty bound to bring some levity into the lives of his friends and neighbors, in particular the children.

Bang, crash, bang. The drums were certainly not making any attempt at all to sound a steady beat, and the tin whistle that could only just be heard was screeching many notes in succession that by no interpretation could be called melodic. It was in fact pure cacophony, and as Matthew came into view, the good folk of Brown Street North erupted in laughter. He and his band of inebriated merrymen were wearing roughly sewn shamrock green smocks over their working attire. Any semblance of uniformity in the smock design was totally missing. One man had short sleeves fitted while another gent had sleeves that were way too long for the length of his arms. Another Mud Holer had a cap, of sorts, on his head made of the all-matching shamrock green fabric while his sidekick had a sash thrown over his shoulder and tied off on the opposite hip. Nothing of the uniform was truly uniform, and of course, Matthew, not to be outdone, had one full-length sleeve in his smock with no sleeve at all on the other arm.

There was no sound or sight of bagpipes. Matthew instead was pushing a very large two-wheeled cart. The type of cart used by the navvies for the on and off loading of cargo from the ships docked in the canal. Loaded onto the cart was one huge timber barrel and two more approximately half its size. Several parcels were also visible. The weight of the load was considerable, and as Matthew held and pushed the two handles at the rear of the contraption, two Mud Holers had attached two short lengths of rope to the front of the cart and were pulling the load with all their might. The event was made even funnier when one of the Mud Holers pulling the cart slipped in the slops-covered street and landed with his face in the mud. The fact that one of the Mud Hole Men was now covered in mud gave the children even more to laugh at.

Colleen leaned toward Finbar and whispered in his ear, "Matthew doesn't own a cart."

Fin replied, "Looks like he does now to be sure."

Colleen then added, "I bought that bolt of shamrock green cloth to make matching surplices for the St. Michael's church choir."

"Maybe the Mud Hole Men will donate their outfits to the church choir," suggested Finbar through a broad smile.

Colleen who was making a poor effort at looking angry to this point simply could not contain herself any longer and began to laugh.

The incline of the street soon brought the cart to a halt. With that, Matthew slammed his huge fist down on the lid of the largest barrel. One plank split in half and that allowed Matthew to remove all of what remained of the lid. The large barrel was full to its brim with freshly caught oysters.

Let us not think for one second that oysters could only be afforded by the wealthy upper class. No. That was not the case in 1846 Manchester. Oysters were very much a staple of the poor. There was no cooking or fancy preparation required. The women had produced bowls and plates from their Brown Street North homes and stood patiently as Matthew's men served up the offerings they had dragged to where they now stood awaiting distribution. The parcels on the cart were unwrapped to reveal an abundance of smoked fish, primarily haddock. One parcel contained only eels, and when Matthew spotted the eels, he quickly took hold of two of them and marched toward Colleen who, by this time, was bursting with pride and inwardly prayed, "Thank you, Lord."

Matthew handed the eels to Finbar so as to free up his arms, and then Mat embraced Colleen, saying, "I have brought to you, your favorite food, my dearest. Mr. Knore, my railway line boss, helped me with this load for the cheer-up. He organized the hand cart and has donated it to the Mud Hole Men, knowing how difficult it is to move things if friends are evicted, but he also said that it could carry the corpses of the dead to St. Michael's for the requiem and then on to Angel Meadow for burial. I remembered you saying what trouble you had trying to get Granny's coffin to the church."

The happy noise of the crowd escalated, and Matthew lifted Colleen several feet off the ground to enable her to see the cart. Killy of the Old Bailey fame had unwrapped the last parcel and was throwing items from it for the assembly to catch.

"Sweeties," cried Colleen. "How, no, where did they come from?"

Matthew puffed out his chest with pride and replied, "Since the Mud Hole Men started setting up the training camps Mr. Knore has given me more and more work to do. He is a good man and knows that whatever he asks of me, I will get done, so long as no laws are broken. He organized the parcel of sweeties. He has a cousin who owns a sweetie shop in York, and he was glad to help. I paid only for the sugar."

The two smaller barrels turned out to be full of gin. Killy asked the women to bring bottles to the cart, and as they did, he decanted the gin into the bottles, much to the joy of the wives of Brown Street North who rarely were able to imbibe because family finances were never much better than dire.

It wasn't long before several of the women were asking for seconds, and two younger girls even proposed to Killy who had not bothered to clean the mud from his face. The women primed with gin and the children loaded up on sugar began to dance, prompting the Mud Hole Men to start bashing their drum once again, and within minutes, two of the women had produced tin whistles, but thankfully, they had the skill that the mud holers sadly lacked, jigs and reels set the Brown Street North folk moving to their happy rhythm. Most of the children had been taught the many dance moves, and the sight was grand. If Mr. Dickens had been in attendance, be assured that he would have been frantically scribbling down notes for his next book.

"Do you intend to keep using the smocks you have so badly put together for your Mud Hole Men uniform?" Colleen chuckled out the question.

Matthew's reply humored her even more, and Fin, standing near and really wanting to talk to Matthew about Angela's dilemma, could not help but laugh along.

"Killy made the smocks. He assured us that he had the skills to do a good job. I began to doubt his expertise when he measured us for a fit and he used a stick, well, actually he used lots of sticks. One stick for the length of my leg, another for the length of my sleeve, and a piece of string to measure around me. He did the same for the other men. Like I said, my beautiful Colleen, lots of sticks. No fancy gear for Killy. Then, when I saw him cutting out the pattern he had scrawled on the green cloth with a piece of charcoal, I just had to have another ale to calm me nerves. He cut the cloth with a knife, and I swear by the dirty sandals of our savior Jesus that with the trouble he was having, he had not even bothered to sharpen that knife.

He then gave the ragged cotton pieces to the fishnet menders to sew up. We decided to just let him finish the job because we knew it was going to give us all a great laugh and didn't the wee-ens love the funny look." Matthew squeezed Colleen once again as he ended the story of the smocks.

Finbar found his mood had lightened, and he said to Matthew, "If ever you have your own tavern, Matthew you might want to call it the Smock and Cart."

Matthew, never one to not respond, issued his decree, "Finbar Denny, I doubt that my beautiful Colleen would ever agree to me running a tavern, so I just might have to settle with the Miracle of the Smock 'n' Cart."

The afternoon played out well into the evening, and at last, Finbar felt it was time to talk to Matthew about the danger that came with Granny's will. Finbar was not a heavy drinker, and he knew that Matthew would still hear sense despite his alcohol intake being well-past excessive.

Matthew was first told that Abraham Rothschild became involved after being asked to give his opinion on the validity of the will and then the value of the locket and its surprise contents. Matthew was already aware that Abraham would have people beaten, men and women, by Asael his shop assistant if they did not pay their inflated debts.

"I believe that Asael has recently broken the fingers of his right hand when he began a fight with a man who objected to the beating he paid out on the husband of one of Colleen's dear friends," Matthew stated with authority.

"Just how would you know that?" asked Finbar.

"A little birdie told me, Fin," replied Matthew with a smile.

"Did that little birdie tell you that the man who broke Asael's hand owned a strange-looking green smock?" prompted Fin.

"He never mentioned it or at least that's what the little birdie whistled to my delicate self."

The humor disappeared from the verbal jousting when Finbar steered the conversation toward Philip, the son of the Drunk Duke. The title deed dilemma was explained, and Matthew sat there quietly digesting the unfolding drama. He did not mention that one of his contacts had discussed with him the arrival of a man in Manchester who was letting it be known that a substantial reward was on offer to anyone who had information regarding a lady who walked with a stick and called herself Louisa DuBois.

Now having been made aware of the imminent danger that Angela had been placed in, Matthew decided to take Fin into his confidence and explain to Fin exactly how he knows so much and is able to step in and deal with situations before they get totally out of hand.

"Fin, I am a Journeyman with the local Freemasons Lodge, and as a group of men who really want to make a difference, we work very hard to get deserving people that are in trouble with debt or about to be evicted out of trouble. There are many of us. We share information between ourselves and other groups of Masons: we call them Lodges. We are able to get cargo and passenger information from France. We know who comes and goes in and out of Manchester as they travel usually between France and Manchester, sometimes to Salford itself.

"The Freemasons started in France. It was the Knights Templar who banded together around 1100 to protect and aid the poor during the Crusades. They first called themselves the Poor Knights, then that was changed to the Knights of Solomon's Temple and then to the Knights Templar. I had to learn a lot of history before I was allowed to be a Freemason. My boss, Mr. Knore, is a Master Mason, and from time to time, he tasks me with Masonic work. I mean, he has me delivering written instructions to Masons throughout the Manchester area. I have had to learn to read and write so we all know who needs our help, and that is how I know so much about Abraham Rothschild, the pawnbroker, and also this new bad man, Solomon Leyman.

"I didn't mention earlier the fact that I have been told about this man who has arrived from Marseille and is looking for Louisa

DuBois. His name is Solomon Leyman, and he is dangerous. I must admit that I am at a loss about what to do, but Fin, there is also some good news, some very good news for you. Joseph Connelly and his family are coming to Salford. I have a friend in the Irish Garda who knows Joseph, and he has persuaded him to accept my offer of transportation. One of my Masonic friends is a ship's captain, and introductions have already been made between him and Joseph. He expects to have them here in three days' time."

Perhaps not the priority number one, but Fin immediately felt his mood lifted. "What great news! Do you know how many of the Connellys are arriving? Where do we meet them? Are they all in good health? Do you need some money for the ship's captain?" Finbar fired questions at Matthew as fast as the pistons fired in a locomotive at full speed.

As he was prone to do, Matthew held up his hand to stop the onslaught and proceeded to answer the pistons fired, one by one. "I have been told that five Connellys will be arriving. I only know that Joseph is one of them. Who has survived the famine, I am not sure. I know nothing of their health, but safe to say, it won't be good. As we did with you, Fin, we will meet them at the Black Duck tavern, and as for any money, you just keep it. No money has been paid on your behalf. This is just good people helping good people."

Finbar and his two offspring had only just moved into their own rented house a few doors up from Matthew, and that allowed Fin to offer a place to sleep for his good friend and family. "My place is small, but I will fit them all in, and I know Michael will be well-pleased to see Benny. They were the best of friends."

Nothing could have prepared the Dennys for the situation they were to be confronted with when finally they were reunited with the Connelly family.

In the span of a life, it had been a few short years since Joseph and Finbar played together in the graveyard at St. Brendan's Catholic Church, Transbridge.

CHAPTER SEVENTEEN

This story has to take a small backwards step now in order that the reader can attain a clear understanding of what was happening in and to the lives of Joseph Connelly and his family during the twelve-month period since Finbar, Angela, and Michael Denny had left the Great Hunger in Ireland and taken up residence in the putrid Salford slum of Manchester.

Joseph Connelly was not a sinner. His sin page was blank. Not even the tiniest venial infraction. He still believed he had a soul, but the sorrow he had endured and with not one pennyweight of cause attributable to himself had convinced him that his god, although almighty, just may not get it right all of the time.

Within the minuscule droplet of spent time that formed the history of forever that contained the story of the life of Joseph Connelly, much more had happened than ever before had happened in human history ever.

The lifetime of Joseph to date had seen the invention of matches, the bicycle, photography, and hugely important was the invention of steam power. Steam powered the hundreds of cotton mills that had sprung up during this the Industrial Revolution. Steam powered the trains that became the rib cage of the massive development taking place throughout Britain but in particular Manchester. Mr. Goldsworthy Gurney had invented steam-powered buses that became very popular, but due to massive protests from the owners of the horse-drawn carriage community, the local authorities imposed license fees so high that Mr. Gurney could no longer afford to run the very popular service. It is an odd fact that the name Gurney has been used to describe so many inventions—e.g., four-wheeled trolly used to move patients around in hospitals, the field stretcher used by soldiers, water-pumping equipment. It seems that if you don't know what to call it, just call it a gurney. The man himself was a surgeon, chemist, lecturer, consultant, architect, builder, scientist, inventor, and gentleman. This man invented the lime light, a far superior method of illuminating theaters and large venues—now a well-used theatrical term with both negative and positive connotations.

The sewing machine was invented, and a whole new industry followed. Clothing could be mass-produced. The world of fashion embraced the new technology, and factories sprung up everywhere. It was an industry that primarily employed women and was regarded as far better employment than in the textile mills because it was much safer and did not come with the problem of lint-filled air.

The sewing machine created an industry that earned fortunes for those who had the foresight to build the factories and employ the workers who were to begin the mass production of clothing. It has to be remembered that through this period, very little or no consideration at all was given to the factory workers, and the workhouses of the era were an abomination with regard to workplace health and safety.

What a fabulous time it was . . . for some.

On the bizarre scale of inventions, the steam-powered pistol should be mentioned. The cumbersome contraption simply did not take off.

The telephone came into existence.

Morse code was invented along with rubber tires.

London Road in Nottingham was covered with tarmac (tar macadam) making roads smoother. Imagine, no more cobblestones.

With the design of every new invention scribbled out on pieces of paper came the need to build the machinery that would prove the viability, or not, of so many ideas. Ideas cost nothing, but bringing ideas to life could be enormously expensive. Victorian England was a time when so much happened in industry. Manchester was at the center of that manufacturing mayhem.

Confectionery grew into an enormously profitable venture. The people who actually designed and then manufactured the hugely popular products were regarded as the highest skilled artisans of the food manufacturing trade. Sugar was as valuable as gold to the top ranking lolly makers.

Mr. Frederick Engel, in his book *Conditions of the Working Class in England*, tried to highlight the damning issues, but change was hard fought for and many suffered as the sad situation continued on well into the next century. Mr. Engels went to great lengths to verify everything he related in his book. He relied on personal observation, not hearsay. He visited the poor. He spoke with them in their homes. He produced a true and accurate account of the conditions of the time.

The book was printed in German in 1845 and was meant to be a warning to the German people not to repeat the sad state of affairs that was playing out in Manchester.

Engels was born in Barmen, Prussia, which was situated in the Wupper Valley. He could see that everything he deemed wrong with the exploding Industrial Revolution in England could be repeated in his homeland, and he obviously hoped that his book might help stem the madness. Germany was not as industrially advanced as England at the time that Engels's book went to print. Sadly, his warnings were not heeded, and his Wupper Valley actually became the epicenter for all the industrial development he was hoping would be better considered.

One of the worst clusters of dense housing, known as slums, in Manchester was referred to as Little Ireland because this had become the area that so many Irish people had resettled in after escaping the Potato Famine in their homeland.

Mamucium was the name given by the Romans in the year 79 Anno Domini to the place now known by the residents of Little Ireland as Manchester. The original name translates to mean breast-shaped hill. Manchester in the1840s had become the breast being fed on by the Industrial Revolution. The massive scale of the bounty being delivered saw Mamucium grow to be the second largest English city behind London.

Not yet forty years of age, Joseph Connelly found himself and his family trapped in a terror that bore witness to the truth that the point of desperation had been overwhelmingly surpassed and the only apt title applicable to his life today was that of hell on earth.

For months, Joseph had prayed, begging for a change in fortune. All to no avail but still he continued to beg his god for forgiveness. His mind had become so obsessed with repentance that his wife, Grace, truly believed he had become insane. "Mea culpa, mea culpa, mea culpa," he repeated, striking his left breast three times with his closed right fist. That Latin plea had been indoctrinated into him for all his life, but of late, Joseph Connelly had begun to falter, questioning the relevance of it all.

On that Sunday morning in 1846, just four days before Christmas, he found himself deep in thought, and when his mind cleared, only one dominant revelation found its way to the surface of his consciousness.

"I am not to blame. This is not my fault." He pushed those words through trembling lips. His soul did not implode. He did not fall down dead to the earth beneath his feet. He knew that the hold his catholic faith had over him was no longer binding. This prison without bars relied solely upon Joseph believing he was born in a state of original sin and the only pathway to his heaven had to be repaved constantly with apologies, hence "Forgive me, Father, for I have sinned."

Three of Joseph's children, Josephine, Mary, and Therese, had died of the Great Hunger earlier that year, leaving three remaining from the original seven: Benedict, Paul, and Ellen. Joseph Connelly had been able to keep abreast of all that was happening with regard to what was left of his long gone neighbors the Dennys through conversations he was able to have with members of the local constabulary and letters that were written by one parish priest in Manchester, Father McCordy, to his counterpart in charge of St. Brendan's Catholic Church, Transbridge.

When Joseph's sister Tess was brutally murdered by her drunken husband, Marcus Eversall, it fell to the small local police force to investigate and then deal with the murderer. Senior Constable John Rostan, the officer put in charge of the case at the time, had only recently moved to Transbridge from London. Constable Rostan took the responsibilities that came with his senior policing position very seriously. He had witnessed countless atrocities during his eleven years of service in London prior to transferring to Ireland, but nothing could have prepared him for the onslaught his own five senses were about to suffer on the day of Tess Connelly's savage death. The limbs of her young body had been axed apart, completely severed, and thrown across the surrounding area with, what would have taken, considerable force.

Senior Constable Rostan spent many hours trying to locate the murderer, and over the course of his investigation, he and Joseph Connelly had become firm friends. John Rostan's mother and father were still alive and living in London. John was very close to them and would visit as often as his busy schedule would allow. There were times when he was required to report to his head office in London in order that he be kept up-to-date with expected procedures and reporting. It was on one of these occasions that he met Matthew Denny, the cousin of Finbar Denny.

Rostan was required to give evidence regarding one of his more serious cases in the Central Criminal Court, renamed so in 1834 but had always been known as the Old Bailey.

It was fate that had control of this day. Two men were meant to meet and become good friends. They met at the Old Bailey because the Manchester court rooms were being given a makeover and were temporarily out of action. Matthew Denny was there on behalf of a friend, and John Rostan was there because of duty.

Matthew Denny had cautiously offered the attendance of his own huge frame to attest to the good and honest character of the man who considered himself to be the sergeant at arms of Matthew's free-spirited band of brigands known throughout Manchester and Salford as the Mud Hole Men. The offender, Declan Killeen, known to his associates as Killy, was facing a charge of common assault resulting from a fight that he had with another patron at the Black Duck ale house during which his opponent's nose had been broken. An insignificant issue, thought Killy, but Matthew was well-aware that he could be sent to prison for up to five years.

Killy was put on the stand to testify on his own behalf, but it would seem that one of the Mud Holers had smuggled in some gin, the English poor man's variation of the Dutch spirit Genever, to the accused, and as he began to speak, he could only produce a stutter. "Plee, ple, pleea youoo onner." It was not going well for poor Killy, but as fortune would have it, that stutter saved the day. Matthew interjected and begged the judge to let him speak on his friend's behalf.

The judge agreed, and with that, Matthew launched himself into yet another prize-winning soliloquy. He convinced the judge that it was "Killy who was the victim here, your honor. As you have just heard the man is mildly addled and has never really been able to talk proper.

"On the afternoon we speak of, in the Black Duck ale house, my friend Mr. Declan Killeen and I were sitting there quietly, having a drink, and planning how we were going to help Mr. Brunel with his current railway line construction."

With the mention of the name Brunel, the judge became very interested. "Is that Mr. Izambard Kingdom Brunel of which you speak, man?"

With the bait swallowed, Matthew quickly embellished the story by telling the judge of his recent appointment as troubleshooter for Mr. Brunel and how, with Killy's help, he was enabling the Great Western Railways reach the completion of many of their projects well ahead of time.

Matthew went on to summarize the events that led to the charge being laid against his good friend. "Mr. Killeen, here, is truly a victim rather than a sinner, sir, and I will explain. He did take offence at something that was said to him in the tavern, and he rightly stood to defend his hard-earned honor, your honor. Now as he rose, he was hit heavily by the real offender without even raising his hands. As he travelled backward, trying to stay on his feet, his sizable head ran straight into the nose of the poor gent sitting over there, but the damage to that poor man was never intended. We are only here because a man who was hurt by pure accident wants some money paid to him for damages.

Matthew went on to explain that Killy's wife had recently passed away, leaving him to care for his five young children, but the judge, having heard enough, raised his hand and asked Matthew to return to his seat. He stared directly at Matthew and rendered his verdict through the slightest smile. "It would appear that this is anything but a common assault, uncommon perhaps?" His gavel dropped. "Not guilty."

Chapter Eighteen

John Rostan was seated in the gallery of the Old Bailey that day. The trial he played a part in was heard prior to the Matthew Denny one-man show. John found himself smiling along with the judge when the Declan Killeen saga took center stage.

At six o'clock that evening, John Rostan was boarding a train at London's Central Station to begin his journey back to the police station at Transbridge in Ireland. He had decided to visit a friend, the owner of the Leek and Rose ale house in Manchester, before boarding the ferry that would take him back across the Irish Sea and home. As he was boarding the train, he saw the two men who had featured so comically at the Old Bailey already seated in the carriage he had just entered.

They must have boarded at an earlier station They were in the company of four other men and one woman. No more than five minutes later, the steam locomotive was hissing, chugging, clicking, and clacking its way toward Manchester. John was not in his uniform but overheard one of the men tell Matthew that he reckoned John was a Peeler (a policeman) Matthew was not a man to ever miss an opportunity to expand his network, and it seemed to him that such an opportunity might just be in the offing. The Mud Hole Men had already begun to celebrate their Old Bailey victory and foul-smelling gin was the inebriant of choice.

Matthew slowly edged his way toward John, and true to his own self-imposed rules of living that demanded he be true, he asked this question, "Are you a Peeler, sir?"

It was rare indeed that John Rostan ever found himself confronted by another human being who would actually displace more water than himself from the bath of Archimedes. Both men were giants.

Rostan had already anticipated the approach and was happy to converse. He found himself quietly admiring the man before him. He had decided after witnessing the farce at the Old Bailey that Matthew Denny could be his friend if the opportunity ever arose.

"Sir, am I to understand by your use of the expression Peeler you have presumed me to be an officer in the police service once governed by Mr. Robert Peel and from whose very name has been struck the two derogatory terms now commonplace when speaking of a police officer, that of Peeler and Bobby?" Rostan replied.

"Yes, the man who now serves as our sympathetic prime minister, sir. Peeler, yes or no, sir?" Matthew theatrically demanded complete with Shakespearean bow.

"I am indeed a proud serving member of Her Majesty's police force in Ireland, and in truth, sir, I am returning to my station at Transbridge," retorted Rostan with an air of the overplayed thespian about him.

Matthew thrust forward his right hand to shake and laughed having noticed that Rostan was off the mark in the same second.

"Did I hear you refer to Transbridge, sir?" questioned Matthew. "Can I believe that the Transbridge to which you refer is the village that sits within the parish of St. Brendan's?" added Matthew, heralding in a tense series of questions and answers that helped both men arrive at the same conclusions. "So tis true, sir, that you personally know Joseph Connelly?"

Rostan agreed that he knew Joseph very well and related that his present circumstances were dire indeed. He told the sad story of Tess, Joseph's sister, who was butchered by her brutish drunken husband, Marcus Eversall.

He told of his relentless but fruitless efforts to bring this murderer to justice. At the mention of the name Marcus Eversall, Matthew showed no outward signs of recognition, but he had heard the name before, and although he was not able to place the memory into accurate context, he decided that he would think on it again later with sober clarity. Matthew was not a man to let the murder of his friend's sister go without resolution. He then asked Rostan to help locate Joseph and his family and to inform them that Finbar Denny had made it to Manchester and wanted Joseph to join him.

Rostan had not seen Joseph Connelly for some time, but he knew where he was living and that the family circumstances were dire. He had offered to pay the passage for Joseph and his family to cross to England, but Joseph would not hear of charity.

From their chance meeting at the Old Bailey, a lifelong friendship was forged that would test both men well beyond the measures endured by most friendships. These two men were not akin to most.

By journey's end, at Manchester Railway Station, Matthew and Rostan had learned much about each other. Rostan was pleased when the connection between the two cousins was realized. "Finbar Denny is your cousin, you say, and he is the same Finbar that farmed next to Joseph Connelly?" Rostan quizzed.

"Finbar Denny is indeed my cousin, and I know that he has been desperately trying to find out the whereabouts of his friend Joseph. He says they were like brothers growing up. Finbar and his wee-ens were staying with me and my wife, but they just took over the rental of a small house just four doors down from mine. Finbar works on the Manchester to London rail line with me, and my wife's friend Mary Burns found gainful work for the two children in a noisy cotton mill owned by a German family. The Engels, I think.

"Mary Burns has been able to help many of the poor souls who have come from the Great Hunger in Ireland hoping to find better lives for their families. The man who manages the mill is Mr. Engels, and he is the son of the owner. I have supped ale with this man and have to say, I have never before met the like. He talks openly of how harsh he believes the treatment of all the workers in Manchester to be, and Mary tells me that he often argues with other mill owners about the horrible conditions in the mills but gets very angry when the craic spins into the subject of the workhouses and poor starved children."

"I think I would like to meet this Mr. Engels one day. He sounds like a good man," said Rostan.

"Well, I surely believe him to be. Can I let you in on a little secret, Chief Constable?" asked Matthew of Rostan.

"Of course you can, sir, and please rest assured that secret will be mine to keep unless you wish otherwise," replied Rostan. Through the course of conversation, Matthew had taken to calling Rostan Chief Constable merely referencing his line of work as a police officer after the offensive terms Peeler and Bobby were off the table.

"Mary Burns is more than a good friend to Mr. Engels. My wife, Colleen, has told me that Mary and Mr. Engels share the same bed, and if true, she actually lives with him in his grand home. She is best friend to Colleen, but many of the Catholics are disgusted by her sinful behavior. Father Tim, who runs the St. Michael's Parish in Salford, has preached from the almighty's pulpit about the sin of adultery, and he actually picks out Mary in the congregation with his eyes when he does."

"What does Mary do when Father Tim does that?" quizzed Rostan.

"Sir, as true as I sit here in your honorable company, Mary stares right back at him, and he is always the first to turn away." Matthew smiled broadly as he told the tale, and as the gin was passed around, the light began to fail.

"But, sir," Rostan quizzed, "surely there's no secret to be kept by me if the whole of the parish knows of Mary Burns's sins?"

"Peeler, Peeler, Peeler!" The gin was now conducting the rhythmical Dublin lilt in Matthew's tone.

The Book

"The book, sir, the secret, the book. Mr. Frederick Engels is writing a book. Mary has told me, and I know it to be true. I knew about the book before good Mary told me. Neddy, my neighbor up five doors in Brown Street North, cleans the floor at Chetham's Library, and he sees Mr. Engels at that place most days. Mr. Engels meets there with another gentleman, and Neddy says that they talk for hours about a book that Mr. Engels is writing. Sir, you and I both know that you have to have a ton of learnin' in your head to write a whole book. The only book I have had to do with is the Holy Bible, and it took a lot of real knowing folk to put it together. Mr. Engels introduced Neddy to his friend, and Neddy says—and I tell you now—Neddy says that Freddie's friend has two first names and that's all of it."

Rostan was now making allowances for Matthew's gin-driven deliveries and couldn't help but notice that his visage had turned a whiter shade of pale.

"Two first names, Matty, and just how does that happen?" Rostan had to ask because by now he just wanted to keep Matthew Denny talking, for the more he spoke, the happier the policeman felt.

"Neddy says his name is Karl Mark , and that is two first names, do you not agree, sir?"

And as Matthew offered that little gem, Killy of the Old Bailey chimed in with a gem of his own, totally unrelated. "Have you met m-my w-wife, Mr. P-p-policeman?" he stuttered as he had done in court.

"But Mr. Killy, your friend Matty here told the Judge in court this very day that your wife had recently been taken to heaven." Rostan had deliberately slipped his interrogator's hat on and questioned further. "So good, sir, I would now have you explain to this assembly just how your good wife could be this morning in heaven but now we all see her again on earth."

Killy mentally scrambled for a reply, and looking Rostan square in the eye, he exclaimed, "In the name of our all that is powerful, almighty God and his sweet son Jesus, sir, I tell you true. What we have all witnessed here today is a resolution. A miracle, sir Peeler. Indeed a divine resolution."

Matthew could not contain himself and stood erect as he declared. "Resurrection, Killy. Resur-bloody-rection, my dear man."

Senior Constable John Rostan did not want this journey to end. He had been given no reason to smile for several long months. He had moved to Transbridge from London sincerely hoping for a good life and, at the same time, to be an exceptional police officer. The priority was a good life. He took up residence in Transbridge, sharing a cottage with his friend Roger Earls. At the time, Rostan was well-aware that Roman Catholic Ireland was probably about the worst place on his God's earth to be living in the way that he was. Roger Earls was an award-winning baker in London, so Transbridge was a huge backward step for him as it was for Rostan whose career in London was going from strength to strength.

The two men loved one another, and to them, that love took prime position as they hoped to have a good life together. The move to Transbridge was to be the beginning of that good life.

CHAPTER NINETEEN

While Rostan found the challenges he faced having to deal with the good folk of Transbridge catered adequately to his personal needs, his partner found himself unable to settle into the cruelly judgmental community. He tried hard to fit in and had gained employment at the Bridge Bakery. The townsfolk all agreed that his oven-kissed offerings were sublime, and word spread throughout the district. His employer was so pleased with the increasing profits that without being asked, he simply began paying extra money to Roger at the end of each week. It was a good life.

Although the Great Hunger was having a devastating impact on the farms and farmers of the district, the Bridge Bakery flourished due to the fact that Roger Earls' heavenly offerings came at a price that was only affordable to the landed gentry, rich landowners, and businessmen of the area.

When all seemed to be going well for the policeman and the baker, circumstances began to mar. The sales at the Bridge Bakery were dropping off. Fewer customers were visiting the premises to purchase Roger Earls' mouthwatering offerings. Both Rostan and Earls had experienced the backlash that good god-fearing folks could mete out when clergy decided to ride roughshod over individual conscience. Tongues began to wag, and several sermons delivered by the latest parish priest of St. Brendan's helped fuel the negative behavior of the good Christians toward their neighbors who were choosing to live differently to themselves but hurting no one.

As profits at the bakery continued to drop, Roger was approached by the owner. He was a kind man but had a large family to feed. He told Roger that he could no longer afford his services. Roger Earls was a sensitive man prone to rash decision-making, and true to form, the decision he was about to make will not only lead to his own death but it will also find John Rostan, his partner, at the brink of insanity.

When told his skills were no longer required at the bakery, Roger Earls simply could not believe that the good life both he and Rostan hoped and prayed for had been shattered. He blamed himself for everything that was going on. He knew his own spirit intimately. "I am a show-off. I do ramble on too much sometimes, nay, often. I know that parents give me strange looks when I talk to their children. I love children. We don't attend Mass, John and I, because people go out of their way to stare at us, and that makes me feel very uncomfortable." Roger found himself going over and over what had just happened but could not steer his mind away from the feeling of self-blame that simply compounded itself within his deepest thoughts. *Rostan does not deserve this. He does not deserve to have me hanging around his neck*, thought Roger.

Roger Earls was a well-read man and came from a family who could well-afford the hefty fees payable to the Westminster School where he attended as a boarding school pupil for two years having already completed four years of earlier education. His father was a hard but fair man who planned to have his only son, Roger, take over management of the family business. Earls Manufacturing was an enterprise that Roger's father had taken over from his own father and was one of London's best known producers of high-end cuisine.

If you were one of London's wealthy families and wanted to show off to your rich friends by throwing an extravagant party, you would most likely engage Earls Manufacturing to provide the food that guests would still be talking about long after the event. The kitchens of the wealthy set were well-able to produce good food, but by bringing in Earls to add its creations to the menu, the end result would be exquisite. The main event of the show-off party was desserts. Suffice to say, Roger's creations were magnificent and never failed to please.

Roger's father had insisted that his only son serve as an apprentice under his best pastry chef. It was due to this that Roger found his passion. He quickly became the king of heavenly creations. Apart from the banquet standards such as syllabub, a boozy fortified wine and cream concoction or brown bread ice cream made with caramelized wholemeal breadcrumbs, Roger had created many additions to the Earls menu, and business was booming. It would seem, however, that life had a different route planned for Roger.

When his father began to realize that Roger was leading a sinful life, he went down the road of conversion and demanded that his son fit into the plans he had divined for him. Roger felt trapped as his father became more determined to have him mend his ways. For fear of the long-term damage to his own reputation and how Roger's lifestyle may impact the company's reputation, he edged him out of the family business and out of the family home.

As Roger sat alone in the Transbridge home, he recalled a poem he had read in a book that he had borrowed from the library at Westminster School entitled "Rime of the Ancient Mariner" written by Samuel Taylor Coleridge in 1798. He had always drawn parallels from the poem that he felt reflected his own life. Coleridge tells the story of a sailor who kills a friendly albatross, believing that the beautiful bird was the cause of the becalmed seas that hampered the ship's progress. The crew were becoming anxious at the lack of progress but told the sailor not to kill the bird because it would surely bring bad luck. He chose to ignore them and did kill the bird but nothing changed. The seas remained calm, so as punishment, the angry crew made the offending man wear the dead bird around his neck.

Roger Earls considered that he, like the mariner of old, had his own albatross to wear around his neck. His homosexuality was his albatross, and after constant reflection throughout his life, Roger always arrived at the same conclusion. A burden to be carried as a penance. "My god is cruel," he mused.

Within the grounds of the Westminster School that Roger once attended, there was a quadrangle on the north side of Ashburnham House referred to as Little Deans Yard. Roger would seek refuge there and hide from the collection of brutes who had made it their mission on this earth to physically bully and verbally demean and torment him. They knew he was different, although Roger doubted that the bullies understood anything at all about his sexual leanings. He was gentle, soft, and kind. He was different. He loved the hideaway he had found for himself in Little Deans Yard, and it came with a bonus. Roger loved architecture and design and could not believe his luck when he found out that Ashburnham House adjoining the yard, as it was often referred to, was designed and built by the great Inigo Jones. Roger appreciated greatness in many people, but Mr. Jones did indeed sit high on his scale of appreciation for great men and women.

The woman he most admired was Mary Wolstonecraft Shelley who assaulted the stuffy minds of the literary world of her time with her novel *Frankenstein*, also known as the Modern Prometheus. It was not just her novel that afforded her the very high admiration ranking allocated by Roger Earls. There were rumors aplenty regarding Mary Shelley's mother, who was a regarded writer herself, but it was her free attitude to sex embarking on illicit love affairs and her efforts to push the rights of women to the fore that amounted to the larger measure of her reputation. Mary Shelley's father, William Godwin, also captivated the gathering mind of Roger Earls. Godwin was a writer, poet, and philosopher, but he was considered at that time to be one of the first exponents of utilitarianism and the first modern proponent of anarchism.

Percy Shelley, the husband of Mary Shelley, held top ranking for poets in Roger's world. The beautiful words in "The Music When Soft Voices Die" always brought a tear to Roger's eye.

The Westminster School motto read in Latin "Dat Deus Incrementum" and translates to English as "God gives the increase." A reference in Corinthians to Paul sowing the seed. Apollo waters the seed. But all for naught without the increase. God provides the increase, the growth. Roger always hated that motto. God had never provided him with the increase, the clarity, the understanding, the comfort—nothing.

No longer having paid work to do, Roger was becoming more and more withdrawn and depressed. At first, he found much to amuse himself with at the cottage he and Rostan lived in, approximately two miles from the police station in Transbridge. He attempted repairs to items that were never used and, therefore, in no genuine need of repair. He added stitches on top of perfectly stitched repairs to Rostan's uniforms while justifying the waste of time with "One can never be too careful." He applied a fresh lime coat to the exterior of the home and even tried to establish a small garden where previously there had been none. His skills as a gardener were very basic, and although every seed he gently tended to did begin to show promise, once it had depleted the nutrients it carried within itself to aid its own beginning, it simply withered and died. As in the school motto from his days at the Westminster School, he needed the increase. He needed his god's help but that did not eventuate.

The relationship between Roger and Rostan became so strained that the policeman began spending some nights at the living quarters provided to him at the Transbridge Police Station. It seemed to him that the harder he tried to comfort his partner simply caused a worsening of the situation. Rostan arrived home late one evening after spending the previous night at the police station. It was dark, but no candles flickered within the house. Roger was gone. A brief note read, "I am sorry I have caused so much trouble. You don't need me. Please forget me.

Please forgive me, and do not try to find me." If Roger Earls believed for one second that his partner of six years was going to forget him, he was wrong.

CHAPTER TWENTY

The Connelly family was destitute. They had abandoned the croft. They were sharing the tenancy of an old shanty at the Dublin dockyards. It happened that when the Connellys arrived at Dublin Docks, Garrett, the gypsy tinker who used to visit the croft trying to sell his wares, recognized them and offered to help in any way he could. His rented shanty was small, but the Connellys were glad of anywhere to stay, so they all moved in, sharing one room and all sleeping on the floor. Joseph Connelly was greatly appreciative of the help from Garrett, but he still harbored his long-term concern with regard to Garrett's tale of the Heartless Black Madonna. The title did not sit with any understanding that he had of a Madonna. Heartless was such a contradiction of the expected.

They were eating the scraps that were thrown out by the numerous ale houses and taverns that had crammed themselves into any vacant space big enough to house two to three full barrels of low-class ale, two to three trestle tables, two to three twin bench pews, and a chest full of glazed clay tankards. The ales were served twenty-four hours a day, and profits were plenty. Almost every dock worker built up a tremendous thirst while slaving hard at the heavy work and long hours expected of them by their wealthy employers, most of whom showed a total lack of social conscience. In addition to the navvies, there was always a huge population of seafaring men who seemed to deem it necessary that they be drunk some of the time and half-drunk most of the time.

Because Joseph was able to read and write, coupled with a basic understanding of arithmetic thanks to the generous efforts of his old schoolteacher, Mr. George Dossett, he was able to convince three of the illiterate bar owners to use his skills to keep their accounts in order where previously there was no order at all. His reward for effort was a pittance, but pennies were mounting.

Joseph Connelly knew that the Dublin Docks were no place for his family, but he was stuck. He found himself constantly in prayer, hoping to be delivered some hope.

Benedict Connelly, Joseph's eldest son, had tasked himself with helping the shipbuilders in the dockyards in an effort to gain paid work. It was almost impossible to break into the tightly knit dockworker community because somebody knew somebody who knew somebody within that community. "Outsiders need not apply." He would just turn up every morning, and wherever he saw men struggling, he would volunteer to assist. His persistence paid off when, one morning, he was spotted by a foreman who was told the story of this young man who was prepared to work for nothing in the hope of being offered a paid job. He was assigned to a shore-up gang. The work entailed the erection of timber retaining walls to ensure against cave-ins of the excavations taking place to expand the ever-extending channel network growing like tentacles surrounding Dublin out of the Liffey River. As the hundreds of men dug the channels, it was the task of the shore-up team to come along behind, building the substantial timber walls required to ensure that cave-ins were avoided. The timbers involved in the construction of these walls came in long lengths. They were extremely heavy and difficult to place in position. No machinery was available to ease the human effort required in construction. It was tough work, and these men were just that.

Benedict Connelly was a strong young man who was faring well while other members of his family were all suffering the ailments that came with two years of poor diet often verging on starvation.

Benny had realized at an early age that gambling was a way to earn quick money. Even when he attended school in Transbridge, he would delight in winning food from his friends by drawing the highest card, but when his victims realized that he was cheating them, they began to distance themselves, and before long, Benny became a very lonely boy, a victim of his own vice. To make matters worse, as Benny tried to gamble with the older men at the docks, it became obvious that the opinion he had of his skills did not match the reality, and he was constantly in debt.

Grace, his mother, was extremely unwell by this time. Her emerald green eyes that had so captivated Joseph Connelly when first they met were bulging and had lost their fire. Her teeth had become loose, and her swollen gums had turned a frightening shade of purple. Her hair was brittle and breaking off. Joseph was well-aware that Grace was suffering from scurvy, and it was common knowledge that citrus fruits could stem the problem, but citrus was not readily available. Crops of oranges and lemons were grown in abundance in Ireland but shipped to England for sale at better prices than the locals could afford to pay. They were a rare item.

Benny, as he was referred to by his family, was doing better than the others because, by pushing his keenness to work in the dockyards, he was now earning money. He could afford to eat, which he did every day while away from family. He was taking care of himself and did not seem too concerned about the precarious situation at home. He would tell his father that the money he earned was far less than the amount he was actually paid and then look for thanks as he handed over the small amount that he grudgingly spared.

Benny was consistently earning the ire of his father. In the four months, that the Connellys had been living at the docks, Benny had changed into a young man that his father no longer recognized. His language had fallen into the sewer, his father told him. He had adopted the navvy swagger and had taken to dressing in a pseudo-military style. The dockworkers were issued with uniforms. Many business owners of that time had decided to supply uniforms, the cost of which was deducted from the meager wages paid. The amount debited to the workers for their uniforms was far in excess of the price paid. The uniforms came into favor because it enabled the employers of the wretched serfs to give the appearance of caring to the many critics who were becoming more vocal about the appalling conditions of workers in general.

Benny and several of his coworkers had coaxed a local seamstress to modify the look of the always-oversized garments, and with a nip here and a tuck there, the end product was quite handsome. To further enhance the look, the prime purpose of which was to intimidate, the group took to wearing an offcut of red cloth around their necks in the form of a rough cravat.

The gang of men that Benny had gravitated to called themselves the Fixers. The name was baptized into being with spilt ale and rum during a particularly wild night at the King and Crossroads public house, situated on the banks of the Liffey River, Dublin Port. Eight men who entered the premises reasonably sober at five o'clock that evening had, by eleven o'clock, become heavily intoxicated. Paddy, the unelected and unlikely leader of the rough-edged clique, put it to members that a name was needed. Paddy was an uneasy atheist. "We have to call ourselves somethin'. We need a name, and I have just the one. I dreamed on it last night. It was like the good lord was givin' me a message. I kept see-in an image of the crucifix. There he was, hanging on the cross for us sinners. I tell you the truth. I think he was telling me that we should call ourselves the crucifixes. We're always hanging off one lump of timber or another on the docks. Do you get my meanin'?"

Yet another god-given message to the uneasy atheist who seemed to have a direct line to the almighty in whom he would continually deny the existence of.

"You're a bloody genius, Paddy," stated Benny. "We do need a name, and I believe that the lord you deny has indeed given that name to us, but of course, it is in the form of a riddle. I think he was testing you, Paddy, and by telling us of your dream, you have passed that test. I believe he actually tells us to call ourselves the Fixers, and that solves the riddle in your dream." Benny was not interested at all in pandering to crazy Paddy; he just loved the tough sound of the name and the other men he was addressing agreed immediately, so Fixers they became.

CHAPTER TWENTY ONE

Paddy was the unlikely leader because, to put it plainly, he was quite mad. He hid a mass of ginger ringlets under a black cap that he always pulled forward down his forehead to a point where his eyes were almost obscured from view. It was those eyes, almost black, that consistently made people feel on edge in his company. He was not heavily built, so his strength came as a shock to those who worked with him. He was as good as two much larger men when it came to lifting the heavy timbers required to complete a day's work.

He had not been under the roof of any church for years. In particular, he had no time for the catholic church. He cussed and swore at anything that referenced religion. But he endlessly quoted passages from the Bible, albeit with his own slants on the stories of the good book. He continually gesticulated the sign of the cross, always finishing with a full-blooded, closed-fisted strike to his own breast. His audiences were always willing to hear Paddy's latest biblical rant because his stories were so absurd, but it was obvious to all that Paddy believed his own outrageous ramblings.

On one occasion, Paddy told his version of the water into wine miracle, and the old ale house building positively shook with the laughter that ensued.

One priceless rant. "Now that rubbish about Jesus turning water into wine at some place nobody's ever heard of. Canaan, they say. Well, I'm here to swear to you that, Mary, the mother of Jesus, had asked him to do that trick, and I was there to see it. It was at Malahide, just north of here, during my cousin Sarah's wedding. I wanted to ask Jesus how he did that, but my Ma said I was too young to talk to the holy man. It was a long time ago, and I reckon that myself, I would have had all of five years." It was clear to all assembled that Paddy truly believed his rant to be true.

Benny Connelly made enemies easily. He would not let a grudge fade away; in fact, under the likeable larrikin façade, he was a true narcissist. There was one foreman in particular that gave Benny a hard time when he was volunteering in the hope of securing a job. This man beat Benny with a wooden staff that he carried just for one purpose: to shock other workers into submission. Benny believed now that he was in a strong position of power. He believed that the time had come for an equalizer, and he knew that the Fixers would help him in his mission. All he had to do was get the Fixers drunk enough, and they would agree to almost anything. He realized that he could easily convince Paddy that his suggested course of action was ordained by god, and if he repeated the sign of the cross often enough in Paddy's presence, he would surely agree to the plan.

In the middle of a particularly heavy drinking session at the Crown and Anchor ale house, Benedict Connelly proposed his plan for revenge. He drank very little that night to ensure that he was sound of thought and missed no details. The Fixers were all in agreement with Benny's vengeful plan, and a majority vote was won.

Mad Paddy was on board with the proposition as soon as he realized that it was god who spoke to him through Benny. "Patrick, you must lead your disciples on this mission to extract penance from this cruel man that has so wronged your true friend Benjamin Connelly, who stands here before us all in my image" was Benny's winning plea.

The way that Benny explained his intentions led the Fixers to believe that they were just going to have a bit of fun and send the cruel foreman a message. It was decided that Tuesday night would be the time to act. The Fixers, to a man, believed that they were simply going to apply a light coat of black pitch to the front of the foreman's house, ignite it, and depart. It was intended that the pitch would burn out quickly, leaving scorched timber behind as the warning. The pitch was easy to obtain. It was used to seal between the planks of the working boats being built in the Dublin Port.

Benny said that he would bring the black pitch and arrived with two buckets and five brushes. It was a dark night, so the vandals were not visible to anyone as they prepared to give the foreman's home a slight toasting. Benny had told the men that he had made enquiries and assured the Fixers that nobody would be home.

The men did as agreed and lightly applied the pitch, but in the dark, Benny was plastering on the highly flammable substance and he slyly went down each side of the home applying thick stripes of the pitch, knowing full well that what he was doing was way beyond what had been agreed to by the other men.

Paddy and the remainder of the Fixers left the crime scene and strolled into a narrow lane opposite the home. This position would give great vantage to the house as it toasted. Benny stayed down the side of the dwelling as the others left. He made sure it was he that got to strike the match.

"Please the lord, no," Paddy muttered to himself. Within seconds, the house was in flames. Paddy knew instantly what Benny had done, and he seethed. He looked over at the house hoping to catch sight of Benny as he had already decided that Benny was poison to the Fixers and should be dealt with. As expected, Paddy caught sight of a skulking shadow, and the moonlight allowed clear vision of the red neck scarf.

Once the fire took hold, the timber at the front of the house was exploding, and the noise reminded Paddy of the cannon fire at the battle of Waterloo. Paddy wished for a second that he was still in the army, but at that precise moment, he tuned into another familiar sound that turned his blood cold. It was the sound of screaming children. The burning pitch caused the smoke to turn black, and it was so thick that seeing anything beyond it was extremely difficult. Paddy shouted at his men to go home, but he, however, turned and headed toward to blazing house.

Through the thick smoke, Paddy could see three small children exiting through the front door of the pyre. Two young boys held the hands of a small girl. Paddy guessed correctly that the boys were her brothers. The two lads appeared to be all right, but the little girl's clothing was on fire. Without giving it a second thought, Paddy launched himself at the girl. As he crossed the narrow street, he removed his coat. He then used it to smother the flames that had attacked her small frame. The little girl was wrapped up in Paddy's coat, and he knew the flames would be gone so he began to unwrap her. As he started her unveiling, he was grabbed hard on his right shoulder by a man screaming "Rosie, where is Rosie?" As the foreman shook Paddy, the young girl exclaimed, "Da, da, it's me."

Paddy recognized the foreman whose home had been attacked but knew he had to help. The foreman embraced his three children, and his wife joined the huddle. Quickly realizing all was not well, she shrieked, "Adam, where is Adam?"

Little Rosie, whose throat was so burned, rasped out the words, "In the house, Ma."

Paddy was already running toward the flaming doorway, and he charged straight into what was left of the home and disappeared. Adam's father followed close behind but faltered as he got close to the blaze. He realized that if anything should happen to him, his wife and three wee-ens would be left homeless and destitute. He got as close as he could and then began to pray.

It only took a short while before he could see a darkened image approaching from within the hell-like zone. It was Paddy, and the foreman could see that he was carrying something. As Paddy emerged into the moonlight, he handed Adam to his father.

Adam's mother screamed, "Is he alive, Tim. Is he breathing?" The boy's father staggered toward his wife and placed Adam gently onto the ground.

"He is dead, luv. He has no life in him. He is dead."

Paddy dropped beside the dead child. He had seen much death and indeed caused much of it when he fought under Wellington at Waterloo where he saw Napoleon defeated. *I have killed many men, but that was war. I have killed this poor child, and this is murder*, he thought to himself as he wept over the body. "Benny Connelly, you have made me a murderer, and I swear now that I will square this debt" was the only consolation he allowed himself to ponder on.

Paddy was the only Fixer who attended the funeral of little Adam Farrell. As he arrived at the church, he was immediately recognized by Tim Farrell, Adam's father. The two men greeted each other with outstretched hands. As they shook hands, Adam's father thanked Paddy for assisting little Rosie and told him that, thanks to him, her burns were only minor. He then went on to thank Paddy for retrieving the corpse of his dead son. "At least the family had a recognizable body to grieve over, and that meant so much especially to the lad's Ma," Tim Farrell whispered to Paddy.

At this point, Paddy asked the question of Tim that had troubled him about the night of the fire. "Why were the wee-ens alone in the house on that sad night, Mr. Farrell?"

Tim Farrell felt the guilt all over again and gave his sharp reply. "Me and the wife never leave the children at home alone. We should have been with them, but my friend Des had invited us to wet the babies head. So we were having a couple of drinks to celebrate the birth of their first child just two doors down. We are always at home in the evenings. Why do you ask such a troublesome question?"

The reply was Paddy gold. "I have no faith, Mr. Farrell, but I wondered how god could have let such a sadness happen." He did his usual multiple signings of the cross and beat his chest with a loud thump.

The question was only posed to validate what Paddy already knew. Benny lied when he told the Fixers that no one would be home on the night that the house was to be singed. "He did not care if anyone would be hurt. He was a bad man," reflected Paddy, and as he pondered, he packed his clay pipe and struck a match to light it. He saw what he immediately interpreted as god's message written across the box containing the matches.

Matches had only just been invented, and the brand name inscribed in flaming letters on the packaging was Lucifer. As he read the name, Paddy immediately thought of Benny Connelly. The message, as he understood it to be, meant that Benny was in fact Lucifer. Paddy's thoughts often drifted between symbolism, idealism, realism, and pessimism with the perceived avoidance of the religion that in truth he relied upon far too much. "Benny, Lucifer, Beelzebub, Mephistopheles, and the Prince of Darkness, all one and the same," he mused.

Paddy actually stayed for the requiem, and thus ended the long-term absence from church that he had imposed upon himself, not meaning to say he would ever attend any other services into the future. His experiences in the army and the suffering and cruelty that he saw under Wellington against Napoleon in France had killed off his religion, or at least that is how Paddy sorted it within his own perception of how he saw the world. When the Mass ended, Paddy thrust five one-pound notes into Tim Farrell's hand and moved away quickly. The money he gave was the entirety of his own wealth.

Tim Farrell felt uneasy about this gesture and made his mind up to learn more about the man who had risked his own life so bravely to help on that tragic night. *Just who is this brave and kind man? Maybe there is more to be reckoned with,* Tim mused to himself.

Chapter Twenty Two

Paddy was seething with anger, and in truth, he was already planning a murder of his own, but of course, he could justify the killing by drawing on his own peculiar mental considerations of justice, retribution, and anger all peppered with medallions of religion placed into wherever he deemed them necessary to allow what he believed to be his valid conscience to be sated.

Paddy let the Fixers know that they had some fixing to do, and he organized a meeting at his own shabby overcrowded tenement to ensure the men remained sober. He made sure that Benny was not told of the gathering as Benny was to be the subject of a judgement. He explained that Benny had made no effort to ensure that the targeted house would be empty, and to make matters far worse, it was Benny who plastered the black pitch on so thick that he fully intended to incinerate the home regardless of anyone being inside.

Paddy pulled no punches as he declared to the others that it had been revealed to him that Benedict Connelly was in truth the Devil himself. He had caused the Fixers to murder a young child, and it was only just that Benny should pay with his own life for such a crime.

"I believe we have the right to do away with Benny and rid Ireland of the Dark Angel, so I need a show of hands in order to seal the demon's fate."

The youngest fixer was a Scottish lad named Malcolm McDonald, and he announced firmly in the thick Scottish brogue of his birth, "I think Benny should pay for his treachery, so I say yes," and he raised his hand.

Two of the Fixers immediately asked Paddy to explain the meaning of the big word that Malcolm had used. "What does *treshury* mean, Paddy?" but as they quizzed, the two remaining Fixers raised their hands in affirmation, and with that, Paddy raised his hand, making four out of six in agreement. Without an explanation for the meaning of the word treachery, used by Malcolm, the two questioning Fixers both raised their hands, allowing a unanimous stand to be taken. That meant that Benny's fate was sealed.

"How shall we do it, Paddy?" asked one of the Fixers. Malcolm immediately suggested that Benny could be pushed into the canal as they worked. Several men had slipped accidentally into the canal as they toiled, and death was certain. No one would jump in to help because no one could swim. That, coupled with the facts that the mud would simply not allow any poor unfortunate soul to scramble back on to land and the water being freezing as it was December, Benny's demise would be quick.

During all that was being said, Paddy could not help but notice that Malcolm McDonald was steering the ship of decision-making. It puzzled him because Benny was, without a doubt, Malcolm's best friend. In fact, he knew that the pair would share a room for the weekend at the King and Crossroads public house, and the thought of them as a couple vexed him. *They must have fallen out*, Paddy thought, but nothing could be further from the truth of the matter as it turned out.

Malcolm volunteered to do the deed. "Tomorrow is Sunday," he said "so we do not work all of the day. Monday we are to unload timbers along the canal banks, so our accident couldn't happen on Monday, therefore Tuesday it will be. In the morning, we should arrive earlier than usual and tell Benny to do the same to allow some Fixer issue to be discussed. Let's say a birthday celebration. Paddy you can say that my birthday is due. I will act really happy and surprised. We can agree to meet at the King and Crossroads for a drink after work, and then we can all walk to the canal side, but being that little bit earlier, no one will see me as I shove that bastard Benny into the freezing canal waters, and that will surely cool the devil down."

It became the quickest decision ever made by the Fixers, and Paddy was suspicious of Malcolm's motives. The agreement meant that Malcolm was in total control of the show, and what a show it turned out to be.

In truth, Malcolm loved Benny, and although he knew that Benny had multiple liaisons with both sexes, Malcolm saw this fiasco as a way to remove Benny from Dublin and start afresh in London, hopefully.

Malcolm knew it would be hard to convince Benny to leave the Dublin Docks because he had become the pauper's version of Lord George Gordon Byron (poet darling of the English elite) whose romantic poetry he once scoffed at, but now, because his father insisted that he be taught to read and write, he had adopted the habit of scribbling short poems expressing his singular love for all and sundry personnel who shared his bed when he stayed at the King and Crossroads public house. He did, of course, reflect on the absurdity of handing over his poetically scripted gems knowing that not one of the recipients could read them. He often referred to himself as Lord Benedict, bard of the Dublin Docks.

As soon as the meeting ended, Malcolm tasked himself with finding Benny and putting a proposal to him that he reckoned his agreement of was beyond doubt.

The hour was late, but his first port of call was the Connelly shanty that Benny's family shared with Garrett, the one-handed wild-eyed gypsy king. Garrett had revealed to Joseph that he was truly a gypsy king, and because he knew that Joseph was planning to move his family to Manchester, he made Joseph promise to take him along.

Malcolm pounded the door of the tiny shanty, and very quickly, he could see candle light through the window. The door opened, and Joseph stood there, not amused. Joseph had met Malcolm on previous occasions, so he let him in from the cold. Joseph was pleased that Malcolm had become a friend of the family. He spoke at times with Mrs. Connelly and would sometimes bring her oranges as he realized she was badly afflicted with scurvy. Joseph woke Benny and went back to his bedspace on the floor.

Benny was annoyed to see Malcolm at such a late hour, but after hearing all that had transpired with the Fixers and their plan to kill him, he was filled with fear. It was at this point that Malcolm put forward his proposal.

"I know you have no money, Benny, but I have managed to save some, and I think we can both afford to go to London and get as far away from here as possible. Paddy is boiling with anger at the death of young Adam Farrell. He says you caused the murder, and we know he is mad, so he will not stop until you are dead, dear friend, and that is the last thing I would want to have happen to you."

Benny was simply a selfish, self-indulgent bastard who cared for no one but himself. He was well-aware of Malcolm's feelings for him, but to him, he was just a mere dalliance, one among many. He did, however, take very seriously the threat imposed on him by the Fixers and instantly agreed to leave with Malcolm for London at daylight.

Malcolm felt that he had just won a great victory. He firmly believed that once Benny had distanced himself from all he had happening at the Dublin Docks, he would be able to see Malcolm in a clearer light and surely that could only lead to Benny reevaluating his feelings for him. "He does love me? I am sure." Malcolm felt hopeful but terrified at the same time. He had every right to be terrified. Benny was a narcissist who saw himself alone as the center of his very limited and toxically stunted universe.

Benny agreed to meet up with Malcolm at five o'clock the next morning so as to begin what Malcolm was now referring to as their safe escape.

Before crawling back to his sleeping space on the floor, Benny emptied out the money from a tobacco tin his father kept under the wood cooker. This money was specifically put aside by Benny's father, Joseph, to pay for any medication that might become available to help save his mother's life. Benny also knew that his sister's had saved up some small change to buy birthday gifts with, so he also stole that. Without one thought given to the survival of his own family, Benny crawled back into his space on the floor, hoping to get some sleep before he had to meet Malcolm to execute their safe escape. Benny went to sleep with only one concern on his mind: He had to get away from Mad Paddy.

As it turned out, Mad Paddy was no longer any threat at all to Benedict Connelly. The lifeless body of Paddy the Fixer was found on the same morning of the safe escape behind the King and Crossroads public house. His throat had been cut from ear to ear. Both hands had been soaked in black pitch and burnt to the bone. Five single-pound notes had been forcefully rammed into his mouth. Paddy left behind no one, but one lone man attended his requiem and burial. Patrick "Paddy" Peter Demsey was a good man, but he died the shattered product of the conflicted life that had been gifted to him by his god.

CHAPTER TWENTY THREE

hanks to the network of friends and their helpers, including Finbar Denny, Matthew Denny, and John Rostan (the Peeler), Joseph Connelly was able to finally put together a loosely formed plan with regard to relocating himself and his family to Salford, more particularly Brown Street North.

The Connellys in transit now numbered five plus one. Joseph and his extremely ill wife, Grace, and the children, Paul, Josephine, and Ellen, made up the balance. Those missing from the full quota were Therese and Mary who died of the Great Hunger, plus Benedict who had chosen to defy his father and left prematurely in a nervous hurry with his friend and fellow dockworker Malcolm McDonald.

Joseph Connelly had promised that when his family fled the famine, he would allow Garrett, their friend, who had helped them and shared with the Connellys his accommodation at the

Dublin Docks, to travel with them, and true to his word, it was Garrett, the gypsy tinker, who filled the sixth position allocated to the Connellys for the crossing.

The journey from Dublin to the Black Duck tavern in Manchester went well for the Connellys, and unlike the situation that Finbar found himself in on his arrival where he and his two children had to sleep over for the night in the cramped, filthy, little room that adjoined the Black Duck tavern, Finbar was able to meet up with the Connellys as they arrived in Salford. Finbar had been made aware via the grapevine that Grace was not faring well, and he had organized to use the cart that Matthew had been given to transport her from the riverboat near the Black Duck tavern to Brown Street North. The bed of the cart had been padded down with clean straw, and two tattered blankets had been placed on the cart for Grace. One to sit on and one to abate the strong cold wind of that day. Michael had arranged with Mr. Engels, manager of the cotton mill where he worked, to take some time off to assist his father with the mission.

When Finbar took in the whole sad spectacle that was the arrival of his friend and family, it was all he could do to stop himself from bursting into tears. His eyes were instantly drawn to Grace. She was utterly unrecognizable. Had Finbar not known they were coming, he truly believed that he could have passed by every family member and not recognized one of them. On the other hand, he immediately identified the smiling face of the irrepressible Garrett who came toward him and clasped him in a warm embrace. Garrett was an astute man, and the embrace was to cover up the expression of sheer shock on Finbar's face.

"Smile my friend, please smile. These people need you to smile," he said, and with that, he released his arms to allow Finbar to approach Joseph who was in tears.

The two men fell to their knees as they embraced. "It's going to be all right, Joey. I've got you now. You are all here now, Joey, and life is better," whispered Finbar, desperately trying to feed some hope back into the spirit of the man he so admired who was obviously no longer the same person that he had left behind.

Michael could see that his father was struggling with the situation and immediately went to tell Grace that he had prepared her carriage, and when she saw what he was referring to, she simply had to laugh, and that laugh was something that Joseph had not heard in such a long time. He turned from Fin, and looking in her direction, he saluted Michael, and the discomfort was overcome. Finbar felt his chest plump with pride because of how Michael had taken the pressure off a situation over which he had surrendered control.

Michael asked as to the whereabouts of Benny. Joseph's reply was short. "I don't believe we can tell you anything about

Benedict. He has gone on before us, and I believe he may be in London. Nothing but trouble, that boy."

Michael and Finbar made Grace as comfortable as they could on the cart, and the slow journey to Brown Street North began. The cart weighed far more than the emaciated cargo it carried. Fin had attached a rope to the front of it, and that allowed Michael to pull the vehicle while he held to two handles at the rear and pushed. The cobblestones made the journey hard to manipulate, but good progress was being made. Paul, Joseph's son, began chatting to Michael and insisted that he help pull the cart.

Joseph was at Finbar's side as they walked, and the conversation was brisk. Fin drew the girls, Josephine and Ellen, closer so that they could hear what was being spoken of. Finbar found himself doing exactly what Matthew had done on his arrival. He was explaining all the dos and do-nots of the Salford slum.

"We Taigs, do not mix with the Prodies. Another thing I must warn you about is the youth gangs. There are many young men in the area. There's work for those who want to, but many of these misfits have formed themselves into gangs, and they survive by stealing from shops and houses, even holding knives to people's throats, demanding that they give over their money. We do hear all the time about the trouble these devils cause, so when we are out in the streets, we always travel in the company of others. Make sure there is at least three of you and you should be safe."

Joseph immediately thought of his boy Benedict. If he had made it to London, Joseph was sure that his wayward son would gravitate to gang lifestyle rather than take on hard work. Benny could work hard, but if there was an easier way to make money, that would be the road for him. Joseph found it hard to stop thinking about Benny, but he was making a conscious effort to concentrate on the people around him who really needed him for direction.

"You will love my cousin Matthew and his good wife, Colleen. I have rented a place on my own, so we do have room for you all"—*I hope*, he thought—"There is paid work for you all, and you too, Garrett, if you need it," Finbar said, desperately searching his mind for anything positive that he could relate to the new arrivals who were all physically far worse off than his family were upon their arrival. "You will all love my cousin big Matthew and his funny wife, Colleen, when you meet them," merely repetition, but it was all Fin could manage as he stared at Grace bouncing like a cork on water in the cart he was trying so hard to navigate smoothly.

Garrett thanked Fin for the offer of work but declined, saying, "In all humility, sir, a king does not have to work, but I do thank you for your kind offer. I have alerted several of my friends in Ireland to let my people who live here in Manchester know of my arrival, so if I could impose on you for one night only, I will be gone by tomorrow morning."

Joseph caught Finbar's eye, and a simple wink was suffice to end further enquiry.

Finbar continued on with his warnings, trying to insert humor wherever possible to deflect the emerging seriousness of the strife going on all around them that Joseph had tuned into as they struggled toward Brown Street North.

"Our local parish is St. Michael's. The church is the ugliest you have ever seen, but Father Tim is a very good man. He offered me a loan to help us survive when we first arrived, and I accepted it as just that: a loan which I paid back quickly thanks to the work Matthew and Colleen had arranged for us. Now please don't think me rude, but I would like to offer you the same deal: a small loan to get you settled that you can repay when you are able."

Joseph's reply was instant. The days of self-containment and bridled pride expected of him because of his faith had been stripped away by the toll that the Great Hunger had taken on the way he felt his life would unfold and be lived. "I would appreciate that loan very much. Young Benny stole all the money he could find at home and left us with nothing before he snuck away. I believe he has got himself involved in some serious crime, and Garrett has hinted to me that someone may have died because of him. He has become a godless little sinner. He has broken his mother's heart, and I can forgive all but not that."

Finbar was an unlikely hero. He loved Joseph dearly because Joseph had opened his eyes to a world that, without Joseph, he would have never known. The times of his youth that he had spent with Joseph delving into the stories that Joseph brought to life for two poor souls who had nothing but could escape into the fantasies of the printed word. Finbar had gained through Joseph a power. The power of imagination, the power of the human mind.

Finbar was determined to make life better for the man to whom he felt he owed so much. He had spent most of what he kept aside for emergencies to prepare for the arrival of his friend and family, and what money he was left with was that which he intended to loan to his good friend, but he was not concerned because there were three wages coming into the home and his children gave most of their earnings to their father without question.

Finbar had brought in extra food. Fresh straw had been laid over the cellar floor, and the three Dennys had done all they could to make life as comfortable as they could for the Connellys. Fin even obtained from Matthew a bottle of gin, reckoning that if Joseph felt the way he did when he first had to take in all the chaos of Salford, he would need a stiff drink.

"Here we are," said Finbar. "We are home. Now, Connellys, I would like to introduce you to Colleen Denny, my cousin-in-law, I think that's how it is. Colleen was our archangel when we first arrived as I intend to be yours, Joseph. She is cousin Matthew's wife and the person to talk to about health problems, and I know from my experience you will have some at least." He glanced at Grace as he spoke.

Finbar led the way up the three steps of his rented house to the front door and noticed that it was ajar. Apprehension immediately gripped him. *Surely we have not been robbed*, he thought to himself. *The Thompsons, four doors away, had been broken into only yesterday, and the thieves stripped the home of anything of value, including the children's clothing. The mongrels even took the kettle from the stove, surely not?*

The lock had not been forced, and Finbar immediately felt relief as he remembered that Matthew had the spare key, and just as he had that thought, Colleen pushed her way to his side smiling. "Come on, Fin. Don't you keep these good people waiting. They must be so tired. I will put the kettle on." Colleen disappeared into the house, and Finbar stood aside as manners dictated to allow his guests to enter.

The first difference that Finbar noticed was the fragrance of fresh flowers, and then slowly the surprise revealed itself. Matthew and Colleen had struck again. Ten beautiful fresh red roses in a vase that was not new but certainly new to the Dennys.

The extra amount of food that Finbar had organized had been miraculously multiplied by four. There was clean secondhand clothing in piles laid out on a long wooden pew that had also materialized from nowhere. A clean flock mattress had been placed on the floor in front of the pew. There were four bottles of gin where previously there had only been one, and to top off the dazzling display, six large ripe oranges sat in a new timber bowl on the kitchen table.

The interrogation began as the four adults allowed the gin to calm their collective nerves. Finbar offered Michael a drink, but he refused and stated that he ought to be getting back to work. He had been placed in a position of demanding responsibility at Engels's Victoria Mill thanks initially to Colleen and then Mary Burns. He was being rewarded admirably for his efforts and had taken to wearing a suit daily with shoes polished to mirror his image. Education had been his savior.

Because Mary Burns knew that Michael had been taught to read and write, she had suggested to the Victoria Cotton Mill manager, Frederick Engels, with whom she was having a de facto relationship, that Michael's obvious talents would be an asset to management if he was given a job in the office rather than the mundane position he was holding as a general hand on the mill floor. The influence that Mary Burns had over Frederick Engels was considerable. He was sent by his father to Manchester in the hope that he would mend his ways, and that is exactly what happened but not in the least the way his father had intended.

Young Engels was quite the rebel back home in Germany. He was a staunch member of the Young Hegelians and had, in his own name, published articles that helped lead to the groundswell of support for the proletariat that began to fight for better conditions for workers. In summary, anti-politics, hence anti-government, anti-religion including anti-marriage; he wrote about fair play and freedom. His exposure was becoming an embarrassment to his father.

Through Mary Burns, Engels visited many slum homes, gaining a complete knowledge of all that was wrong with the working conditions and appalling living situations that the laborers and their families found themselves in. How Engels met Mary is unknown. Some say she worked in the mill. Some say Mary and her sister, Lizzie, worked as domestics, and that is how they were able to manage his stately home for twenty years. Some say Mary sold oranges in the market at Manchester's Hall of Science and that term, used at the time, referred to prostitution.

However they met, she became a huge influence on how he lived, and it has often been said that if Engels was the father of socialism, Mary was certainly the mother. Engels had a healthy social conscience, and that was extremely rare among the rising numbers of factory owners who had become so powerfully wealthy in such a short time. Wealthy people who considered their workforce as expendable and easily replaced.

CHAPTER TWENTY FOUR

inbar was still bringing Joseph up-to-date with life in the Salford slum. Colleen had pushed the flock mattress, an absolute luxury, into the corner of the small lounge area that adjoined the kitchen which was even smaller. She moved the recently arrived pew to form a barrier alongside the mattress. She draped a blanket over the back of the pew, hoping to afford Grace some semblance of privacy. After devouring two oranges, some cheese, and bread with a small portion of the smoked cod on offer, Grace retired to her alcove and probably was asleep before Colleen could cover her with the heaviest of the new-old blankets on offer thanks to herself and Matthew.

Finbar was ensuring that Joseph's family be included in the conversation. He put forward a proposition that he hoped would suit them all. "I think we need a plan here, Joey," he said. "It is plain to see that none of you are in any condition to work, and I was hoping you would take up my offer to have you stay here with us at least until you are able to begin earning money, and only when you have enough, and only then, you might be able to find a house to rent close by so that we are all able to support each other the way Matthew and Colleen have helped us to get started with our new lives. The town is a great shock, I know, but you will get used to it and probably quicker than you are thinking at the moment. What do you say, Joey?"

Joseph was a broken man. "Anything you say, Fin. You view our troubles in the light of day and nothing is right at the moment, so I agree, with thanks, to all you have proposed."

Joseph's children only had one question between them. "Where do we sleep, Uncle Fin?"

The Dennys had decided Joseph and Grace would be best suited to sleeping on the newly acquired flock mattress because Grace would benefit greatly from the heat given off from the coal-burning stove in the kitchen. Michael volunteered to stoke the burner during the night to keep the house warm because the weather had turned bitterly cold and the snow was falling on Brown Street North.

Michael and Angela, who usually slept in the cellar, had agreed to share their father's bedroom and sleep on the floor. This allowed the three Connelly offspring to sleep in the cellar where fresh straw had been laid and was quite dry despite the weather. Michael decided to return to the cellar during the night because, when he was stoking the stove, he heard one of the girls whimpering. All three of Joseph's children were awake when he descended the cellar steps. They were in such a state that Michael talked with them hoping to calm their anxiety into the wee hours of the morning when at last they were all asleep, Michael included.

Joseph, Finbar, and Garrett arose early the next morning, and all three were eating a hearty breakfast of bread, cheese, and smoked cod all washed down with cups of tea. Several loud knocks sounded on the front door. It was just after five in the morning, and Finbar hastened to open it.

He did not recognize the two men that stood in front of him, but he immediately knew what, rather whom, they had come for. Their attire announced that they were gypsies. Garrett had already made his way to the door and was standing to one side of Fin. He moved forward past Fin and on to the small porch where the garishly clad pair stood.

"It has been a long time, my father," said the taller of the two men.

"Indeed, indeed, it has, my son. Shall we go?" asked Garrett.

"Who are your friends here, Father?" asked the same man.

"Please forgive me. Where are my manners?" said Garrett, and with that, all the proper introductions were made.

Finbar asked the two gypsies to join them for something to eat, and not wanting to appear rude, they agreed. As they sat deep in conversation, Joseph could hold back no longer. He had been told by Garrett, when he was just a young boy living on the croft, that Garrett was a king among his own people.

"Garrett has always told me he was a king, and that must mean you are a prince, sir," Joseph quizzed the taller man claiming to be Garrett's son.

"I can see doubt and pity in your eyes, sir, as you ask the question. I am a prince among my people. I am called Manfri Garrett, and my father here before me was indeed a king. I doubt, sir, that you would know this, but the sad exile of his life was not caused by himself but because of the importance of the man that he killed, he was banished to live a life on his own. I have often tried to find him, but every time I get close, he seems to know and simply moves on. I was pleased and relieved to get the message that my father was finally going to allow us to meet again. There are things he needs to know."

Garrett senior interrupted. "Manfri, I know I had been forgiven by our people a long time ago, my boy, and that my title had been restored, but I felt that if I returned home, I would be hated by all, and that would cost you also. I just chose the life of a tinker, and I hoped you would eventually give up the search, but you have never stopped. I am very happy that you never stopped."

It was not long before Finbar, Joseph, Garrett, Manfri, and his friend were on to their third cup of tea, and the stockpile of food had been levelled somewhat Joseph had finally found himself comfortable enough with the company that he allowed himself to ask the question that had bothered him since the first day he met Garrett all those years ago.

"Manfri, will you tell me how your father lost his hand?" and as he asked, he pointed to the decorative silver hook that had replaced the missing limb at the end of Garrett's left arm. "He has told the story many times in the past, but every retelling of the story is different."

The three gypsies snapped a look at one another, and immediately, Joseph realized that he had pushed the conversation too far.

Manfri looked at his father and said, "Papa, I can see that these people have become like family to you, so if you want to tell the story, I think they have earned the right to know."

It was obvious to the assembly that a raw nerve was hit, and Garrett proceeded to bury his head in his hand while stroking his forehead with the silver hook. "Manfri, tell them, tell them, please for me," Garrett said quietly.

"My father lost his hand in a fight with his brother, Waa. Waa was a beast of a man. He was a thief, a heavy drinker, he was paid to hurt people, and he loved my mother. Yes, he wanted my mother for himself, but she was already promised to my father, and so they were married. I know my mother loved my father. I was too young when it happened, but the gypsy stories still talk of the love between my mother and father, the king and his queen.

"One night, while my father was away selling horses, Waa overpowered my mother, and he raped her. He hurt her so badly. He broke her leg and caused some blindness in one eye where he hit her so hard. I remember how sick my mother was after the bashing, and I remember that I never heard her laugh again. When she stopped laughing, I felt my world was ending.

"When my father returned and saw the state my mother was in, he went to Waa's wagon where he found him still drunk and asleep. They began to fight, and my father stabbed Waa in his rotten heart. Waa was dead, but during the fight, my father's hand was almost cut off. Our blacksmith who helps with wounds tried to save my father's hand, but it started to turn black, so it had to be cut off with a red hot knife, and I can remember him screaming when my mother's sister sewed up the wound with fishnet cord. The hook you refer to was fashioned by one of our men who does beautiful work in silver, and because my father was king, he made a special effort as you can see.

"Our people secretly buried Waa's body, but we knew that someone had told the police about the dead man because they came to our camp asking questions. My father stayed hidden in the forest until we moved camp, and then he was able to spend more time with Mother and me. My mother was so sick. Waa had hurt her so much. One day, she went for her usual walk before our evening meal, and she never came back. I went looking for her. She was dead when I found her. She had climbed up into a tree, tied one end of her shawl around a tree branch and the other end around her neck. She dropped from the limb and hung herself.

"My father tried to look after me. I remember that he did so, but the police kept turning up and making life hard for our people. I was having to spend more and more time with my aunty Agnes, and in the end, my papa left me with her and disappeared. The police lost interest after a while, but my father stayed away. Some of our people, who thought at the time that my father should have been handed to the police, began to realize that he had been punished enough, but I have not been able until now to tell him that. We still have to worry about the police, but they have not asked about my father for a long time. Our people are always in trouble with the police, but maybe my father will be left alone."

Joseph realized that it would have been far better if he had not been so curious. Garrett stood and asked his son to take him home. Manfri placed some coins on the table and thanked Finbar for his hospitality. Garrett promised to stay in touch, and then they were gone.

Chapter Twenty Five

When the three gypsies arrived back at their campsite, Manfri was greeted as Garrett had been when he was leader. Manfri had assumed his father's role.

Garrett was amazed to see just how many wagons there were. A countless number of children ran around in the central area formed by the perimeter of wagons. Many women sat chatting, but all seemed busy with various craft projects. Some were weaving on small looms, some were engaged in intricate needlework, and one group of gaudily dressed women were toiling in the art of beading: that is either jewelry-making or decorating the beautifully ornate dance dresses worn by the vibrant, life-loving gypsy women.

Garrett took special note of a young girl who was being fitted with a crimson dress because he saw the family resemblance.

He turned to Manfri and asked, "Is that her, Manfri? Is that my granddaughter?"

Manfri replied, "She is my beautiful little girl Ingi, Father, and yes, your second grandchild. We will wait until the women are finished with her because it is for you that she asked for that dress to be made. It is to be a surprise, so I don't want her to be disappointed."

The two men moved toward a beautifully ornate wagon and entered. Manfri explained that the number of gypsies in the camp had swelled because the police were constantly raiding the smaller communities and most times with good reason. These communities are being so intimidated that many have opted for the better security that a larger camp should offer.

"It is becoming harder by the day to earn enough legally to feed our families. Many of the young men have put gangs together. They are breaking in to houses and even robbing people in the streets."

Garrett was relieved to be at home at last, but he could not contain his excitement any longer, and so he asked, "Manfri, is it true that the statue of our beautiful Black Saint Sara-la-Kali was stolen and then returned without her heart in place? Is the Madonna here, Manfri? Do we still hold her? Can I see her? What of her heart?"

"Yes, yes, and yes, Papa. We have her back. It turns out that the people who stole her only did it for the value of her heart. What they did not know was that someone had already removed the Madonna's heart, and we had replaced the beautiful jewel that was once mounted at her breast with a piece of well-fashioned glass.

"When the thieves realized that the replacement heart was made of glass, they left the statue, undamaged, near where we used to dip our water for drinking, and it was Ingi who found the Madonna. She grew ten feet on that day, or at least that is what she thinks. We had such a party to celebrate the return of the Madonna."

Saint Sarah, who was also known as Sara-la-Kali, is the patron saint of the Romani gypsy people. Garrett remembered being told as a child that Saint Sarah came from Upper Egypt where she first appeared as a black maid.

Garrett was finally able to embrace his son. Manfri, however, was not as willing to simply accept his father's return without hearing the answers to all the questions he had thought of since Garrett had let him know via the gypsy grapevine that he intended to come home.

The old man embarked on a long drawn-out explanation of the whys and the why-nots that led him to behave the way he did and turn his back on his family. He presented many valid arguments that might just allow an outsider to believe that he was trying always to do the right thing, but after almost one hour of the to-and-fro, Manfri brought the conversation to an end as he looked directly into his father's eyes and said, "Did I hear an apology in all you have offered so far, Papa? Do you understand how let down and alone I felt when you finally stopped coming back to the camp, do you, Papa?"

"Manfri, please forgive me," sincerely pleaded Garrett. "I have not been the father that I wanted to be. After your mother decided that she could take no more, my world fell to pieces, but I never wanted you to be hurt. Because the police just kept raiding our camp to find me, I was told by the elders that it would be better for you if I just disappeared. Manfri, I have always known what was happening to you and how you were growing into a fine man. My sister Agnes, who became your mother, has always passed information on to me so that I could know you but from afar. I made Agnes swear not to tell you anything about me. I thought what I was doing was the best for you. Manfri, please understand. I will always love you."

Manfri's puff and bluster were born more of ego rather than anger. He knew his father had always been kept up-to-date with what was going on among the gypsies. His auntie and de facto mother felt it necessary that the old king should still be shown the respect due to him, and she also firmly believed that Manfri was, in her eyes, the new king. She dreamed that one day her brother, Garrett, would be able to return and that father and son might rule together.

As father and son (king and king) were endeavoring to create some even ground to further their discussion, Agnes entered the grand gypsy wagon; both men immediately stopped talking and diligently looked her way. If an observer had been present, there would be no doubt as to which person in that wagon commanded the most respect.

"I don't know whether to laugh or cry," said Agnes. "I have waited so long for this day to come, and here you are, both behaving like enemies. Forget what has happened in the past, and I beg you, look to the future. Our people have lost their way. They need a strong leader. They need someone who can take control of our young men who are in so much trouble with the police. Our young girls don't want to continue in the old ways because the young men don't understand anymore about what is needed to be a good husband. Manfri, you have done your best, but our people see you as too young to lead. Gypsy kings are old men with the wisdom of the ages in them. The sons of gypsy kings become gypsy kings, but our old king has been away too long. Our people want to follow, but it will take a miracle to hold them together."

Garrett took his sister's hand and said, "You are always right, Agnes, and we do need a miracle. I know of such a miracle. Our God has instructed me to return to my people, and through me, he will reunite the gypsies and bring new hope. If I am able to remain as the king of our people, I can make that miracle come true."

Manfri addressed Agnes. "Mama, the old fool thinks he is bloody Moses coming down from Mt. Sinai holding the two lumps of rock with the shiteful ten commandments scratched on to them. Back then, the people of Moses were rebelling, surely you are not asking us to believe that you have the power of Moses, Papa. I think you are mad. All I hear are the ramblings of an old man who is too tired, too afraid, and too bloody old to live on his own anymore. A miracle, Papa," said Manfri in a mocking tone, "do you realize how stupid you sound? What is this miracle you speak of and how could God possibly be working through you to make anything happen, never mind a miracle?"

Garrett fiercely tried to stand tall in his bent frame, and beating his fist on the table, he announced, "As king and through God, I swear I will make the heart of our Black Madonna beat again. I believe all our troubles started when her heart was stolen, and when I return it, all our prayers will be answered and our people will unite."

"The people see me as the leader, and that is how it will stay," shouted Manfri.

"You both know how troubles are settled," shouted Agnes above them both. "The council will have to meet and listen to the pair of you behaving like little bloody children. There is no easy answer here, but the council will judge you both, and I tell you now that whatever is decided is how things will be. We all have to obey the rules, and I hope for the sake and survival of our people that each of you understand that."

Manfri knew, as was always the case, that Agnes was right. It had to be left to the council of elders to decide how the situation that had developed between father and son should be resolved. He was so incensed that he stormed out of the wagon without offering a word.

Agnes had remained relatively calm, but as soon as Manfri was gone, she quickly moved toward Garrett. She had made a fist with her right hand and closed her fingers together as tightly as she could. She knew how to fight and knew that a tight fist lessened the chance of fingers being broken when delivering a blow. Garrett had misread her action and thought he was about to receive a warm embrace. Before he could draw another breath, he found himself hitting the floor of the wagon bum first. Agnes stood over him, and the look on her face was one of long overdue satisfaction. She had struck Garrett hard on the jaw, and he wavered between consciousness and blackout.

"You bloody cow. You have broken my jaw. Why did you do that?" cried Garrett.

"Shut your bloody childish wailing. Your jaw is not broken. I would have heard the snap and anyway you would not be able to talk," said Agnes, almost smiling. "If I hear one more word from you about the beautiful heart of our Black Madonna, I swear I will have to kill you. I know what you did, you bastard. I know it was you who stole the gem in the first place. We were not robbed. When you decided to disappear altogether was at the same time that the heart was so roughly removed from our beautiful lady. You needed money, and you helped yourself. You will not be forgiven."

"What you say is not true," offered Garrett. "I would not do such a thing. I am a king. I am a businessman. I work for my money. I have no need to steal. How dare you accuse me of such a thing. I did not steal the heart, but I promise you, Agnes, that I will have it returned."

"Do it then. No more of your lies. If you deserve to be king, you should see to it that the red heart is returned to its place of pride before the council of elders meet, and maybe they might consider you to be our king," Agnes teased.

Agnes was not guessing that Garrett had stolen the gem. She knew exactly where the stone was first sold on. A good friend of Agnes who belonged to another gypsy community had told her that around the time that Garrett disappeared, she had seen him in the pawn shop run by the dubious Abraham Rothschild, and he was being extremely secretive as he spoke to the owner. She overheard Abraham tell Garrett that to get the best price for the beautiful gem, he would take it to London where his Jewish friends would have far better access to the sort of money needed to complete the sale. Agnes's friend felt that the whole affair was so secretive that she was obliged to tell her. At the time, Agnes knew exactly what was being sold, but the loyalty she felt for her brother took first place over doing the right thing by her gypsy community.

The importance of the Black Madonna cannot be overplayed. The gypsies were very devout Christians, but above any devotion, there was another aspect of gypsy beliefs that was far more powerful than prayer. That major driving force was superstition. So much of the gypsy lifestyle depended on how well-satisfied their superstitions were.

If a knife falls on the floor, you will have a gentleman visitor; a fork will bring a lady visitor; a spoon heralds the visit from a child.

Counting magpies: One for sorrow, two for joy, three for a girl, four for a boy, five for silver, six for gold, seven for a secret never to be told.

The boogeyman played a prominent part in decision-making.

If you meet a red-haired woman first thing in the morning, you will have bad luck all day.

It is true that some gypsies were literally driven mad by superstitions.

Agnes weighed in heavily on the side of superstitions, and she firmly believed that the theft of the heart began the decline of the gypsy lifestyle that she so loved and was still continuing to erode traditions that kept the communities bound together. Quite literally, things were falling apart for Agnes and her community. And for that, she held her brother, Garrett, to blame.

CHAPTER TWENTY SIX

G arrett had stolen the gem, and yes, he had used Abraham Rothschild to get the best price he could for the stone. Garrett also correctly guessed that the money he was given by Abraham for the sacred artefact was far less than he was due. He knew Abraham would cheat him and keep an amount for himself that was far greater than the commission he had agreed to pay, but Garrett was desperate. He did not want to burden his gypsy community, and he surmised that simply disappearing would take all the pressure off his people.

Abraham had told Garrett that when the gem was sold, it was purchased by the agent of a French marquis from Marseille who was a man of great wealth. Garrett also remembered that although this agent was English, her name was Louisa DuBois.

Garrett had been told by several travelling gypsies that the French marquis had died and his son was desperate to find the English lady that married his father because she had stolen several items of value from the marquis and her name was Louisa DuBois. Garrett was told that a considerable reward was on offer for the return of these items, which consisted of two title deeds for land at the Port of Marseilles, one beautifully cut two-carat diamond, and one heart-shaped ruby. Yes, the red heart of the Black Madonna. Garrett knew it had to be the stone that Abraham Rothschild had helped with the sale of. He was told that the reward on offer was being handled by a man named Solomon Leyman on behalf of the son of the Drunk Duke.

Garrett knew that if anyone was aware of the whereabouts of the ruby, it would be Abraham Rothschild, and of course, he was right. When Garrett visited Abraham's pawn shop, he was told by the man himself that he had arranged the sale of the diamond on behalf of Angela Denny, and when he casually enquired of her about the whereabouts of the ruby and the title deeds he had been told that everything was being kept safe in the strong room at St. Michael's church in Salford.

Both men agreed that Solomon Leyman must not be told anything about what was happening with the items on which the reward was being offered. Abraham explained to Garrett that by selling off the stones individually, he would end up with far more money than the reward on offer. He also told Garrett that the gems were of little consequence to Leyman because it was the title deeds that the young marquis back in France was frantic to get hold of to enable him to expand his Marseilles Port development.

"I have a proposition to put to you, my old friend," said Abraham to Garrett.

The old gypsy felt his skin crawl, but of course, he knew he needed the Jew's help if he was ever going to fulfil the promise that he had made to Agnes and Manfri to return the heart of the Black Madonna.

"What is it that you think we should do?" questioned Garrett.

"We must blow the door off the strongroom at St. Michael's and steal the treasures, but although I can obtain the black powder, I do not have the understanding of how this explosive works. I would kill myself, I know," blurted Abraham, wringing his hands together with expectation.

"What would you have me do? A man with only one hand and no better understanding of the black powder than you have admitted to yourself," retorted Garrett sharply.

"You are indeed useless, Garrett, my friend," with more hand-wringing, Abraham went on. "But Manfri, your son Manfri. I know for fact that he is one of the best explosive men that Mr. Brunell has in his charge."

"I could not ask Manfri to help us. Why should he help us?" said Garrett with a quiver in his tone.

"I can tell you something of your good son that I know you are not aware of. He drinks gin at the same ale house that I often frequent in order to sometimes buy stolen goods that thieves are desperate to rid themselves of. Not always but sometimes, your Manfri, my dear friend, sometimes drinks far too much, and that is usually on a Saturday night when he knows that he does not have to be at work on the Sunday morning. A few weeks passed now, I helped him stagger home, and as we sang together on that occasion, he began to cry like a baby. Tears ran like a river down his cheek."

"You lying bastard. You are full of black shite. I don't want to hear another word from your miserable mouth, you bloody thief," blasted Garrett. "My son wouldn't cry in front of the likes of you. In fact, my son does not cry at all."

"Garrett, Garrett, my dearest friend," pleaded Abraham, wringing his hands obsequiously. "Manfri is in fear of death. He told me he has nightmares of being blown up by the black powder while working on the rail line, and lately, superstition has been sending bad fortune messages his way. Many of the signs have made him believe he will die in an accident caused by the black powder. He asked his foreman to take him off the powder jobs, but he is too good. His boss man said no. He spoke of turning to crime to feed his family. He is desperate, I tell you, my dear friend."

Garrett could handle the groveling no longer. "I am not your dear friend, and in fact, I would never want you for a friend at all, so stop calling me friend," he shouted at Abraham, "but if what you say is true, you might be right about getting back the precious heart. Leave it to me. I will talk to Manfri, and let's see if we can make a plan."

CHAPTER TWENTY SEVEN

Abraham was confident that Manfri would help because everything he told Garrett about his son was true, and when Garrett told his son about how they could both bring the Black Madonna back to life, Manfri agreed to help his father.

Manfri saw that blowing the door off the strongroom at St. Michael's could not only turn the fortunes of his gypsy community by restoring the heart of the Madonna, but he knew that the church held money in that strongroom that belonged to many of the rich catholic parishioners who did not trust the banks because they were mostly run by protestants. He was also aware that many of the rich folk kept prized possessions and jewelry with the church because the strongroom at St. Michael's was regarded as the best in the area. Manfri reckoned that some of that money could tide him and his family over until he found other employment.

Manfri and Garrett met with Abraham the next day to work out a plan. Garrett immediately went on the offensive when Abraham insisted that his henchman Asael would help them carry away the booty. He insisted that he was too slow to be of any use, whereas Asael was young and powerful.

"I have all the equipment you will need, and I have already enough black powder to blow up the whole of that ugly old church. You will need Asael, and if you think about it, you will agree," insisted Abraham.

Manfri laughed quietly to himself at Abraham referring to the old church as ugly. "It truly is an ugly old monster of a church, but I think removing the strongroom door will be enough for me," he said, "and Father, Abraham is right. We will need a strong man to help us with the plan."

Garrett let it be known to all that he was not happy but knew he had to go along. "So how will it work?" he asked Abraham.

Manfri interrupted before anyone could speak. "I went to St. Michael's today with two other men for morning Mass. After the service, my two friends kept Father McCordy busy while I crept into the rear of the church to find the strongroom. When I saw it, I could understand why it has such a reputation. I will do my best, but it will take a very powerful explosive to blow apart the two massive steel hinges on the strongroom door. I do think it can be done, but it will be dangerous. I worry about Father McCordy getting hurt if he hears us."

Abraham interrupted. "I have already thought of how to deal with him. I keep a supply of chloroform. You will take some with you, and if the priest interferes, you can knock him out with that. No harm will be done."

At eleven o'clock that evening, the three men, Garrett, Manfri, and Asael, were already in the church, and with the aid of one oil lamp, they were gathered at the strongroom door. Manfri told Asael that the stonework next to each of the hinges had to be chiseled away sufficiently to allow the black powder to be packed in tightly but very gently. He then held up two steel plates that he intended to secure to the wall between the stonework and the strongroom frame, covering the black powder. This would hopefully cause enough back pressure to allow the explosive to shatter the hinges. Manfri had predrilled several screw holes in the steel plates to allow for options when getting the best fix to the wall. His idea was pure experimentation, as he had never been called on to perform such a difficult task for the railway.

Asael began to chisel away at the stone, and only a short time had passed when the men heard a voice calling out, "Who is there? What's happening in there?"

As they expected, Father McCordy had heard the din and was coming toward the sound. Manfri had been given the task of putting Father McCordy to sleep with the chloroform, and he did so with medical precision. He bound and gagged the priest, hence eliminating any further interference from him.

The chisel work took less time than expected. Where the stone had already been cut to allow for the installation of the strongroom, it was found to be quite flakey in places, so Asael completed the task of chiseling the sizable holes in less than thirty minutes.

It was now up to Manfri to pack the black powder gently but tightly into the holes, and this he did with further surgical precision. "This is the dangerous part," said Manfri. "I have to secure the steel plates, and if the black powder is going to explode due to friction caused by the movement of the screws, then I am surely dead, so you two should stand around that corner so you are not killed with me. Please, Father," whispered Manfri into his father's ear. "Take care of my children and their mother for me if anything should happen, and Father, I do not trust Asael, so I have two men waiting outside to help us as soon as they hear the powder explode."

Abraham and Asael had already decided when planning the robbery that neither Manfri or Garrett would survive the exploit. Asael had agreed to kill the pair as soon as the strongroom door had been removed, and Abraham had arranged for two of his men to help Asael carry off the booty.

The two men that Manfri had appointed to help had arrived well before Abraham's duo of thieves. Manfri's men were told by him to expect treachery and quickly knocked both men into unconsciousness with the chloroform and securely bound them as if preparing two pigs for the spit. The pig-binding was deliberate as they knew that it would rub copious amounts of salt onto their black Jewish hearts.

During the planning, it had been discussed as to how the men would identify just where the precious heart would be kept in the strongroom, and Abraham, of course, knew exactly what the trio would be dealing with once they entered the room.

Abraham had announced with considerable arrogance, "There is a huge set of timber drawers along one wall of the strongroom, and each drawer bears the family name of the people who have placed things for safekeeping in those drawers. One of the wealthy catholic families often come into my pawn shop intentionally to buy gold jewelry. They melt these poorly crafted items down and create superb pieces in their workshop in Manchester. If they have too much gold, they simply leave it for safekeeping with Father McCordy at St. Michael's. They own Brenton's jewelry shop in Bridge Street, Manchester.

"Mr. Brenton never stops bragging about his wealth, and he told me just how things worked in the strongroom on the day he bragged to me that his family had their names on three of the timber drawers, so that tells us that the gem we seek will be in the drawer that has the name Denny inscribed on to it, but do remember, my dear friends, that it is the French land deeds that will earn us the reward that Solomon Leyman will pay on behalf of the French marquis of Marseille. Now that reward money will be mine alone for helping you. I will require nothing more. What else you find in that room will be yours."

But of course, Abraham did not intend to let Garrett or Manfri share even one ounce of the booty retrieved that night. Asael and the two men that he sent to help him were instructed to bring everything found back to the pawn shop where it would be divided among the thieves. Abraham knew that Asael and the others would do as he ordered them to because they would need him to turn any precious items into cash through his shop and the network of dubious characters he dealt with in London. He had them hogtied, and he knew it.

The charges were set, and the fuses lit. Manfri rushed to join his two fellow thieves where he had told them to wait. The noise of the two blasts was almost simultaneous, and the three men felt their ears pounded in with the pressure of the explosion. Manfri tried to give direction, but the temporary deafness made that impossible. When all three moved to see whether the strongroom door had been breached, they smiled at one another. The huge door was lying flat on the stone floor.

As the pall of black smoke was clearing, Asael saw two men approaching the strongroom and incorrectly assumed that they were the men that Abraham had told him would be there to help him eliminate Garrett and Manfri. Reckoning that he had the superior manpower on his side, he drew a bone-handled dagger from his long boot, and with one thrust to the abdomen, he brought Garrett to his knees, screaming in pain. As he raised the blade to strike again, Manfri grabbed his arm, and the two men fell to the floor in a deadly struggle. One of the two men that Manfri had in waiting was quickly upon Asael, and without hesitation, he stabbed him in the neck, immediately severing his jugular vein. Asael made no sound at all as his life bled away.

Manfri had not been hurt and was quickly to his feet. It was only then that he realized the scream he heard seconds earlier came from his father, who by now was lying silently on the floor. Manfri scrambled to him and cradled his head in his arms. Not enough had been said between father and son. All animosity faded to pale as the two men realized that their love for one another was all that was left. Kings or commoners: nothing mattered.

"I will not die here, Manfri. I need to know that the Madonna has a heart that beats again. Please tell me that you have it." Garrett knew that this was one fight he was not going to win, but he desperately needed to salvage something from the wreckage that he had created when he so roughly removed the beautiful ruby from the Madonna.

Manfri asked one of the men to comfort his father, and he immediately entered the strongroom in search of the drawer marked Denny. Everything was as Abraham had described, and he found the prize quickly. He pulled open the drawer. He could see the land deeds in French, and under them was a small wrapped box. He tore the wrapping apart, and as he lifted the lid of the small box it had covered, he revealed the stone that had caused so much sorrow. He rushed back to his father and held the stone for him to see. The transformation on Garrett's face was miraculous. He smiled and looked as calm as a man about to enter heaven, and then he was gone.

Manfri was numb. It was left to his friends to round up as much treasure as they could hold in the two sacks that they had brought along for that purpose. Within a few short minutes, the men had mounted the two horses that they had arrived on, only now Manfri was astride one of the beasts, holding his father in front of him while the other two gypsies doubled up on the second mount.

A very special burial was provided for Garrett. His sister, Agnes, had made sure that it was a celebration fit for a king, and at the center of all that was happening was the Black Madonna held high by Manfri who had been officially recognized as the king now that Garrett had been laid to rest. The heart of the Madonna had been reinstated, and Garrett's Agnes sat quietly as she found herself forgiving him and thanking him also for what she considered to be the return of a bright future for his gypsy community.

All the drama could have ended there, but Abraham Rothschild was not about to let that happen. He knew that the gypsies had to have the land deeds, and he was about to put a diabolical plan into action

CHAPTER TWENTY EIGHT

Benny and Malcolm had made good their safe escape from Dublin and deliberately avoided Liverpool, Manchester, and Salford. They knew that if anyone was sent by Mad Paddy to have Benny pay for his sin of murder, those places would be the obvious destinations to be searched, so they passed through those busy ports quickly and headed straight to London.

London was not at all what the two novices to big city life had imagined. The noise was deafening, and the wafting smells of sewage, rotting flesh, putrid smoke, and close contact with human body odors was causing both men to look and behave as though they were part of a mime act in a low budget circus. Benny was using his right hand to block his nose while trying to damp down the noises by cupping his left hand over one ear and then the other. Malcolm was faring no better, and because of these antics, the pair caught the notice of one of the countless street urchins that hovered around the many points of arrival to London with only one purpose in mind, and that was survival which required a myriad of skills including, begging, pickpocketing, stealing, and sadly even prostitution.

"New here, you are? Are ya not? Maggie's my name. Who are you?" The interrogation spouted out from between the dirty lips housed by the even dirtier face of Maggie Dorn. Maggie would announce to all prepared to listen that she was thirteen years old when in truth she had just turned eleven, facts that she could not truly attest to because she really had no idea of her true age, never mind an actual birth date. Maggie had escaped from a workhouse six months earlier. Her job in the workhouse, along with fifty other starving children, was to smash and pound the bones of butchered animals into grain-sized pieces that would be bagged and sold on as farm fertilizer.

The workhouse owner was a miserable and cruel misshapen little man who called himself Lord Ennis. He wore his tar black hair longer on the left-hand side so that he could brush it across the dome of his bald skull where no hair grew at all. He held the bald head hair in place by slicking it down with his own concoction of sugar and wax mixed with water. He wore expensive suits that had been tailored well to accommodate his odd dimensions. He was never without a top hat because he reckoned it made him look taller than was real. He had no royal entitlement, and his true name was Alfredo Pennis. The Pennis surname certainly carried some weight in the Vatican

States where it had originated several hundred years earlier, but such a name in the London of the 1840s was never going to be taken seriously. Coupled with Alfredo, the jokes came thick and fast. Lord Ennis was created as soon as Alfredo was old enough to leave the home of his impoverished family in Birmingham.

He stole, embezzled, and cheated his way to accumulate enough money to buy a derelict old factory, and without one improvement to the premises, he rolled in his first team of children straight off the streets. They were offered the world but received nothing but beatings, bad food, and straw to sleep on. Ennis never missed an opportunity to make money. It happened on occasions that one of his wretched team would be found dead, either in the straw at the 5:00 a.m. wake-up whistle or at the allocated workstation when the toil ceased around 7:00 p.m. Ennis had come to an arrangement whereby, for a hefty profit, he would direct that the body be taken to a nearby coffin maker who would in turn deliver the poor dead child to the science department of the university for anatomical studies. In truth, his weaker workers were worth more to him dead than alive.

Lord Ennis was despised by all those who knew him, but he had one redeeming trait in his behavior that he would never admit to a single living soul for fear of exposing the ruthlessly tough reputation he had fought so hard to create as a mere sham. Alfredo Pennis would regularly send money home to his mother in Birmingham to help her stave off the misery of the workhouse that threatened herself and his two younger sisters.

Ennis would lock up his team in the workhouse at night. Maggie Dorn had used an iron bar that had been provided by Ennis to pulverize the bones to smash enough bricks from the factory wall, enabling her to squeeze through to freedom. Maggie was a resourceful child as evidenced by the way she was managing to live on the streets without incurring the wrath of the police and evading the grasp of the child protection people who would have simply forced her into a similar workhouse situation from which she had escaped.

"Do you two need somewhere to stay?" asked Maggie.

"Bugger off, you filthy little piece of shite," yelled Benny.

"Please, girl. What is your name?" asked Malcolm, who was in possession of all the money the pair had between them. He was aware that the total value of the coins that jingled in his pocket was one pound, five shillings, and sixpence and that was that. "Yes, girl. We do need somewhere to stay," said Malcolm.

"My name is Maggie Dorn, your honor, and I can 'elp."

On leaving Dublin, Benny had forced Malcolm to give him one pound that he promptly gambled away, along with the money he had stolen from his family, to the sailors on the boat in which they had escaped from Mad Paddy believing that Benny was sure to be murdered if he chose to stay at the docks where he worked. That extra pound would have served them well given that they knew nobody in London and had absolutely no idea how they were to survive until they could start to earn money.

"Nice to meet you, Maggie. My name is Malcolm, and this here is Benny. We are new in town, but then you already know that. I am not your honor, just a simple dockworker looking for somewhere to work and somewhere to sleep and keep dry."

Malcolm was looking solemnly into Maggie's eyes. Despite the dirty face, he could not help but find himself staring. He realized his bad manner but could not look away. Maggie was beautiful. A mere child but beautiful nonetheless. Her eyes were as blue as the clear summer sky, and despite the dirt in her hair, Malcolm could see clusters of blond strands, its true color. He wanted to call her Helen. Malcolm had left his own comfortable home almost two years past because he could no longer live with his tyrannical father after his mother had died. He had only one regret. His sister had been placed in the care of his kind aunt Bessy, but she could not take them both. Malcolm missed his baby sister, Helen, and could not believe the likeness as he looked at Maggie Dorn. *She could be her twin*, he mused.

"Well, Mr. Malcolm, I can tell you that I can find you lodgins. I have a dear friend that runs one of the best lodgin' houses in all of London. Real mattresses and no bedbugs, and you'll need nearly no money at all." Maggie rattled off her lines and sounded far too well-rehearsed.

"And just how much money is nearly no money at all, my pretty Maggie?" quizzed Malcolm. Pretty Maggie, as Malcolm continued to call her, negotiated a price of five pennies per head for one night in one room.

Benny had to tag along with Malcolm and Pretty Maggie because he had no money of his own, and he knew that, because he had gambled away a whole pound of Malcolm's savings during the crossing between Dublin Docks and London, there would be no more pennies coming his way.

Pretty Maggie talked nonstop as she led the two men from fashionable streets into narrow darkened laneways that led into even narrower spaces, and just as Benny was about to halt the procession, Pretty Maggie announced with a smattering of pride, "'Ere we are, gents. Whatta ya reckon at that?"

The look on Benny's face was priceless. Malcolm who had spent some time living on the streets of Glasgow prior to crossing to Dublin was less shocked, and in fact, he smiled at Pretty Maggie.

A flea-riddled almost-hairless brown dog was baring its teeth in the doorway of the building that looked as though it had been hit with cannonballs, and an ancient man was urinating against the red brick wall of the dilapidated structure.

"The bloody place is falling down. Jesus, the front door is lying flat on the ground. There's no glass in the windows, and lots of the roof tiles are there in the street. Give us our money back, you dirty little shite, or I'll blacken both yer eyes," and as Benny ranted, he moved threateningly toward Pretty Maggie, but Malcolm moved between the two of them.

He said quietly to Benny, "You so much as touch my Helen, and I will kill you, Benny Connelly."

Benny had never seen this side of the man that he was just using. The man who had saved his life. The man who loved him. There was something in his manner that made Benny stop immediately. *Who is Malcolm McDonald?* he thought and then asked, "Who in the name of Jesus is Helen?"

"Just a slip, Benny. We are here now, so Pretty Maggie, lead on. Show us to our room," said Malcolm, who by this stage of the proceedings could only see humor in the whole scenario.

Pretty Maggie pushed her way past the nasty-looking dog, and it paid her no heed and treated the newcomers with the same indifference. The men were led down a long hallway, and just as they felt they were about to be escorted out the back door, Pretty Maggie stopped and opened a door on her left. "'Ere we are, gents. I'll be leaving ya now. I've work to do."

Benny entered the room and immediately returned to the hallway. "You little witch. You said we would have a single room. There's two men sleeping on the floor in that room. What's going on, and where is the dear old friend that runs this shite hole?"

"I told you gents you'd 'ave a single room and a single room it is. I did not say you'd 'ave it to yerselves, and as for my dear old friend, you almost met 'im on the way in. He was havin' a piss on the wall outside. He always does that." Maggie quickly explained the deal, and then she was gone.

"We need to work, Benny," said Malcolm

Benny and Malcolm had to stay in the room because night was falling, and along with the two gents that were asleep on the floor when they arrived, by the time they awoke in the morning, the room had accommodated a further four disheveled occupants.

Benny was the first to stir, and after doing a head count, he renewed his resolve to physically damage Pretty Maggie by any means possible, and of course, it would have to be done without Malcolm knowing.

He woke Malcolm, and both men determined to seek out Maggie Dorn's dear old friend who ran the flea pit, as Benny had named it, realizing that he could possibly be of some help to them by way of finding work. Benny opened several doors along the hallway, but the rooms beyond were full of guests in various stages of wake. Malcolm had gone straight to the entrance to inspect just what the street might have to offer, and there he was. The ancient old man, Maggie's dear friend, was urinating over another section of the front wall of his grand establishment. Malcolm remembered with a smile how Pretty Maggie had said about the old man pissing on the wall. "He always does that," and so it would seem.

Malcolm waited until the old man had completed his relief, and as he turned to reenter the building, he was startled at the sight of Malcolm. "Who the 'ek are you, young man?" he asked, trying to force some strength into his voice but only managed a heavy breathed whisper.

Malcolm immediately thought that this man had to be the oldest human that he had ever seen. He mentally toyed at guessing an age, but most people were dead by fifty years, so beyond that, he had no comparison to make. A figure of one hundred sprang to front of mind, but of course, that meant nothing.

"My name is Malcolm, sir. Me and my good friend, Benny, stayed in one of your lovely rooms last night. I wondered if

I might ask you for some help to find work. We are new to London and have no idea on what to do."

"Lovely room indeed, says you. Well, you forget that shite talk, and you and me will be just fine. Did my Maggie fix you up with the room and 'ow much did she get you ta pay? No, don't tell me. Best I just let her be. I know she keeps some for herself on top of what she gets from me, but she's a real charmer, that one, and always makes sure that I have money enough coming in to keep the bailiff away. She'll end up owning this pile of shite one day. She had the cheek to tell me so. She has got a good head on her, that wee lass. Now my name, you ask," said the ancient man. "My friends call me Captain, and until you upset me, young Malcolm, that is what you call me. I'm too old to tell lies. I think we are all born with a quota of lies that we have to tell, and thank Christ, I have filled that number probably before you were born. I was a ship's captain for twice as many years as you have walked the earth, I'm guessing. I have survived six shipwrecks, and I have killed twelve men. All in the legal ship way, and that is why I never had a mutiny against me. I have three children that I know of, and I have taken care of their mothers without them knowing who the money was coming from. I always look after my ladies. I am a godless man, and because of that, I will die a happy man. I have a kettle on the boil and some gruel for a penny a plate if you want to fill your belly, young Malcolm, you are welcome to join me."

Malcolm could not believe what he had just heard. No one had ever impressed him more with sheer power of story and show of will. He introduced the Captain to Benny and was taken aback further at the remark passed by the Captain as he shook Benny's hand. "This one won't be calling me Captain for too long, young Malcolm."

As the three men sat together, drinking tea and supping gruel, more bodies presented themselves, and seeming to know the routine, simply dropped a penny each on to the table in front of the Captain and helped themselves to tea and gruel. The room they all sat in had tables and chairs aplenty.

The low tone of the conversation in the room was suddenly brought to life with the arrival of Maggie Dorn.

"So 'ow did we all sleep then, gents? You there, Mr. Snow, 'ows your gout? And you gents in the corner. Did ya do any good with the man at the stables who needed some strong workers?"

"Gout's fine, Miss Maggie," exclaimed Mr. Snow, with a broad smile pushing its way through his huge moustache. The three men in the corner followed Mr. Snow with their cheerful response. "The lead hand at the stables gave two of us a job, and then he sent young Johnny to a farm nearby, reckoning because he is small he might be needed as a strapper. As it 'appens, Miss Maggie, Johnny was brought up with horses in Ireland, and he landed himself a plum job. Now we can't pay the sixpence each that we owe you for helpin' us, but as soon as we are earnin', we promise to settle the debt."

The Captain leaned toward Malcolm and said, "Looks like our little lady has just bought another small piece of this pile of shite. You want to work, you say? Well, little Maggie might be able to help you like she has a lot of gents who land here. There will be a fee as you 'av' just 'erd."

After eating their fill, Malcolm told Benny that he would find out from Pretty Maggie if she could help them in any way to find work. Benny said he would mix with the other gents for the same purpose, but his twisted mind had already conjured up a completely different plan. Benny found out, after quizzing several of the men, that Maggie had a small room of her own in the building, and it was always kept locked.

He reckoned that after he saw how she operated in the breakfast room, there had to be a pile of cash behind that locked door. He knew that Malcolm would have nothing to do with his evil plan, so he decided to wait until Malcolm was off seeking work. He would invent a story that would have him heading elsewhere. Of course, he intended to use this opportunity to break into Maggie's room and steal whatever he could. He just had to bide his time.

Several days passed, but no work had become available. Malcolm was becoming anxious as the funds were slowly decreasing, but then a ray of hope. As Malcolm and Benny ate breakfast with the Captain, Maggie, who always ventured out early, came breezing into the room and went straight to Malcolm's side.

"You said you was a baker back when you was young, did you not?" she asked.

A broad smile broke out across Malcolm's face. His first point of amusement was Maggie's reference "back when you was young." It had only been five days since his first meeting with Maggie Dorn, but he appreciated her sense of humor and bright outlook.

"Less of the old, Pretty Maggie, and I told you that my father was a baker, but you are right in thinking that I know much about it. He had me as a slave in his shop in Glasgow, and if truth be told, I did most of the baking while he just talked to customers about how hard he worked and what a useless piece of shite I was. If he had been a better man, I would not be in the mess I find myself in today. Have you found something for me, Maggie? Please say you have."

"Reckon I have, but it will cost you six pennies if you get the job, remember?" Maggie said excitedly.

"If I get the job, I swear that there will be a shilling in it for you, Pretty Maggie. Please, please tell me more." Malcolm could barely contain his excitement.

Chapter Twenty Nine

The Captain, who looked on as he listened, could not help but notice that since the arrival of Mr. Malcolm, young Maggie had been making a great effort to improve her appearance. Her pretty face was spotless at the start of each day. She was taking much care in brushing her long blond tresses, and the fact that her hair was clean daily was something new. He also noticed that Maggie had acquired better clothing, not grand but certainly better.

Maggie Dorn could instantly throw color into a story with all the skill that John Constable would have had to muster over many months of pallet scraping to turn out his masterpieces such as *The Hay Wain* and *Dedham Lock and Mill*. He was able to draw inspiration from the likes of Gainsborough, Reubens, and many more, whereas Maggie's pallet of inspiration sprang solely from her unique ability to absorb everything that was happening around her, and then with well-measured conviction, she could deliver an oral masterpiece capable of holding her audiences spellbound. Her words could indeed paint many thousands of pictures.

Maggie replied, "I have had to put some great effort in on your behalf, Mr. Malcolm, and ask so many questions that a lesser person than me would 'av' to write it all down just to remember the half of it. I 'av' worked it out that writing can waste valuable time, and I know for fact that writing kills off memory in people and yer mind can shrink up. If ya write it all down, the memory has naught to do, and that's why I 'aven't taught myself the letters and numbers, and that is why I 'av' such a big mind.

"So I remembered that you 'ad told me you was a baker, and around about question number twenty, thirty, twelve, I said to an old hag sittin', feedin' sea birds down by the old Tunney Bridge, not the new beauty, no the old bridge that was smashed when that wobbly legged loony sea captain, not my Captain, got 'imself overly drunk and smashed his ferry side way on straight into it. A right mess, he made and reckoned it weren't his fault because he doesn't remember ever 'avin' done it."

"The job, Pretty Maggie. What of the job?" Malcolm felt he had to steer the tale to a conclusion. The effect was that Maggie now felt she had more pictures to paint.

"Bide yer wish, Mr. Malcolm. All in my good time. The old lady was feedin' the sea birds with bread, black-headed terns, they was. Who wastes good bread on birds? Questions 'ad to be asked, and so I set myself to the task.

"'Ow is it that you is able to feed perfectly good bread to the terns, my fine lady? She tells me that a baker up on Cider Street, and a good baker she says he is, saves some stale pieces of his loaves for her so she can feed the birds.

"Baker was all I had to hear and straight up Cider Street went I to get you a job, Mr. Malcolm. Quite a big walk I 'ad to take, and the more I walked, the posher the shops got. Some shops 'ad dresses in the windows the likes of 'em I 'ad never seen in all of my life. There was a green one, I reckon would 'av' fitted me self, and it was the prettiest in all of the shop. It had white lace at the collar, so fine it looked to float like clouds around the neck, and the middle was drawn in by somethin' that looked like a shawl tied under the belly and drapin' down one side from the hip to the knee. It was an eye-waterin' sight to behold, so I went in and asked the snotty-nosed old bag that run the shop 'ow much it was. She did not even tell me 'ow much, she just shouted out loud like, 'Get out of here, you filthy little heathen.' I was 'avin' none o' that, so I went to touch that beautiful dress, and she smacks my 'and. So I smacks her back. She starts screaming like she's about to pop out three bairns, I know three wee-ens at the one time does 'appen, and I reckon she was about to 'av' 'em. I ran out of her shiteful shop and kept looking for our baker. Posh shop after posh shop. Beautiful they was."

"Maggie, Maggie, Maggie. The job." Malcolm tried once again to obtain the information he so desperately needed.

It did not escape Maggie's notice that he omitted, this time, to call her Pretty Maggie, and she took that as her cue to put him out of his misery.

"'Old yer 'orses, Mr. Malcolm. We are nearly there. One other shop I 'ad to go into sold sweets and those new chocolate pieces that folk talk about. Before I was told to scram, I showed the owner my purse. Now it don't look much, but it's plain to see that it is fat and heavy. I bought one piece of chocolate, and the man went to wrap it with a piece of paper. No bother, I says. I paid for it. He put it in my hand, and I started eating it right there in the shop. Now I am here to tell you all that if any of you gents make it to heaven, and not much chance of that I bet, it's chocolate that the Holy Ghost will be serving to you at the table. Made in heaven, I reckon it is."

Noticing that Malcolm was about to explode, Maggie blurted out, "And then I spies it. The baker I had just put so much hard work inta finding. But not just any baker shop, Mr. Malcolm. This place was like looking into a magic show. Stuff I'd never seen before and big prices, I bet. Loads of fine ladies and gents were in there, pickin' through the wares and handing them to the man at the counter who was so busy, he was fair run off his feet.

"I could see straight away that this man needed help, so I waited till he had some time and told 'im all about you, Mr. Malcolm. I was going to mention that you had baked for Queen Vic 'erself, but I thought better of it. He was a pleasant fella and told me he was desperate cos his assistant had just walked out for no reason, but no one has no reason. He said you'd have to be quick and prove that you could do the job, and then he got busy again."

Malcolm's frustration was almost at boiling point. Maggie was told that he had to be quick and had just wasted half an hour on storytelling. He could have been there.

"Can you take me there? Please, Pretty Maggie, and did you get his name?" At the risk of Maggie taking another eon to divulge the name and directions, Malcolm simply dragged her by the hand and out into the street. "Right, off we go, and tell me all as we move. Did you get his name?"

"You 'av' to remember, Mr. Malcolm, that I 'ad little chance to talk to the baker, but I do know that his name was a royal one, and I reckon he called himself Mr. Duke. Yep, that was it. Mr. Duke or was it Baron?"

With Malcolm almost running, poor Maggie, being dragged by the hand, found herself battling for breath. "Slow it, Mr. Malcolm, or you'll 'av' us both dead," she pleaded.

Malcolm apologized and allowed Maggie to compose herself before he slowly began to up the rate of transit once again.

"Here it is, Mr. Malcolm. Now ain't that 'ansome? And there is Mr. er Duke." Maggie spoke in a tone of obvious relief. "Shall I wait out here, or do you need me inside to 'elp? I could do the talkin' if you want me too."

"Pretty Maggie, you must rest out here but wait for me. I have to talk to the baker on my own. He will ask me many questions, and I have to keep a clear head. I need this job because Benny and I are down to our last few shillings. Wish me luck, and a small prayer might help because I reckon a fine young lady such as you would get a kindly hearing from the Lord," said Malcolm, and it did not escape his notice that Pretty Maggie's face was ripened to red in an instant.

There were several people in the baker shop, but the shelves had been almost stripped, so Malcolm was able to immediately introduce himself and stretched out his right hand. The baker, without hesitation, shook Malcolm's hand, and the relieved look on his face was obvious.

"My name is Roger Earls, and if you are half as good at your trade as the young lady reported to me, then you will certainly find yourself employed, and again if you are as good young Maggie says you are, I will pay you handsomely."

Malcolm was amused without showing at how Maggie had confused the baker's name. "Something royal, Duke, Baron, but no, it was Earl in the plural. Earls. Roger Earls."

When Roger Earls left Ireland, Transbridge, and John Rostan, his life had become an absolute shambles. He and John had both given up substantial careers to try and find a good life, a life where they could live together and hopefully be left alone. The dominantly catholic community of Transbridge was never going to let that happen. Roger found himself sacked from his job, utterly depressed, and quite convinced that he was responsible for the quiet sadness of the only person in the world that he loved and would ever love, John Rostan.

When Roger fled Transbridge, he returned to London. He had become very successful with his heavenly creations that fore-fronted the helm of his father's catering business, which was now the talk of London's elite. His father, who alienated him because of his sinful lifestyle and caused the move to Transbridge, had died while Roger was away.

When Roger returned home, his mother and two sisters could not have made him feel more welcome. His mother apologized for not doing more when it was becoming obvious that Roger's father was going too far with regard to removal of his son from the family business. Roger was just glad to be back among friendly faces, and when his mother asked him to rejoin the family business, he jumped at the opportunity but with one proviso. Rather than be thrown in at the deep end of the elite catering, Roger proposed that he open a shop of his own to allow distance between what his father had established and just test the waters with regard to how London society might accept him back.

His two sisters had taken over the running of the business after the death of their father, and from what Roger could glean, they were doing a fine job. The prime motive behind Roger's proviso was to allow his sisters to keep their station as business managers because it was well-deserved, and he knew a separate shop would only strengthen the business.

CHAPTER THIRTY

Malcolm very quickly proved himself to be every bit as good as his Pretty Maggie had promoted. Roger was very quick to realize that his newly acquired assistant had special talents when it came to new ideas and cake presentation. The skill of decorating the creations was new to him, but once he was shown the basics, Malcolm began to create products that even astounded Roger. As promised, Roger saw to it that Malcolm was being paid handsomely for his effort.

Back at the Captain's guesthouse, things there had also begun to improve. The front door had been reattached, the roof tiles that had taken up residence on the street below had been returned to the roof from which they had fallen, fresh wallpaper had been hung in the cavernous hallway and some of the rooms. The smell of paint now overwhelmed all the putrid stenches that had, up to now, caused most guests to complain bitterly.

All in all, the Captain was very proud of his efforts and had even stopped urinating on the front wall.

The scabies-ridden nasty-looking dog that had greeted Malcolm and Benny on their arrival had also been reborn. Boson, as the Captain had named him, had been put on a better diet all under the guidance of Maggie Dorn. She furiously attacked Boson's flea problem, and he in turn showed Maggie such affection. Something she had never known. His fur had mostly grown back, and although he was never vicious, he now wagged his tail as guests arrived and was frequently stroked and patted by the same men that only three months previously would have rushed past him to enter the dwelling.

At breakfast one morning, the Captain announced that a parcel had arrived for Maggie Dorn. Maggie, as was the norm for her, had risen early to be about her business but was due to arrive back for her breakfast, so the Captain had placed the parcel on the chair that she always sat on next to him.

"'Ow are we all, gents?" Maggie asked. The room replied to her now awaited catch cry, and once she had made everyone feel that they did matter, she proceeded to her chair. "What's this then?" she asked as she spied the parcel.

"Arrived for you this very morning, Maggie. Penny mail did not quite cover it, so I paid the extra tuppence," said the Captain who could barely contain his excitement. "Go on, open it, Maggie. Let's see what ya got."

Maggie was already ripping at the brown paper before the Captain's request had finished. Having removed the wrapping, Maggie placed the item on the table in front of her. It was a large pink box, and she just stood staring at it. The box alone would have been enough for Maggie. To her, it was beautiful. After what seemed an age, the assembly had all drawn closer when Maggie lifted the lid ever so carefully. She then removed some soft paper that had obviously been placed over the precious item to safeguard it.

"Shite, shite, shite, who did this? It is beautiful." Maggie instantly recognized the stunning green dress with the lace collar and white waist shawl that she had fallen in love with on that day weeks ago when she was searching out employment for Malcolm.

Maggie quickly replaced the lid of the box, picked it up, and ran into the hallway to her room. "What will it look like? What will I look like?" she wondered.

No one left the dining room, as it was now being referred to as, because they all hoped to see Maggie on her return. After well over twenty minutes, Pretty Maggie Dorn returned, and a uniform gasp erupted.

The transformation was magical. Maggie was resplendent in the green gown, and using several combs, she had arranged her flaxen locks in a style that would be the envy of all of high society's grand ladies.

The Captain walked toward her and took her by the hand. "This dance is mine, my darling," and that being said, the ancient sea captain and Maggie Dorn waltzed around that dining room as though they were the only two people on earth.

Once the waltz was over, the Captain turned to his guests as though they were all in attendance at a grand society ball and announced, "It is with pride that I would like to introduce to you my granddaughter, Maggie Dorn-May, on her fourteenth birthday."

Something the Captain had said on their first meeting jumped straight into Malcolm's recollections of that day. The Captain had said, "I always look after my ladies." There he was announcing to all that Maggie Dorn was his granddaughter. He had tracked her down after hearing that her mother (whom he knew to be his daughter) had died and left only one child. His granddaughter. He tasked several of his ex-crew members to help him search for Maggie.

It was not easy, but when she was discovered in a terrible state, having just escaped the clutches Lord Ennis (Alfredo Pennis) by pounding a hole in the brick wall of Lord Ennis's dismal workhouse, she was taken to the Captain who offered her a room of her own and keep if she would help bring paying lodgers to his premises. Maggie jumped at the chance. All she needed to hear was "room of your own." Her only request was that the room had a key so that she could feel secure. Something she had never really known.

The Captain had absolutely no experience with children but was prepared to try. He did not tell Maggie that she was his granddaughter because he needed to take it slowly. If Maggie had turned out to be a "badin," he did not want to become too close in case he had to turn her away.

His apprehension drained away very quickly as he got to know the delightful creature that was his kin. He could feel a renewed reason to live, and for the first time in years, he could also see a reason to love. He had told Maggie one week earlier that he was her grandfather, but she just laughed. It was not until the Captain had explained how much he knew of her mother and after answering many, many questions that Maggie tentatively held his hand and then they embraced, both in tears. The Captain made Maggie promise not to tell a soul until he thought the time was right.

Malcolm put it all together. Maggie was responsible for the new spring in the Captain's step. Of course, there now was a reason for the door, the wallpaper, the tiles, and all the paint. Malcolm did not really understand why, but he felt so happy.

The day after the big announcement, the Captain asked Malcolm to come and see him after he finished work at the bakery. Malcolm did as asked, and the Captain ushered him into a room he had never been in before. This was the Captain's office, and Malcolm could not believe the vision. The large room was decked out exactly as you would see a captain's cabin presented on a posh ship. It was spotless and charming. It had become obvious to Malcolm that the Captain was indeed a grand man.

"What are your intentions toward my granddaughter?" asked the Captain mincing no words.

Malcolm was dumbstruck and could only hold up his right hand. "Maggie, me, no, sir."

"You bloody fool, young Malcolm, you must know she thinks she is in love with you?"

Malcolm burst out laughing, and that was not the response the Captain was looking for. He drew a whip from the draw in his desk and was about to let fly when Malcolm screamed, "Captain, I love her as a sister, but I don't see women in that way. I do not just share a room with Benny."

"You mean you're bloody bent then?" blurted the Captain who, after many years at sea, had learned to turn a blind eye to so much he deemed wrong with his world.

The Captain expressed a relieved laugh but still wanted to know what Malcolm was going to do about Maggie's infatuation for him. After some discussion, both men agreed that Malcolm should let Maggie know that he was far too old for her, and in fact, there was someone else.

Sadly for all concerned, that someone else was Benny. Malcolm was finding it harder and harder to cope with Benny's selfish and cruel behavior. Since Malcolm had begun working for Roger Earls and bringing home some decent money, it was obvious to all that Benny had no intention to gain employment for himself. He expected Malcolm to pay him an allowance. "Until I find work," he would say.

"Benny is no good"

Chapter thirty One

Benny had in fact started hanging around with a local gang of like-minded layabouts, but unlike the Fixers, headed up by Mad Paddy back at the Dublin Docks, Benny was finding it hard to fit in. These men, mostly comprising tough battle-hardened ex-soldiers, saw Benny as a bit of a joke and treated him as a lesser entity, a bit of a mouthy oddball. He bragged about murdering a man in Dublin, and that only lowered the opinion of him held by the other gang members.

To try and gain some credence within the gang, Benny began blathering on about a robbery he was about to commit that would bring in a substantial amount of cash. The robbery he was planning was never going to reap a high return, but Benny didn't care. He just wanted to do something to prove himself. He did not like Maggie Dorn. He reckoned she kept cash in her locked bedroom. Since the Captain had announced to the world that she was his granddaughter, Benny incorrectly imagined the bedroom was as good as a bank vault. He was desperate to prove himself.

Benny had decided to raid Maggie's room months earlier, but because of all the activity in the guesthouse regarding painting and decorating, there were too many people around. The work was nearing completion, so Benny found himself lying awake in the evenings, fine-tuning his criminal plan.

The gang that Benny was desperately trying to attach himself to had decided that he was more of a problem than an asset. They did not trust him, so they decided to put the pressure on, in the hope that he would deliver the big haul he kept endlessly bragging about. Benny was given an ultimatum, and having had his hand forced, he decided that the coming Thursday was going to be the big day.

Benny knew that Maggie and the Captain went shopping for provisions on Thursdays and could be gone for several hours. They would walk to the food market but come home in a horse-drawn cart heavily laden with produce. The Captain had decided that evening meals could be supplied to the guests at a reasonable cost, thereby adding to the ever-increasing profits being made by the now smart-looking guesthouse. A new name sign had even been fixed to the brick wall above the gleaming red front door. Good things were happening for these good people. The sign was quite large and read in fine letters of black, gold, and green.

Maggie and the Captain
Proprietors Captain May and Maggie Dorn-May

Thursday came, and as Benny expected, the Captain and Maggie headed off to the food market. Benny waited twenty minutes, and then he made his way to Maggie's bedroom door. He had borrowed a three-foot-long iron wheel lever from a gang member, and with this, he gained entry to Maggie's room with minimal effort. He proceeded to ransack the place.

"Nothing, nothing," he ranted. His anger reached fever pitch, and when he found Maggie's beautiful green dress with the fine lace collar, his face contorted into an evil diabolical countenance that would make a believer out of the staunchest anti-religionist. As Mad Paddy had predicted, Benny was the Dark Angel himself. He tore Maggie's pride and joy to pieces and was not satisfied until shreds of green cloth were strewn all across the room.

"Jesus, Benny, what are ya doin'?" Maggie had returned home to find an account the painters had dropped off the previous day. The Captain had forgotten to bring it with him, and he wanted it paid.

Benny swung around to face Maggie. She was rushing toward Benny, driven by pure anger. She did not get close. Benny still had the iron lever in one hand, and he lifted it and brought it crashing down on the left side of Maggie's face. A stream of

237

blood erupted immediately, and Maggie dropped to the floor. Benny's twisted mind only brought one thought forward: "I do kill people." He was not concerned at all about what he had just done. The only thing that bothered Benny was that he had nothing to take back to show off to the gang. *No money. They would laugh*, he thought, but then he remembered the Captain's office. Surely that is where all the treasure is hidden.

Several guests had appeared in the hall, wanting to know what the commotion was all about. Benny struck one of the men a glancing blow, and with that the others all returned to their rooms. Benny battered down the door to the Captain's office and became even more infuriated when he saw that the Captain had a large heavy iron safe in one corner. "Of course, all the treasure will be in that, and this iron bar is bloody useless," Benny seethed and ran out into the street.

One of the residents had plucked up enough courage to look into Maggie's room, and he also ran out into the street. "Peeler, is there a Peeler about? Our Maggie has been murdered. Help, dear lord. Our Maggie is dead."

Benny was absolutely frantic but could not get past the thought that he still needed to impress the gang, and immediately, he ran in the direction of the Earls Bakery where Malcolm was at work. With barely an ounce of breath left in him, he crashed through the bakery door and ran toward Roger Earls.

"Give me all the money you have, or I will smash your head in. I have no problem with killing people, so do as I say." Benny had moved behind the serving counter, and although he was still carrying the iron lever, he picked up a large knife from the workbench. "Money, money, money, you bastard. I know you have money in the shop, so get it for me."

Benny was so enraged that he had not taken into account that Malcolm was also at the bakery, and hearing the screaming, he came running in from the work area at the rear of the shop. "Christ almighty, Benny. What in god's name do you think you are doing?" demanded Malcolm.

Without hesitation, Benny swung the iron bar at Malcolm and hit him on his arm as he raised it to defend himself. He swung another blow, this time hitting Malcolm on the top of his shoulder. Malcolm shrunk to the floor, screaming in pain.

Roger was demanding him to stop. "I will get you the money, you piece of shite, but you must stop. You will kill him."

Malcolm was writhing on the floor but still conscious enough to hear Benny's reply to Roger's demands. "I kill people. That's what I do, and I will gladly kill Malcolm if I have to. You just get the money."

Roger had just been paid a large amount of cash as deposit for a huge order that Malcolm had taken. "I have cash. Here it is in the money tin. Take it, you stinking bastard, and get the hell out of here."

Benny moved close to Roger and snatched the money. He had dropped the iron bar. Roger stood there motionless, offering no resistance, and the last thing he saw on this earth was Benny Connelly slowly lift the knife and plunge it directly into his heart

Malcolm was still on the floor and screamed at Benny. "You bastard. Why? You will rot in hell."

Benny picked up the iron bar and brought it crashing down on Malcolm's head. He then picked up a blue iced cake and began stuffing it into his mouth as he left the shop.

Chapter Thirty Two

Back at Maggie and the Captain's guesthouse, the situation was pandemonium. One of the residents had gone to find the Captain at the food market. When he told the Captain that Maggie had been murdered by Benny, he slumped to the ground clutching his chest. With the aid of a passerby, the Captain was taken to St. Thomas's Hospital. He had suffered a heart attack, but the doctor seemed to think it was only mild; however, he would have to stay at the hospital and in bed for two days at least.

The Captain had regained consciousness and determined that he was not staying in hospital when he had a killer to dispatch. Three residents of the guesthouse were by his side when he awoke. He arranged to wear the clothing of one of the men because the hospital staff had taken the liberty to hide his, knowing full well he would try to leave. The unclothed gent took the Captain's place in the bed and pulled the blankets over his head to complete the subterfuge.

As the Captain was making his escape, he heard faint whimpering coming from a room they had just passed. "My beautiful green dress, that bastard tore up my beautiful green dress."

"Maggie, my dear Maggie, they told me you were dead. How, what, why are you? Maggie, I can't believe it," uttered the Captain, as he came to her bedside. He steeled himself as he looked down on her smashed face. *I will not cry. She mustn't see me cry.*

Maggie was fully conscious and was able to tell the Captain that the doctor who came to the guesthouse thought she was dead, but as she was being carried out, she moved, and he immediately brought her to the hospital. "I feel mighty poorly, but I am not dead, am I?" Maggie asked.

"You surely are not, my dear one," said the Captain ever so quietly. As he spoke, a doctor entered the room, and after the Captain explained who he was, he asked the doctor to step outside so that he could speak to him.

"She has taken a powerful blow to the cheek, but we don't think the bone is broken. There is much swelling, and until that goes down, we can't really say how much her face will recover, but I have to say, she is one very brave and one very lucky young lady. There is damage to one eye, and again only time will tell whether she will have eyesight back because at the moment she says she can see nothing from it."

The Captain felt nothing but relief. Maggie was alive, and she would recover. The next standing order only demanded one outcome. "Benny Connelly will be found and dealt with."

Maggie was not coming home anytime soon, and the Captain spent more time at the hospital than he could really afford. He had so much to do. His first priority was to alert as many of his ex-shipmates to help find Benny. One of the residents at the guesthouse had taken it upon himself to make sketches of Benny's face, and several of his friends were helping him show the likeness in the streets, hoping to unearth the whereabouts of the murderer.

When the Captain saw how good the sketches were, he had two hundred copies printed, and the manhunt ramped up in earnest.

Malcolm McDonald did not die of his injuries. He was in a far worse state than Maggie and was told his recovery would take a long time. He really did hope that he would die in hospital. He was weighed down with mind-crushing guilt. He had brought Benny to London. Roger Earls would still be alive if not for him. He thought sure that the happiness he had just begun to experience was ripped from his grasp on the morning of that terrible attack.

Malcolm had been in hospital for a week, and although he imagined that he had spoken to visitors, he was not able to establish just who these people were. Because of the beating, Malcolm's memory was not serving him well, but the doctors did assure him that things would improve, and gradually they did.

"And 'ow is Young Malcolm today? The doc tells me you are starting to recognize some of us who have been talking to the bloody bed for the past week. What say you, son?"

Malcolm instantly knew he was listening to the voice of the Captain. His mood was immediately lifted, but as he learned about what had happened to Maggie, he pushed his face into the pillow and began to sob. Malcolm was shattered at the news, and of course, the guilt he was now feeling was unbearable.

"None of this is your fault, Young Malcolm. You are a good man. You have proved that to me, and now I have a big favor to ask of you," said the Captain who had already decided that Malcolm would have to say yes to his request.

"What could I possibly do for you, sir?" asked Malcolm.

"Christ, you are not quite right yet," exclaimed the Captain. "Remember we agreed that—well, actually remember that I told you to call me Captain as my friends do. None of the sir shite, Young Malcolm. Now here is the favor I ask and I 'av' to say it's a biggen. Maggie is in another hospital close to here, and I want to have you moved to that same place to be close to her because she asks about you all the time, and I know seeing you every day would surely help her get better quicker. What do ya say to that?"

"Captain, I just can't do that. I just cannot imagine why Maggie would want me anywhere near her. I have caused her so much pain, and if her injuries are as you say, I don't think I could live with myself."

As Malcolm pleaded with the Captain, a lithe-figured young lady entered the room. She had heard the conversation going on as she waited outside, and when she picked up on Malcolm's negativity, she decided to join the Captain on his mission.

Malcolm was struggling to identify the newcomer, but as the clouds lifted on his memory a little further, he said questioningly, "Emily Earls, is that you?"

"Malcolm, yes, it is me, Emily. I am so pleased to see you looking—or should I say, sounding much better. You have had us all so worried. I could not help but overhear what the Captain is asking of you, and I hope you agree to help. I have met Maggie since the unfortunate affair, and I know she wants to see you. Please, I beg you do as the Captain asks."

CHAPTER THIRTY THREE

The Earls family, one and all, had become involved with Malcolm's troubles since the murder and assault. They had agreed to pay all of Malcolm's hospital costs and to help wherever possible in his recovery. They knew that Roger Earls would have wanted it this way. Malcolm, in such a short time, had become a great friend to Roger, and the Earls had never seen him so happy. Unbeknown to Malcolm, Roger had been discussing with his family the possibility of Malcolm taking over his bakery, thus freeing up Roger to open another shop. A plan had been agreed to, but Roger was murdered before it could be carried out.

The Earls had also become well-acquainted with the Captain during the long hours they spent beside Malcolm's bed, and of course, it was through him that Emily Earls, in particular, had met Maggie and knew she had to help.

"Please help me with Maggie," asked the Captain

"Malcolm, it would do you good to get out of here and help Maggie. You know how much she can help you also. What do you say? Please, Malcolm."

Malcolm finally agreed, and Emily left to make the necessary arrangements.

"Captain, are you not afraid of Maggie still thinking she loves me?" asked Malcolm sheepishly.

The Captain burst into relieved laughter. "She does love you. She told me that herself only three days ago. Before I could explain your situation, she proclaimed to me, 'I don't care what you think of the matter, Captain. He might be bent, but he is my best friend.' It seems she knew from day one that she saw you as her brother."

Later that day, Malcolm was moved to St. Thomas's Hospital. Two nurses helped him into a wheelchair and delivered him to Maggie's bedside. Malcolm had been prepared by the Captain with regard to Maggie's injuries and how she looked, but no amount of mental imaging could have prepared Malcolm for what he was about to see.

Maggie was unrecognizable, but as instructed by the Captain, Malcolm found himself desperately trying not to cry. His dry throat had closed over. His jaw was trembling. He was blinking as though he had just come in from a wild dust storm. The tiniest of tears, just one, had escaped from where Malcolm thought he had total control. Another and then another. Neither Maggie nor Malcolm had spoken a word as yet, but both had done their best to be brave. Maggie leaned toward the side of the bed, and Malcolm was doing his best to form an embrace. Their tears combined, and Malcolm felt comforted by the briny taste that hit him as he kissed Maggie's hand. He felt he had let the Captain down, but as he searched him out in the room, he saw the Captain was nodding his approval as tears also ran down his face.

As the days passed, both patients in this oddest coupling began to improve much faster than the doctors had surmised. Doctor White, who was the chief surgeon and the man responsible for saving the use of Maggie's right hand, was taking a very keen interest in this case. He was trying to understand and learn as much as he could about the relatively new field of psychology.

He could not believe how both Maggie and Malcolm were improving beyond anything he had hoped for and at a faster rate of time. He was trying to understand the power of positive thinking that he was studying about, but now he had patients in his keeping who were showing him just how powerful positive thoughts could be.

The Earls family had sought out John Rostan, the policeman. He and Roger shared their life together in Transbridge, Ireland. They felt obliged to let him know that Roger had been murdered. With the news of Roger's death, John Rostan's world had collapsed. He had not seen his partner in some time, but he was never far from John's thoughts. John had arranged for permission to assist the local constabulary in apprehending Benny Connelly.

John also seized this opportunity to stay with his aging parents who still lived in the same comfortable home that held so many memories for him. John was only young when his parents decided to leave Ireland and settle in London. His physical size and obvious strength intimidated all the pupils at his new school, and his serious nature made it hard for people to get to know him. He was not a happy child.

Things changed for John when he met Roger Earls while playing rugby for his school. John had rampaged his way down the rugby field and completely flattened four members of the opposing team as he ran. He travelled well over forty yards to score the try that won the game for his school. As John went to stand up, he was illegally tackled, bashed around the head by one of the opposition bullies. As he was coming to his senses, he realized he was lying flat on his back. Someone was mopping the blood out of his eyes and off his forehead with a pure white linen handkerchief. Roger Earls tried to introduce himself but realized that John was not making sense. His teammates had gathered, but when Roger volunteered to deliver John home in his carriage, that made the most sense. Roger Earls was attending the Westminster School and was only at the game hoping to see his school's team of "spoilt little rich brats" being given a sound thrashing.

John introduced Roger Earls to his parents in that house. John's parents, although strict Catholics, forced themselves to adopt a broader attitude when they began to realize that the bond between their son and Roger went well beyond that of an uncomplicated friendship. They had to constantly remind each other that when John was born, they vowed to one another that they would do all within their power to ensure his happiness. They could see that their very serious son was totally different whenever he was with Roger. He was happy, not acting for their benefit as he sometimes did; no, he was happy.

John and Roger were as unalike as milk and whiskey. Individually, they were both coping well, but in combination, one man took from the other that ingredient that they both lacked. Hope for the future.

Weeks had passed since Maggie was beaten and Roger Earls was murdered, but Benny Connelly had eluded all attempts to capture him and bring him to justice. John Rostan was quietly making headway but chose not to bring the Captain in on his findings in case he went off half-cocked and Benny could be gone forever.

Rostan had found out about the gang that Benny was so desperately trying to impress. He actually knew one of the gang members through dealings he had with this man when he was a Peeler in London prior to moving to Ireland. The gang member had told Rostan that Benny was being given some protection as pay back for the sizable bundle of cash he delivered to the gang the day of the murder. The cash he had stolen from Roger's bakery.

The informant was not sure where Benny was being hidden away but told Rostan that the gang would certainly dump him back into the streets once the money was spent. He said he would get a message to Rostan as soon as he knew where Benny was.

It was just one week later that Benny's savagely beaten body was found at the bottom of Tunney Bridge. He was not dead. The doctor that treated him at St. Thomas's Hospital concluded that the beating was so severe the patient should be dead, but whoever was responsible for the punishment knew exactly how far to go to extend the painful suffering but at the same time to prolong the assured death. Benny Connelly lingered on for three agonizing days and then died.

Both Maggie and Malcolm were recovering well, and the Captain noticed, once Benny was no longer a threat, they both seemed far more positive and ready to move forward. Malcolm's wounds had healed well. His ginger mane hid most of the scar across his head, and he had regained almost full movement of the arm that was hit by the iron bar as he defended himself. Maggie's recovery was nothing short of a biological miracle. Her pretty face that looked unfixable after the beating had almost reshaped itself back to normal. The injured eye that had greatly concerned the doctor had healed well. The pupil looked almost normal, and apart from some loss of peripheral vision, the sight had returned. Close scrutiny could find fault with facial alignment, but to do that, the observer would have to look beyond Maggie's smile and that was nigh on impossible.

The police officers who were put in charge of Benny's murder barely bothered to investigate the crime. The senior inspector knew Roger Earls through the family catering business and functions that he had to organize. In particular, he fondly remembered how much effort Roger had put into making sure that a recently retired officer was given the send-off he so well deserved. "Nobody gives a damn when one of our own leaves the force, but Roger Earls created an evening that was spoken about well after the event. A true gent, he was," he said. "Don't bother wastin' too much time on this investigation. Whoever did this did the bloody world a favor."

CHAPTER THIRTY FOUR

Amid all the trouble and seeing that both Maggie and Malcolm were well and truly on the mend, the Captain decided to throw himself a birthday party. He announced at breakfast one morning, in the dining room of the guesthouse, that he would be turning seventy-two years of age on the thirtieth of July, and that just happened to be a Saturday. He deemed Maggie well enough to organize the function on his behalf and allocated a generous budget to ensure that the evening would be a success.

Malcolm was shocked at hearing "72 years of age." He had always imagined the Captain to be much older, and in fact, he remembered seizing upon the number 100 when they first met. He had got to know the Captain very well and quietly wished that he had been the father who was so sadly lacking in love in his real life story.

Malcolm asked Maggie to let him organize the food for the evening, and Maggie, knowing full well how skilled Malcolm had become at catering for functions, she jumped at the opportunity. He asked if he could invite Emily Earls to the party. Emily was close to Malcolm's age and had endeared herself to all those concerned with him, Maggie, the Captain, and the guests at Maggie and the Captain boarding house.

Everything was in place for what promised to be a grand evening. Maggie was wearing a new dress. "Nothing will ever be as beautiful as my green dress," she said to Malcolm who assured her that she looked beautiful.

"Come and say good evening to Miss Emily," said Malcolm with more than a hint of mystique.

As soon as Emily spied Maggie and Malcolm approaching, she moved toward them with her timidly unsure friend beside her. "Let me introduce you both to my dearest friend Sarah," she said and then instantly blushed.

After exchanging pleasantries, Malcolm and Maggie wandered on to mingle. Maggie embarrassingly asked, "Are they both bent like you?" Maggie could not contain her curiosity. Malcolm took her hand, looked her straight in the eye, and said nothing.

The party was a huge success, and it was obvious to those who knew him that the Captain was using the excuse to have a party for more powerful reasons. People needed to mend. There was too much sadness. There had been far too much hurt. People's tensions dissipated at the same rate as did the gin and the sublime food.

At one stage, mid evening, Malcolm was sitting alone, just relieved that his food had left everyone more than satisfied. John Rostan very deliberately headed in his direction and seated himself at the table beside him. The ordinary conversation that began between the two men very soon took a sinister turn. John took a length of roughly cut red material from his pocket and began folding it and then unfolding it. Malcolm instantly recognized the article. It was Benny's neck scarf. It was part of the uniform that Benny was so proud of when the Fixers tried to rule the roust at the Dublin Docks. Benny was never without his scarf. It reminded him of better days, and he often bragged to Malcolm that with his new gang, he would take power again. Of course, he never had power but then Benny could not see himself that way.

The two men talked for several minutes, but neither one mentioned the scarf. As John Rostan stood up to move on, he handed the red scarf to Malcolm and said, "Please take this. It may be of some comfort, one day."

The police department had dropped off a small parcel to Malcolm containing several personal items found on Benny's body. The scarf should have been in that parcel. How was it that John Rostan had it, and how did he know the significance of it?

The Earls family invited John Rostan to their home, advising him that they had some business to discuss with him. Mrs. Earls and her two daughters greeted John warmly and ushered him into an office where it seemed much of the family business records were housed.

"We have some good news for you, John, and we hope you receive it with our blessing," said Mrs. Earls. "Our Roger left a will, and in it, he has bequeathed to you a considerable amount of money."

"There was no need for him to do that. I don't know what to say. As you know, I had his love, and that is all I ever want from him," said John.

"Be that as it may, John, but we will insist that you receive what Roger wished you to have," added Emily Earls.

It took no less than three cups of tea and several biscuits before John realized that there would be no escape. Mrs. Earls placed an envelope in his hand, and John left, thanking his hosts without opening the letter. When he returned to his lodgings, he did open the letter and could not believe its contents.

There was a letter written in the hand of Roger Earls. He stated in the letter that he always knew his path would cross with John's at some stage of their lives. He hoped that John had found someone else to share his life with but knew that he himself never would. "If you are reading this letter, it must be that I am dead. I do hope I reached a reasonable age and died in peace in my own bed. I thank you for all you have done for me and hope in some small way this money will help you remain comfortable, and as I know you will, please feel free to use some of it to help others." Signed Roger Deacon Earls.

The envelope also contained a banker's draft for the sum of one thousand pounds. The money was left to Roger in his father's will by way of an apology. John Rostan, due to his latest promotion, was earning fourteen pounds and five shillings per week.

CHAPTER THIRTY FIVE

John Rostan had decided to travel to Salford to let his old friend Joseph Connelly know what had happened to his firstborn son, Benedict Francis Connelly. He would do his best to euphemize the horrific tale but knew that Joseph and Grace would be shattered to hear of their son's demise and the circumstances that lead to his death.

John Rostan had another reason to visit Salford. Matthew Denny, the cousin of Finbar Denny and the man he had befriended on a train trip from London to Manchester, had let him know through a mutual Masonic friend that he needed to see him.

John Rostan had told the tale over and over of his first encounter with Matthew Denny at the Old Bailey where he so graciously spoke on the character of his friend Killy and got him off on a minor assault charge. They had stayed friends and met up occasionally when John was able to travel to Salford.

Matthew Denny was not there when John Rostan arrived at his home unannounced. John had decided to delay telling his friend Joseph Connelly about the death of his son until he had spoken to Matthew first. He wasn't sure of the Connellys' current situation, health- and wealth-wise, but he did know that when he assisted their departure from Ireland, none of the Connellys was faring well and in particular Joseph's wife, Grace.

It was Colleen Denny who greeted John on his arrival at her Brown Street North address. "As I live and breathe, John, is that yourself?" asked Colleen.

That typical form of Irish greeting had always brought a smile to John's eyes, and today was no exception. He was tempted to reply, "To be sure, I'm sure it surely is me, myself," and if it had been Matthew greeting him that way, he surely would have responded as he thought. He loved Matthew's sense of humor and was looking forward to catching up with the big man and hearing about all of his wild exploits.

Colleen had immediately taken John by the arm and already had him seated in her kitchen with the copper kettle at the boil. She explained that Matthew was not due to return for two days and then asked the reason for his visit.

John knew Colleen well enough to trust that anything he told her would stay with her and not be repeated. He asked all about the Connellys and was pleased to be told that their situation had improved. She explained that they were all still living with Finbar and his two children. Grace's health had improved greatly, but Finbar insisted that none of the Connellys was yet fit enough to work.

"It's such a tiny house, but you will see. They all seem happy, and that's the best Finbar had hoped for. Fin and his two bairns, Angela and Michael, all work, and they pool their money so everyone gets well fed. Fin is very proud of his Angela and Michael, and he has every right to be," said Colleen.

After John had finished taking Colleen into his strictest confidence and telling her all about Benny and how he died, she just sat there in her kitchen, numb. John knew it was a lot to take in, so he just sat in silence and waited for her to process everything she had just been told.

"You are so right, John. I think we do need to wait for Matthew to come home before we let either Joseph or even Finbar know what has happened. I did not know Benedict, but when the Connellys arrived here and he was not with them, Matthew did say that something was badly wrong. Joseph had said that he had turned out no good, but who could have ever imagined that things would turn out like this?" Colleen spoke as if she was miles away.

John decided to stay in the area until Matthew returned so that, between them, they could talk to Finbar and decide on how to proceed with Joseph and his family.

Colleen had much news of her own, and several cups of tea later, she was bringing John up-to-date with the current situation in Salford, but he was more interested in finding out whether she knew why Matthew had asked to see him. Colleen was scant on detail but did not hesitate to tell John as much as she knew of what was behind the reason for Matthew's request.

"Matthew told me he needed to talk to you about a murder that had happened over in Manchester proper. He talked about a poor young woman being killed but not just killed. I really did not want to know any more, and I do not really know why he wanted to speak to you," said Colleen.

"What would interest me about a murder in Manchester? Do you have any idea, Colleen?"

"No, John, but I have to tell you something else because I think this was important to Matthew. The body was chopped up. The arms and legs were separated and just thrown away like rubbish. He said a couple of times that it sounded like a murder you had told him about, and he wants to talk to you about a man called Marcus Eversall."

The mention of the name Marcus Eversall hit John like a bullet from a gun. Joseph Connelly's sister Tess had married an animal named Marcus Eversall. He brutally murdered her and chopped her body up, and just as Colleen had described, he threw the severed limbs around like garbage.

Colleen had much to tell, but it was obvious to John that he would have to wait until Matthew arrived home to understand more regarding Marcus Eversall. However, several of Colleen's news snippets piqued the interest of the policeman.

He was told about how Granny, the English wife of the French marquis referred to by Granny as the Drunk Duke, had sought haven with them after escaping France and a cruel marriage and how, on her death, she left her estate to Angela Denny. "Angela had made Granny's last days on earth an absolute joy," said Colleen. He was told of the huge diamond, the beautiful ruby, and the title to some land at the Port of Marseille in France. Colleen expressed concern about a rumor she had heard regarding a bad man who had been sent by the son of the Drunk Duke, now dead, to bring home that family land deed at any cost. John heard that Matthew had some of his helpers keeping an eye out in Manchester to hopefully identify this bad man.

Colleen told of how Michael Denny, Finbar's son, had become quite the gentleman thanks to her friend Mary Burns and the kindness of her friend, Mr. Frederick Engels. Because Joseph

Connelly had insisted that Michael Denny learn to read and write back in Ireland, he had worked himself into a good job at Engels' mill. He was working in accounting, and while doing business with one of the other mills, he met and fell "shovel over shamrock" in love with Sarah. She was the daughter of the mill owner that Michael was doing business with. Engels' mill had just upgraded several spinning machines called mules. The upgrade enabled more cotton to be processed and at a much faster rate. Michael was set the task of purchasing extra cotton to allow the machines to keep running until the next shipment of cotton for Engels mill arrived from America.

Sarah Thomlin worked at her father's mill doing similar tasks to Michael. He saw her as exceptionally beautiful. That was how he described her to his sister, Angela, after his first encounter. "Angela, she has the palest skin and the brownest eyes I have ever seen. She is tall for a young lady, and that suits me given my own height. She has read so many books and knows so much about the world. She has been to America with her father buying cotton. She has been to Vienna where she met the composer Richard Wagner. She went to the opera with her mother and saw his latest work *The Flying Dutchman*. I would love to experience an opera. Just imagine, Angela, a room full of musical instruments all playing the same music together. What would that sound be like? I swear I will go to the opera one day, and I will have Sarah on my arm."

Colleen went on to explain how all the hopes that Michael had for Sarah and himself were shattered. "She is a bloody Prodie, John, and Michael is as Catholic as the Pope himself. Finbar warned his boy that there would be trouble. Matthew had said over and over to his nephew. 'Do not mix with the Church of England people. If you do, you will get hurt.'

"The cowardly bastards did not come for Michael. They knew that my Matthew would always see that they came off second best if anything was to happen to Michael. You see, Matthew had heard that Michael had been threatened and told to leave Sarah alone, so he put out the word to 'leave young Michael alone or it's me you will be dealing with,' and so they did leave Michael alone," said Colleen in a foreboding tone.

"But they didn't leave poor wee Sarah Thomlin alone. She had let her family know that she loved Michael and that she intended to marry him. Some of the Prodies got hold of her as she and some of her friends were walking home from choir practice. They roughed her up badly, and then they raped her. The friends she was with were made to watch as a warning to all the young girls. Sarah was taken to hospital, and I have heard that because of the way she was abused, she will never be able to have children, but at least she is still alive."

"How is Michael after all of this?" asked John. "He is not likely to do anything silly, is he?"

All Colleen could add to the matter was that "Sarah Thomlin's father came to see Michael personally at Engels' mill to let him know that he had nothing to do with what had happened to his daughter. Michael called him a hypocrite and insisted that it was Mr. Thomlin's constant criticism of Michael and Sarah that allowed the cruel rapists to justify in their twisted minds that someone had to be punished. Mr. Thomlin then insisted that Michael apologize, and at that point, Michael hit him. He has been charged with assault and is being held in the Manchester gaol awaiting trial. Matthew has organized a good solicitor for him, but we have been told that he most likely will be transported to Australia."

John was astounded that two people simply loving one another had led to so much sadness and savagery. He had not even thought to consider his own personal situation. He had just murdered Benny Connelly, and it was his love for Roger Earls that had caused him to act so out of character.

John Rostan had no idea how he could help Michael. All he knew was that he would get involved. He did not stay any longer with Colleen. He was made aware that Finbar Denny and his family lived nearby and that the Connellys were temporarily living with them. He did not want to face his friend Joseph Connelly and have to inform him of the death of his son Benny without speaking to Matthew first.

Rostan knew he could stay with a friend in Manchester. He was a Freemason and ex-police officer. His name was Osian Jones, and he was as Welsh as the best choir ever heard. Osian had bought an ale house with the inheritance he received after the death of his mother. He shared the amount with his two sisters as instructed by the will but was still left with enough money to allow him to own the ale house unencumbered.

The premises already had a name attached over the front door, and in fact, it was when Osian was told the name, he knew he would buy the establishment, and this was well before he and his wife had actually inspected it.

It was known as the Rose and Leek. Osian only made one small change to that sign after taking over the business. It became known as the Leek and Rose.

Osian's wife, Joan, who was a noted signwriter, fabricated a square sign by joining three short lengths of ship planks together and painted a bright red dragon on the surface. This fine artwork was hung above the bar to announce to all who drank within that the Welsh had arrived. Osian was a master when it came to dealing with drunks, and Joan could calm the wildest storm. Their gamble had turned out to be a great success, and the Leek and Rose had become one of the most popular ale houses in Manchester.

John Rostan had worked with Osian Jones when he first joined the police force. The characters and personalities of the two men were as different as sand and water. John's approach to policing was rigid and staunch. The laws were there for a reason, and he was there to ensure people played by the rules. Osian Jones, on the other hand, saw the laws of the land as a framework within which people were expected to live, but that framework did not always allow its citizens to do what was best. He could see no benefit in bringing a child to court for stealing food items such as bread and fruit. Rostan often saw Osian press two pennies into the palm of a very young offender while simultaneously extracting a promise through trembling lips from the urchin that he or she would never be caught again.

Osian had caused John to reconsider his own moral stance regarding right and wrong on many occasions. It fascinated him that when Osian delivered his reprieve to some of the wretched poor souls, he used the phrase "never be caught again" rather than never offend again. Osian, of course, was well-aware that they would most likely offend again, but the message he hoped they would take from his advice was simple: two pennies' worth of kindness might, in some small way, positively affect that one child's attitude toward society in general.

When John Rostan arrived unannounced at the Leek and Rose, it was Osian who sighted him first. "Well, will you look at what the bloody dragon has dragged in now, Joan," and as he spoke, he moved toward his old friend, and both men genuinely embraced. Joan also moved to her husband's side and completed the trio. "I owe my wonderful life to this good man," Osian announced to the twenty or more drinkers who were seated, mostly in pairs, at tables in the bar. "This big bastard took a bullet that was meant for me, and it was no accident. He jumped in the way of that bullet. As sure as I stand here, I owe him my life."

It was true. The pair were trying to arrest three men who'd been accused of bashing and robbing a local jeweler. They accosted the man in his shop and got away with several expensive bracelets and brooches. Witnesses had stated that they could identify the men and, in fact, knew where one of them was living.

Armed with that information and nothing more, John Rostan smashed his way through the front door of the nominated premises, and Osian followed behind. John had hit the door with such force that it splintered, and he clumsily fell to the floor. As Osian went to move forward past him to arrest the culprits, John saw that one of the men was holding a gun. The man raised the pistol and aimed it directly at Osian. As John screamed "No, no," he leapt to his feet, and the bullet intended for his friend ripped straight through his left shoulder. His anger countered the pain, and he proceeded to knock two of the villains to the floor while Osian took control of the third.

John was awarded the police Medal of Valor for his bravery. Any time the medal was mentioned, John had a stock standard reply to make light of his effort. "Well, I just couldn't let the Welsh bastard leak all over the bloody floor now, could I?" John was not a man who was comfortable with making wisecracks, so those that knew him really appreciated the effort he must have made to come up with that little gem.

During the time that John and Osian had worked together, they became firm friends, and John regarded Osian as the brother he never had. With this in mind, when John was able to get Osian alone, he decided to tell him about everything that had happened in London and that included confessing to the murder of Benedict Connelly. He needed to talk to someone, and Osian was the perfect choice.

Having got the confession off his chest, he proceeded to tell Osian of the trouble that Michael Denny had found himself in after striking Mr. Thomlin. It was indeed a serious charge, and Osian agreed with the information John had been given with regard to probable transportation to Australia.

Together they hatched a plan that, with the help of several Masonic friends, could mean a better outcome for Michael. John Rostan did not really know Michael Denny, but it was after listening to Colleen, his aunt, explain just what an effort Michael had put into improving his own lot and also how actively he was helping his own family and now the Connellys since their arrival in Salford that he felt he just had to help.

For their plan of salvation for Michael, many pieces had to neatly fit into what would end up being a very complicated puzzle.

The first thing the men needed to know was if Sarah Thomlin, Michael's intended, had recovered sufficiently and if she still wanted Michael by her side. It was decided that Osian's wife, Joan, could help with this, the first part of the plan.

Joan visited Sarah in hospital under the guise of delivering flowers from some of the concerned mill workers where Sarah was employed by her father. When Joan arrived with the flowers, she found Sarah alone in her room. The poor girl looked as though her world was in tatters and really was not in need of any company. Joan whispered that the flowers were in fact from Michael, and that being said, Sarah's face began to come alive, and she even managed a slight smile through all the bruising.

"Oh, how is he? Is he well? Is he really in gaol?" Sarah sobbed, and Joan moved closer to console her.

As she did, Sarah's father rushed into the room. "And who might you be, disturbing my daughter?" blustered an ever irate Mr. Thomlin.

"She is a good friend of mine from the mill, Papa, and look at the beautiful flowers she has brought here for me," said Sarah, totally disarming the possible crisis.

Joan seized on the situation and left immediately but not before she whispered into Sarah's ear. "We have a plan," and as she drew away, she said cheerfully, "See you again soon, my darling."

John Rostan spent three nights at the Leek and Rose, and while he was there, he along with Osian and Joan met with all the personalities that would each play a crucial part in the salvation of Michael. John knew that if he went ahead with the plan, it would sound the death knell on his policing career, but there were already totally unrelated factors that had begun that erosion anyway.

Matthew Denny was home when John Rostan arrived to discuss with him just how and, more importantly, what to tell Joseph Connelly regarding the murder of his son Benny.

Matthew thanked Rostan for the way he had decided to deal with Joseph Connelly as he was only too well-aware that the most important thing to Joseph Connelly was the happiness of his family. He had come to this conclusion after speaking with Finbar Denny about the demise of Benedict Connelly as told to him by Rostan.

Matthew had taken the liberty to talk to Finbar at work, well away from Joseph, about everything that had happened to Benny. The two men agreed that although Joseph had to be told of Benny's death, it would be dangerous to make him aware that it was his good friend John Rostan who had terminated the murderous Benny. From what they both understood of the events leading up to Benny's death, they agreed that he got exactly what he deserved, an eye for an eye and all that.

What John Rostan had not made them aware of was how he left enough life in Benny's body to have him exist for several days in extreme pain but with no hope of survival. John Rostan believed he had sold his soul to the devil on that frightful night. He believed all the honor he had so valued was gone, and although he prayed to his god for forgiveness, he knew he would never forgive himself. He had become a dangerous man, and woe betide anyone he would judge to be deserving of punishment.

Since the Connelly family had arrived in Salford and were now living with Fin and his family, it was obvious to all that knew him how tormented Joseph Connelly was about the whereabouts of his eldest son.

It was agreed that John Rostan should be the bearer of the news regarding Benny Connelly's death. Rostan sat alone with Joseph in the Black Duck tavern where he had arranged through Finbar to meet him as news had come to light of Benny.

Rostan came straight to the point with Joseph as he explained just what he understood of the fate of Joseph's son. The tale, of course, was an invention, but it was hoped that the lies that Rostan was about to embark upon would ease the pain he was about to deliver to the man he respected greatly.

"Joseph, I will tell as much as I have been able to learn about just what happened to Benny after he arrived in London," explained Rostan. "It seems that Benny took up with a bad lot when he arrived there. He became part of a gang, and the reason he chose this path was forced upon him because, although he tried, he just could not find work and had become desperate. The friend he travelled with, a young man named Malcolm, whom I believe you were acquainted with, told me that he offered to assist Benny with money, but like you, Joseph, his pride would not let him accept Malcolm's offer."

John Rostan began to choke on his own words as he arrived at the difficult juncture within the maze of lies that he hoped would explain the death of Roger Earls.

"Benny needed money, so it seems that he decided to rob a shop that he reckoned would be carrying lots of cash. He was in the process of gathering the cash as he held the shopkeeper at bay when a worker unknowingly came into the front of the shop from the workhouse behind. It would seem that Benny immediately felt threatened and lashed out at both of the men with an iron bar he was carrying. He only injured one of the men, but unfortunately, in sheer panic, I guess, he hit the first gent on the head with the bar and that poor man died later."

He made no mention of Malcolm by name and omitted the fact that the dead man was actually stabbed to death.

Rostan made no reference to the fact he knew the murdered man who was indeed the same man he lived with in Transbridge. He did not relate to Joseph that the second man was Benny's only friend, Malcolm. He told a tale that was meant to have Joseph Connelly believe that the whole sad affair was purely random. He went on to explain how Benny was found dead, and the police had decided that the gang he had tangled up with had disposed of him because the murder could have come back on them, and by association, they would have all landed in gaol.

At no point in the telling did John Rostan so much as mention Maggie Dorn. What Benny did to Maggie was what upset Rostan the most. A slip of a child beaten across the face with an iron bar. Rostan could not get the frightening image of Maggie's damaged face from his mind, and he knew it was that image that drove him to deal with Benny Connelly in such a cold-blooded manner.

Joseph Connelly listened in total silence and offered no questions at the end of Rostan's explanation. He knew the story had been softened for his benefit because he knew that his son

Benny was far more evil than his friend John Rostan would have him believe.

He recalled how Benny had skulked away from the Dublin Docks before his family were due to leave. He remembered how Benny had stolen every penny the family had to assist his escape. He remembered the rumors that were circulating the Docks at that time. The rumors that hinted at Benny being the prime suspect in the murder of a small boy who burnt to death in a house that Benny had set fire to.

John Rostan suggested that a memorial service could be offered in the hope of saving Benny's soul from everlasting damnation. Joseph thanked John for his concern but stated sadly, "You and I both know that Benny is in hell right now, and the only comfort I can draw out of any of this is that he will stay there. In hell, just where he deserved to be. John, I thank you for your concern, but I suggest that Benny be never mentioned again. If you please, I would like to explain to Grace and the children that Benny had died in an unfortunate accident while working at the London docks. The truth would serve no purpose here and certainly would bring no comfort to Grace. I know in her heart of hearts that she will be relieved to hear of his death because she constantly worries about what trouble he might be in."

Rostan was greatly relieved that Joseph took the news with quiet acceptance, and so he gave himself permission to embark on his next quest. The second reason for his visit to see Matthew Denny was to find out what Matt wanted to tell him about Marcus Eversall, the man who murdered Joseph Connelly's sister Tess.

Chapter Thirty Six

Matthew met with Rostan away from the family home, and he had Finbar Denny with him. He was told by both men about a murder that had been committed in Sheffield. They were working on the rail link between Manchester and Leeds when they heard the story. Now murders in that area were not uncommon, but this one stood out.

The female victim's limbs were severed and scattered about the scene as though the killer wanted to totally humiliate and demean her. Finbar heard the news giver refer to the suspect as the man the poor woman had been living with. She apparently tried to escape his cruel beatings but was murdered as she attempted to leave with her two small children. The killer did not harm the children but did make them watch the brutal killing.

The partner was well-known to the local police, and his name was Marcus Eversall. The three men agreed that Joseph Connelly should not be told any of what they had just found out. He was already grieving over the death of his son, and this news, regarding the killer of his long dead sister Tess, could well drive him to desperate action.

John Rostan offered to make some enquiries through the Sheffield police as to what was happening with their endeavors to apprehend Marcus Eversall. Finbar mentioned that one of the railway workers admitted that he knew Eversall, so Rostan also agreed to follow up with this man to find out whether he could help in any way.

Matthew asked Rostan about not returning to Transbridge. "Will you need to get permission to investigate this case, John? Surely you are due back in Ireland now that Benny Connelly is finished?"

"I have been given permission to take some extra time off if I needed it," replied John. In truth, no such permission had been given. John Rostan had actually resigned his position with the police force. He knew he had things to do that would need time to complete and resignation was the honorable way out rather than be asked to leave.

The three friends parted company with Matthew and Finbar heading back to their homes while Rostan boarded one of

Goldsworthy Gurneys steam-driven buses that would deliver him to Manchester Central railway station where, after a two-hour wait, he got on to a train headed for Sheffield.

John Rostan had no intention of seeking out police help; he merely put forward that suggestion to placate the mood of the meeting. He did, however, use the map that Finbar had drawn for him to find the home of the railway worker who had said he knew Eversall and found out from this man that Eversall had a sister living in the same town. Rostan met with her, and it was very obvious as the conversation began that this woman greatly feared her violent brother.

"We don't know where he is, and we don't bloody well want to know," she told Rostan who continued to badger her for information because his experience told him that she certainly knew more than she was offering.

"I am staying for one night at the tavern in town, so please, if you remember anything, come and find me," Rostan said in a beseeching tone.

It was getting late into the evening, and Rostan had almost given up on hearing from the murderer's sister as he sat alone at the bar of the tavern he told her he would be staying in. "Hey, copper, I can help you find that bastard who butchered his missus," said a voice that came from behind where Rostan was seated.

As he turned to face the sound, Rostan recognized the man who stood before him as the husband of Eversall's sister whom he had met that afternoon.

The man introduced himself properly to Rostan and apologized for the rudeness his wife had shown to him on that afternoon. "My name is Will Quinn, sir, and my wife, Iris, is a grand woman, sir, but she fears that animal of a brother so badly that whenever he is mentioned, she flies into a mad panic, and she has good reason to, sir, if I may tell you."

John Rostan knew he had good judgment when deciding whether people he was expected to deal with were being honest with him or possibly trying to lead him into a trap. He looked hard into the eyes of Will Quinn and arrived at the opinion that told him he was dealing with an honest man, but he saw much more.

Rostan had been a copper for a long time, and he had looked at many people whose eyes told a similar story to the picture he saw in the eyes of Will Quinn. Rostan could see that Quinn loved his wife and his children. He was an honest man, but overarching all else in the vision was genuine fear. Will Quinn was terrified of Marcus Eversall. He knew that this man would not hesitate to kill anyone who got in his way.

"If you are able to assist me in delivering justice to Eversall, I promise that no harm will come to you or your family," said

Rostan. "All I need is information, Will, and you need not involve yourself any further."

Will went on with his offer. "The police up here have asked all the right questions, but we know that they will not pursue Marcus because they told me that they would sooner see him move away from Yorkshire. The police also fear him and with good reason. They all have families, and they all know what Marcus is capable of.

"Marcus Eversall came to our home about ten days ago," said Will. "He does not visit often, but when he does, it is only when he needs money or to steal anything of value that he can sell. I am ashamed, but I never try to stop him. This time, however, was different. We had no money to give him, and he became furious. My wife wears a small golden cross with a tiny ruby mounted into it on a chain around her neck. Marcus knows that the cross was given to Iris by her mother when she was alive and that cross was given to Iris's mother by her father when she was married. It is the only thing of value that Iris has ever owned, and she loved it.

"Marcus pulled the cross from Iris's neck, and the chain broke. Iris flew into a rage, and she hit out at Marcus. He punched her in the stomach, and when she fell to the floor, he proceeded to kick her. I tried to drag him off, but he punched me in the eye. There was so much blood. I could not see properly. I ran to protect the children, but Marcus kicked his sister one more time and then left, cursing us all as he rode off."

Rostan was incensed and demanded of Will, "Just tell me where he is. Tell me where I can find him. I promise I will end the problem."

"Sir, I believe I know where he is hiding, but it is difficult to find. I cannot direct you. I will have to go with you. Marcus often poaches deer on a large estate about ten miles from here. There is a cave in the woods that Marcus has been known to stay in. I did go with him several times when I needed food to feed my family, but I have not done so for a long time. I try to have nothing to do with him, and I know he has no friends, so if he is at the cave, he will probably be alone." Will Quinn began to tremble as he spoke.

"Are you able to get us a horse each?" asked Rostan.

"I can do that, sir. Do you have a plan?"

"If you can get me close to the cave, that is all I expect of you. Once we are there, you have to tell me now that you will return home and leave me there alone. I will not let you be seen by Eversall. I will deal with him on my own. If you agree to this proposal, we can leave in the morning," said Rostan.

Will Quinn timorously agreed. "Tomorrow is Sunday, sir, so there is no work for me on the rail. I will borrow two horses from a good friend who runs a cartage business. What time do you want me to meet you in the morning, sir?"

Rostan replied, "We need to make best use of the daylight, so because the sun rises around five o'clock, it would be good if we left then. Does that suit you, Will?"

Will agreed, and Rostan insisted on buying him a drink in the hope that it might calm his nerves.

The two men set off at five in the morning as agreed. After leaving the village, the terrain became harsh and quite steep in places. Will knew what to expect, so the two horses he had chosen were hardy and used to heavy going. Rostan could see why someone like Eversall would hide out in such rough country. Unless you had some knowledge of his hideout, you may well be kept looking forever. Will had to stop several times to assure himself that he was headed in the right direction. As he had stated, it had been a long time since he had made this journey, and the vegetation had grown considerably, making several of his sought after landmarks hard to find. After four hours, Will reined in his horse and said to Rostan, "We are close now, sir. The cave is beyond that outcrop of rocks about five hundred yards on our left."

The men dismounted and tethered their horses to a tree, allowing enough rope for both animals to pick at the scant growth of grass that surrounded them. Rostan and Will climbed the outcrop of rock because Will said that they should get a clear view of the cave entrance from there. Before arriving at the summit, Will grabbed Rostan's arm and pointed to a thin ribbon of smoke emanating from the area beyond the rocks and in the direction of where he had said the cave would be. As they arrived at the summit, both men peered over the top toward the cave. They quickly ducked back down again.

"That is him, sir. That is Eversall," whispered Will.

Rostan had no doubt that the man he spied in front of the cave was indeed Marcus Eversall. Yes, he was older, but Rostan had pawed over the old reward posters back in Transbridge after the murder of Tess Connelly and knew every evil curve and crevice of that countenance.

Rostan signaled that they should return to the horses, and Will did as directed.

"Now this is where we part company, Will. As we agreed, you will head for home, and I will attend to the problem at hand. I will wait thirty minutes before I confront our friend so that if anything goes wrong, you will be long gone and Eversall will be none the wiser."

Will wished Rostan the very best of outcomes, and with that, he hastened away from the scene.

Rostan was only armed with a small pistol and a large knife that he kept hidden in his boot. He allowed his anger to get the better of him, and rather than consider a plan, he decided to simply walk up to Eversall and meet him head on.

As Eversall saw Rostan walking toward him, he immediately picked up his rifle, aimed it at Rostan, and fired. Rostan dropped to the ground motionless. Eversall ran toward him to make sure he was dead. As he drew close to the body, Rostan sprang to his feet, screaming, "You should have taken better aim, you murdering bag of shite because you are now about to die."

Will and Iris Quinn never saw John Rostan again. They assumed that borrowed horse must have made its own way home as there was no rider to be seen, and Will had made up his mind that Eversall had claimed another victim.

A good month after their encounter with John Rostan, a small parcel was delivered to Iris Quinn via the penny mail. She unwrapped it and dropped the contents to the floor. Will picked up the golden cross with its small ruby still intact, and for the first time in a long time, the couple entered into a peaceful embrace.

CHAPTER THIRTY SEVEN

Meanwhile, back at Salford, life was falling all over itself for the Dennys and the Connellys. The major concern for all was Michael Denny, who was still in Manchester gaol being held for assaulting Mr. Thomlin.

Money was needed to mount a good defense, so Angela Denny had agreed to trust the sale of the diamond bequeathed to her by Granny to Abraham the pawn broker. She did not trust him, so she insisted on going with him to London to find a suitable buyer for the exquisite gem.

Angela proved to be quite the businesswoman because when Abraham was seated with her during the negotiation of the sale, a price was agreed to by Abraham but Angela declined the offer and immediately rose to leave. Abraham blustered his disapproval, but the gem dealer began to laugh. "You have a smart one there, Abraham," he said, and he immediately offered an additional fifty pounds. Angela had no idea of the value of her prize. All that concerned her was being able to get enough money to help her brother. She agreed to the sale, and in the company of Abraham, she returned to Manchester.

During the journey, Abraham kept enquiring about the ruby that was also left to Angela in Granny DuBois's will. "I have a buyer for that beautiful stone, and they will pay a good price." He badgered Angela, but she said that she had not yet decided what to do with it. "There was also a title deed to some land in France, Angela. What has become of that?" asked Abraham.

"I have left the deed and the ruby with Father McCordy at St. Michael's Church. He has a large strongroom there to keep all the church treasures in, so I know the deed is safe with him," said Angela in a tone that left little doubt in the mind of Abraham that there had been enough questioning.

A court date had been set for two weeks from the day that Angela returned from London. She and her father, Finbar, met with the solicitor who would be representing Michael, and he assured them that Michael had nothing to fear. "He has an honest and diligent reputation, and I know this will carry considerable weight with the judge. He is a good man, and the law will recognize that" was the best the solicitor could offer.

John Rostan had returned to Manchester after his devastating run-in with Marcus Eversall and was staying with his friend Osian Jones at Jones's ale house, the Leek and Rose.

Rostan had dealt with many court cases, and he knew the reputation of the judge that would be adjudicating the trial. He told Matthew Denny that Judge Pomroy-Forth had no time for the Irish, and to boot, he was a staunch Anglican. Rostan could not help but tell Matthew that "as sure as I stand here, Matt, that lad will be sent to Australia, and he will be made an example of. I have heard that the worst of the transported prisoners are being sent to a small island called Norfolk. This place has a brutal reputation where men are beaten and starved. I think with what we know, it is likely that young Michael will be sent there, and if that be the case, he will die on that miserable island. No amount of money is going to stop that from happening. To make things worse, Matt, the judge is a good friend of the man that Michael stands accused of assaulting."

With Michael awaiting trial, it was hard to imagine that things could get worse for the Connelly and Denny families of Brown Street North, Salford, but that is exactly what happened.

It was just after Angela Denny had used the services of Abraham Rothschild to sell the diamond bequeathed to her by Granny DuBois that the strongroom within St. Michael's Catholic Church, Salford, was broken into and many items stolen.

The French land deeds left to Angela were stolen during that unfortunate incident and that resulted in Abraham allowing his anger and greed to overrule his usual calm demeanor. He had orchestrated the robbery, but things had gone so wrong. He enlisted Garrett and his son, Manfri, to blow the vault door but had also ordered his evil off-sider Asael to kill them both and bring all the treasure from the strongroom back to him. Unfortunately for Abraham, Asael was killed after he took the life of Garrett during the robbery, so it was Manfri and his two accomplices who made away with the loot.

Abraham wanted the reward on offer for the return of the deeds to the French marquis, and that reward had been increased considerably since the robbery. Abraham knew that Manfri would have the documents, and he was determined to collect that reward.

Chapter Thirty Eight

The man acting on behalf of the French marquis, Solomon Leyman, was prepared to do anything to resolve the task set to him by the marquis who was now sending messages to Solomon expressing with anger that he wanted and now demanded a result. Abraham decided that the best way to bring about a quick resolution was to kidnap Angela Denny and demand that the land deeds be delivered to him along with two hundred pounds cash or Finbar Denny would not see his daughter alive again.

Solomon could see no sense in the plan. "Sir, it was Manfri Garrett the gypsy who stole the deeds, so how can Finbar Denny be expected to arrange for their return?"

Abraham snapped back his reply, "I intend to let Finbar Denny know that it was Manfri who broke into the church strongroom, and I know the Connellys and the Dennys were great friends with Garrett, so I believe that they will convince Manfri to help them. We know Garrett was buried by the gypsies two days ago, and he must have died during the robbery. Manfri will surely want the reward on offer but is being too careful. The kidnapping will surely make him act."

Solomon saw the whole scheme as badly thought out, but he was desperate to get his hands on the deeds, so he agreed to the kidnapping.

Solomon Leyman and two of Abraham's henchmen were able to capture Angela Denny on the following evening when she was returning home from the mill at the end of her shift. She was in the company of three female coworkers when the ruffians put a chloroformed rag to her mouth and knocked her out. Her friends tried to stop the abduction, but the men hit two of the girls with heavy blows to their faces, and the third girl ran away to raise the alarm.

Finbar Denny was inconsolable after he had read the ransom demand letter that was delivered to the Denny household by a small child who was obviously just a paid messenger randomly chosen from the street.

That letter clearly stated the demands but also intimated that the deeds that were to be handed over in exchange for Angela's life were held by Manfri the gypsy who was the son of the now-deceased Garrett. Finbar did not know Garrett well, but he knew that Garrett had traveled to Salford from Dublin with the

Connelly family, so he immediately showed the letter to Joseph Connelly who agreed to do all within his power to ensure the safe return of Angela.

The letter allowed three days for Finbar Denny to put together the two hundred pounds that Abraham demanded in addition to Angela's return. He knew that the church robbery would have yielded cash as well as items of value, and his greed would not be sated unless he saw some of that cash come his way.

The instruction stated that the deeds and cash had to be left with Father McCordy of St. Michael's Church, the church that had been robbed, and he would deliver it to an address only known to him, and Angela would be released to him only after the ransom had been checked and deemed to be correct.

Both Finbar and Joseph agreed that Matthew Denny and John Rostan should be brought in to help with the safe return of Angela. Only Joseph Connelly had been informed by Rostan about the demise of Marcus Eversall.

John Rostan felt he had to tell Joseph because he should know that the brutal murder of his sister Tess had been avenged. Rostan did not elaborate on the cruelty he had inflicted upon Eversall before sending him to hell, but suffice to say that Eversall lived out every ounce of pain he had ever inflicted upon any of his badly damaged victims. When the body was discovered by shepherds in the area, it was reported that only a torso and head remained. The arms and legs had been hacked off and were nowhere to be found.

It was agreed that Joseph Connelly and Finbar Denny would meet with Manfri and plead with him to help them save Angela from certain death. Manfri had insisted that his aunt Agnes sit in on the proceedings. Finbar told the story of the kidnap and the ransom demands. Agnes, on hearing of the crisis, looked at Manfri and asked, "What are you going to do, Manfri? We cannot allow this young girl to die."

Manfri had already decided that he and the gypsies would help free Angela. He recalled the first day that he met Joseph Connelly and how Joseph had quizzed him and his father about Garrett's finely crafted silver hook. After that meeting, Garrett often spoke of Joseph in conversation, and he always referred to what a good and honest man he was. Manfri was not a killer, and his conscience weighed heavy because Garrett and Asael were killed during the robbery. He believed that in helping Angela Denny to be saved from death, it would in some way bring a little relief to his troubled mind.

Solomon Leyman was absolutely correct when he objected to the kidnapping, stating that it was a poorly thought out plan. Prior to meeting with Manfri, Angela's father, along with Uncle Matthew, Joseph, and Rostan, had no idea who had kidnapped her, but Manfri explained in great detail just what had happened during the robbery, but most importantly, he made it absolutely clear that Abraham Rothschild had orchestrated the whole misadventure.

A loose order of happenings was decided upon by the five men, and Agnes had decided quietly to herself that she would ensure that every gypsy woman and man would be warned not to have any further dealings with the man who had stooped to the lowest ebb by stealing a child.

It was agreed that Finbar Denny and Joseph Connelly would meet with Father McCordy to tell him what was expected of him by way of the instructions contained in the cruel ransom letter. He agreed to help wherever he could but refused to agree to tell the two men where the ransom was to be delivered. He told Finbar and Joseph that no one had been in touch with him thus far but reiterated that he would not divulge the address of the drop-off site because he did not want any further bloodshed. He explained that if he met with the kidnappers alone, he was sure in doing so, lives would be saved.

Matthew and Rostan were left to consider just how they might secure Angela's safe return. Rostan considered bringing Abraham to heel but knew that if he was to do so, Angela would certainly be killed, so he and Matthew decided to spread the word through the Masonic community that help was needed. Maybe some people had seen a young girl being mistreated. Perhaps somebody knew where she was being kept. It was not much of a plan, but it was all they could come up with.

Manfri sent five gypsies out into the streets of Manchester in the hope of gaining some helpful information.

Agnes had her own ways when it came to finding out what all the bad people were doing. She had established a network of women who would report to her whenever they saw any young members of the various gypsy communities pushing their behavior beyond the law. She would alert the elders within the communities, and more often than not, the young offenders could be given help and positive support in the hope that they would mend their ways. Times were very hard for all members of the gypsy communities, but the work that Agnes was involved in saw her rise in prominence among her people, and when she put out her plea for help, only a few short hours had passed before her efforts were rewarded.

Angela had been held against her will for almost thirty hours when an older gypsy woman rode slowly into Manfri's encampment. The gray horse she was mounted upon was a sad sight indeed. It looked to be lame, it was obviously blind in one eye, it showed almost every rib, its spine protruded through the thin hide, every vertebrae could be counted, and its hide hung off its huge old frame looking like a ruffled wet bedsheet hung on a cloth line. No gypsy horse was ill-treated, and such was the case with Sultan. His appearance was solely due to old age. His rider was known throughout the gypsy world as Queeny. She asked to see Agnes. She was assisted in her dismount from

Sultan by two young men and courteously escorted to Manfri's wagon.

Queeny told Agnes and Manfri that the limp body of a young lady had been secreted into the rear living quarters of an old disused factory in Baker Street, not far from the ancient market square that had been temporarily taken over by her people.

Three men were said to be involved, but while two had left the site, one still remained with the girl. The area was known to all inhabitants of Manchester as a no-go zone. It had a reputation for harboring criminals, and more dead bodies would turn up around Baker Street than anywhere else in the industrial powerhouse. Manchester was growing at an extraordinary rate, and the local police force, which was just in its infancy, was fighting a losing battle.

Manfri thanked Queeny for her help and insisted that he escort her home. He harnessed up a small gig drawn by one mule, sat Queeny beside him in the cart, and tied Sultan to a draw rail attached to the rear of the gig. As Queeny left the campsite, she gave an imitation Queen Victoria wave, and the humor of it all was not missed by anyone who witnessed her departure.

Agnes wasted no time in saddling up her own mount and headed out to find John Rostan. He had told the searchers that he could be reached at the Leek and Rose ale house run by his friend and ex-policeman Osian Jones.

Agnes was pleased to find that John Rostan had just returned to the Leek and Rose shortly before her arrival. She found him in the bar, and by his demeanor, she could see that his search for Angela had so far been in vain.

"Mr. Rostan, I think I have found the girl," said Agnes. "But I want you alone to help get her home safely to her family."

"Agnes, if you know where she is, we should all of us rescue her," said Rostan, noting the strong emphasis that Agnes had put on "you alone."

"I know who you are, sir," continued Agnes, "and I know that you can save the young lady. I do not want any family man getting hurt or, heaven forbid, killed trying to free Angela. I know you have no one who will miss you. I know what I say is cruel, sir, but I do know who you are."

"I think you need to explain yourself, Agnes, and who the hell it is that you think I am?" demanded Rostan, who due to lack of sleep, reacted far out of character.

"My Manfri returned from York last week where he had been using the black powder to remove stone from along the area where the new rail line to Sheffield is to be built. He was staying in the railway workers camp near a small village in that area, and it happened that one day, the local policeman returned to the village with a corpse laid out on a flatbed wagon. Manfri saw this happening, and he told me that although the corpse was covered with potato sacks, it was obvious to all the people looking that somebody had removed the arms and legs from the body."

Agnes's speech was faltering, so Rostan demanded, "And just what does any of what you have just told me have to do with anything I have done?"

"A man working in the gang where Manfri was camped lived in the village, and he told the workers that a policeman had been in the area looking for a man who was accused of murdering his wife, and although he did not know for sure, he told his friends in the gang that he reckoned the policeman just might be the one who delivered the justice that this animal deserved. I believe you to be that policeman," stated Agnes, whose voice by now was even, calm, and most deliberate.

"Of all the policemen in England, how do you arrive at the conclusion that I am that man?" quizzed Rostan, trying desperately to appear calm.

Agnes continued. "Sir, I mean you no harm, and I know you want to help. The rail worker from the village told his friends that this policeman was the biggest man he had ever seen. In fact, he said that this man was as big as a barn door, and he also said that this policeman knew the murderer from the time he spent in Transbridge as a policeman. I asked some questions of your friend Joseph Connelly, and he said that he knew you from Transbridge. He also told me that you are a man alone. You had recently lost a dear friend, and he told me also that both your parents are deceased. That is why I beg you to deal with this matter alone so that no man with a family to care for and provide food for is hurt. Please, sir, I beg you."

Rostan was speechless. Not because of everything Agnes had found out about him but because she skipped over the death of his parents as so matter of fact. His mother and father were barely cold in the ground, and here was this woman skipping past their existence as if it was just another hurdle she had to negotiate to reach her goal.

John Rostan's father had certainly reached an age that all his close friends had not. He had been suffering from consumption for almost two years, so his passing was no surprise, but when John was informed that his mother had also died just two months after her husband's passing, he was shocked.

The notice of her death caught up with him when he returned to the Leek and Rose ale house after taking care of business with Marcus Eversall. He had missed the funeral, and the heartache was still raw. And now here was this woman talking about his parents as though they had been past history for a long time.

Rostan had learned through a police report that his mother had died of what seemed to be starvation. The truth, in fact, was that she died of a broken heart. Her husband was gone, and she had noticed a great change in her son. She felt that the bond between them had been broken. John had become distant, and his mother could see no reason to go on. She died believing her place in heaven was secure because refusing to eat surely could not be called suicide. "Surely this is no mortal sin," she tried to convince herself.

At first, Rostan just wanted to scream at Agnes and tell her to go away, but as he was about to do just that, he reheard in his anger something that Agnes had just said. "You are a man alone," that is what she said.

"I am just as you say, Agnes. I am a man alone," Rostan reaffirmed in a whisper that was barely audible. "Why is it that sometimes it takes an utterance from a virtual stranger to clear another's mind. I am alone."

Rostan had been sad on many other occasions throughout his life but not this sad. He asked Agnes to sit with him. She did as he asked, but Rostan did not utter a single word for at least ten minutes, and when he did speak, he told Agnes everything about his parents and how much he loved them. He told her that the family home was sold and for a considerable amount of money.

"Agnes, I am no longer a policeman, so you see, I simply cannot help you, and expecting me to deal with this situation on my own is just asking too much," said Rostan.

Agnes did not try to hide her disappointment, and as she rose to leave, she threw the crumpled up piece of paper she had been fiddling with directly at Rostan. He had guessed correctly what was written on the note, and as soon as Agnes was out of sight, he asked the young lad who attended to horses in the ale house stables to make ready his steed.

Within the hour, Rostan found himself in Baker Street. The crumpled paper that Agnes had angrily thrown at him had a crude map drawn on it. The map had Baker Street clearly marked, and the only other writing on the page read Pier Street and an x had been placed almost half way along Pier St. on the right hand side.

To avoid drawing suspicion to himself, Rostan entered the Ox and Horn tavern in Pier Street and asked the price of a room. "You rentin' by the hour or do you intend to stay all night, sir," queried the ruddy-faced, balding little man who was barely visible behind the bar.

"I intend to grace your fine establishment for two nights, and no, sir, I will only be requiring a single bed. I must have light, sir, as I have some writing to do, so do you have a room that faces the south?" Rostan knew that the tavern faced south, and the x marked on the map was close enough to opposite the tavern. Any room facing in a southerly direction would give a fine view of the spot where Agnes believed young Angela was being held.

Rostan had been canny enough to pack several items of clothing into a saddle bag. This adornment made his story of having business to do in the area and therefore having to stay two nights at the Ox and Horn sound plausible. Once in his room, situated on the first floor, Rostan sat in the one chair near to the window, and as he had expected, he could see everything that was going on out in the street.

Mid-afternoon was slowly sliding toward evening, and Rostan was straining to stay awake when he saw a man with a parcel in his hands banging on one of the doors opposite. The door opened only slightly, and the parcel was handed toward the darkness. The man who gave over the parcel quickly turned and left immediately. Rostan reckoned that he had pinpointed the kidnapper's lair. The parcel was probably food. Rostan was feeling exhausted, so he laid down on the hard bed and was asleep within seconds. It was not a deep sleep, and he counted off each hour as the bells of St. Thomas's Church sounded their end. Twelve bells had just peeled loudly. Rostan was fully awake as he crept down the unlit stairs and was remarkably quiet for such a large man. He saddled up his horse in the stable and quietly led the handsome beast out into Pier Street, tethering him near to the door that, behind which, Rostan believed held the prize.

The almost full moon was being kind as it lit Pier Street. The big man had faced several of these dangerous situations lately and had to admit to himself that the thrill he was experiencing was not something his conscience found easy to condone.

Rostan removed the bone-handled blade from his boot, and when he arrived at the door that had received the parcel, he proceeded to force the lock by jamming the sturdy blade into the gap between the old door and its weathered frame. Age had weakened the timber, and given the power that Rostan was able to apply to the task, the door sprung open with a loud *crack*.

Rostan had no idea as to what he would be facing, but a loud bang and then a bright flash of light accompanied by the familiar smell of black powder sent a musket ball directly into his right shoulder. He had taken the precaution of wearing a second thick jacket over his usual attire, and as he had hoped, the penetration of the shot fired was lessened considerably. He felt no pain at all as is often the case with extreme trauma, and he ran toward the flash. He tackled the shooter who was only several strides away, and both men fell to the floor. Rostan tried to hold his opponent down but was unable to exert pressure with his right hand, so he was overpowered and felt himself being repeatedly bashed about his head with the butt of the musket that had neutralized his right arm. Rostan still had raw power on his side, so he brought his left fist crashing into the jaw of his oppressor.

What was it that Agnes screamed at Garrett when he insisted that the full-blooded blow she had delivered to his face had broken his jaw? "Your jaw is not broken. If it was, I would have heard it crack."

Well, Rostan just heard that crack loud and clear. The recipient of the hammerlike blow was indeed Solomon Leyman, and as Rostan's fist landed squarely on his jaw, he let out a short sharp gasp and fell, unconscious, on top of Rostan.

Rostan quickly extricated himself from the tangle and immediately began looking for Angela. The moonlight allowed him to take in the full size of the room, and as he scanned the space, he sought out what looked to be a small crumpled parcel in one corner. He went to it, and when he was able to realize just what he was looking at, anger surged. It was Angela Denny. He knew it to be her because he had been told just what she was wearing when she was abducted. If he was left to rely on identifying Angela by face alone, it would have been impossible. He instantly recalled the face of young Maggie Dorn as he looked down at Angela. She had been badly beaten and was barely alive. He knew he had to get help for her as quickly as possible, and that meant carrying her over the street to the Ox and Horn where he awoke the landlord who, upon seeing Angela, summoned his wife to help.

As the landlord went to fetch the doctor who lived nearby, Rostan returned to Solomon Leyman who by now was staggering around the crime scene, trying to make some sense of what had just happened. He need not have wasted the energy.

"You are nothing but an animal, and before I kill you, I want you to know that you are about to feel pain that you never believed could be possible," said Rostan to the man who was about to wish had never been born. Rostan did not take the life of Solomon Leyman immediately, but as he had done with Benny Connelly, he inflicted such wounds that Leyman would linger for several agonizing days without hope of recovery.

Having dealt with Leyman, Rostan returned to the Ox and Horn where he was able to satisfy himself that Angela, although badly beaten, would mend well. He left instructions with the landlord and his wife to alert the police and wrote down Angela's name and address. "Please don't mention anything about me other than I left Angela with you. I did not pay for a room here, and you don't really remember what I looked like. Do me this favor, and I will be forever in your debt," asked Rostan. He explained about the kidnapping and told them that there was a very sick man in the building opposite where the door is still open. "He is the kidnapper, so make that known to the police."

Once his instructions were given, Rostan handed twenty pounds to the landlord and began to leave.

"Rest assured, kind sir. My wife and I will do all that you ask, but what of your shoulder, sir? I have seen enough injuries in the war to know that you have a gunshot wound there. Please return to your room, and the little lady and I will take care of that problem."

Rostan knew that he was losing a lot of blood and did really need to have the wound attended to. He looked hard into the faces of his would-be benefactors and relying on his good judgement. "Would you please attend to my horse, good sir?" he asked as he ascended the stairs and fell on to the bed in the room he had left only forty-seven minutes previously.

The landlord of the Ox and Horn was good to his word. He restabled Rostan's horse. He sent a message to the address that was written on the note he was given, and when the police came, he was vague with his description as Rostan had asked.

Finbar Denny arrived at the Ox and Horn, along with Father McCordy, at five o'clock on the morning that Angela was rescued. He was not sure how badly hurt his daughter was, so he brought the kind priest along with him just in case the last rites were required. By the time her father arrived, Angela was faring far better than was expected. She smiled when she saw her father and rushed to his daughter and held her in his arms for a long while. He kept thanking the landlord and his wife over and over. He offered them all the money he had on his person, only a small amount, but they refused.

"How did my daughter come to be here? Who was it that helped her? Where are they? I must thank them," asked Finbar, and as the landlord told his tale, it was obvious that the mystery was meant to remain unsolved.

Angela was unable to walk, so the landlord offered Finbar the use of his horse and cart so that she could be taken home. Finbar asked Father McCordy to stay with his daughter while he went with the landlord to the stable to help him harness the horse to the cart. He commented to the landlord on the fine animal housed in the end stall. He knew who belonged to that beautiful animal but did not say a word. He had been told of the frightful condition that Solomon Leyman had been left in. He knew that the police would be looking for answers. He decided to quietly take his daughter home, but the events that took place with regard to her rescue were no longer a mystery.

"Please tell me your name. I can't just go on calling you landlord," asked Rostan of the man who had just removed the shot from his shoulder and was in the process of sewing up the wound.

"Edward Gould, sir. But my friends call me Teddy, and my good wife is called Sheila," replied the landlord. Rostan proceeded to quiz Teddy with regard to the reason that he saved him from the police, and Teddy explained that he had two daughters of his own, and when he saw how badly young Angela had been treated, he realized that in good conscience he should help the man who had saved the young lady from any further suffering.

Rostan spent a further three days recovering at the Ox and Horn before he ruled himself well enough to leave. He had to admit to himself that he could have left earlier, but he was so enjoying the company of Teddy and the stories he told that in truth he simply did not want to leave. Teddy had led a hard life even by the standards of the time. He was forced into child labor at the age of four because his father had deserted the family and his mother simply could not keep her family adequately fed. Teddy was forced to work in a leather tanning factory where he was cruelly treated and given very little food to eat.

Rostan listened intently to every sad tale but could not help but realize that with every anecdote that Teddy related, there was an element of hope. No story was without some sunshine, and Teddy became brilliantly animated as he told of his life. Rostan felt his spirit lift every time Teddy regaled him with another piece of his own history.

Rostan was reminded of the first time he met Matthew Denny on the train trip back to Manchester from London after Matthew had secured the freedom of his friend Killy who faced assault charges at the Old Bailey courthouse. Matthew entertained Rostan with the carefree attitude he displayed while telling story after story of his exploits. He recalled that he did not want that train journey to end just as he did not want his time with Teddy to conclude, but he had to get back to Brown Street North because he knew he would be needed if Michael Denny was to have any chance at all of beating his assault charges.

On the fourth morning, Teddy informed Rostan that the man who had treated young Angela so badly had died in police custody, and with that information to hand, Rostan knew that he had to leave the safe haven that had afforded him so much joy. He knew that he had to be gone from the Ox and Horn so as not to jeopardize the freedom of Teddy and his good wife, Sheila. He did not want them implicated in any way. He embraced both his carers as he left and told Teddy that he considered him to be the elder brother that he never had. He treated Osian Jones, Matthew Denny, and Joseph Connelly as his brothers, but they were younger, whereas Teddy fitted well into the senior position. Teddy insisted that he wanted Rostan to keep in touch, and after hearing that genuine request, Rostan felt that maybe, just maybe, he was not altogether a man alone as Agnes had described him.

Rostan's right arm was still being held in the roughly fashioned sling that Sheila had insisted he wear, and after trying to discard it along the way back to spend some time with his friend Osian Jones, Rostan realized that the sling was still needed but just for a short time. He needed to put together a plan that would secure the freedom of Michael Denny, but more importantly, that freedom had to be guaranteed to last.

CHAPTER THIRTY NINE

Michael Denny's court hearing was only days away, and the men who had banded together to secure his release had many obstacles to overcome.

With a plan in mind, Rostan asked Matthew to arrange for himself, along with Finbar and Joseph, to meet at the Leek and Rose to discuss Michael's escape. Rostan had explained everything he had arranged in great detail to Matthew and insisted that Matthew present the plan as if it was his. Rostan was well-aware that he was a fringe member of the group and believed that Finbar and Joseph would take better heed of anything Matthew was to propose rather than present the plan as his. Matthew strongly opposed the idea, but after Rostan explained his reasons, he reluctantly agreed.

"We have to make sure that Michael escapes from Manchester gaol before his court date because if he does not and is found guilty, as we all know he is, he will be whisked off to one of the death ships moored in the Thames River near London," stated Rostan.

Finbar Denny informed the others of a rebellion that had taken place on one of the hulks named the *York*. The hulks or death ships were old cargo vessels that were no longer seaworthy but made good makeshift prisons for the huge number of petty criminals who had been sentenced to transportation to the English colonies. The *York* had over 500 prisoners on board. The conditions were described as absolutely appalling. Disease was running rampant through the prisoner population and the guards. The food supplied to the inmates was totally inadequate and oft times rotten.

"Our Michael wouldn't last a week on one of those prison ships," said Finbar who looked to be a broken man. He was so grateful to have his daughter back and wished he could thank the people who so bravely came to her aid, but they still remained anonymous, but "What of Michael? What do we do?" He looked imploringly at cousin Matthew, best friend Joseph Connelly, and the ubiquitous John Rostan.

"I am well-confident that we men here can assure the freedom of Michael Denny, and I think there is only one way to assure that he, once free, is not tracked down and brought back to gaol," said Matthew. "I have had a friend of mine visiting Sarah Thomlin, Michael's intended, and my friend assures me that whatever happens to Michael, she wants to be with him.

Sarah is home from hospital and has been told to expect to see Michael soon," continued Matthew.

Finbar Denny added another piece to the plan. "My son is truly in love with Sarah Thomlin, and I want no more than to see them both happy. I visit Michael when I can, but the hours I work make it hard. I thank you, Matthew, for everything you have done to help me see him. I have whispered to Michael that we may be able to organize his escape, and when he heard that, his face lit up, and he only had one request for me. He insisted that Sarah be part of the relocation plan but only if she wanted to, of course.

Matthew Denny proceeded to add some further ingredients to the forming puzzle. "One of my Masonic connections knows the two private contractors who are employed to drive the prison cart from the Manchester gaol to the court house delivering the prisoners backwards and forwards all day long. The police department uses private drivers because they need the prison cart drivers to be skilled. The cart has to go fast, and the department insists on this because they believe it is a huge deterrent to anyone wanting to help prisoners escape. Some years back, two policemen who were unskilled and driving the cart tipped it over, and sadly one of the officers was killed, and that is why we now have contractors."

"But just how is that going to help us?" asked Finbar.

"Cart driving skills they may have, but common sense is not something either of these men can claim to possess even in the smallest of quantities. They both gamble badly, and they drink heavily. I put a proposition to them, and they jumped at it," explained Matthew.

"How are they able to help us, Matthew?" Finbar interjected yet again. Of course he did. He had almost lost Angela, his daughter, to a foul kidnapping plan, and while living through that nightmare, his only son was suffering in gaol awaiting a terrible fate that was beyond his imaginings.

Matthew laid out the plan. "The two drivers will be on the cart together. They have both agreed to make it easy for us to bail them up at the Tower Street corner on the way to the court house. I told them that we will have to rough them up a bit so that suspicion doesn't fall back on them. They are tough men and saw no problem with my plan. The money I have offered them both was enough to ensure that greed overruled any loyalties that they might have had."

"This money, Matthew, can you deliver on that promise? Where is it coming from? I have a little if you need more," asked Finbar.

Matthew took the floor once again. "Rostan has agreed to meet the cost demanded by the two drivers. He says he will pay it himself directly to the two men so that no blame can fall back on you, Finbar, or you, Joseph, and that also leaves me in the background where no one can identify us directly."

Finbar was concerned, "But what of you, Rostan? What if you are caught?"

"I do not intend to let that happen. You men have families that need you, whereas I can simply disappear very quickly, leaving no trail to follow," stated Rostan with his usual confident way of understating the danger he will be placing himself in.

"The plan, gentlemen. We all have to play our parts, so please listen," said Matthew. "We will not know when it will be Michael's turn to be in the transport cart and because it is completely covered in. We will not be able to see him. The only opening is a door at the rear of the cart, and it is fitted with a small window that has four steel bars in it. I have smuggled in a length of blue ribbon to Michael and told him to tie the ribbon to one of the steel bars in the opening so that we know he is in the cart. There will be no guards in with the prisoners to stop him because it was decided some time ago that putting guards in with the prisoners was too dangerous.

"In truth, the crimes are so petty that the police see no need for heavy security. The prisoners charged with more serious crimes are escorted to court under a totally different system." Matthew continued. "Joseph, you are to be stationed a short distance from the Tower Street corner, and it will be your job to alert Rostan and myself with a wave of your hand when you see the blue ribbon tied to the iron bar in the cart window. Once you have done that, you just join the crowd and move closer to us, but please do not get involved unless absolutely necessary. When you give the wave, two men from my railway gang will pretend to begin a fight with one another. I have chosen Killy to start the fight. He has the loudest voice known to man. I would not be surprised to see birds falling dead from the sky due to shock. If any Peelers happen to be close by, I am sure Killy will win their attention. Finbar, you will be waiting a further distance along Tower Street with three saddled horses tethered near to the barbershop. No suspicion will arise as folk passing will just think that the barbershop must be busy with the extra horses being there."

Finbar stammered out, "Just three horses. There will be me on one, and that only leaves two horses for you, Matthew, and you, Rostan, but what of Michael?"

Rostan was quick to reply. "My horse is a strong animal, and he will easily carry myself and Michael. Michael will have to ride with me because he will be manacled, and with his hands bound, it will be better if I was able to help him mount in front of me so that we can move away quickly without causing too much of a scene."

"Now remember this," ordered Matthew. "We will all have our faces covered by our black scarves. As we jump into action, we simply pull the neck scarves up and over our noses to hide our faces. We need to make it as hard as possible for witnesses to identify us in case a reward is offered, and that Thomlin fella is just the type to try and hunt us down. We should all practice with the neck scarves. We don't want 'em falling down in the middle of the job."

Matthew then proceeded to throw another competitor into the mix. "I only mention this now because I did not want to create any panic. The cart that Michael will be travelling in has two heavy timber doors held shut by a large inbuilt iron lock. The drivers do not carry the key, so I had to come up with a way to open it quickly."

The panic that Matthew was hoping to avoid gave birth immediately. Finbar, almost out of control, screamed, "And just how in god's shitey name do you beat a lock of that size?"

"Black powder, Finbar, and we have a very good man who has agreed to help us. Manfri the gypsy king. As you well know, it was Manfri who very successfully blew away the hinges that held tight the strongroom door in St. Michael's Church. He has agreed to help us for two reasons. Firstly, to honor the memory of his father, Garrett. Garrett spoke often of how kind both the Dennys and the Connellys were to him when he was barely surviving in Ireland, and secondly, because Angela Denny had decided to lay no claim to the ruby that was left to her by

Granny DuBois, and it has now been returned and remounted as the heart of their Black Madonna."

Matthew explained, "Manfri had been able to inspect the lock from a distance and had put together an explosive charge that he assured would be powerful enough to disarm the lock. The cart was always in front of the court house or the Manchester gaol, so Manfri has passed it by on several occasions, and that has allowed him to inspect the same lock in a shop that sells such things. He has made a double-ended S-shaped iron hook about two feet long. The explosive and back pressure plate will be mounted on a hook at one end while the hook at the other end will simply be hung from the small window in the door. The two-foot measurement will allow the explosive to sit directly in front of the lock. Michael has been told to huddle as far forward in the cart as he can, and if there are any other prisoners with him, he should tell them to do the same. Once Manfri has hung the explosive, he will jump onto a cart being driven near the scene by his aunt Agnes. Now I hope all that is clear, and are there any questions?"

The four men stood in silence. There were many questions, but silence ruled. The plan was a desperate one, and after what seemed to be an age, only Finbar spoke. "I believe I am the luckiest man in the world to have such fine friends. I will never forget how brave you all are, and I pledge my life to each and all of you. Yes, I would give it gladly. I say thank you, but do know this: thank you is simply not good enough."

Chapter Forty

The day of the trial arrived, and it was dismal. Rain was sleeting down. The sun had failed to make an appearance, and the wind rattled and shook every form of vegetation and installation, causing sounds to constantly erupt and then ebb only to be immediately repeated.

The cart which was the center of attention had made several passes by the Tower Street corner, but the blue ribbon had yet to appear. Midday slowly gave way then yet another hour, and then it happened.

Not only was Joseph Connelly waving madly, but he decided to add his voice to the warning. Rostan cringed, hoping Joseph was not drawing police attention to himself. Relief came when Killy began the feigned fight. The volume he produced totally drowned out any noise being made by Joseph.

Matthew and Rostan had taken hold of the harnesses fitted to the two horses dragging the cart and had brought it to a standstill. The two drivers were soon both on the ground, receiving a beating that looked real but in fact was not causing much damage. Both assailants had agreed to deliver a final blow to both drivers that would be sure to knock them out thus affording the whole scene considerable credibility.

While the Shakespearean performance was taking place at the front of the cart, Manfri had already approached the rear door. The fuse was lit, and Manfri hung the custom-built S-shaped hook on the window frame, but as he pulled his left hand away, the sleeve of his jacket was caught in the bottom hook of his rig.

Three short seconds was all it took. Manfri was able to free his jacket, but his hand had not travelled that safe distance required to stave off any damage. The explosion was loud, and the backing plate flew straight at Manfri's left hand, shattering many bones and causing blood to erupt out of a long jagged laceration to his wrist.

Matthew and Rostan arrived at the rear of the cart together. Rostan immediately realized the trouble Manfri was in. He removed the neck scarf covering his face and wrapped Manfri's shattered hand tightly.

Agnes with her small pony and cart full of hay was exactly where the plan had marked her to be. Rostan quickly picked up Manfri with no more strain than a less powerful man would lift his pint of ale when offering a toast. He raised him over the hay in the cart then lowered him down and into it, providing instant cover. He could see that Manfri was in shock and was not making a sound.

While that was happening, Matthew had pulled open the prison cart door, and Michael jumped toward him. As he did, he grabbed hold of the blue warning ribbon, tore it from the bar to which it had been tied, and stuffed it into his pocket.

Finbar was right there with the horses, and just as easily as he had with Manfri, Rostan picked up Michael and lifted him high enough that he was able to straddle the shoulders of Rostan's horse. Seconds later, Rostan was mounted directly behind Michael and was spurring the horse to a gallop along Tower Street and toward freedom.

Matthew and Finbar headed off in different directions. This was all part of Rostan's plan which had been enacted without a hitch except for the damage to Manfri's hand.

Matthew returned to his home. Finbar returned to his home. Agnes took Manfri back to the gypsy encampment, and again as planned, Rostan rode to the ale house of his friend Osian Jones, the Leek and Rose.

It had been agreed that Michael would stay with Osian and his wife, Joan. Michael would take on the role of general hand as Rostan had convinced the others that hiding the escapee in plain sight was the best way to avoid his detection.

Three days after Manfri's hand had been so badly damaged by the explosion, Agnes and the gypsy elders met to decide what they felt would be the best course of action. Infection had set in, and all the fingers were turning black. Manfri was in so much pain. He had told Agnes that he would agree to anything they decided. He knew what had to happen. Agnes plied Manfri with large amounts of gin, and when she deemed him drunk enough, she insisted he smoke her opium pipe in the hope that the pain to come would be considerably numbed.

Agnes had not seen John Rostan since the strange rescue of Angela Denny from the brutal hands of Solomon Leyman, but she had no doubt that he and he alone was responsible for Angela's safe return to her family. It happened due to sheer coincidence that Rostan had decided to visit the gypsy camp on the day that Manfri was to lose his hand.

Rostan was there to find out how Manfri was faring after the explosion that allowed Michael Denny to be free had shattered his left hand. He had hoped that some part of the limb could be saved, but instead, he was given the job of holding Manfri down on the bench that served as a kitchen table in the wagon owned by the gypsy blacksmith who had removed Manfri's father's same hand all those years ago.

Agnes had raised Manfri as her own son when his father, Garrett, disappeared, enabling himself to avoid being tried for the murder of his own brother, Waa, who had assaulted his wife, Manfri's mother.

Agnes was a very strong woman but found herself sobbing uncontrollably in the smithy's wagon. Manfri had just passed out due to the combination of alcohol and opium. Before the amputation could take place, Rostan decided that he would escort Agnes back to her own wagon, telling her that he personally would make sure that Manfri was made as comfortable as possible.

As they walked together, she thanked Rostan for not involving any of the family men when he rescued Angela. "I know you did it all on your own, John, but here we are now with Manfri so badly damaged. We went from one man acting alone to a situation where up to ten people could be caught and sent to gaol. I want to apologize to you, John, for speaking to you the way I did when I came and pleaded with you to rescue Angela. What I said was too cruel. I called you a man alone, John, but in truth, that is not the way things are with you. I watched how the men looked up to you when you tried to fool us all into believing that Michael's rescue plan was Matthew's idea. You proved that we all need one another, and far from being that man alone, you indeed have many friends who, it seems, would go to gaol for you if that is how things have to be. I hope I am considered a friend of yours, John, and if I can help you at any time in the future, you must ask me."

CHAPTER FORTY ONE

Finbar Denny knew that he could only meet up with Michael in secret, and those meetings had to be carefully planned. The local police would surely be watching his movements in the hope that he might lead them to his escapee son.

Osian Jones had quickly set out a list of duties for Michael Denny, and one of those chores was to drive the horse and heavy duty cart to the brewery each week to load on the barrels of ale required for the upcoming week. This task was always performed on a Friday. Michael had made the four-mile round trip on two occasions since his escape. A lesser man would have rebelled against the plan that had been explained to him with regard to his future. He knew he had to wait and was prepared to obey all the rules set before him, but those who were looking out for him knew that one hunger had to be satisfied if their plan for Michael was work.

Michael was driving the cart alone, having just set out from the Leek and Rose to pick up the weekly load of ale. He was only fifteen minutes into the journey when a familiar horse and rider pulled up beside him. There was a second person on the horse who wore a hood. Rostan drew up close to the driver's seat of the cart, and his passenger quickly boarded, taking Michael by surprise, and what a surprise she was. Sarah Thomlin had completely recovered after being assaulted and raped eight weeks earlier. Michael could not believe how much better his life had just become. They embraced immediately. Michael had actually let go of the reins, and it was Rostan that drew the cart to a halt. He let the young lovers have several minutes to compose themselves, and then he addressed Michael who by now was so energized, he probably could have unharnessed the cart horse and pulled the wagon all the way to the brewery on his own.

Immediately after the long embrace, Michael reached into the pocket of his long coat and produced the length of blue ribbon that he had tied to the iron bars on the prisoner transport cart to let his rescuers know that he was inside. He explained to Sarah that it was his symbol of freedom and more importantly his constant reminder of the love he had for her. Sarah took the ribbon and tied it into her hair, promising as she did that she would never be without it.

It had been almost four months since Michael and Sarah had seen one another. His rescuers had insisted that Michael make no attempt to see Sarah in case the police were having her watched, and Rostan strongly enforced his belief that they would be. Sarah's father was a vengeful man, and he blamed Michael for all that had happened to his daughter. Rostan informed Michael that there was a reward posted for his capture by Mr. Thomlin, and he had made it clear to all who would listen that he did not care what condition Michael Denny was in when the captors came to collect the bounty.

Michael and Sarah had been in touch with one another by letter. Because Rostan was not part of the family circle, he reckoned that he would be of no interest to the police and far less likely to be followed, so he agreed to pick up and deliver the love letters written by the pair to one another. The fact that Rostan had retired himself from the police force also meant that he had plenty of free time which the others definitely did not. He arranged to meet Sarah Thomlin once weekly, when she, as part of her work with her father, had to deliver letters of guarantee to the bank. Sarah had been handling the banking for her father for over twelve months, and while he insisted that she be accompanied at first, she saw no need for a bodyguard and was soon able to do all that was required on her own.

The pair met in Phillips Park near to the bank. Sarah had suggested the meeting place because the park had been lobbied into existence by Mr. Mark Phillip, a local MP and friend of the family. The park was new. It had just been set out on thirty-one acres of land purchased by council from the owner Mrs.

Hoghton. Bounded on one side by the Medlow River, it is one of the oldest municipal parks in the UK.

Mr. Phillips hoped the parklands, three of which were opened on the same day, would become a meeting place for all classes, and it was his wish that people should better understand and care for one another. Mark Phillips had spread the word to all who would listen to use the park to ensure its permanence.

Phillips was aware of the constant street fighting among rival youth gangs, and he wanted these designated areas to be used for games and sport. What he was doing allowed the birth of all team and individual sports to be enjoyed by the commonfolk where previously these activities only took place in privileged schools. He encouraged the games of the elite to be played by all.

Sarah could see the tremendous benefits of such a meeting place, and so it was that she chose this place.

Rostan always allowed Sarah to find a spot to sit while he would stand some distance away, ensuring that she was not being followed. Sarah would hit Rostan with a barrage of questions about how Michael was faring. "Was he talking to any other girls? Does he say he still loves me? Is he eating enough?"

Rostan assured her that all was well with Michael but also made sure that he did not tell her where Michael was staying, and he had insisted that Michael not tell her but now that they had met, it was becoming more urgent to relocate the pair to somewhere safe before they allowed their love for one another to lead them both into trouble.

Rostan knew he could not keep the pair apart any longer, so he suggested a plan that would allow them to disappear and get on with their lives together. He had visited an old friend in London, and it was agreed that Michael and Sarah would elope to that big city where they would not be known and hence their safety far more secure than if they were to remain anywhere near Manchester.

Since the murder of Benny Connelly, John Rostan had firmed up a friendship with the man who was instrumental in his salvation following the cruel demise of Benny. Rostan was overcome with guilt after he had meted out such terrible retribution on Benny. He found himself considering the only black option he believed open to him. There was, however, one person who could place himself in Rostan's shoes, and that was the Captain. The man who ran the guesthouse where Benny Connelly had savagely beaten young Maggie Dorn prior to murdering Roger Earls. The man who had admitted to killing eleven men, all according to the law of the sea, during his time as a ship's captain. He had faced similar torment of his own, and he could see that Rostan was struggling with his own conscience.

"You only did what the law would have done to that evil bastard. You made a judgment, and I tell you straight that no man in the land would condemn you for what took place here except for the lad's father, but that is proper. You should not take a bad stance on this," was how the Captain slowly convinced Rostan that what he did was just.

Rostan had stayed several times at the Maggie and the Captain guesthouse when he had to visit London, given that his family home had been sold after the death of his parents. The guesthouse was prospering well under the strong arm of the Captain and the shrewd management of the delightful Maggie Dorn.

Maggie had completely recovered from the injuries she had sustained at the hands of Benny Connelly. Her indomitable spirit had returned to full strength, and no guest who stayed at the Maggie and the Captain guesthouse left without having a grand experience, and all patrons promised to return and to recommend the premises to their associates.

The renovations that had begun around the same time as Benny Connelly stayed with his friend, Malcolm McDonald, at the guesthouse were almost completed, and the co-owners, the Captain and Maggie, were able to charge new guests more money for the rooms, but Maggie insisted that six rooms on the lower floor be kept at a low rate per night and that multiple occupancy be allowed in those rooms to cater for the men who had kept the business afloat when the premises was in a very poor state.

On one of his visits, Rostan had explained to the Captain the trouble that Michael Denny had found himself in and how he and his betrothed needed to get as far away from Manchester as possible. In earlier times, the Captain would have been less receptive to the plight of the two young lovers, but since Maggie Dorn had arrived on the scene, he had mellowed. His granddaughter had given him a renewed reason to live, and when he saw that his friend Rostan genuinely wanted to help the young couple, he immediately offered to assist.

Rostan had good reason to take the pressure off himself with regard to Michael and Sarah. He needed to free up his time because there were two problems he deemed needed his attention. He knew that Angela Denny would never be safe until the dilemma regarding the land deed that had caused all the trouble, because of the reward that had been offered by the young marquis for its return, had been resolved.

Rostan knew that the gypsies had the deed because it was with the ruby that was stolen from St. Michael's Church on the night that Garrett was stabbed to death by Solomon Leyman. Solomon was the key to the reward being paid, but with him being dead, the gypsies were at a loss as to how to collect the money. They knew that if they approached the marquis directly, they would be putting gypsy lives in danger, and Manfri as the new king had forbidden anyone to take action until a better plan could be made.

CHAPTER FORTY TWO

Four months had passed since Michael had escaped, and of course, it was during that daring venture that the explosive rigged to blow open the rear door of the prison cart had so badly damaged Manfri's left hand that it had to be amputated.

Rostan wanted to see an end to the problem that was caused when Granny left her estate to Angela Denny. The land deed ownership had to be sorted out, and he decided to take the matter in hand. He journeyed by horse to the gypsy camp and asked to see Agnes. He did this deliberately because he knew that Agnes felt she owed him a positive consideration because he had rescued Angela Denny alone. Agnes had pleaded with him not to risk the lives of the family men that would surely have offered to help with her rescue. Agnes greeted him warmly and agreed to do all that was in her power to help. She then insisted that Rostan take up the matter with Manfri and led him to his wagon. Rostan knew that Manfri had to have his hand amputated and was at a loss as to what to say. When he and Agnes entered the wagon, Manfri was seated at a table, playing cards with two other men. The first thing Rostan noticed as he entered was Manfri reaching forward to drag the cards he had just been dealt toward him with the aid of a silver hook that had been fitted to replace his missing left hand. The hook was instantly recognizable. It was the same finely crafted piece of artwork that had been worn by his father, Garrett.

Rostan was not sure just how well he would be received by Manfri. It was, after all, John Rostan who had enlisted the expertise of Manfri to blow apart the lock that led to the loss of his hand.

As he saw Rostan enter the wagon, he rose immediately and moved toward the retired policeman and shook his hand. "I am greatly surprised that you have taken so long to come and see me. We have business to do, you and I, do we not?" Manfri's tone was calm and measured. "If you are troubled about what happened to me, please do not be. It was an accident of my own creation. But Rostan, look at me now. I always loved my father, and here I am wearing a constant reminder of the man who helped save our gypsy soul. Since the Black Madonna has been brought back to life, our community has been blessed many times over. Our young people seem to have turned their backs on the gang life that they were chasing. Several couples have asked to be married. We have four of our fine women with child and due soon. Your friend Matthew has arranged work for eight of our young men on the rail line, and he visits on the odd occasion with sweeties for the wee-ens. Young Angela, the poor lass who was stolen from her family, visits with several of her friends on Sunday afternoons to help some of our young folk to read. She tells them stories of a grand lady that she once knew, and she calls her Granny. Her stories of Granny are beautiful but just stories. Sure the children love her though."

Rostan, realizing that Manfri was in a far better frame of mind than he had imagined, addressed him more directly than he had originally planned. "Manfri, I am pleased that you are faring so well. I am not going to beat about the bush with you. I am simply here to ask you to help me secure the safety of the young lady that comes here to help with reading. The young lady that you say was stolen. Yes, Angela, the storyteller, and Manfri, I am pleased to tell you that the Granny in her stories is no made-up character, she was indeed real. Manfri, do you have the land deed that was stolen along with the heart of the Black Madonna from St. Michael's Church?"

Manfri knew exactly the item that Rostan was referring to and very quickly replied, "We do hold the deed. We know that there was a grand reward on offer for its return to some marquis in France. We also know that the man who was handling the payment of the reward was the same man who stole the girl and was butchered for his trouble."

"Can I stop you there please?" asked Rostan. "I know who the deed has to be returned to. It was said by Solomon Leyman, the kidnapper, that the marquis that you refer to does not care who is hurt or even killed so long as he gets the title deed back. There is one problem with all he proposes. The land referred to in the deed is not his. It truly belongs to Angela Denny, the young lady that visits your camp, and it was given to her by the Granny in her stories, and her name was Louisa DuBois."

After a short pause for effect, Rostan continued. "I believe that anyone trying to deal with the marquis will surely end up dead. Manfri, I have a plan that will put good money in everybody's pocket, but to make it work, I must have the deed, and you must trust me to work alone."

Manfri hastened his reply. "If all that you say is true about this marquis person, why would you risk your own life in dealing with such a man?"

"I will do it for my friends" was the reply that Rostan offered, and Manfri could see the determination in his eyes.

"I know you are a good man, and I agree to let you have the deed. As you say, we don't know this marquis, so if you are able to make the girl safe and see that we gypsies get some money for our trouble, then everybody wins, surely they do?"

Manfri insisted that Rostan sit in at the card game, and after relieving him of ten pounds and three shillings, the gypsy king handed over the deed and bid him a safe farewell.

Agnes escorted Rostan to the edge of the gypsy camp and wished him luck. "You are the strangest man that I have ever known, Mr. Rostan. I could see that you deliberately let Manfri and his friends win your money, and you took pleasure in losing. You made yourself look vulnerable, but I know that you are no such thing. Instead of fearing you, those men now think you are a bit soft. You have disarmed them in the quietest way. Just what do you intend to do with the deed?"

"Agnes, all I can tell you is that I am going to France. I have a plan, but I think it best that I keep it to myself."

Prior to leaving for Paris, Rostan had arranged to obtain a letter of authority from Angela Denny. Correctly signed and witnessed, this letter would allow Rostan to act for Angela regarding any dealings he could initiate on her behalf regarding the land deed.

Rostan had the good fortune to have worked with one of Paris's best detectives when he was stationed in London. Allain Batteux was a dominant figure working for law enforcement in Paris.

Batteux first met John Rostan when he had occasion to be in London to take over custody of a man wanted in France who was being held by Rostan in the London gaol. The French and English police forces had combined efforts to apprehend this criminal who was accused of grand theft and assault against a shop assistant resulting in that man being no longer able to walk.

Rostan recalled his introduction to Batteux with a smile.

The man presented as a proper dandy, and although Rostan had been told what to expect, he was taken aback, somewhat, all the same. He saw in front of him a man whom he judged to be over-stylish and, after their first brief conversation, considered him to be self-absorbed. Batteux was six years younger than the man giving him the once-over. He was thin and stood a good few inches shorter than Rostan, but that only made him of average height, and that is where average stopped. He had a dark complexion, and his eyes were a disarming light brown. He wore his wavy hair long, and it was as black as pitch. His ears protruded, and the long hair helped to cover the issue. He wore a cut-down top hat tilted to the right as it sat on his head. The suit he was wearing was like nothing Rostan had seen before. It had been beautifully tailored to fit tightly, and the lapels of the top coat were narrow in total contrast to all the wide-cut lapels worn by the gentlemen of London. He wore a tortoise-shell rimmed monocle that sat perfectly in place in front of his right eye. Rostan was fascinated by the way this eyepiece sat there because it seemed that Batteux did not display any of the usual squints that other men seemed to be continually contorting to when their monocles were pressed into place. A well-waxed moustache sat perfectly in place, and in fact, it did not look real.

On first observation, Rostan actually thought to himself, *This person before me does not look real,* and he had good reason to think that way. He had seen wax figures in Madame Tussaud's museum in London with skin that appeared to give off the same appearance as Batteux's face did. There were no blemishes, no wrinkles. There was an unrealness to his countenance. He had a presence that made Rostan feel uncomfortable without actually being able to pinpoint why.

Rostan did not judge the man on observation alone, and once he got to know him, he realized that Batteux was very proud of his achievements and certainly took his position as law keeper very seriously.

"Sir, my name is Allain Batteux, and as you have already been made aware, I am a detective working for the Surete in Paris. This is my first visit to your dirty town, and I do not intend to return to Paris immediately. I have arranged to stay in a hotel nearby so that I can get a better understanding of how you people do things here. Your police force has been in place for a long time whereas the Surete, sir, was born in 1827 and has much to learn. Would you be able to tell me how and show me how you people get things done over here? And another thing, sir. Why is it that the English police force calls itself Scotland Yard?"

Rostan had already been told by his superiors that he would be expected to do as Batteux asked, so he immediately got to work, and so began a most unusual friendship.

Unlike Batteux, Rostan had taken the time to find out exactly what the Surete was and what kind of men made up its numbers. He smiled unnoticeably when Batteux mentioned the infancy of his Surete when, if he had bothered to find out, he would have been informed that Scotland Yard was two whole years younger than the Surete. So much was obvious but simply overlooked by the cocky Frenchman. Scotland Yard simply referred to Great Scotland Street where the police station was situated. The most interesting facts regarding the Surete, as far as Rostan was concerned, was that it was formed to run independently to the Paris police force. He also found out that the detectives of the Surete worked undercover, and this aspect excited Rostan who by now realized that he himself derived an unhealthy pleasure from dangerous situations, and so he was keen to find out more. The most astonishing fact that came to light, however, was that many of the now-twenty-plus detectives working for the Surete were, in fact, reformed criminals. Rostan had decided that he would have to find out whether Batteux was one of those reformed criminals.

The two men spent a considerable amount of time together before Batteux returned to Paris with his prisoner. Rostan did find out directly from Batteux that he had spent five years in gaol for forgery and fraud and felt extremely blessed to have been offered the position he now held and that was all down to his good behavior in gaol.

The two men had been involved in four other cases and would write to one another whenever either party deemed he had some new information regarding police work to pass on. On one occasion, Rostan visited Paris and got to see Batteux's Surete team in action. His behavior was at odds with that of his cohorts, and one day while Rostan was talking to one of the Parisian detectives, he was given a clear understanding of why Batteux behaved the way he did.

"Our friend Batteux lives in a different world all of his own creation. You may be aware of a very popular book written by Charles Batteux. The book is thought to be a great work, and as far as I can make out, it helps the reader to understand fine arts. He keeps a copy on his desk. His claim to fame. The book is titled *Les beaux-arts reduits a un meme principe*, you can see it there on his desk. It is a book only a lofty scholar would read, but I believe it is why our Batteux puts on such airs and graces. God, man, the thing is nearly one hundred years old. I have asked our Batteux if the author is a relative, and I have to say that he has never actually claimed that to be so. Because

Batteux behaves like a member of the Paris elite, he has been accepted into that society, and in doing so, he does wonderful police work among their numbers. I know he was left some money, and that has allowed him to take up residence in a beautiful apartment that overlooks the Seine. He is most odd but gets great results. You don't have to like a man to admire him."

Rostan had got over the "like" opposition because he found it far easier than most when it came to understanding people who were different.

When Rostan let Allain Batteux know that he was coming to Paris on business, Batteux insisted that Rostan should stay with him. Rostan wanted to enlist the aid of Batteux in some way to help him with the mission he had taken on. That of resolving the problem with the young marquis and the land deed that he now had in his possession.

When Rostan arrived at the apartment his friend was living in, he couldn't believe the opulence on show. He understood from what he had been told about Batteux that he would have a taste for fine things, and although he acknowledged within himself that he was no judge of quality in art, he did at least have some basic information to go on. His deceased friend, Roger Earls, had a great eye for beauty in objects, and Rostan had learned much from him.

"My god, man, your home is beautiful, or perhaps I should say magnificent. Is this all yours? Oh, please excuse my bad manners, but I have never been in a home so grand. You must really enjoy what you have accomplished here, my friend," said Rostan apologetically.

"I am a lucky man indeed. I had two maiden aunts who died four and five years ago. They left me a small fortune, and because we Batteux's have appreciation of fine things running through our veins, what you see before you mostly came to me from their mansions after I had sold them. It does look a bit like a museum, and I do intend to thin things out by selling off some of the lesser items, but my problem is that every time I try to select an item to be auctioned, I can see nothing that I would consider to be lesser." Batteux chuckled at his own humor.

"I am a fortunate man," said Batteux. "I grew up surrounded by beautiful things. My father was a master cabinet maker and timber worker. He had his own workshop and received commissions from far and wide to produce pieces of furniture for those people who could afford his considerable charges. His reputation was such that quite often he was paid in full for the orders even before he had cut the first piece of timber or planed the first board. His favorite cabinet timber was rosewood, and it is still very popular here in Paris. He would organize imports of large quantities of this divine wood to come in from Brazil, and indeed, I once traveled with him to South America to inspect the quality of the product before he placed his largest order.

"He told me once that he believed if he could create a piece so fine that families would keep it forever, handing it down to following generations, then the tree it was made from never really dies. It could live on. His skills were unmatched, and like his trees, I thought my father would live on forever, but his god took that dream from me so cruelly that I can no longer bring myself to follow the faith of my father and the thought of that makes me sad.

"My father died alone in a muddy laneway not far from here. He was beaten and robbed for what probably would have amounted to a few lousy francs. The doctor seemed to think that the assailant kicked him so hard directly into his heart as he laid on the ground, it simply exploded. He died at the age I am now. Thirty-six years.

"That desk over there, that I use as my own, is the only reminder that I have of his workmanship. When I was old enough, he insisted that I help him in his workshop. He wanted me to become his apprentice, and I would have wanted for nothing more, but alas, my dexterity and his were poles apart, and try as hard as I could, I was all thumbs. Even today, I cannot sharpen a pencil without making a mess of it."

Rostan thought of his own father and the patience he had shown while dealing with his son's troubled younger years. "Fathers and sons, Batteux. The stories told. The books written. Just like your father's trees. It will be so forever. A continuum is what it is. And as it has to, faith just comes and goes." Rostan spoke just loud enough to be heard as he walked over to the beautifully finished desk, gently sliding his fingers across its surface and thought to himself, *My fingers are skating on glass.*

Rostan only had a vague mental outline of how he was going make the marquis pay for his cruelty. He had decided that the kidnap and assault of Angela Denny had to be avenged. Garrett indirectly died because of the same man, and an old lady had lived in fear of him for years.

Rostan told Batteux the whole sad story and then asked if he was able to help resolve the matter. While Rostan was explaining his plight, Batteux had poured out two glasses of wine. He had asked Rostan to be seated, and by the end of the tale, the two men were well into the third bottle of red happiness.

Batteux did not respond to Rostan's request immediately; rather, he seemed to be formulating a plan of his own. He stood up and walked toward the window that afforded him a sweeping vista of the beautiful Seine river and Paris beyond.

"You say this villain lives in Marseille. You do realize that the Surete does not have jurisdiction in that area? I know you well enough to know that you are well-aware that we have no authority there. Would it be that you are asking me to do something that is not altogether legal, my friend? No need to answer that. Of course you are. Well, I would like to show the land deed in question to some friends of mine because I have some tricks up my sleeve that just may allow us to stay within the bounds of the law.

"I have been invited to one of the regular parties that my friends often throw, and I have told them that an associate will be accompanying me. So how do you feel about mingling with some of the elite of Paris? These occasions are not for the fainthearted, but I am sure you will enjoy the spectacle," said Batteux with even further affectation to his tone.

"Yes, indeed," Rostan replied. "I would be delighted to join you, but I have to say that I have no idea as to how one should behave in the company of the elite."

"Oh, that problem, if indeed it is one, has a simple solution, John. We arrive suitably late to join the company so that they are all the merrier for the drink, and believe me, the champagne flows by the gallon. Their finesse drops dramatically within the first hour. Now you must not mention that we are detectives. These people think I make my money by dealing in the trade of buying and selling fine arts. I think you should be a mill owner, but be vague about details. They will be paying you no attention anyway." Batteux was pacing the floor by this stage, and it was obvious that he was getting very excited at the prospect of the upcoming skullduggery.

"Just who are these friends that you think will be able to help us with a plan?" asked Rostan.

"Two of the best lawyers in Paris," answered Batteux. "They are good men, and I often find myself having to change some of my court times to avoid them discovering just who I am. Fortunately, my commander appreciates the crime I am able to uncover among some of the most highly thought of members of Paris's high society, so he allows other officers to run my cases in court, and that means that I am seldom there, but as I have just said. I always have to be careful. Some of the crime I have discovered is very serious, involving large amounts of money, and my life has often been in danger. The two friends I speak of are brothers and have their own law office. They specialize in land titles, and the deed that you hold will be something they will be very familiar with.

"The party is two nights from now, and I think I will buy you a new suit just for the occasion." Batteux poured the last of the wine and then added. "John, you have been a good friend to me, but more importantly, you have taught me so much about my chosen profession. To begin with, in England and subsequent to that, with all the advice you gave in the letters you have written over the years. I owe you much, so please let me do this small thing for you."

"Do I really need a new suit?" asked Rostan. "Surely I don't look that out of place?"

"You do, and yes, you really do," replied Batteux with his exaggerated laugh.

Rostan found himself well-rested by the next morning when, at seven o'clock, Batteux knocked on his door asking John to join him for breakfast. Batteux knew how to live well, and the breakfast he had just prepared for his friend was sumptuous. Bacon, eggs, cheeses, sausages, and croissants. As Rostan feasted, he picked up a croissant and just had to ask, "What on earth is this, my friend?"

"Of course, you English would not know the like. You have to admit that we French lead the world when it comes to fine food, and what you are holding there is a croissant. Maybe twenty years from now, some British chefs may be brave enough to serve some of these delights to you backward folk over there. Oh, excuse my forwardness. You do have such people as chefs in your cloudy city, don't you? Most people you meet would tell you that the croissant is a French-designed pastry, but as you know, I am a man who knows all about the finer arts, and alas, I will have to give Mr. August Zang, originally from Vienna, full credit for the creation of the mouthwatering treat you have before you. He opened his Boulangerie Viennoise at 92 rue de Richelieu here in Paris several years ago. Something else I feel I should add about this great man. He was the entrepreneur who

347

commenced the printing of the *Viennese Daily*. I make a point of knowing such things."

After what Batteux described as the "matutinal repast" had been enjoyed by both men, the host insisted that Rostan be escorted by him to his tailor.

"You may find Phillipe Sartre, my tailor, a little strange, but I can assure you that he is the finest creator of suits that I have ever come across. I need to know who I am dealing with, as you can appreciate, so I took it upon myself to find out what I could about him, and as good as I am at digging up information regarding certain people, I have to admit that I was unable to unearth anything about the man who calls himself Mr. Sartre. Given that his surname is merely a play on the word tailor, I suspect that he is play acting and that he has a past he would rather people not know about. He calls his business Sartre and Son, but I have never seen the son. He employs women to do the stitching and sewing, but it seems that he has no wife, or at least that is what I have concluded after several conversations where he has avoided discussing anything of a personal nature," explained Batteux.

Rostan had been measured for clothing in the past, uniforms and such, but never had the process been so thorough, and he found himself agreeing with Batteux. *Sartre is an odd chap,* he thought to himself, *but he was easy to like*. Rostan felt very awkward throughout the procedure, but Sartre kept a conversation moving along that helped to markedly ease his embarrassment.

Sartre laid several bolts of material on the shop counter to allow Rostan to choose the pattern and quality of cloth for his new suit.

"No, no, no, and again I say no, Sartre. None of those will do," Batteux exploded with enthusiasm and went straight to a roll of beautiful material, still on the shelf, that he had already decided would be the one.

"Mr. Batteux, you have expensive taste indeed. The roll you have chosen is the most costly in my shop. Are you s—" Sartre was cut off mid-sentence.

"Nothing but the best for my good friend here," shouted Batteux. "You see, he is from London where the people dress as drably as their miserable weather, and I feel it is my duty to send him home looking as bright as a Paris summer morning. He is a good man. He owns a cotton mill but sadly has no taste when it comes to the finer things. Now, Sartre, I know this is short notice, but I will make it worth your while if my friend's suit can be ready by tomorrow afternoon. Will that be a problem?"

"The timing is tight, Mr. Batteux, but for you, being such a good customer, I am sure my ladies and I will fill your request with time to spare in case any small adjustments need addressing. I do believe that I have never had the honor of providing my services to a man of such large proportions. If, sir," Sartre looked at Rostan as he spoke, "you can return to me at three o'clock tomorrow afternoon, we can accommodate a fitting that will allow me to make sure that you have free movement with the jacket on."

With the formalities gladly over and done, Sartre asked one of the seamstresses to set out three glasses on the shop counter and asked the two gentlemen to join him for a drink of cognac.

"Sorry, Sartre, I have work to do," Batteux excused himself, but Rostan agreed to stay and told Batteux that he would find his own way home.

Sartre finished his drink quickly and apologized to Rostan. "I must start your order sir, or it will not be finished in time."

"Please go ahead, but would you allow me to observe just how it all happens?" asked Rostan.

Sartre nodded his affirmation and pulled a stool over to the front counter where he then asked Rostan to be seated.

The observer sat there for over an hour, watching Sartre draw chalk lines and cut the cloth with such skill. Tacking stitches were placed with what seemed to be such ease. Sartre spoke with Rostan the whole time, but as Batteux had forewarned him, Rostan was not able to lure the tailor into any discussion with regard to family.

By the time he had left the tailors small premises, Rostan's spirits had been lifted. He had been made to feel special.

CHAPTER FORTY THREE

Rostan arrived on time for his three o'clock fitting with the tailor on the following day, but the man he met the previous day was not the man who was clumsily caring for him now. The same person, yes, but something was well out of order.

The steady hand that had so carefully cut and stitched the previous morning was barely able to hold a needle. Sartre was visibly upset, and despite his efforts at bravado, he was physically shaking, and his mind was certainly not on the job at hand.

Rostan had been involved with criminals and victims far too long not to recognize fear when he saw it. He did not question Sartre's demeanor, he simply hoped that if the tailor needed help, he might feel comfortable enough to ask, but then Rostan remembered that the trembling man before him believed him to be a mill owner. Not anyone he could turn to for real help.

"Please, Mr. Rostan, could you kindly take your new suit to the fitting room over there, and try it on. We will see if the fit is good, and if so, then you can be on your way."

Rostan did as he was asked and walked to the rear of the small shop where he found the fitting room hidden away behind shelves stacked high with rolls of material. He proceeded to undress and began to put on the new garments. The trousers fitted perfectly. The jacket, he thought, was a bit snug. Rostan had worried that the cloth chosen by Batteux would be far too loud, too gaudy, but when he saw the end product, he was positively delighted and remembered a term used often by Roger Earls: "What sartorial splendor do we have here," and of course, as he said it to himself, he remembered Batteux saying that the tailor's name Sartre was a wordplay.

Rostan quickly snapped out of his musings when he heard raised voices coming from the front of the shop. "I cannot pay you any more money. You have taken all I have. I have wages to pay. Goods to buy, and rent on top of all of that," Sartre was shouting, and he sounded terrified.

"God damn you, man, you will pay more when I say to pay more. Get the money from your family, and if you don't, their name will be shamed along with yours," yelled a scruffy, rough-looking man standing menacingly close to Sartre.

Rostan had reentered the shop and was heading for the front counter when he saw that the man who was yelling the demands had drawn back his fist and was about to deliver Sartre a hefty blow to the face. Rostan rushed forward, and with one quick fluid motion, he struck the attacker in the kidney area, and the man crumpled to the floor. A second offender had entered the shop to help his associate, and by the time he realized the size of his opponent, it was too late to turn and run. Rostan struck him fair on the chin, and he joined his companion writhing in agony at Rostan's feet.

"Just what is going on here?" demanded Rostan.

"I cannot, no, I will not explain, Mr. Rostan. Let me just tell you that these men know some details from my past that would ruin my name if it became common knowledge. I am from a good catholic family, sir, and most of my customers are catholic. I will just have to continue paying them whatever I can afford. My mother would die of the shame, and I know that my father would no longer allow me to visit him on the family estate if rumors were spread. I beg you, sir," pleaded Sartre.

Rostan's thoughts immediately took him to Transbridge. "I don't need to hear any more. What these men are doing to you is called blackmail or, to give it its original name, reditus nigri. It is a criminal offence, Sartre, and these men will go to gaol. You must have them charged. I will be a witness, and you will have no more trouble from them."

"You don't understand, sir. I can do nothing to them. They can ruin me." Sartre was sobbing, and John Rostan found himself consoling his tailor. He held him as he shook. Both men felt more than simple consolation.

The two blackmailers were beginning to get to their feet, and as each one rose, Rostan took them to the shop door and sent them sprawling to the hard pavement with one kick each from his sizable right boot.

"I live nearby, and Mr. Sartre here is a dear friend. If I see either of you anywhere near his shop or his home, believe me, sirs, I will not kill you, but you will wish I had." Rostan's venom spewed out so thick it could have been spread on bread.

"I don't know how to thank you, Mr. Rostan. Do you think they will stay away," asked Sartre with obvious doubts.

"Firstly, Phillipe, if I may call you Phillipe, no more Rostan. Please call me John. I promise you that I will make it my business to be seen several times each day for one week near to this shop. If the men are watching, this will surely put them off. Secondly, I have a friend in the Paris police force. I am going to find out whether my friend knows either of these gentlemen. Maybe he can help you, and thirdly, I will simply tell him that they were demanding money but mention nothing of their threats to damage your reputation. We will simply call it a robbery."

With everything going on, the two men had completely forgotten the two ladies who worked for Sartre and had hidden themselves in the fitting room during the melee. One woman had plucked up the courage to reappear and was already pouring out two glasses of cognac.

"Please, my dear ladies, pour yourselves a large drink each also and be so kind as to join us," said Sartre who had stopped shaking.

"I do have one more favor to ask, Phillipe, if I may," said Rostan.

"Anything, John, just ask away," said Sartre.

"Do you think you could possibly reattach this sleeve?" Rostan replied with a wry smile.

The day had been a wild one, and Rostan, knowing that Batteux would not be at his apartment, went directly to the offices of the Surete where he found Batteux busy delving into a mound of paper that was becoming one of the biggest cases he had ever worked on.

"How did the fitting go, my friend?" asked Batteux.

"Very well indeed, and I must thank you for the introduction to Phillipe," replied Rostan, "although I feel I should tell you of the afternoon's events," and he proceeded to lay out the whole unhappy episode.

"Could you describe the two men to me? Was there anything about them that made them stand out?" asked Batteux.

"Indeed there was. The man who went to strike Phillipe had the sole on his right boot raised by two inches with the addition of extra leather, and he walked with quite a limp. The fellow with him called him Caliban, and he could easily have been the son of Shakespeare's witch. Now this second fellow was Chinese-looking and wore his hair in that hanging tail look that they all have," replied Rostan.

"Quite the score, my friend," offered Batteux, "I know of both these criminals. What you see before you is the immense file that I am compiling, hoping I will bring those two and at least ten other thugs to face our courts and have them all pay for their cruelty. They are an organized gang, and I know for a fact that they are simply the soldiers that do the dirty work, but I am quite convinced that they get their information and instructions from a catholic priest. He is a Spaniard who goes by the name of Father Francisco. He lives here in Paris and works in the Basilica of the Sacred Heart situated on Montmartre. I have suspected for some time that he is carrying out his own inquisition and making considerable amounts of money at the same time. I have to be very careful when it comes to any accusations made against the church, but there is one bishop here that has agreed to listen to what I have to say, and if I have a strong enough case, he has agreed to attend to the matter. I need him with me, but I suspect that the priest will only be moved elsewhere and his whole scheme will simply be relocated with him. I have decided that once the bishop has agreed to act, I will then ask that the Paris police arrest the culprit, and hopefully, he and the gang members will face court."

"Well, good luck with that Batteux," said Rostan, "but I think you know that the church will have the last say in the matter. If something similar was to happen in sunny England, I know for sure that no priest would face the courts, catholic or not."

"Indeed, we will have to wait and see how the cards fall, John," said Batteux, "but tell me now how does your suit fit? And, oh yes, a letter has arrived for you. It is on my desk, and it must be urgent because the writer has paid extra money to ensure quick delivery."

CHAPTER FORTY FOUR

Rostan opened the letter and went straight to the bottom of the page to find out just who had written it. It was signed Colleen Denny, but a notation beside the signature explained that the letter had been dictated by her to Father McCordy of St. Michael's.

It had been quite some time since Rostan had heard of any news from his friends back in Salford. He had spent months with Michael Denny and Sarah Thomlin in London at the Captain's guesthouse. He wanted to make sure that they had truly settled in and were living quietly so as to avoid bringing any attention upon themselves by the police.

Rostan knew that the families would have many questions, but the situation with the young couple had to be sorted out, and it had to be legal. They were living together as man and wife because that is exactly what they were. Rostan knew that the legal age for a boy to marry at the time was fourteen years of age without parental permission, and girls only had to have twelve years, again without parental permission. The age had been set at twenty-one years but was lowered in 1823 simply due to the fact that young couples were pairing off under age and the government of the time needed to tidy things up.

Fearing future family fallout, the Captain had persuaded a Catholic priest, who was a friend, to marry the couple, and then he had arranged for the ceremony to be repeated in a nearby Protestant parish by an Anglican clergyman. Maggie Dorn was delighted at the prospect of two weddings, and she was asked to be bridesmaid at both services.

The young married couple had not much money between them, but Maggie Dorn was not going to let that stop them having at least one reception, and so with the help of Malcolm McDonald, she and the Captain made sure that the newlyweds were given a celebration to remember.

The letter began with some very sad news.

"Mr. Rostan, I feel I have to let you know that Grace Connelly died at Finbar Denny's home several days ago. She was so poorly when she first arrived in Salford, but she was getting better. Poor Joseph Connelly was by her side tending to her wounds and trying to bathe her, but after some good signs, she started to become sicker, and despite all his efforts, she died one night in her sleep. Joseph was sleeping beside her throughout the night and held her close to keep her warm. He told us that he knew she was gone some time early in the morning because she turned so cold, but he couldn't stop holding her. He said he prayed. He prayed so hard.

"Poor Joseph has not really settled here in Salford, and my Matthew is concerned that he is drinking too much. His three children, Paul, Josephine, and Ellen, are all working so they have money. Poor Finbar does not want them to leave his home because he fears for his friend and what might happen to him if he continues to behave the way he has been.

"I have tried to encourage Joseph to come to Mass at St. Michael's with me, but he seems to see no value in faith anymore.

"Please tell me what has happened to Michael and Sarah. Fin has heard nothing from his son and is worried for his safety. Young Angela has told her father that she wants to become a nun. After the ordeal of the kidnapping, she tried to be so brave. She was teaching the gypsy children to read and everything seemed to be going so well, but lately she has changed. Finbar thinks that since the kidnapping, she just wants to hide away somewhere. Her beautiful spirit has been broken. I hope you return home soon, John. You are very close to Joseph, and he really does need a good friend."

The letter ended with a scrawl and Father McCordy's signature.

Rostan recalled Joseph, the man of strong faith that had dealt with so much back in Transbridge where they first met. The death of his young daughter, Katherine. The tragic murder of Tess, his sister. The deaths of two of his daughters, Therese and Mary, due to the Great Hunger. The loss of the croft. The squaller of the Dublin docks. His son Benedict, the murderer and now the death of his once beautiful wife Grace. *No man on earth could blame him for abandoning his faith*, was the one and only thought that came from his pondering.

Rostan asked Batteux if he could be seated at his desk, and with permission granted, he immediately began writing his reply to Colleen. He told her that he expected his business in France would keep him away from England for at least another month. He did not give any indication as to how the land deed problem would be resolved, and if he spoke the truth, he really did not know how a resolution would be arrived at.

He added a letter within his letter to be given to Joseph Connelly in which he reminded his friend of how strong he was and asked him not to give up hope while promising that he would be home soon to help him regain the strength and see the light ahead.

CHAPTER FORTY FIVE

The evening of that most eventful day arrived far more quickly than Rostan had hoped for. He found himself dressing for Batteux's soiree and becoming more nervous as the minutes began to collide in quick succession.

"I speak very little French. I will know no one. I am the trout out of the pond," he said to Batteux. "Perhaps you should go on your own?"

"Stop being so disagreeable, John," said Batteux, slightly angrily. "You will meet some wonderful people. I am giving you a chance at an evening that, I promise you, you will never forget."

As previously decided, Batteux and Rostan arrived late for the party, and as Batteux had predicted, the majority of the guests were well on their way to the state of inebriation.

The party was being held in a grand mansion owned by one of Batteux's associates, and he had explained to Rostan that this man was a merchant banker. Batteux had also told Rostan that he was investigating the owner because he believed that the man was living well beyond his means.

"I have the ear of several prominent bankers who live here in Paris, and they all agree that it would be impossible to live in such lavish style if a person's sole income was from banking. They love to gossip, so I just fire the questions at them and they are very keen to oblige me with information that, I know, will see our generous host in gaol one day. And our host is very generous indeed. As you are about to bear witness to," stated Batteux.

Prior to arriving at the venue for the party, Rostan had tried to imagine just what the spectacle would look like, and he thought he had allowed for all the grandiosity possible, but he had to admit to himself that his mental musings fell well short of the reality that was confronting him.

Everything was catered for. He had not even thought to consider music, but there it was. A small orchestra consisting of ten virtuosos was providing the glorious sound that allowed many couples to glide across the polished timber floor as if they were skating on ice. The combination of violins, cello, mandolins, piano, and one man on percussion produced a magical sound but with the addition of one oboist Rostan imagined he was listening to music that only deserved to be played in heaven.

A team of three of Paris's best chefs was preparing an enormous amount of food items all delicately placed on either trays or trollies to be served by six waitresses to the awaiting guests. The hors d'oeuvres were, each and every one, a sumptuous work of art. Batteux warned Rostan to go easy on the first course because there was much more food to come, and as Batteux had preempted, champagne seemed to be the only drink on offer, and three spritely, well-chiseled young males were wafting about the ornate ballroom, making sure that every glass was constantly topped up.

Given that no one in the room was standing still, it was hard to count just how many people were in attendance. Rostan tried twice to arrive at an accurate figure but gave up and opted instead on an estimate of eighty, but possibly, ninety souls. Elegance of style and presentation seemed to be the order of the evening. The gentlemen were dressed formally but not to the extent of black tie. The ladies, on the other hand, had all gone to considerable lengths attempting to appear as though they had just stepped from the posters of the latest fashion printouts that adorned the walls of the many dress shops in Paris.

John quietly wished that Roger Earls could be having this experience with him. Roger would have appreciated the spectacular beauty that was on offer and would have spoken about it long after the last candle had burnt itself away.

The new suit caught many an eye, and the wearer found himself conversing freely with the merry company, most of whom had a far better understanding of his English than he did of their French. He caught up with Batteux who was mingling and thanked him for insisting that he should attend. "You are so correct, as always, my friend. I have not had such a good time in such a long time, and please accept my apology for being such a dreary Londoner."

"I knew you would have no trouble fitting in, John. You are very easy to get along with. It is just that you don't know it to be so," said Batteux. "Now let me introduce you to my two legal advisers. I have told them about you, and they have agreed to help with no charge as a favor to me. I was able to assist them in decorating their new offices with several fine pieces that I procured at a very reasonable price, so they insist on returning the good deed."

The two gentlemen that Batteux had spoken of were actually brothers, Louis and Edouard Lavigne, and Batteux had in fact taken it upon himself to tell them the whole story of the land deed or at least as much as he knew. He had done this the previous day, so Louis, armed with the deed number, had already been to the Paris Land Registry Le Cadastre and had verified that the deed in question was still in the name of Louisa "Granny" DuBois.

The introductions were made, but Rostan could see that the two wives of the young brothers were looking on impatiently as the pair began to talk options with regard to the deed.

"Gentlemen, gentlemen, please where are my manners," said Rostan. "These two beautiful young ladies look to be far better company than my friend, Batteux, and I. Now business is business and here is certainly not the place for seriousness. Your wives deserve your good company far more than I, so please let me know when I can meet with you at your office to discuss the matter at hand. Besides, Batteux here would not forgive me if I were to return to London without seeing how he has organized the decor of your new premises. I am seriously considering giving him an open budget to transform my own drab business offices into something more modern and eye-catching such as the suit I am wearing after he insisted that I desperately needed an upgrade."

The two young wives found themselves looking at Rostan and admiring the way he had just put their interests ahead of his own, something that just did not happen in Paris. As they moved away, he overheard one say to the other, in English, loud enough for him to discern, "Isn't he quite the darling?"

It was announced to the assemblage that the main course of the evening was about to be served, and with that announcement, two huge oak doors were drawn open to reveal the dining room which was half the size of the ballroom but still enormous.

The tables were set with sheening white cloths and silver cutlery. The porcelain dinnerware was of sublime quality. Each plate had been fired with beautiful hand-painted floral motifs and were edged in gold. The hand-engraved crystal wine glasses stood tall and proud. Huge platters held the food and had been covered over with dome-shaped silver lids to retain the heat within.

Rostan could not believe the vision and felt odd that it was the ornate candelabras that impressed him the most. He quietly thought that none of what he beheld could be seen without light and the candleholders did just that. He reckoned them to be the stars of the show. That thought was just momentary, but as Rostan thought on, it occurred to him that he had learned far more from Roger Earls than he had previously imagined.

The seating arrangements were not formalized, and guests were asked to sit where they pleased. Batteux, however, had been asked to sit to the left of the host, so Rostan simply moved around the room looking for a vacant chair. It was then that he spotted a late arrival.

"Would it be possible for me to sit next to you, John?" asked Phillipe Sartre with a wide smile.

Just when John Rostan thought that the evening could not be bettered, it was. He and Sartre chatted throughout the meal as though they had known one another all their lives.

Batteux seemed not to mind being ignored when the meal was over and all the guests had regathered in the ballroom to continue dancing and, of course, drinking. In fact, he was in his element. He enjoyed dancing, and every time Rostan caught sight of him on the dance floor, while he himself was still absorbed with the company of Sartre, Batteux was waltzing with a different woman each time.

As the evening wore on, the guests began to bid their fare thee wells to one another, and when Rostan realized that midnight had come and was long gone, he sought out Batteux to ask when they would be returning home.

"Oh, John, I am so sorry," he said. "I should have told you earlier. I won't be coming home directly. It seems that one of the fine young ladies who has graced me with her company on the dance floor this evening is in need of some help. She is recently divorced, poor pet, and tells me that she will have to sell off some expensive items of furniture to allow her to pay the lawyer who was able to secure her sole ownership of the family home. Usually the man ends up with it all, but it seems the husband was a well-known brute, and she had the ear of a very sympathetic judge. Anyway, I may not be home until the morning, so please, you and Sartre use my carriage to get home. I must say, I see similarities between yourself and the horse that draws my carriage, John, if I may say."

"Well, it seems you have said, Allain, but I can make no connection," replied Rostan to the strange remark.

"Oh, you must see it, John. You are both dark," and Batteux turned away, emitting one of his strangely affected laughs.

Chapter Forty Six

On the morning of the next day, it was true. Batteux had not returned home, and as Rostan prepared breakfast for himself, he hoped his friend had fixed a fair price for the furniture that he had offered to help sell. He also hoped that his friend had satisfied himself with the real reason he did not return home.

As arranged during the previous evening's festivities, Rostan found himself at nine o'clock on the following morning seated at the desk of Louis Lavigne, hoping to come up with a solution to the problem of the land deed. After filling in all the blanks that Batteux was unable to when he summarized the dilemma that Angela Denny was stuck with because of the will of Louisa DuBois, he found himself looking hopefully at the lawyer.

"Mr. Rostan," said Louis. "Firstly, let me congratulate you on the way you have presented the documentation we will need if we are able to do anything. We needed to establish that Angela

Denny does own the land, and the fact that you have presented the original will of Louisa DuBois to us along with the letter you obtained from the English judge confirming that the will is legal and correct, you have done that. The second letter that we have here stating that you have the power to sign documents on behalf of Angela Denny means that we do have options before us, but I must say, you may not like them."

"Well, Louis, I have not come this far to give up without considering the options no matter how poor they are, so please, tell me more," stated Rostan.

"The marquis has placed two caveats over the land deed in question. His lawyers have tried to be very cunning, but my brother and I both agree that if tested in court, neither of these caveats would be upheld. Miss Denny's proof of ownership is too strong," iterated the lawyer.

"Well, there we have it then, Louis. We can have the caveats lifted, and the land can be sold. Is that not so?" said Rostan enthusiastically.

"If only it were that simple, John. The lawyers for the marquis will be well-aware that the caveats will not be upheld, but it is the time it will take to have the whole case run through our court system that will be the main problem for you, John." It was Edouard Lavigne's turn to have a say. "The matter could be fought for months, John, and given what you have told us about this marquis, my brother and I fear that more good people back in England could be hurt."

"You said options, Louis. What would they be?" asked John decidedly crestfallen.

"You could deal directly with the marquis yourself. That is an option," offered Louis.

"If I were to see this animal, I expect I would kill him. The state young Angela was in when she was rescued was heartbreaking. I am hoping to raise enough money from the sale of the deed to allow Angela to buy a home for her family, but she has asked me to ensure that the sale brings in enough money to help her brother Michael and the Connelly family. If the land was sold fairly, without the marquis being so ruthless, I have verified that a genuine sale price could make all of Angela's dreams come true. If I am only able to deal with the marquis, he will want to pay a pittance of the true value." Rostan was looking worried.

"Edouard and I have a suggestion to make what we think will get you a far better price, and we have also allowed ourselves to dream up a plan that will vex the marquis to no end," said Louis at his turn.

"Please tell me all, gentlemen," said Rostan.

"My brother and I believe, in reality, that the marquis will want a quick sale, so we should offer him just that. If he needs the land to put in a road to provide access to other land that he owns, it would make sense that a quick sale would suit. He probably thinks that Angela can only deal with him because of the caveats, but what if another buyer should come forward? This marquis would surely have to be prepared to pay the better money. We propose that Angela Denny advise the marquis that her lawyers, Louis and I, have told her that the caveats are simply a ruse and she intends to have them lifted because she has been approached by a mill owner in Manchester, that would be you, John, who wants to buy her land so that he can have a base in Marseille to expand his business into. She will tell the marquis that this mill owner is desperate to have the land and has agreed to a fair price. Don't you see, John, by simply introducing another buyer, all the pressure is put back on the marquis."

"You have my head spinning, sirs, but I think you are on to something here. Just where do we start?" said Rostan whose mood had lifted considerably.

"Edouard has had a brilliant thought. We think you should travel to Marseille and, as openly as possible, let the authorities at the docks know that you are looking to buy the land we hold the deed for but ask if they know of any other land on offer. It will make our story all the more credible if we are able to place a real person at the waterfront asking all the right questions.

Now the next step in the plan is to try and arrange a meeting with the marquis. You can do this under the guise of possibly becoming his neighbor as he owns the adjoining land. There should be no suspicion created there, but it will really give strength to the story. If he does not agree to meet you, it is of no matter because he will get the message anyway." Louis then sat back looking very satisfied with himself.

"And this false buyer will be the vexation you mentioned," said Rostan.

"Oh no, no indeed. We have left the best till last," both brothers spoke in unison.

After the brothers had explained the vexation, John Rostan began to roar with laughter and was still laughing when he left the offices of Louis and Edouard Lavigne.

When Rostan caught up with Batteux that evening, back at his apartment, he told him of all that had happened between himself and the Lavigne brothers. Batteux was obviously under the influence, and as Rostan spied the empty wine bottle with a second only half empty, he poured himself a drink.

"Are we celebrating, my friend?" enquired Rostan.

Batteux's attitude and affectations slipped into well overdone as he declared. "Did I not tell you, John, that I would put you in touch with the greatest lawyers in Paris, and haven't I done just that? Now before you thank me, I have been giving some thought as to how we both should hurt Marquis de Maggot even more so, but this proposition does not have legality in its corner."

"I am not confident that the Marquis de Maggot, I like that, as you now call him, will fall for the plan that the brothers Lavigne have devised," said John. "He has proven himself to be a ruthless man, so it just might be that when I go to Marseille, you may never hear from me again. That being said, yes let us hurt him more. An attack on two fronts might just be what is needed to gain some satisfaction."

"You have told me that he has continued on with his father's business of marketing fine ornamentations, artworks, and furniture. Is that true and how do you know that to be the case?" queried Batteux.

"Before coming to Paris, I found out everything I needed to know about the Marquis de Maggot from a man named Solomon Leyman who had been sent by the marquis to retrieve the land deed. He was the animal who kidnapped young Angela. I was fortunate enough to be able to question him just prior to his death," answered Rostan with a judgmental tone.

Batteux was no man's fool. He knew immediately that the interrogation his friend was referring to was extracted by force.

"My father," explained Batteux, "had much to do with the port of Marseille when importing timber for his workshop. He would go there often to sign off on deliveries of timber, and sometimes he would take me with him. They were some of my best memories. We would take a coach to St. Jean de Losne on the Saone River south of Paris, and there we would board a riverboat that would take us into the Rhone River and on to Marseille. When everything was in order, the timber would be offloaded in Marseille and then loaded on to the riverboats, and we would travel with it back to St. Jean de Losne where it would be unloaded on to wagons and brought the last two hundred miles to Paris. My father estimated it to be a five hundred mile trip all together." Batteux was wandering along an alcohol created road of nostalgia, and Rostan needed a point to be made.

"Allain, do you have a plan, or shall we both wait until morning where a clear head might begin to make some sense?" quizzed John.

"No, no, and may I say no again," exclaimed Batteux, and he deliberately let his faultless monocle drop into his right hand. "I have good reason to want to do some dubious business with Marquis de Maggot, the son. You see, John, it was not I who conjured up that inglorious name because that credit should go to my dear father. He had the misfortune to trust the Maggot in a rather large business transaction. The marquis placed a substantial order through my father's business to produce many fine pieces of furniture to dress the appearance of ten extra rooms that he had built as an extension to his original Chateau de Maggot In Marseille.

"My father always insisted that a substantial part of the contract price be paid before the commencement of any work. The marquis was a bully of a man, and my father made the sad mistake of trusting the man and his word. One payment was made, but it was such a small amount. My father was committed, and so he had everything made as promised. The marquis insisted that his own men load on the finished pieces, tables, chairs, so many chairs, chiffoniers, credenzas, wine racks, bookcases, beautifully upholstered parlor and lounge suites. There was even a grand billiard table complete with ivory handled cues. The Maggot never paid my father the balance of the money he owed. He simply said that the goods were of poor standard, and he refused to pay.

"My father had the overheads of a factory to run. He had wages to pay. The upholsterers were paid separately. Families were not able to feed their children. There were so many people demanding money from my father. He sold off everything of value he owned just to try to pay his workers.

"He never recovered from the evil done to him by our friend the Maggot. I told you that he died after being beaten and robbed. That was a lie, John. I awoke one morning to the sound of a gunshot. I ran to my father's office and found him dead on the floor. He had taken his own life. He was a good man and maybe, just maybe, the Maggot might be made to pay back in some small way." On finishing, Batteux was uncorking yet another bottle of wine.

"Slow down please, Allain, or we will never make sense of this evening," said John. "Now what plan is it that you have in mind?"

"It is no small thing, John, and I will tell you some of the history of my plan."

Having spoken, Batteux drove the cork back into the bottle and proceeded to tell Rostan a most astonishing tale.

"I have always believed that I would make the Maggot pay one day, John, and it was while trialing my plan that I was arrested and charged with forgery and fraud leading to me being sentenced to five years in gaol. I was caught because I was not a very good forger, although my skills concerning fraud were described by the judge as most adroit, but I have to tell you, my friend, that after spending five years locked up, being mentored by the best forger France has ever known, I can say surely that my skills are now at an undetectable level. I can say this with proof because I have not been found out for five years now. I will leave you to think on that, John, but I will not be questioned on the matter.

"I want to place an order for a full shipment from the Maggot Marquis. I am talking about a full shipload of goods worth many thousands of francs. I have created false identities. Lawyers who do not exist, bankers who do not exist, and most importantly, money that does not exist.

"I have already established a strong rapport with the lawyers used by the Maggot. I have paid them to help with some of my clients regarding the marketing of chattels from deceased estates in and around Marseille.

"I have a Belgian friend, Arvin Bergin, who actually studied law but failed, running a bogus legal office near the port. I needed a premises to strengthen the fabrication, so I set him up. His law accreditation certificates, some of my finest work, are hung on the walls of his plush office, and of course, most people believe what they see. That office has been in operation for over a year. I don't have to fund it as my friend has developed a good legal business independently to the work he does and will do for me.

"I have been moving funds in and out of two banks in Marseille and, in doing so, have established a sound credit rating with them both. All I do is arrange for letters of escrow to be held in the two banks. These letters give the banks the authority to pay out large amounts of money from my accounts when I give instructions. These accounts are not in my name, of course, and none of the payees of the escrow letters are real people either.

The whole enterprise consists of me paying myself considerable amounts of money and then just repeating the process over and over. There is never a problem, and Mr. Allain D'Aboville, myself, is a valued client.

"Mr. Allain D'Aboville has expressed an interest in doing business with Marquis de Maggot and has asked his bankers to arrange introductory letters to be sent to the marquis. Once a sound business relationship has been established, I will have that full shipload of goods. I will withdraw the letter of escrow just prior to the arrival of the goods from China and the Middle East. Timing is all important, John, and I have a solution to that problem.

"The Maggot uses the same pilot boat to inform the docking authorities of the arrival of a new shipment. This advice always arrives at least twenty-four hours before the ship docks because the pilot boats sight the vessels at the port entry and are able to travel much faster than the bulky cargo ships. I intend to have an official instruction delivered to the captain of the cargo ship explaining that docking arrangements had been altered. The letter will carry the marquis's signature and seal so no suspicion will be aroused. There is a smaller docking facility at the entry to the port, and that is where the ship will be unloaded directly on to wagons that I have arranged and quickly transported to Avignon, sixty miles away where I have purchased a storage facility.

"I have convinced the Surete that I soon will be needing to spend some time in Marseille to bring together all the evidence I need to present a case against our host from the other evening. This part of the story is true, so again no suspicion will arise.

"When I visit Marseille, I will stay with my Belgian friend, Arvin Bergin, and between us, we will monitor the port action so the plan can be executed. Arvin has already mocked the plan several times so that we both know what to do."

"It seems like an enormous amount of trouble to go to, Allain. Are you sure it will be worth all your effort?" asked Rostan.

"Maybe you did not love your father enough, John?" replied Batteux, and then he added, "I do not intend to keep any of the money that will come from the sale of the stolen shipment. The man I have placed in charge of the storage facility in Avignon is the man who was my father's best friend. He was also the overseer of my father's furniture crafting workshop. He calls himself the Foreman. Apparently, you Englanders use the term in your factories."

Rostan could not help jumping on to the fun of it all.

"I must remember that when I return to my cotton mill. Foreman, you say?"

"Seriously, John, you do not handle your drink well at all," quipped Batteux, and having said that, he re-extracted the wine cork and poured two generous glasses. "I have to explain, John, because if you are to have dealings with the Maggot, I feel it is important that we do not clash while executing our separate plans," Batteux went on. "The Foreman is a very astute businessman in his own right. I have set up introductions for him to several of the leading fine furniture shops in Paris, and he has been selling some items of mine to each of them and has established a good reputation for himself. He also buys items at various auctions and then sells them on. There may be little or no profit, but his credentials are strengthened and that is what I need to happen.

"Now when I prepare the manifest for the shipment that will disappear, I have ensured that the cargo will be well-laden with fine porcelain. There will be dinner sets, jardinieres, vases, lamps, and fantastic ornaments. They are less bulky than furniture and easier to sell. Once the money starts to come in from the sale of the stolen items, the Foreman will take on an additional role. He has a list of all the people my father owed money to when he died. I will make it my mission to ensure that the Foreman repays every one of my dear father's debts. So there you have it, John. Yes, it is a complicated matter, but I swore over my father's dead body on that sad morning that the Marquis de Maggot will pay and only my own death will prevent that from happening." Batteux was visibly shaking as he delivered his oath.

John Rostan had felt he had taken on a huge task when he promised Angela Denny that he would ensure her safety and bring home enough money to see her and her loved ones living comfortably, but his small mission absolutely paled compared to the brilliance of the plan proposed and being carried out by the man who stood by his side, uncorking yet another bottle.

CHAPTER FORTY SEVEN

Rostan and Batteux rose early on the next morning. Batteux explained that he was meeting with a young man who has been confronted by two other members of Father Francisco's band of thugs and forced to pay them money. "He seems a brave one and has agreed that he will testify in court against the gang members. I am going to ask him to tell his tormentors that he knows of a man who would have much information about the goings-on among some of Paris's elite, and for an agreed consideration, he would be prepared to meet the leader of the gang to pass on his information. If I can meet with Father Francisco, I am sure that I will be able to trip him up and hopefully see him sent to gaol," explained Batteux through bloodshot eyes and carrying his head in both hands as though it had been detached.

"Be careful, my friend," said Rostan whose eyes were crystal clear as he stood strongly erect. "I have promised Phillipe Sartre that I would keep an eye on the goings-on near to his shop in case the thugs return. I will begin to make arrangements to travel to Marseille to get my meager plan under way. From what you told me last evening, Allain, you may be able to put together some documents for me so that I can quickly convince the Marquis de Maggot that I am who I am not and get the sale of this wretched deed document done once and for all."

Rostan was keen to catch up with Sartre and found himself feeling very self-conscious when, as he arrived, Sartre asked the ladies of his business to continue on in his absence as he was taking his friend to his favorite restaurant for lunch.

CHAPTER FORTY EIGHT

Back in Brown Street North, an event had taken place that cast a devastating sadness over all those who lived in Salford that knew Joseph Connelly. The poor man was beaten mentally. He had lived through so much sadness but always had his faith for support. That faith had been so utterly tested and cruelly attacked that he was simply hanging on to his sanity by thread, but that thread finally fractured with the death of his once beautiful wife, Grace.

Paul Connelly had left work early on the Wednesday because he just felt he had to be with his father. When he arrived at the Denny household where the remaining Connellys were still living, he called for his father whom he expected would be home alone as everyone who lived in that house would be at work. With no answer being returned, Paul ran into the second room of the dwelling, but his father was not there. His heart sank as he ran down the cellar steps. His father was hanging from an oak floor support. Paul struggled to take his father's weight. He screamed for help. The limp body was still warm, but Joseph Connelly was dead.

He was gone. The man whose own opinion of self-worth had slid below the scales of such judgements. The man who had so positively impacted the many lives that had been granted the gift of knowing him. The man who, when living in Ireland, had fought to better the miserable conditions endured by the crofters. The man who was physically damaged by the gentry's overseers simply because he could no longer afford to pay the exorbitant rent demanded of him. The man who, as did his father, dared to ask the catholic church to lighten the financial burden imposed by it on the parishioners of Transbridge who were mostly, in the end, unable to feed their own children. The man who insisted that his own children battle to be educated as he taught them all to read. The man who asked his children to promise to teach others to read whenever the opportunity arose. The man who sat every evening on the front steps of his friend Finbar's home in Brown Street North and read to the children of the street who would gather around him as though he was the Pied Piper. The man who would not leave his wife's side as he watched her spirit falter and her life fade away. And most sadly of all, the man who took his own life knowing that the mortal sin he was committing would exclude him from his heaven. He damned himself, sincerely doubting the existence of heaven at all.

Finbar Denny sent a message to his son, Michael, who was still living with his wife, Sarah, at the Maggie and the Captain guesthouse in London. He told him of Joseph's death but begged him not to return to Salford in case he was spotted and arrested. Finbar knew that Michael would want to help but hoped he would heed the warning.

An unexpected victim of the sadness was Matthew Denny. He had only got to know Joseph Connelly since his arrival in Salford but had found himself sometimes sitting with the children as Joseph read to them. There was a calmness about Joseph Connelly, and Matthew Denny found himself wishing he had more evenness of temperament. Matthew had not much faith at all, but when he heard of what Joseph had done, he quietly made a sole pilgrimage to St. Michael's Church and prayed that god would turn a blind eye to the sin and give his poor soul the reward it so richly deserved.

The funeral of Joseph Connelly was a quiet affair. St. Michael's was packed, but because of circumstances, the church would not celebrate the traditional requiem. Instead Father McCordy broke with the rules and at least offered the church as a venue whereby people could drop in and pay their respects.

There were no flowers, but Father McCordy could not believe what awaited him when he entered the church on the day of the burial. A pile of books had been stacked in the apse. Father McCordy counted thirty-four. The note that sat atop the pile simply read, "A gift from your friend Joseph Connelly." Sad and all as it was to see Father McCordy instantly recognized the clumsy writing style of Matthew Denny.

"If ever I was asked to name the most unlikely saint, I simply could not pass by the name of Matthew Denny." Father McCordy smiled to himself as he began to read through the many book titles.

There would be no honorable burial for Joseph Connelly. His suicide was a sin, and therefore, the church would not allow him to be buried in consecrated ground. There was an area of the graveyard where such sinners and excommunicated believers were permitted to be buried, and Joseph Connelly was laid to rest in that neglected place.

Such a sad judgment did not sit well with Finbar Denny, so in the dead of the night of that same day, Finbar and Matthew dug up the corpse of Joseph Connelly and reburied him where Grace, his wife, had been interred those few weeks earlier.

Colleen Denny had written a letter to John Rostan informing him of the sad event. She did not pay the extra postage that would guarantee a quick delivery. Not out of meanness but out of kindness. She felt that if she could delay the delivery, she would delay the sadness that Rostan would surely be upset with.

Chapter Forty Nine

Back in Paris, Batteux, who used the alias, Emile Natsor, had two separate meetings with Father Francisco, the self-appointed judge of his own Inquisition. The priest was tight-lipped about his band of thugs, but as Batteux fed his ego by telling him of what a fine job he was doing by making so many sinners pay the price of their errant ways, his guard began to slip.

"Father, our Lord would be so happy with you because of the great work you are doing. I know that there will be a special place in heaven for you, and you so richly deserve it." Batteux felt like vomiting all over the cleric as they spoke.

"Well, I have to admit, Mr. Natsor, I do believe that I was chosen by our Savior to do his work here on earth. I was particularly pleased to hear that only today, two of my men were able to inflict a deserved punishment on a young woman who was working as a prostitute out of a brothel along the Boulevard de

Clichy not far from my Montmartre home," stated the priest so casually it was as though he was discussing the combing of his hair. "It was Caliban and the Chinaman who made sure that evil woman answered to the lord."

Batteux had already heard about the young woman who had been made to answer to the lord. He now knew her assailants to be the same two men who had terrorized Sartre. She had been found near death in her room at the brothel by two of her friends who ran to her aid on hearing her screams. Batteux had made a point of reading the police report prior to meeting with Father Francisco, and he presumed by the severity of the attack that the Inquisitor would probably be behind it. Not only had the victim been badly beaten, she had also been raped by the two men.

Batteux now had one victim ready to have his day in court, and he had an oral admission from the Inquisitor that he organized the attack on the young prostitute who was almost dead because of it. He decided that he had enough proof to approach the sympathetic bishop and hopefully bring the Inquisitor to justice.

Bishop Cordello of the catholic faith was the man that Batteux hoped would help him bring the Inquisition to an end. The morning after speaking with Father Francisco, he had arranged to meet the Bishop whom he was led to believe would give him a fair hearing and, in doing so, would instigate a resolution.

While Batteux pleaded his case to the Bishop, he began to realize that, as he had expected, the Bishop was not prepared to take any serious action against the man he described as "one of the most dedicated priests it had ever been his privilege to know."

He actually told Batteux that "it would be best for all if Father Francisco was returned to his native Spain where his methods would not be judged so harshly."

Batteux could not believe the absurdity of it all. He knew then that he would have to put the case to the Paris Police. His major concern was that his position with the Surete meant that he had to remain anonymous to the street patrollers. He worked undercover and simply could not afford to go public with what he had found. It was then that he arrived at the conclusion that Rostan would have to be his cover. *Rostan*, he thought, *could present Sartre's story along with the testimony of the young man. Rostan would have to agree, of course, and lie that it was he who heard Father Francisco admit to organizing the band of thugs and that should be enough to see Father Francisco charged and brought to justice*. To any other man, such a plan would seem too Quixotic, but Batteux was not any other man.

As Rostan listened to Batteux explain the plan that he seemed to believe would oust the Inquisitor, he thought to himself, *Surely this plot is coming straight from the mind of the mighty Shakespeare himself*. Nothing about Batteux's plan was doable, he thought, and even as he agreed to the whole scenario, he deemed himself to be utterly mad for doing so.

Rostan had intended to head straight to Marseille after he and Batteux had agreed on their separate plans for bringing down the Marquis de Maggot, but now that he had his sights re-set on the Inquisitor, it would mean that more time would have to be spent in Paris. Only one positive thought was born of this change of plan. He would be able to continue his vigilante watch over Sartre.

As Rostan sat in front of officer Yolande of the Paris Police Force, he tried to appear comfortable but felt as though he was giving himself away with every lie he told. The young officer had only been in the force for less than one year, and the story he was listening to had set his mind racing. If what he was hearing was all true, and if he was able to arrest the Inquisitor, surely his actions would greatly enhance his chance for promotion.

"The accusations you are making are very serious, Mr. Rostan," he said. "Are you prepared to write down a statement of everything you have told me, and are you prepared to swear that all you have stated is true, Mr. Rostan?" asked the young officer.

"I once was a policeman in England, sir, and know just how serious this matter is. I swear that everything I have told you is true," stated Rostan, and after he had written out and signed the statement, he asked officer Yolande, "What happens now?"

"We will ask Father Francisco to come here to make his own statement. We will verify if what you say is true by talking to the victims you have told us about, and once that is done, my superiors will decide whether to act or not," said Yolande confidently.

Two days after Rostan had tendered his statement, he was sitting with Sartre having lunch. He was surprised when Batteux appeared by his side.

"Good god, man," said Rostan with a jump. "Did you just fall out of the sky? You have unnerved me, Allain. To what do we owe this pleasure?"

"John, brace yourself please," said Batteux. "Nothing I am about to tell you is pleasant."

"Spit it out, man. You don't look well. What in god's name has happened?" asked Rostan.

"The young man who agreed to testify against the Inquisitor is dead, John," exclaimed Batteux. "I have seen the body, and he has been stabbed many times. A witness said she saw a Chinaman and a man with a limp coming from the small apartment where the young man lived. He is dead, John, and

I know that it is all my fault. The prostitute is still alive, but out of fear for her safety, I have had her moved to a different hospital. We simply cannot allow her to act as a witness, John, she has a child, a young girl. I have arranged for her to be placed in an orphanage."

"What of Father Francisco?" asked Rostan.

"To hell with him, John. We will just have to let it go. He is in a position to hurt too many people and do remember, John, your friend Sartre is one of them." Batteux was looking directly at Sartre as he spoke.

John Rostan's mind rushed, filled with memories of Eversall and poor Tess, Benny Connelly and the poor bairn he had burnt to death, Solomon Leyman and the brutal beating he had meted out to Angela Connelly. The switch had tripped once again.

"Are you sure there is nothing you can do, Allain?" demanded Rostan.

Batteux replied, "I am telling you. For the sake of all who could still be hurt, John: just leave it alone." But even as he spoke, Allain had taken note that John said "there is nothing *you* can do," but no mention of *we*.

Allain Batteux knew that the best thing he could do for his friend was to make sure that Rostan was on his way to Marseille as soon as possible. He knew he had to get John thinking about other matters, so he booked a passage for John and told him he had to be on his way.

To quote himself, Rostan felt as though he was a "trout out of the pond" when he was seated in front of the young police officer Yolande giving his statement. John did not cope well with not being in control of the situation. As he was packing his bag in Allain's apartment prior to heading to Marseille, he felt completely in control.

Father Francisco had not met John Rostan. John had made a point of finding out when it was that the Inquisitor heard confessions.

"Forgive me, Father, but you have sinned," said Rostan as he sat in the confessional ruled over by Father Francisco in the Sacred Heart Basilica situated on Montmartre, Paris.

As he spoke, Rostan tore out the square-framed wire mesh that separated him from the Inquisitor. He stretched both his hands through the small opening and gained a firm grip on Father Francisco's head. As he drew the shocked face toward himself, Rostan pushed Francisco's throat down hard on the framework. The priest would surely have suffocated, but Rostan did not have the luxury of time. His anger-driven strength was such that the downward pressure he exerted snapped the neck of the Inquisitor within seconds.

It was late evening when Rostan was returning home from the scene of his satisfaction. He knew his size would never allow him to simply slip away unnoticed, and that is why he had arranged to go straight to the coach depot where he was met by Sartre who held his bag. He farewelled his friend, and the coach lurched several times as the horses took up the weight of the heavy load. Rostan was surprised at how comfortable the seats were. He was also surprised at how exhilarated he felt as he breathed in the night air.

Rostan had left a letter with Sartre to be given to Batteux on the next morning.

Dear Allain,

I do believe that the Inquisitor will no longer be in a position to rule his evil empire. I took the liberty of hearing his last confession last night. Do not think harshly of me, my friend, I will never see heaven, but I am damned if I will give up the chance of sending monsters to the hell they so wretchedly deserve. At least your hands are clean.

One favor please.

Sartre has agreed to testify against the men who attacked him. There is no fear of reprisals as the serpent no longer has its head, but could you look out for his safety? In fact, I ask two favors of you. Could you please make sure that the young girl who was bashed and raped by Caliban and his Chinese collaborator receives all the care she needs, and please, favor number three. Could you make sure that her daughter is cared for. You told me that you believed the child's name to be Lizette.

As Batteux read the letter from his friend, he shed tears. He knew Rostan was a tormented man, but never in his wildest imaginings did he realize the depths to which his friend was prepared to go to, to see justice done.

Batteux had seen the corpse of the Inquisitor. The head had almost been completely torn away from the body.

CHAPTER FIFTY

John Rostan used the time it took to travel from Paris in the north of France all the way down to Marseille in the south to mentally plot out just how he would coerce the Marquis de Maggot into the trap he was about to spring.

It was imperative that Rostan get to know Arvin Bergin, the failed law student that Batteux had set up an office for near to the docks. Arvin was a larger than life character. What he lacked in physical stature he amply made up for with ego. Not ego in an unpleasant way, but an ego that could make people feel comfortable in his presence while also allowing them to feel his control. He bore an air of trust.

At first, Rostan did not know what to make of Bergin, but because Batteux had handpicked him, he knew the man before him was trustworthy.

Rostan estimated that Bergin would be in his early thirties. His hair had receded considerably, but what was left was almost orange, not red and not blond. He greeted Rostan with a warm, disarming smile. He wore glasses, obviously only needed for reading because he perched them on the end of his nose and only looked through the actual lenses when trying to focus on a page; otherwise, he looked straight over the rim to see distance. Without a doubt, Rostan recognized the sartorial skill of his friend Sartre in the suit he was wearing. A gold ear ring hung from his left lobe, and he sported no less than four rings, two on each hand.

"Have you found any other parcels of land that I may look at Arvin?" Rostan wanted to get straight to business, and he needed the marquis to hear about the Englishman looking to buy land in the docks to further his milling business back in Manchester.

Arvin Bergin had already sent a letter to the marquis asking whether he would be prepared to sell any of his holdings to the miller from England. Everything that was done was done to establish the bona fides of the enquiry to buy land.

The marquis sent a message to Rostan via Arvin Bergin asking that they meet under the pretense that he might have some land that would suit the Englishman. A time was set, and Rostan rode to the Chateau de la Roche, owned by the marquis, and the two men finally met.

Rostan had been involved for hours, in total, discussing the Marquis de Maggot and had never really known the family name. It occurred to him that he had never heard a good word spoken either about the Drunk Duke, Granny's husband, or his son the marquis who was now seated across the small table from him. He looked the man up and down and was amazed yet again at how normal evil people can appear to be.

The marquis sported a mop of unruly black hair. Rostan doubted that hair color was natural as it was just too black. A compact moustache sat above his lip, and the few gray hairs within exposed the lack of honesty attributable to the coiffure. The face was attractive, but Rostan felt that the eyes were too close set. Four heavy dark moles on the right cheek also led to identity points being deducted by the ex-detective. Yes, this was a face that could be easily recognized.

Rostan had the urge to kill him there on the spot, but the Marquis had two sturdy men standing close by, and it was obvious that they were not there to tend the magnificent gardens. A table had been set for tea under the shade of a huge oak tree that had born witness to nine generations of the Roche family.

The Lavigne brothers of Paris had informed the marquis that a buyer was looking at the land he really needed to expand his empire into, and now with that buyer sitting in front of him, he concluded that the threat was no bluff. His immediate thought was to dispose of the opposition, but too many people knew that Rostan was seeing the marquis, so killing him was not an option, at least not at this stage.

"I believe, Mr. Rostan, that you have inspected a piece of land that just might suit your needs. I wonder if you have been made aware that the land you are looking at once belonged to my family, and in fact, the deed was lost to us because my father became so besotted with his second wife, he just transferred some of what he considered to be secondary assets to her for what reason I am still at a loss to understand. I still believe that the deed should have remained with my family," explained the marquis, making no attempt to cover up the obvious contempt he held for his deceased stepmother.

"All you say is news to me, sir. I only know that the land is held in the name of a young English lass. I do not know her. I have not met her. All the dealings I have been involved in are through a lawyer in Paris, Mr. Louis Lavigne, and I am only dealing with him because he is the agent for my English law firm," the words rolled off Rostan's tongue like water over silk. He felt the excitement building and was so pleased that he had taken the time to go over and over all he wanted to say to the marquis during his long trip from Paris.

"Well, Mr. Rostan, I have some very good news for you. I have been told by my lawyers in Marseille just what you require from the land you wish to purchase, and I believe that I have a plot that would far better suit your needs. It is situated along the street we call La Canebiere and is six hundred perches in total. I know you intend to build a large warehouse and other buildings for workers and to house wagons. There are already structures on the property. This land is perfect for all those needs, and I believe that I could be persuaded to sell it if you meet my price," stated the marquis in a tone that suggested the deal had already been done.

"In fact, sir, I believe I have already walked over the ground you speak of, and you must remember that I am an Englishman," jousted Rostan.

"What is it you mean me to understand by that remark, sir?" blurted the marquis with his finesse gone.

"The whole of the land you mention, sir, is scarred by deep wheel ruts. It is obvious to all that trying to move heavy wagons to and fro across that property has been near impossible in the past. The land sits too low, sir, and the ocean wants to rise into it. As I said, I am an Englishman and know only too well about wet land. It simply would not suit my needs at all," stated Rostan, knowing full well that he had either just forced the marquis to purchase the illusive deed from Angela Denny or he had just signed his own death warrant.

"I believe we have nothing more to discuss, and it probably is best that you leave," said the marquis curtly.

Rostan chose to ignore the rudeness and saw an opportunity to further force the hand of the Marquis. "I must say," stressed Rostan, "I am so glad we have met as it looks likely that we will be neighbors in the near future. Neighbors in business at least. Oh, and by the way, sir, I must mention. I noticed when I inspected the property I intend to buy that a poorly made road has been constructed across one end of it. It seems to me, sir, that your workers use that road for wagon access to your warehouse. Once ownership transfers to me, all that will have to stop. I am sorry, but my plans would have buildings erected over that track."

John Rostan could not believe that it was all over so quickly. He knew he would have to wait to see if the sale was actually going to happen, but he was sure one of the two options left to the marquis would be acted on swiftly. He did not take the commercial route back to Paris. To stay one step ahead of the marquis, he bought a stout horse in Marseille and rode for three days, almost covering one hundred miles. He then boarded the horse and himself on to one of the smaller riverboats and made very good time back to Paris. Even so, the journey took six days.

While sailing back to Paris, Rostan dared to dream. He recalled the proposition put to him by the Lavigne brothers, Louis and Edouard. They referred to it as the Vexation, and it went so:

"The caveats that the marquis has placed on the title only inhibit a sale. They do not inhibit anything else happening to the deed. They cannot stop you, John, as Angela's agent, adding a restriction to the body of the deed. You say the marquis needs this deed to build road access to his own land which otherwise is next to useless. My brother and I suggest that you approach the department of land in Marseille and note with them that the current owner wants to place an encumbrance over a section of the deed stating that that small area should be designated as parkland and any construction on it should be prohibited. The section we refer to, John, is the area where the marquis would have to build his road."

John remembered how he was laughing when he left the offices of the Lavigne brothers those few weeks back, and as he relived the Vexation proposition, he laughed again, and it dawned on him just how seldom it was that he ever laughed.

Rostan, on his return to Paris, quickly brought Batteux up-to-date with everything that had happened in Marseille. Rostan had arrived just after 1:00 p.m., so he went straight to the offices of the Surete, and fortunately, Batteux was there, seated at his desk.

"John, you obviously have not heard," said Batteux. "The marquis has instructed the Lavigne brothers to forward to his solicitors the contract to purchase Angela's land. He has agreed to pay a price that is considerably more than you apparently offered, and he wants the matter settled as quickly as possible. The lawyers say the matter will settle before he physically has the deed because he has insisted on such a rush, and of course, he expects everything to be in order because he thought he restricted any activity concerning the deed document. It appears, John, that your visit accomplished everything you had hoped for and more. I will say this though, John. When the Marquis de Maggot realizes how he was duped, I suspect he will want to take revenge on Angela Denny. You will have to make sure she disappears and very soon."

"I will wait until the money is available from the land sale and then return to Manchester," said John. "I am hoping that Angela has given up on her fool idea of becoming a nun. If so, I will move her to London to be with her brother, Michael, at the Captain's guesthouse. Hopefully, Finbar Denny and what is left of the Connelly family will join us. It is all too much to deal with at the moment, but I will have to act soon.

CHAPTER FIFTY ONE

"**A**llain, did you do as I asked and take care of the young girl who was beaten and her child, Lizette?"

"I did, John, but I am sad to say that the mother of the young child died in hospital. I made sure she was comfortable, and I supplied sufficient amounts of laudanum to help relieve the suffering. I suppose the child will be adopted or sent out to work as soon as she is able to earn money. A shame, John, but what can be done?" Batteux was obviously upset as he spoke.

John Rostan had no sooner heard the news of Lizette's mother when he found himself pounding on the door of the small apartment where he had been told she lived with two friends. A young woman answered, and after Rostan had convinced her that he meant her no harm, she asked him inside and offered him a drink.

"My name is Adelaine, sir. Just what is it that you need to know?" The young lady spoke well, and her English was understandable. That relieved Rostan because although his French had come on in leaps and bounds since his arrival in France, he was still experiencing great problems with the speed at which the French could deliver a sentence, and he found himself constantly asking people to speak slowly.

"Could you please tell me if Lizette's mother had any family here in Paris or even France for that matter?" asked Rostan.

"Camille, Lizette's mother, has lived here with me for two years, and in all that time, she never talked about family. If she had family, they certainly did not seem interested in her. She only had love for Lizette, and she was a good mother. I have another friend living here with me, and between the three of us, we used to take good care of little Lizette. She is at the orphanage now, and we have been told that she will have to stay there. We love the little girl, but we have been told that she cannot still live here," said Adelaine, visibly upset.

Rostan's next stop was to see either of the Lavigne brothers. He had made up his mind that the little girl was not going to be left and forgotten.

"I need for you to arrange an adoption for me please, Edouard," said Rostan. "There is a little three-year-old girl at St. Maria's

Orphanage. Her mother has just died. She needs help, and I know that I can help her. What do we have to do?"

"John, John, slow down," said Louis Lavigne who had come to his brother's rescue. "You cannot just sign a piece of paper and the child is yours. There is a process, and it can take some time. The nuns at that orphanage have a very good reputation when it comes to care of the children. It may not be as easy as you think, John, but Edouard and I will try our best."

Rostan settled down and explained to the brothers that he really wanted to help the little girl, and although they attempted to be positive, Rostan left their office knowing full well that taking Lizette into his care may not be feasible legally, so he was already conjuring up alternatives.

Batteux told John that he was crazy. "How in god's name, man, do you think you can look after a small child living the way you do. John, I don't want to put too fine a point on this, but here goes. You are a murderer, John. Now you know I love you as a friend, but you would be the last man I would choose to become the father of this orphan, John."

"I fully intend to settle down back in London, Allain. I have all the money I will ever need. I want to help that child, and I believe I can be a good father to her," proffered Rostan, almost pleading with his friend.

"I will help you, John, but you must promise me one thing," said Batteux.

"Anything," replied John.

"If she, Lizette, is too much for you, if she is too hard for you, you must find a suitable home for her away from you, John. Will you promise me that?" said Batteux.

Rostan looked straight into the eyes of his friend. "Yes, you have my word," was all he said.

CHAPTER FIFTY TWO

Things were starting to fall into place for Batteux with regard to his plan to relieve the Marquis de Maggot of a full shipment of prized goods. The request for goods had been submitted months earlier, and he had heard from Arvin Bergin that the shipment was on the high seas and due to be landed within the month. The marquis had buying agents acting for him all over the world. The shipment consisted of goods brought across land from as far away as China, India, and Persia and delivered to ports along the Mediterranean coast where they were loaded on to a sailing ship to be delivered to Marseille. The exercise was cripplingly expensive and, at times, left the Marquis dangerously financially exposed.

The ship carrying the booty was called the *Asturius*, and Batteux explained to Rostan that he would be travelling to Marseille to execute his plan but promised that he would help him to somehow take charge of Lizette although neither of the two men had any idea as to how they would make that happen.

As planned, authentic-looking documents were delivered to the captain of the *Asturius* as he was entering the port of Marseille. He had no reason to doubt the change of plan, so the goods were offloaded exactly where Batteux had planned. The wagons were loaded quickly, and Batteux's Foreman took charge of the lead wagon and headed to the storage facility in Avignon. The letter of escrow guaranteeing payment for the now stolen goods had been cancelled on the same day.

Batteux knew his friend Arvin Bergin would most likely be implicated in the theft, so the legal office in Marseille was also closed, and Arvin was asked to travel with the Foreman to help him with the legal side of running the Fine Wares business that would eventually see all of Allain Batteux's father's debts repaid.

When Batteux arrived back in Paris, he could not wait to tell Rostan about the latest news in Marseille. "John, apparently a certain Maggot known to both of us took possession of a prime piece of land adjoining an allotment he already owned. It seems he needed a permit from the department of land to allow him to build a certain road. When he presented the title deed to the department, it was pointed out to him that an encumbrance had been placed over that exact area, and the department had just been charged with turning that area into parkland as stipulated by a certain John Rostan who had designated it so, as legally appointed agent for one Angela Grace Denny.

"It is a fact, John, born out by Arvin Bergin, that our Maggot has upset many people in Marseille. He has continually pushed his luck with various local government departments, and that being said, the inspectors at the land department were being deliberately difficult with regard to the park allocation. They would not rescind it, and to make matters even better, John, they sent a sizable account to our little Maggot for reinstating the ground that he had laid his own road over." Batteux was so excited, he was dancing around his apartment like a man possessed. He was possessed. He was possessed by the long-awaited knowledge that finally, the Marquis de Roche had been brought down from his self-imagined pedestal back to earth where things that were bad for him at present were about to get much worse.

Batteux could only imagine how the stolen shipment might impact on the reputation of the marquis. He had no information detailing the financial situation that the marquis found himself in immediately after that ill-fated shipment. The total value of the cargo had to be prepaid. The cost of the shipping also was paid prior to delivery once the marquis knew that the load was nearing Marseille. The marquis had a pecuniary predicament on his hands. Trouble did not hit immediately because the marquis was able to obtain further credit. After all, he was the marquis. He owned a substantial estate. He lived like a king and spared no expense when it came to catering to his many whims. He had several follies built on the estate, and because of the nature of these useless edifices, the amounts that designers and builders were able to charge were beyond exorbitant. He had extended the magnificent gardens left to him by his father but not for aesthetic value; everything the marquis spent money on was to impress.

He also collected beautifully ornate carriages, and prior to the shipment going missing, he had just taken delivery of his thirteenth such beauty. Payment was due, and he did not have it. In fact, many accounts began to roll in that he was no longer in a position to honor and the reason for that was simple.

The reputation in business circles that the marquis enjoyed was extremely solid, however, he was addicted to gambling and had always just been one step ahead of financial insolvency, but that was no longer the case.

The killing factor was a dashed reputation. Many clients had been dealing with the Roche family name for years, but word of the missing shipment had undermined their confidence, and orders for goods began to dry up. This caused a spiral that the marquis was unable to escape from. He began selling assets, including all thirteen of his prized carriages. People who knew the marquis all judged him to be a strong man, but that was not the case. He was a bully who was always able to pay someone to come down hard on anyone who opposed him, as was the case with Angela Denny, but now that he was no longer a wealthy bully, he was just a bully that people no longer had to pay any attention to. He became the local laughing stock. The estate did eventually right itself, but the marquis was just a shell of the man he once was and was seldom seen in public and never entertained.

Having digested all the information that Batteux had just unloaded with regard to the marquis, for it was indeed a feast, Rostan asked his friend if he had come up with any ideas as to how he might gain custody of Lizette.

CHAPTER FIFTY THREE

Batteux was hoping that John had cooled off on the idea, but obviously he had not. "Short of kidnapping the poor little wretch, there is nothing else to be done, John," replied Batteux rather flatly.

"Well then, Mr. Batteux," touted John, "and how do you propose we go about doing that?"

"I sincerely wish that you would reconsider this craziness, John, but if you are determined to go ahead, there is possibly one way that might just work," said Batteux cautiously.

"Tell me then, Allain, because with or without you, I will give that wee-en a better life than she would have slaving away at scrubbing already spotless floors," said Rostan with anger in his tone.

"I have made some enquiries about just what it is that the orphans are expected to do, and scrubbing floors does seem to sit high on the list of work that the children are forced to endure. If they misbehave or refuse to work, the nuns do beat them as well as sending them to bed without being properly fed. I have had a friend visit the orphanage, and she has found out much that could help you win the prize," and Batteux started to become his usual animated self as he got to the meat in the sandwich.

"Spit it out, man. What do you have in mind?" demanded Rostan.

"My friend says that she will adopt the little one as long as you, John, take delivery of your new daughter immediately after the papers are signed and leave this country on the same day. I will magically produce all the documentation you will need to convince any of the port authorities that you are her father. Birth certificates are somewhat of a specialty of mine, and I guarantee you will have no issues," stated Batteux with obvious pride in his workmanship.

"Who is this angel, and how did you get her to agree to such an outrageous proposition?" asked Rostan.

"She is the divine creature that I met on the night we attended the grand party. She is called Antoinette, and she asked me to evaluate some of her possessions, if you remember. She insisted that I escort her home from the party on that evening. Well, I have to admit, John, that since the party, I have spent many evenings with Antoinette, evaluating her assets, you understand. Now as it happens, she is a widow who married well, and on the death of her husband, she is a wealthy angel. However, she does not come from wealth herself, in fact, she was orphaned very young, and when I told her of your plight, she offered to help immediately. She has very sad memories of the orphanage she spent ten years in as a child and believes that helping you is absolutely the right thing to do. So there you have it, my friend. All tied up in a neat little parcel with a pink bow around it. What do you say to that?" said Batteux, who now was positively glowing.

Rostan said nothing. He just walked over to his friend and put his arms around him. He held him in a tight embrace as tears rolled down his cheeks.

From the time it was first discussed to the day that the adoption was formalized took four agonizing weeks. Antoinette was told by the nasty old nun who seemed to be in charge of adoptions that the matter could be expedited if she was prepared to make a substantial donation to the orphanage. She agreed, knowing full well Batteux and Rostan were prepared to pay whatever the cost.

As he waited delivery of the prize, Rostan enlisted the aid of Sartre, the tailor, to help him select some suitable clothing for

Lizette. The two men were totally out of their depth but loving every moment that it took to assemble the wardrobe for the little girl.

All documents had been signed, and the adoption was pronounced legal. All forged documents had been meticulously created by Batteux, and so a huge adventure was set to begin for Lizette Rostan. The ferry tickets paying for the channel crossing had been pressed hard into the inside pocket of Rostan's still relatively new suit jacket, and he had dressed Lizette in the new outfit he best preferred.

"London, here we come," said John, and he could not wait, but wait he knew he had to because before he could escape the company of Batteux and the beauty of Paris, there was a Bon Voyage party to attend.

Departure time for Dover was scheduled for five in the morning from Calais and was two weeks away. The send-off was to take place at Batteux's apartment, and only people who could be trusted were invited.

Rostan had spent the better part of that Friday in the company of Antoinette, making sure that all went well with the adoption. It wasn't until late afternoon that Antoinette, Rostan, and Lizette finally arrived at Batteux's apartment.

Lizette was asleep in Rostan's arms when they entered the apartment but quickly woke due to all the noise. Rostan could not believe the trouble that Batteux had gone to. He was dressed as a clown, and several of his friends were also in costume. One man wore a tiger outfit, another was dressed as a cuddly bear, while one young lady was dressed to appear as a cat. There were ten guests, and Rostan immediately recognized Arvin Bergin who was dressed as a pirate. The Foreman, whom Rostan had only met once, was seated at the piano, and although John did not recognize the piece he was playing, he thought it sounded beautiful.

Rostan, with Lizette still firmly held in his arms, went to Batteux with a panicked look on his face. "I thank you, Allain, but do you not think that this is all too much for the child?"

As he spoke, Lizette was awake, and she immediately produced a huge smile accompanied with laughter. She wriggled in John's arms, and Antoinette said, "I believe she wants to play, John."

Rostan nervously lowered her to stand and as soon as he let her loose, she ran to Bergin. She was able to speak in a fashion, and as she held Bergin's hand, she uttered the word *funny*.

Rostan had just experienced his first "proud father" moment. Lizette, he realized, was used to company and late nights, and soon she became the life of the party. The Foreman sat her beside him and let her plonk away on the base notes of the piano as he held the melody together with considerable skill on the higher end of the keyboard. Rostan's little girl danced with Batteux and the cat lady. It seemed she was only satisfied once she had spent some time with each of the guests. The seemingly boundless energy put a full stop to itself after two hours of complete fun. Lizette came over to John, looked up at him, and said, "Lift me." His heart almost burst as his little girl fell asleep, once again, in his arms.

CHAPTER FIFTY FOUR

The trip from Paris to Calais for the channel crossing was arduous, but where once he would have been annoyed with the uncomfortable coach, Rostan enjoyed every minute. He had so much to learn, and Lizette was such a delightful teacher.

The channel crossing the next morning was brutal. The wind seemed to be lashing the sails from every direction all at once. The mountainous waves drove into one another from the north, south, east, and west, simultaneously causing the raging waters to rise like pyramids and surround the small vessel only to come crashing down on to the exposed decks, allowing yet more to appear as the assault continued. Rostan did not stay in his cabin. He thought if the ship was to sink, he could be trapped there, so he picked up Lizette and held her close to him, under his long overcoat, near a doorway to the upper deck. He knew himself well, and that being the case, he could not understand what was happening. If he had been on his own, there would be no fear. As he held the small child close to his heart, he was terrified. Rostan had given up any efforts at prayer years prior, but he found himself making all sorts of promises to any god that was listening during that crossing. He asked nothing for himself, but he begged that the small child he held so close would be spared.

The crossing took hours, but eventually, the battered ship limped into Dover. Rostan allowed good manners to dictate his behavior, but as soon as his courtesy had been dispensed to those passengers who forced themselves past him and the small child to disembark, he took his bag in one hand after lifting Lizette on to his shoulder and stepped on to the gang plank with a feeling of great relief.

Rostan looked up at the sun as he peered out from the coach window carrying himself, Lizette, and four other passengers to London.

"What a glorious day," he mused. "I have never seen the sun shine so brightly. I know the blue sky above is a brand-new shade to me. The air is sweeter, and I swear the grass is greener. I thank the lord that my prayers were answered. Whichever lord wants to claim responsibility, I thank you for the life of my Lizette, and I vow to keep her safe."

He realized, as he pondered over the events of the crossing, just how fragile life can be. He then found himself dwelling on the many sins he had committed to avenge the cruelty that he saw all around him.

"Who am I to think I have the right to force myself into the life of this young child? What a fool I am to think I could get away with such deed. I have no plan. I have no right to this innocent soul." Rostan's self-examination of conscience was damning, and he realized that he needed help, and he knew of only one man who could provide the help he so desperately needed.

John Rostan had built up a huge respect for the Captain, and he knew that if any man could advise him on how he should proceed with his new life, the Captain was that man. When he and Lizette arrived at the Maggie and the Captain guesthouse, he had to stare hard at the premises to reassure himself that he had arrived at the correct address. The place was in the throes of a rebirth when he left all those months ago to inform his friend Joseph Connelly of the death of his son and then to go on and put a final chapter to the life of Marcus Eversall.

The transformation is such a credit to the proprietors, he thought. The word *proprietors* came out of nowhere, but it was the correct use. "My goodness, Lizette," he said as he lifted his small charge from the coach. "I believe you have just arrived at your palace, young princess."

A piercing scream overwhelmed all the cacophonous goings-on in the street and then this: "Mr. Rostan, sir, is that truly you?

Is this Lizette? Oh, sir, she is beautiful. Have you come to stay? Please tell me you have." Maggie Dorn had lost none of her enthusiasm, but John hardly recognized the young lady that stood before him.

"My god, Maggie, you are beautiful. You are the perfect picture. How you have blossomed in my absence," said Rostan, realizing that his enthusiasm was overdone, and with that, he put the emphasis back on to Lizette. "Yes, Maggie, this is my Lizette, and judging by what you seem to already know, I can take it that you and the Captain got all of my letters," said Rostan, having put a calm back into his tone.

"Can I hold her, sir? What a little darling she is." Maggie's enthusiasm was infectious, and as she held out her arms to Lizette, the little girl looked up at Rostan who was stilling holding her in his arms and said, "Down, Papa." This was the first time that she had called Rostan Papa. He had no idea how she could even know what the term meant. It was as though she had decided that all was right with the way things were and she just decided to give it her seal of approval. As John let her go, she ran to Maggie. He could not believe the relief he felt. Maybe, just maybe, he could be a father after all.

Rostan had much news to pass on and also much to learn. He was able to tell Michael Denny that he had sold the troublesome deed as Angela's agent to the Marquis de Maggot for the grand sum four thousand six hundred pounds. Angela had hoped that the money would be sufficient to help herself, her family, and their friends rid themselves of financial worries and have a more promising future to look forward to. This amount could well and truly make all of her wishes come true.

Rostan took great delight in telling the Captain in strictest confidence of how the Vexation had negated any plans that the marquis had for the land. He also told the story of the stolen shipment. How the cargo vessel *Asturius* had been given forged documents instructing the captain to dock well away from the original planned berthing, allowing the cargo to be offloaded and smuggled away to help pay for debts incurred by Batteux's father.

"I once captained the *Asturius*, John. She was a sizable craft. If the cargo was stacked well, she was capable of hauling many tons. I don't like the idea of theft from ships, but it seems it was all for a good cause," stated the Captain.

Rostan thought later that he should not have bothered the Captain with his bragging, but he just needed someone to talk to. He also spent time with Maggie, catching up with her story, and the revelations were entertaining. She told Rostan that the Captain had arranged for her to learn to "speak more proper, and I don't know why that is."

It was obvious to Rostan that the Captain was doing all in his power to groom Maggie, to improve her credibility, to make a lady out of her. His motives were simple. He loved his granddaughter and wanted her to have all the skills she would need when he was no longer around. John remembered that before he left for Paris, the Captain had celebrated his seventy-second birthday. This was a huge achievement given that most adults at the time were old at fifty-five. It was even more staggering when taking into consideration the hard life that the Captain had lived.

John was also delighted that he was able to spend some time with Malcolm McDonald. He was still living at the guesthouse and seemed very contented. The Earls family had taken him under their collective wings after the death of Roger Earls. He had been put in charge of the shop where he had been introduced to Roger. The Earls sisters had made Roger a junior partner because he had proven himself to be a huge asset to the business. He and Maggie Dorn had both suffered cruelly at the hands of Benny Connelly, but somehow they had formed a bond. Maggie became the sister that Malcolm so missed, and in turn, Malcolm had become the brother that Maggie never had.

CHAPTER FIFTY FIVE

Brown Street North was not a happy place to be after the death of Joseph Connelly, but Finbar Denny found himself considerably cheered up because he had noticed that Angela, his daughter, seemed to be in a far cheerier mood over the last month. After her abduction and beating, she had become withdrawn and seemed always to be looking over her shoulder in fear.

It was Sunday, and as usual, Joseph Connelly's three remaining children Paul, Josephine, and Ellen were accompanying Finbar and Angela to mass, but the usual procession had changed formation over the last few walks to church. Where usually the five churchgoers would walk in a huddle, Paul and Angela had taken to dropping behind the group by a distance that put them out of earshot but not so far that Finbar could not hear Angela laughing and Paul echoing her cheer.

Finbar was so happy that his daughter seemed to have given up on the prospect of becoming a nun. Like Joseph Connelly, Finbar realized that his firm belief in all things catholic had been severely diminished as the result of so many unanswered prayers. He knew that Paul Connelly was truly his father's son. He was good, honest, and kind, and if Angela was falling in love with him, Finbar knew that he, like his father, would be a fine choice.

Ellen and Josephine, on the other hand, were still struggling with the sadness that they had fallen into after the cruel death of their father. They both wanted to leave that sadness behind and had decided to tell Finbar that they wanted to move to London. The girls and Paul were still living in the home that Finbar rented, and he had made it very plain that they were welcome to stay as long as they needed, so the girls had allowed him to take on a paternal role. To put more weight to their argument, Josephine and Ellen decided to ask their brother Paul to come with them to London. Paul explained to his sisters that he felt he might be in love with Angela, and rather than see that as a problem, the two girls exploded with enthusiasm and insisted that he should marry Angela immediately and all four could leave for London.

"I cannot expect Angela to leave her father alone here in Salford. Our father is dead, and Michael has left for god knows where. I will not be so cruel." Paul did not tell his sisters that Angela had received several letters from her brother in London. He told

Angela that he and Sarah Thomlin had married but begged her not to tell their father because Finbar had enough to worry himself with. What with the death of Joseph Connelly and the added burden of having to take care of the three Connelly siblings, Michael did not want to burden his father with additional worries. The letters that Michael wrote to his father simply stated that he and Sarah were staying in a respectable guesthouse and both were working, hoping to build a bright future together.

Angela did, however, drop her guard and decided to tell Paul the truth about Michael and Sarah being married.

"We could be married, Angela. We love each other. Maybe my sisters have the right idea. The church folk only pretend to care about my sisters and me. I know they all talk about us. I feel the cruelty every time I go to Mass. 'Oh, what a shame it is that their father was such a sinner. Not much hope for that lot.' That's what they say. The girls have told me that mill workers who were their friends barely talk to them anymore. My boss is still kind to me, but things are different. We need a change. What do you say, Angela?"

"Yes, Paul, yes. If that was your idea of a marriage proposal, I accept." Angela threw her arms around Paul and kissed his cheek. "So what will we do, Paul? Does this mean you have to have a talk with my father?"

"Angela, it does, and our future still rests with him. I will agree with whatever your father asks of me. He is like a father to me and my sisters, and if it was not for the love and care he has shown us, our lives could be totally different. I will have to show him the respect he has earned and truly deserves." Paul spoke with such conviction, Angela realized that she could add no more to the conversation. All she could hope for was that her father would see the sense in it all.

Paul decided that the conversation he had to have with Angela's father could not wait, and so after the evening meal was over, he asked Finbar to join him for a drink at their usual ale house situated a short walk away at the end of Brown Street North.

Finbar knew immediately what was about to happen, but he hadn't considered all of the situation.

Paul very cunningly asked firstly if he could be considered as a husband for Angela and was surprised at how quickly Finbar replied to his request.

"I wondered when you were going to pluck up enough courage to ask me for Angela's hand, lad, and of course, I say yes to your request," replied Finbar. "Paul, I could not wish for a better man to trust my Angela to. I am luckier than any other father of the bride because I have you living under my own roof, so I know what a good man you are, and I have no doubt that you will make a fine husband."

"Sir, there is one more thing I have to ask, and before I do, I vow that whatever decision you make, I will honor it. I swear on my father's name," stated Paul almost shaking.

"Before you go on, I have an idea that I hope you will consider, Paul," interrupted Finbar. "What say if my daughter agrees to marry you that we all pack up our home and move to London. The air here in Salford is too full of idle gossip, and I think a change will do us all good."

Paul instantly regretted the extra-large swallow of ale he had just taken. In the middle of Finbar's revelation, he spat the whole mouthful back out all over the bar with some of it landing in Finbar's hair.

"Did you know, sir? Did Angela . . . how, are you sure you would do that?" Paul was so taken aback, he decided to stop talking. He just raised his hands in front of Finbar's mouth and continued to make gestures as if he was trying to drag out more information.

"Paul, a man would be a fool if he had not noticed how the death of your father has changed everything. I would never expect you and the girls, and I include my Angela here, to remain living in the house that has so many bad memories. The slow, agonizing death of your mother and the tragic end that your father chose for himself. I hear the gossip in the street. Matthew and Colleen have done their best to cheer us all up, but I need to see smiles back on faces. I need to hear laughter again, and I know that staying where we are is not going to help bring back those smiles or the laughter."

The two men continued drinking until the candles were all blown out and they were cordially asked to vacate the premises. Paul purchased two bottles of gin, and the pair staggered back down the length of Brown Street North, waking nearly every household as they sang loudly and proudly in Gaelic while telling each other to *sshhhh*.

Ellen and Josephine had gone to bed and were asleep, but Angela knew of the mission that Paul was on and would not sleep until she knew what the future held for her.

Finbar was the first to come crashing through the front door, closely followed by Paul who was apologizing to the doorknob, then the wall, and eventually the kitchen table.

"*Ssshhhh*," muttered Finbar.

"Well, there you are, Missus Connelly," stammered Paul, and as the words spilled out, Angela ran to her father and thanked him over and over, completely covering his face with kisses.

Paul tried to stand erect like a soldier on guard duty. He struggled with the cork in one of the bottles of gin. As it came free, he announced with all the aplomb of the town crier.

"All those going to London, please find a cup and drink a toast to our captain." Paul lost his balance as he spoke, and Finbar relieved him of the bottle of gin as he slumped into a chair.

Ellen and Josephine had arrived from the cellar by this time and began firing questions at Finbar and Paul.

"Is it true, Paul? Are we really able to leave this miserable place? Will we be seeing Michael and Sarah soon? Oh, please tell me it is true." Ellen could not contain her joy as Paul nodded yes again and again and then began pouring his sister a large gin.

Josephine was so overcome, she sat down on the old church pew, dropped her face into her hands, and sobbed loudly.

CHAPTER FIFTY SIX

The next day began with members of the Denny household trying to pack up their meager belongings in preparation for their move to London. Finbar told his motley crew that he would take charge of the money. Each traveler gladly gave Finbar all the money he or she had, but with fares to pay, food and drink to buy along the way, and accommodation once they reached London, the escapees from Brown Street North would be lucky to survive two weeks, possibly three at the most. Finbar had heard nothing from Rostan regarding the sale of Angela's land to the marquis.

While the escapees huddled together in Finbar's kitchen trying to apply a positive spin to their somewhat dire situation, Matthew Denny appeared like a huge brown bear at the front door.

"I am here personally to thank you one and all. You . . . the merry makers for the wonderful entertainment you provided to all of us that live here in Brown Street North this evening passed." Matthew had obviously been sharing some cheap foul-smelling gin with several of his gang men during that same evening, and he still wreaked of it.

Matthew had placed himself in front of Finbar and was coaxing him to move away from the eavesdropping group by winking one eye and nodding his head to the direction he wanted Finbar to follow, and Fin did as suggested.

"Finbar, my dear cousin, Colleen and I had a visit from Angela this morning, and she told us that you all plan to move to London. We don't want you to leave, but the reason is obvious to all, and so we would like to help you. I have done some reckoning, and by my reckoning, your little band of travelers are going to run out of money before you will be able to settle," Matthew stuttered due to the combination of fading inebriation and dry retching.

Finbar knew that Matthew Denny never presented a problem without being able to couple it to a solution.

"Now I just might be able to help you and all your wee-ens, cousin Fin," said Matthew, now minus the stutter and only kindness in his tone. "I would have you accept this money as a loan, and you can pay me back once you and your new lot of bairns get properly settled. Please do as I ask, Fin. The last thing you need when you get to London is to lose the girls to the streets. Here is the address of the guesthouse that Rostan stays in when he is in London, and oh yes, I almost forgot. I have a letter here for you from that very man." Matthew handed over two envelopes to Finbar. One envelope contained one hundred pounds. The London startup money. The second envelope held the future.

No one in Finbar's household had heard from Rostan since he left for France. Fin took hold of the second letter and noticed that it was addressed to himself and also to Angela. In case the contents of the letter was bad news, Finbar decided to read it before Angela saw it.

In the letter, Rostan explained what had taken place in Paris and Marseille, and in typical Rostan style, there was no gilding of the lily or, in this case, the Maggot.

> Dear Finbar and Angela,
>
> I retained the services of Lavigne Brothers Lawyers in Paris to ensure all dealings with the Marquis De Roche were legal under French law.
>
> A contract of sale was entered into regarding your Marseille property. The price agreed to by the marquis and myself, acting as your agent, was four thousand six hundred English pounds.

The legal charges and government documentation fees amounted to two hundred and ten English pounds. I have transferred the balance of the money to my account in London. I am returning to London to stay at the guesthouse where Michael and Sarah are living. You have that address, so please send me further instructions and let me know where to deposit your money.

I hope to hear from you soon.

Yours sincerely, John Rostan

After reading the letter, Finbar handed it to Angela who began to scream as soon as she read the amount that the land sold for.

Finbar handed back to Matthew the envelope he had just been given containing one hundred pounds, and to be heard above the noise of Angela's screams, he spoke into Matthew's ear, "Thank you for your generous offer, cousin, but it would seem that Angela has just become rich beyond belief."

Having almost exhausted herself with the screaming, Angela finally sat down and explained the contents of the letter to her about-to-be fellow travelers. Angela could only contain her exuberance long enough to ensure her companions that money was not going to be a problem but that was in the future. Plans still had to be made for the now of it all.

It was decided that between them, the group certainly had enough money to get them all to London with enough left over to survive on for a week to ten days. Many of the calculations put forward by Finbar were pure guesswork. He had no way of measuring what would be the true cost of living in London, and he certainly could not be sure how long it would take Angela to access her money.

Matthew pulled Finbar close to him and handed back the envelope. "It is a loan, Fin, please take it," and having said that, Matthew left after separately wishing each traveler "the best of Irish luck."

CHAPTER FIFTY SEVEN

Finbar and family were glad to finally arrive at Maggie and the Captain guesthouse. They had made the journey to London by train. By the time Finbar had settled on a price for a coach to deliver himself and his charges from London Railway Station to the Captain's guesthouse, he realized that the survival calculations he had made back in Brown Street North were going to fall well short of the reality. He bargained with three coach drivers before he found one who was prepared to show some sympathy, but even then, the fare was three times more than he thought fair. As Finbar sat in the coach that would deliver them to the guesthouse, he reached for the inside pocket of his jacket and was much relieved having satisfied himself that Matthew's one hundred pounds sat safely within.

Michael and Sarah had no idea that they were coming. The surprise was deliberate. Angela insisted that they should arrive unannounced because she just wanted to see the look on her brother's face, and she insisted that she be the one to tell her brother that they were now rich. "I just want to tell him that he doesn't have to worry about the police anymore because I will give him enough money to make a fresh start somewhere where the police just won't be looking."

The travelers arrived at the guesthouse just after midday, and Angela felt let down when the Captain informed her that Michael and Sarah would not return home until the evening.

"Michael and his wife both found work in one of the banks in town and usually do not return home until six o'clock," explained the Captain.

Angela was beside herself. " So they did marry. They are married. This is the best news," exclaimed Angela.

"That they are, miss, and in fact, they were married twice," said the Captain.

Angela's joyous shrieking soon caused the others to gather, and the Captain explained about the two weddings. Finbar raised his hand to interrupt the proceedings and rudely fired questions at the Captain in a tone that varied from anger to bewilderment.

"Stop there, man," demanded the Captain. "You have a fine son, and he has a loving wife. Everything they have done is out of their love for one another, and I have never heard him utter a bad word about his father or his sister. You should be proud of the man you have as a son." The Captain had done it again. He calmed the seas with empathy and truth.

Just as the heated conversation dissipated, Maggie Dorn returned home from the fish market with supplies for the evening meal. After the Captain had explained to her just who the new guests were, she flew up the stairs to introduce herself to her new friends.

Maggie lived every minute as though it might be her last. Every question needed an answer, and every answer needed to be understood. Kindness was not a duty: to Maggie Dorn it was a gift to be given away as often as possible. She found her new friends settling into the two rooms that the Captain had allocated to them. Maggie proved yet again that kindness was key. After all the necessary introductions were made, Finbar thanked her for helping him to realize he need not worry about Michael and Sarah.

Angela, Josephine, and Ellen were to share one room while Paul Connelly and Finbar were to share the other. Maggie soon made herself known and suggested that a surprise party should been given for Michael and Sarah when they returned from work. The three girls jumped at the opportunity for a bit of fun, and with that, Maggie Dorn suggested that they come with her back to the market to buy the extra food that would be required for the evening. Before arriving at the market, Maggie took the girls to the Earls Bakery and reacquainted Josephine and Ellen with Malcolm McDonald who was now manager and part-owner of the business. They only had scant memories of Malcolm from the Dublin Docks days and were far more interested in the array of wonders laid out before them.

"Maggie, could we please buy some of these beautiful cakes for Sarah and Michael's party? Please. Please." The girls shared the question, and of course, Maggie was quick to reply.

"Why do you think I brought you here? What do you say, Malcolm? Are we able to purchase some of your masterpieces?" asked Maggie very correctly.

Malcolm replied, "Pretty Maggie, it would be my pleasure to provide you with whatever your collective hearts' desire. Please choose whatever you think will be necessary, and I will parcel them up and bring them home with me to the guesthouse. I can close the shop early so as not to spoil your surprise."

When Michael and Sarah arrived home from work at the bank, they entered the unusually quiet guesthouse. Even Boson the dog was nowhere to be seen. Sarah called out. "Where is everybody? Where is anybody?"

As she spoke, Angela appeared in the doorway of the dining room.

"Mr. and Mrs. Denny. Good day to you," and no sooner had she uttered the words than the rest of the company spilled into the room and surrounded them.

Finbar stood in front of his son. "So you are a married man now, my boy. I want to be angry because I think that is what would be expected of me, but here you are with Sarah, and I know you love her as a good man does love. I can only say that I am proud of you both."

Michael put out his hand, and Finbar took it. The gesture soon rolled into a full embrace, and as soon as Finbar got close to Sarah, he swept her into the fold. As apologies were made and accepted. As praise was delivered and well-received.

The party was in full swing when John Rostan arrived home carrying Lizette, who was asleep in his arms. He had taken his little girl to the London Zoo. Although it had only been in existence for eight years, Rostan and Lizette were thrilled with the experience.

John found himself once again to be the trout out of the pond, as he would put it, while trying to fathom the reasons for the reverie that confronted him.

Finbar and his entourage had not been told that Rostan had returned from France a week earlier nor had they been told about Lizette. Maggie went to make the introductions, but Finbar stopped her by shouting out, "As I live and breathe. Here he is, our hero, our giant. The man of the hour. Please everybody make sure you have something in your glass. I will propose a toast."

Maggie had appointed herself to the role of master of ceremonies and made sure that everyone was holding the necessary requirements to complete the toast.

Finbar laughed as he raised his glass, ready for the formality. "I have already said everything that makes up John's toast, so please just let me add. Here is to our good friend, John, and should I go so far as to congratulate you on becoming a father, John?"

As the toast was being clumsily proposed, Lizette was wriggling her way out of Rostan's arms. She stood, trying to recognize the new faces that surrounded her. "Sahla, Sahla. Sahla not here?" She glanced back at Rostan with her arms outstretched and palms facing skyward. She was asking to see Sarah. Since their arrival back in London, Lizette had started to call Sarah Mama. Sarah bore similar features to the little girl's murdered mother. Similar height, face, and skin tone. Sarah, having had the advantage of better education, also spoke French, and that was an obvious comfort to Lizette who often looked sad and reflective.

Rostan stumbled out an explanation that he hoped would pre-answer any questions that might be coming. "I have adopted this little bairn as her mother was no longer able to care for her. As a father, I still have much to learn, so any help and reasonable advice would be greatly appreciated," said Rostan almost apologetically.

Rostan then realized that he had good reason to talk to Finbar. He suggested that the information he had should not be bandied about in general conversation.

"Since my return to London, I have made it my business to call in on some of my old friends who are still in the force," said Rostan. "And it seems Mr. Thomlin, Sarah's father, has offered a 200-pound reward for her safe return. He is telling anyone who will listen that if he ever catches your Michael, he will make sure he is sent to the gallows. I think Angela is correct to suggest that he and Sarah disappear, and I do have a plan that can make that happen and yet still keep the extended family together. I have found out a great deal of information about the plan, but I will keep it all to myself until I am firmly convinced that it will work."

John Rostan had really settled into the fathering role, and he had plenty of folk on hand at the Maggie and the Captain guesthouse to take charge of the little one if he had to go out on business. Maggie Dorn was a great help during the day, and Sarah Denny made herself available for the evenings.

Rostan thanked everyone for all the help he was getting and he needed it. He was putting together his grand plan to relocate his companions. He seemed unstoppable, but then one day, a letter arrived. He recognized the handwriting to be that of Father McCordy of St. Michael's Church, Salford, but the message was from Colleen Denny.

> Dear John,
>
> Matthew is in serious trouble. Could you please come as soon as possible? Please we need you.
>
> Father McCordy for Mrs. Matthew Denny.

CHAPTER FIFTY EIGHT

That was all the letter contained. John Rostan knew Colleen well enough to know that her plea for help would be genuine. He felt his blood begin to run cold. He told the Captain the true contents of the letter and asked him to explain to the others that he had been called away on business and would be back to formalize his plan as soon as possible.

The train trip to Manchester seemed to take forever, and with every mile traversed, Rostan began to imagine that he knew exactly what the trouble was that Matthew Denny was in. When he finally arrived at Colleen's door, he could hardly recognize the woman. Her face was so pale, and little dirt tracks had formed on her cheeks, marking out just where the many tears had traveled.

It only took minutes to explain the events that caused her to write to Rostan and all that took place on the front doorstep.

Rostan did not enter the house, he simply handed his travel case to Colleen and stated, "Your Matthew has nothing to worry about, and I will fix the problem right now."

John Rostan ran from Brown Street North to the Gaol House in Manchester proper. He stood outside the cruel gray-looking building for several minutes, trying to compose himself. He knew he would be recognized by some of the prison officers because he was often at the gaol delivering prisoners when he was a policeman himself.

He travelled up the eight steps that led to the front door, and as he stepped inside, he was immediately recognized by a burly copper who was charging some petty crook at the booking desk.

"Well, as I live and breathe, if it ain't the big man himself. Rostan, in god's name, what are you doing here, man? It has been a long time. What brings this welcome visit, John? Have you a fine to pay?" The burly officer's questions came loud and fast.

"I am here to sort out a bad situation," replied Rostan. "You are holding a man in your cells. His name is Matthew Denny. Could someone please tell me what he has been charged with?" Rostan already knew the answer to his question but hoped against all else that Colleen had got it wrong.

"Murder, John. Vicious murder. That's what he is in here for. He butchered a man named Marcus Eversall in the poaching hills just out of Sheffield. He was seen in the area where the body was found. He had been telling friends that the sister of a family he knew from Ireland had been married to the man and that he supposedly killed her and chopped her up. He came to the notice of our Sheffield office when another of his wives received the same treatment.

"It seems Mr. Matthew Denny tracked him down and dished out back to him a similar gruesome death. If it's all true, the lads here reckon he should be given a medal, but sadly, John, it will be the rope for him for sure."

"What evidence is there to prove the guilt of Mr. Denny?" asked Rostan, and by this time, several more curious police staff had joined in on the discussion.

One senior officer stepped forward and looked directly at Rostan and said, "Sir, we have three honest and reliable witnesses who have given statements that will damn the man we are holding. All three have written down that the man they saw in the area at the time of the murder was a giant. No mythical creature, sir, just a very large man."

Rostan looked into the faces of the police officers. "The giant you want, sirs, is not in your cell. The giant you want is standing right in front of you. I, John Rostan, do confess to the murder of Marcus Eversall, and if it had to be done again, I would take great delight in the repetition."

Rostan had considerable trouble while trying to prove his guilt. The Manchester constabulary reckoned they had their man and asked Rostan to leave. It was only when he began to describe in detail the condition that the body was found in that they had to reconsider the situation. Rostan stated that the body had only one fatal wound and that was caused by the knife he then produced from his boot.

"You found one stab wound only. Straight through his black heart. I did the butchering later. No animal deserves to be carved up until it is truly lifeless," Rostan spoke with no emotion. He had drifted into the trancelike mood that would always overtake him when his excitement began to run high.

Rostan was charged with the murder of Marcus Eversall, and the immediate release of Matthew Denny was ordered. The police officer who first spoke to Rostan as he entered the building was the man given the task of explaining to Matthew just what had transpired. He asked Matthew if he knew John Rostan.

"Yes, I know the good gent," replied Matthew. "Would I be able to see him, to thank him for what he has just done?"

Matthew was overwhelmed when he was taken back to the cells to talk to Rostan. "What a brave and good man you are, John.

You did not have to come forward. When I was told that the main cause for my arrest was that I fitted the description of a giant of a man seen in the area asking about that bastard Eversall, I just laughed. I honestly thought the whole thing was simply a joke, but here we are."

The faces of the two men were nothing alike. Matthew Denny had gleaming blue eyes, dark laborer's skin, and his hair was brown and wavy. John Rostan's eyes were dark brown, almost black. His skin was fair, and his hair was glistening black and straight.

"What will you do, John?" asked Matthew. "What can I do?" he added.

"Nothing and nothing," replied Rostan. "The world is a better place because of my crime, but murder is murder, Matt, and I will have to take whatever it is that is coming for me, and we both know just what that is."

CHAPTER FIFTY NINE

When the news of John Rostan's arrest for committing murder reached the Captain, he knew it had fallen on him to continue on with the plan that Rostan had been discussing with him prior to his arrest. He referred to this plan as the Exodus, and it relied very heavily on the unlawful expertise of Rostan's friend Allain Batteux back in France, but what happened next made the Captain appreciate even more just how far reaching Rostan's friendships had extended.

The Captain, having read through some of Rostan's correspondence with Batteux, was able to find his address, and he promptly apprised Batteux of Rostan's dire situation.

Fourteen days after that letter was sent, Batteux arrived at Maggie and the Captain's guesthouse, and he was not alone: Phillipe Sartre was by his side.

Sartre only stayed for introductions and then headed on to Manchester to help in any way he could with Rostan's defense.

Batteux was far more concerned with the Exodus because Rostan had informed him that Sarah's father had been told that Michael Denny and his daughter had been seen in London. Batteux also knew through the Surete in Paris that Sarah Thomlin's father had convinced the Manchester police to add the crime of kidnapping to the charge of serious assault that he had brought against Michael Denny. If the matter went to trial, Michael Denny would be facing at least fifteen years transportation to one of the colonies.

Rostan's Exodus plan was easily said, but getting all parties to agree was the devil in it. Through the Captain, Rostan had been gathering information relating to what relocation would offer all parties the most promising future, and they had concluded that Australia should be their aim.

Reports were coming back to England about the fortunes that could be made in this colony. The discovery of gold in places with strange names meant that a decision had to be made as to a suitable destination, but when Rostan read that the precious metal had been found in abundance in the town called Bendigo, he felt his mind had been put at rest. He had read that many of the town names had been taken from the languages of the aboriginal people, but Bendigo was a name he knew well, and it definitely was not native.

Rostan was a keen supporter of boxing, and although he would rarely place a bet, he did wager twenty pounds on the outcome of the English Heavyweight Championship bare-knuckled fight between James Burke and William Abednego Thompson on February 12, 1839. The bet was placed at odds of five to one on Thompson to win. He did win and made Rostan a happy man in the process. Thompson's nickname was Bendigo, which was a play on Abednego, and the fact that his supporters would say he had a bendy body. That comment may well have arisen from the fact that he boxed Southpaw, and in fact, he was credited with introducing that stance.

"Bendigo the boxer was good luck for me, and maybe luck is tapping me on the shoulder once again by showing us that there is a town called Bendigo named after him in Australia. A town where gold aplenty was able to be had by all."

The Captain quickly realized, with Rostan gone, it was left to him to carry out all the arrangements and to deal with the added on skullduggery. Just as Rostan had explained things, it was now up to the Captain to work with Batteux while Sartre seemed to be a man certainly able to bring his brand of expertise to the party. But the ragtag band was about to receive another member who could create false credit ratings. A man who under the tutelage of Allain Batteux had sorted out all the avenues of business that enabled Batteux's Foreman to pay all the accounts left unpaid by Batteux's father prior to his tragic suicide. That man was Arvin Bergin.

Batteux met Bergin at the door of the guesthouse and was shocked to see him there. "Is all of bloody France following me here to where I now live?" snapped Batteux.

"Dear sir," stated Bergin, "we both know you cannot go back to France. Your game is up, sir. The Surete are making great efforts to find you at the continual insistence of your Marquis de Maggot, and if you do go to trial, I have been told that you will go away for a very long time, and policemen do not fare well in French gaols. Now, sir, my name has been linked with yours, so I would like to help you manage the plan of escape for both our sakes. I believe that those who know refer to it as the Exodus."

"What a shiteful bloody mess," stated Batteux. "It seems to begin with that I only had to produce false documents for Michael and Sarah Denny. As I am now a wanted man, and we can presume that you too, Arvin, are being sought by the Surete. There are two more identities I have to work on. Rostan hoped that Finbar Denny, along with his daughter Angela who intends to marry Paul Connelly, would see the advantage in moving to another country because the danger would always be there that the Marquis de Maggot could come seeking revenge for the land deed triumph. Last but certainly not least, in Rostan's Exodus plan were Ellen and Josephine Connelly. He knew Finbar had agreed to care for the girls, and if Finbar agreed to the plan, the girls would surely follow."

The Captain asked all parties to meet for a discussion in the dining room on the Friday evening of the next day. Once he and Batteux had laid out the plan in full, the various participants stood quietly, saying nothing.

Michael was the first to speak, and the question was not at all related to the discussion that had just taken place. "With John Rostan in gaol, what will happen to little Lizette here?" He pointed to where Sarah was cradling the child as she peacefully slept.

Sarah then spoke almost through tears. "Michael and I love the wee thing and would be glad to call her ours if that was possible. I was told by the doctors after I was beaten that I would never carry my own child, but this little girl needs love, and we have plenty to give."

Finbar then spoke, "Now there is a question that, as yet, none of us can answer, but let me say this. If sailing off to Australia is the best way to keep my family safe, then I would row the bloody boat there myself."

The two Connelly girls screamed in harmony. "Yes, yes, yes, when do we leave?"

No one had noticed that Maggie Dorn had entered the room and was listening intently. Her now more cultured self shone through as she dreamed to herself. "Oh, how divine it would be to sail away to a new land and leave dirty old London behind."

CHAPTER SIXTY

Rostan was faring well in Manchester Gaol. Sartre was allowed some visitation and made sure the guards were paid well to ensure that his friend came to no harm. One month had passed before a court date was set. Rostan had arranged for a reputable lawyer to represent him, but he told Rostan that there was little he could do on his behalf. The confession had sealed Rostan's fate. Sartre had begged him to arrange an escape, but Rostan knew that any such effort would endanger other people, and so all he asked of his friend Sartre was to pray for him.

Matthew and Colleen Denny also visited Rostan in gaol. Matthew, as was always the case, was able to lift Rostan's spirits by entertaining him with stories of his Mud Hole Men. It seemed that not much had changed with the rail gang. The Mud Holers usually lead by Killy were always mixed up in some trouble, and Matthew was always sorting things out.

"I tell you now, John," said Matthew, "that bloody Killy will be the death of me. It seems he took up with another woman, and his dear missus found him out. She came looking for him at the Black Duck tavern, and she had a knife as long as a sword in her bag. It was so long, John, that the handle was sticking out for all to see.

"'I'll kill him, I'll kill the little weasel for sure this time.' That was what she was screaming in the bar. The bloody barman, to get rid of her, told her he was in the small room off to the side of the tavern. She was out the door before I could get out of my seat. I'd had a couple me-self and was not moving real fast. When she opened the door to that little room, Killy was there on his own, seems his lady friend had just left, but Missus Killy shoved the blade at him anyway. She stabbed his arm, and at the sight of all the blood, she fainted, poor thing. When I get there, Killy is beside her, and when he sees me, he says, 'What in Jesus's name do I do?' Well, I quickly got him to start writing her a letter declaring his undying love. Those of us that know what that room is really used for call it the letter-writing room, so there is always scraps of paper and something to write with. He had scribbled down a few words when she started to come round, and of course, we had a bit of an audience by then. He explained to his dear lady that he was in the room silently composing a short note just for her, and of course, the also guilty men that had gathered around helped convince her of the truth in it all. The poor thing burst into tears and started ripping pieces off her underdress to bandage the wound. The day was saved, but I swear that man was put on this earth to see me into an early grave, John, I surely do."

Rostan recalled when first he met Matthew Denny after another dilemma Killy had dropped him into at the Old Bailey. Only a few years had passed, but it seemed like a lifetime ago.

With John's day in court pending, Batteux made the sad journey to Manchester to bring him up-to-date with all the goings-on concerning the Exodus. There was nothing gracious about their meeting. The guards only allowed Batteux to speak to him through the bars of his cell.

"John, before I talk to you of all the plans so far made for the Exodus, I must discuss the most important reason for my visit. You know what will happen to you, so you must make a decision about the future of your little one, Lizette." Batteux was to continue on, but Rostan cut him off mid breath.

"Allain," he declared. "I have no fears for her future. It is obvious to me that Sarah Denny loves the child dearly, and I believe Michael feels the same way. I have had quite a bit to do with Sarah since we freed Michael from gaol. She is a fine lass, and I am a lucky man to know, before I die, that my daughter will have a good home. You know I am a rich man, Alain, so I will arrange for my estate to fall to Lizette with Sarah and Michael as trustees. That is what you wanted to talk about, was it not?"

Batteux actually laughed. It was a relieved laugh. "My god, John, you made that so easy for me. I should have known you would have already made plans for Lizette. Well, let's talk about the Exodus."

While Batteux was there, Phillipe Sartre had bribed one of the guards so that he could also meet with Rostan, and he couldn't believe his luck to find Batteux there as well.

"Mr. Bateux. You and I have important plans to make," Sartre spoke quietly. "I have decided to send John off in fine style, so as much as he is not interested, I am determined that I shall make for him the finest suit that I have ever created. Now Mr. Batteux, I need you to convince him that he must be properly attired so as to end his days with dignity."

As Sartre spoke, Batteux saw tears welling in his eyes, but they seemed to defy gravity as they refused to fall. He could not believe Sartre's ramblings about a new suit. *He must be mad*, he thought, but then he concluded that it was not madness but simply an odd outpouring of grief for the man that he so obviously loved.

"A fine suit it will surely be then," declared Batteux, "and that will be the end to it, John."

Batteux returned to London, but Sartre remained in Manchester. He had been introduced to Colleen Denny, and Matthew insisted that he stay with them until the ordeal was over. Sartre had sold his tailor shop in Paris well before Matthew had been arrested. He and Rostan had written letters to one another, but Rostan offered no options one way or another to Sartre, so he had decided to surprise John in London with a visit. He felt awkward about the whole idea, but when Batteux informed him by letter that Rostan had been arrested and charged with murder, he immediately made his way to London and then on to Manchester.

Rostan's case was reported in the *Manchester Examiner*, and the story was written with a great deal of sympathy. It seems the people of Manchester felt that any man who had put an end to the life of someone who had brutally murdered and then butchered two women did not deserve to be hanged. A crowd had gathered on the first day of the trial, and when the public gallery was full to overflowing, the remainder waited on the steps of the courthouse and listened to reports of the events as they were delivered to them by the writer from the *Examiner* who had written of the case so favorably.

The trial lasted five days, and although the judge was obviously sympathetic, he had no option but to deliver the death sentence. The jury had found Rostan guilty, and he was due to be hanged in four days.

Chapter Sixty One

Sartre had done as he had promised. Rostan looked dignified as he stood on the trapdoor that would be opened, allowing him to suddenly drop to his death. He refused the comfort of an appointed priest as he said, "Father, there is no god, and the sooner people like you realize that fact, confession will no longer be the veil that sinners can escape through. Some may see me as a bad man, but it suits me to believe that what I did, I did to better this world."

The hangman fiddled with the hood that was drawn down over Rostan's face. He tightened the noose around Rostan's neck and then positioned the rope just behind the left ear so as to ensure the procedure was correctly performed.

"I thank you, sir," said Rostan to the executioner, and as he spoke, he realized he had drifted yet again into that feeling of excitement that he so enjoyed. As the strange euphoria took hold of Rostan, the hangman grabbed the lever next to the trapdoor, and with one quick motion, Rostan disappeared through the floor of the gallows. Because of his size and weight, the whole structure shook as the frightening thud finished the job.

A sizable coffin had been purpose-built to accommodate the large corpse. An officer at the gaol helped the two undertakers to roughly manhandle Rostan's body into the coffin, and as they did, Sartre assisted wherever possible. He was only there because twenty pounds, once his, was now folded in half and pressed deep into the pocket of the head undertaker. The lid was then fixed, the coffin was slid on to a low cart, and the short but last journey of John Rostan began.

Sartre openly wept as the funeral service was being held at St. Michael's Church. Matthew and Colleen Denny sat with him in the front pew. The traditional requiem was not permitted. The church was packed, more due to curiosity than respect.

Very few people knew John Rostan, but those who did all turned out. Manfri Garrett sat with his aunty Agnes, Osian Jones was there with his wife, Joan, and many police officers attended in uniforms as a mark of respect.

He was laid to rest next to his good friend Joseph Connelly, who also died in a state of mortal sin. Like Connelly, Rostan also was not permitted interment in the sanctified graveyard, but Father McCordy, again as a favor to Matthew Denny, had played a little game with the church-defined boundaries. Sartre had arranged for a small stone to be erected at the site. It read, "John Rostan. Died bravely. There are stars in the heavens and that is all there is."

It was decided by Batteux that none of the folk that had agreed to the Exodus should attend the funeral. They all agreed that bringing any attention to themselves could jeopardize the plan.

Maggie Dorn had told Batteux that she desired to join the Exodus group. She was visibly upset and begged Batteux to talk to the Captain in the hope of gaining his permission to join the group who are constantly talking about nothing but the Exodus to Australia.

Maggie, who had initially baulked at the idea of reading was, these days, quite the bookworm, so she had found two very good volumes relating to Australia in the Captain's library room, and she devoured the knowledge that readily sprang out at her from each page. Along with the wealth contained within the texts, Maggie was astonished at the hundreds of illustrations. She wanted to share her enthusiasm and discoveries, and she had a captive and very appreciative audience in every member of the Exodus expedition.

Maggie allowed her singular enthusiasm to wash over the onlookers as she spoke of the aborigines. She showed pictures of the unusual flowers, wombats, giant lizards, eagles, emus, and even went so far as to suggest that she would keep, for herself, a pet kangaroo. With all that fascination aside, it was when Maggie spoke of gold nuggets the size of shoes that most held their attention.

The Captain, of course, had given his permission for Maggie to travel abroad, and Batteux was exacting in all the documents he prepared for her. Rather than have any problems with her age being brought into question, Finbar Denny had agreed to be named her guardian, and the documentation was there for all to inspect.

The Captain outwardly encouraged Maggie's ideas. He needed her desperately to stay with him in London and manage the Maggie and the Captain guesthouse, but he also knew that his little bird had to fly. He could demand that she stay, and he knew that she would, but he also realized that he, possibly, would break her heart with that demand. Maggie's love was the most precious thing that the Captain had ever had in his lifetime. He sadly realized that he had to let that love go if it was to survive.

The time to book passages had arrived. Sartre had returned from the funeral at Manchester and announced that he also intended to travel with the group if he was permitted.

"My life in Paris was a misery, and the power of religion there continued to stop people using my services." Sartre deliberately stopped speaking and allowed himself to seek out any sympathetic glances in the room, and he was not disappointed, so he continued. "I let the good ladies who worked for me buy the shop on credit with no interest to be charged. Mr. Bergin seated over there prepared the contract, and I trust the ladies to be fair. I will have payments coming to me for eighteen months until the debt is cleared. I will not be a burden to you. I have enough money right now to get me settled in Australia, and if what Miss Maggie says is true about the cost of things, and if people are getting rich with the gold, surely they will need to greatly improve their attire and their style. I will need young ladies to help with stitching and cutting. Oh, indeed, Mr. Finbar, your two young charges may be able to work for me. I have finances enough to buy cloth and tools here in England, and they will land with me saving the added cost of purchasing the same goods in this Bendigo place."

Finbar's reply was short and cheery. "Another man in our company would be an advantage and a skilled man even better. I can see, by their smiling faces, that Ellen and Josephine would possibly like to take up your offer of work. I know them both to be well-trained in needlework. Grace, their mother, was a fine teacher, and some of their samplers were entered in local fairs, and there was never a shortage of winning ribbons when they returned home. Their father, Joseph, bless the man, often used to show my Angela their winning pieces."

The Captain learned that the steel-hulled vessel named the SS *Great Britain* engineered and built by the genius Izambard Kingdom Brunel was to embark on its first voyage to the antipodes in August 1852, and he was keen to have Maggie travel on that very ship. He believed it to be the safest vessel afloat. It was to leave Liverpool, and its destination was Melbourne, Australia.

Many men returned to England having made their fortunes in the Australian goldfields. Several of these men had stayed at the Captain's guesthouse and spoke at length while dining about all the goings-on in Australia, and if the Captain had been a younger man, he knew he certainly would have made the goldfields his destination. He would invite Batteux to join him and Maggie at his table, knowing that in the absence of Rostan, it was Batteux that the members of the Exodus were looking to for information and advice. Batteux questioned the men that had returned from Australia, and he very quickly realized that the information gathering was as much to help himself as it was the others.

"Captain, I have to make an announcement," said Batteux after finishing his meal one evening. He raised his wine glass and demanded all in the dining room to listen. "Please, my friends, I would like to propose a toast. I have information that I know will please you all. I have decided that you will need my services to continue on into the future as you settle in the new land, so here it is. I propose a toast to Allain Batteux, yes, me. I have decided to join the Exodus and will be traveling with you all to Bendigo in Australia."

It was no sacrifice that Batteux was making. He knew that he had to escape Europe. He knew that the Surete in Paris had issued several warrants for his arrest on fraud and forgery charges. He had been told by Bergin that his associates at the Surete, many of them ex-criminals, were delaying the inevitable all that they could, but he would eventually be made to pay for his crimes. So his intentions were a convenience rather than a noble gesture. What he did have in his favor was his ability to be liked and admired by all those who knew him, and the fact that he had been such a good friend to John Rostan also carried great weight.

The Captain was the first to raise his clay tankard in support of the toast. If Maggie was leaving, he knew that traveling with Batteux in the group was an added safeguard.

"Damned fine idea," he bellowed. "One less Frenchy in England is a grand plan indeed." The Captain winked at Batteux as he spoke.

"I feel you will have to make room for just one more. If my business partner Mr. Batteux thinks he can escape to the antipodes without me, he is sadly mistaken." The statement came from Arvin Bergin who was seated next to Finbar Denny on a large table that catered to the majority of the Exodus party.

The sound of one person clapping very loudly began immediately after Bergin had spoken. The whole room then erupted with laughter. Without intention, Ellen Connelly, the quietest of Joseph and Grace Connelly's remaining daughters, had just announced to the assembly that Arvin Bergin had at least one supporter and a very keen one at that.

The SS *Great Britain* carried just over six hundred passengers, and the estimated time of travel between Liverpool and Melbourne was six weeks. The members of the Exodus decided to arrive in Liverpool in two's and three's rather than draw attention to themselves in a large group.

Michael and Sarah Denny, to avoid the wrath of Sarah's father, had forged identity papers, compliments to Batteux, and little Lizette was listed as their daughter. It was felt best that Paul Connelly and Angela Denny should travel as man and wife. Their papers had also been forged by Batteux to avoid any recognition. Batteux knew that the Marquis de Maggot was not a man to give up on revenge. The title, owned by Angela Denny, that he desperately needed to expand his empire of greed had been rendered useless to him by Rostan, and that being the case, Angela could never feel safe in England. The three remaining originals of the Exodus were Finbar Denny, Josephine Connelly, and her sister, Ellen. The two girls were to travel as themselves, but Finbar Denny was to travel as their father, Joseph Connelly, to avoid the name Denny appearing anywhere on the passenger list. The newcomers to the group, Batteux and Bergin, were to travel as business partners. Batteux prepared the papers, and he insisted that his new surname be Natsor; only the Captain seemed to recognize the humor in it. Last but certainly not least, Sartre intended to travel as himself.

The combined nervousness of the Exodus group could have driven the steam-powered pistons inside the two motors of SS *Great Britain* without the need for one ounce of the tons of coal she had to carry just for that purpose.

The day of boarding was chaotic, busy, and visually stimulating but, most of all, extremely noisy. As Michael and Sarah were boarding, Lizette was crying inconsolably.

"She is scared of all that is going on," said Michael to Sarah. Sarah did not respond to the remark at all. She was gripped in a fear of her own. She had convinced herself that her father would arrive on the scene accompanied by the police and both her and Michael would be whisked off to gaol. She was so overcome with the dread of that happening that she had asked Colleen and Matthew Denny to be there for the departure to ensure that Lizette could be taken into their care if the worst should happen.

Every boarding had been planned, and indeed every plan was carried out without one single mishap. The Exodus group had all made it to their cabins, and the ship was making good time as she headed away from Liverpool into the oft times treacherous waters of the North Atlantic Ocean. In truth, not all members of the Captain's last supper did make it on to the SS *Great Britain*: one passenger was missing.

Back in London, the Captain was sitting on the grand chair in his office. He glanced around at the walls, allowing his eyes to see his collection of beautiful artworks, he also mused over the many handcrafted pieces from all over the world that hung like Christ's stripped robes. He even imagined that he could spy the crown of thorns, still dripping blood, hanging in the furthest corner, making him feel like the whole picture formed a bewildering obscenity.

"Am I drinking from the holy grail?" he asked himself. "Have I not dined with twelve apostles who have simply deserted me? Is my Maggie to be my Judas? I should not drink gin."

At ten in the morning, he had already consumed the best part of his usual daily quota of gin. He had packed his pipe with the finest opium available on the London docks, procured by himself during the wee hours of this morning. Everything he was looking at was slowly disappearing into his smoke haze. Reality had left the Captain, and the few thoughts that he was still able to muster were just coating the walls of his mind with dark images that were fading to black. The Captain knew he was slipping away from caring.

The love that he had in his life was gone, and soon he too would be gone. Maggie had only been away for three days.

The Captain did not need to muster up any courage in order for him to put an end to it all. He had always been a courageous man. He reached into the top draw of his desk and removed the flintlock pistol from it. He shook in the powder, dropped the ball into the barrel, squeezed in the wading, and them rammed down the barrel to ensure the charge was secure. He placed the gun on his desk and began one long draw on his opium pipe. He drained the last dregs from the bottle of gin into his beautiful cut-crystal glass.

He laughed to himself when he rethought of all the religious imagery he had allowed to play in his mind. It had always fascinated the Captain when the many men he watched die ended their lives ranting about religion. Although his mind was being overpowered by opium and alcohol, it never came close to a belief in god, but there he was, like all those others, allowing his childhood indoctrination to return in dark clouds and have him relive the last supper.

"Jesus, Captain! What in the name of damnation is all this smoke about?" shouted Maggie Dorn as she sought out the clearest path to the Captain. "Just what is it that you are up to, Grandad?" she asked.

Maggie Dorn had decided that she simply could not leave the one person on her earth that truly loved her.

The End

As the SS *Great Britain* steamed along in rough waters, Sartre and Batteux had made it their business to find the first-class cabin numbered two hundred and one. Sartre knocked loudly on the door, and after what seemed minutes, the door slowly opened.

"We are so glad to see that you made it, John."